S

_y of the Fey, book one.

Emma Miles

[signature: E Miles]

All rights reserved. No part of this book may be used or reproduced in any form without written permission from the copyright holder, with the exception of brief quotations in critical articles and reviews.

This book is a work of fiction and is not based on any real persons, living or dead.

Chapter One	5
Chapter Two	34
Chapter Three	57
Chapter Four	80
Chapter Five	101
Chapter Six	122
Chapter Seven	141
Chapter Eight	156
Chapter Nine	180
Chapter Ten	213
Chapter Eleven	250
Chapter Twelve	282
Chapter Thirteen	303
Chapter Fourteen	320
Chapter Fifteen	341
Chapter Sixteen	355
Chapter seventeen	370
Chapter Eighteen	405
Chapter Nineteen	425
Chapter Twenty	437
Chapter Twenty-One	472
Chapter Twenty-Two	506
Chapter Twenty-Three	525

Chapter One

The boy stirred under the blanket but didn't wake. Reaching out Mya lay a hand across his forehead feeling the heat coming off him even before she touched him.

'Oh, Jack.'

She rocked back on her heels, closing her eyes momentarily as her heart clenched. They didn't have the money to pay the village's miserly healer, and the fever had hit Jack so suddenly she'd had no chance to gather medicine of her own before night had descended. Her little nephew whimpered again and with a sigh she made her choice. She would rather brave the fey than watch him suffer.

She left the candle with him and clambered back down in darkness. Feeling with her fingers she picked up her sharpest kitchen knife, and taking up a horseshoe hanging on a ribbon, placed it about her neck. The fireplace was a black wound in the wall, the neatly stacked wood waiting to be lit for the morning cooking. She wrapped a cloak about herself, slung a bag over her shoulder and stepped out into the night. Despite her resolve she found herself rooted to the spot for a moment, her ears straining and her eyes trying to pick out shapes in the gloom. She held her breath. Somewhere in the meadow a fox barked, but it wasn't wild animals she feared; it was the Fey.

Mya's heart skipped a beat when an owl dipped low across her line of sight. She touched the cold metal of the horseshoe for luck and hurried across the open meadow; the grass clutching at her long skirt. The white willows grew half a mile into the forest where a small brook snaked toward the larger river that had formed the Valley. Water was one of the most dangerous places to visit even in the daytime. Mya stepped as silently as she could, her nerves on edge; heart jumping at every sound. There was the lightest of breezes; enough to stir the new spring leaves and tease the ends of her hair. It was hard not to imagine the trees were whispering to each other; or hiding other voices. She placed her feet carefully, cringing every time she snapped a twig or rustled the undergrowth.

She sighted the willows; this would be the most dangerous part. She drew in some long deep breaths through her mouth and forced her feet forward, eyes straining in the dark for any sign of danger. The brook itself was silent here; deep and dark. She reached the nearest willow, ducking under its pale finger-like leaves. Reaching tentatively, she touched the rough grey bark and was about to cut into it with her knife when a movement caught her eye and she recoiled in fear. A tiny man stood looking up at her with a finger to his lips as he flapped a hand to frantically 'shush' her. A brownie! The fear drained from her leaving her lightheaded. He was no more than a foot tall with a wide flat head. His hair was a greenish-brown, short and tightly curled; his ears large and pointed, his nose sharp and long. His body was as squat and wide as his head giving him the appearance of a taller creature that had been stepped on. His little dark eyes showed he was afraid, and he removed his finger from his mouth to point at the brook.

Mya followed the direction he was pointing in and her stomach turned to ice as she saw something dark moving just below the water. The brownie waved his hand at her, gesturing she should get on with what she was doing whilst he himself backed away from the water toward her. Mya cut at the bark; her hands shaking and her eyes darting to the brook. She placed what she had in her bag, wincing at the sound the fabric made. The brownie hissed at her and she didn't need telling twice; she ducked back under the tree. Every part of her screamed at her to run but instead she moved slowly and carefully, trying not to make a sound. Glancing down, she saw the brownie had stayed with her. Only when she reached the meadow, did she dare to speak in a hushed whisper.

'Thank you!'

'It would have found me too had you made too much noise!' The brownie gave a shake of its head. 'What foolishness brought you out?'

'My nephew; he's ill, and I needed willow bark. I didn't think we had any brownies in Briarton? I thought you had all been…' She hesitated, wondering how angry the brownie might be at the exile of his kind; though it had been years ago.

'Thrown out of our homes?' The brownie supplied for her. 'Driven away like unwanted vermin?'

Mya shrank back. 'I wasn't even born–'

'No, you weren't, girl.' The brownie sighed.

'Can I… I don't have any milk left but I can offer you some butter and a bit of yesterday's bread?'

The brownie tilted its head and regarded her steadily. 'You are strange for a vallier. Most scream and run at the sight of even a brownie like me; or reach for the iron. You never even touched your horseshoe.'

Impulsively she reached for it now and realising moved her hand away. Now she thought of it, she had no idea why she hadn't reacted that way, other than the little creature had helped her, and appeared to be no threat at all.

'You have the Gift,' the brownie stated.

'The Gift, no!' Mya protested. Having the Gift meant death. Power, fame and money, maybe; but death in the end. Once people had queued at the Journeyman fairs hoping to prove they had magical ability and be taken off to the Lord Vallier's castle at Ayresport. Now though; now people with the Gift lived in fear of being taken away to the castle. No Spellward, it seemed, lasted long in service to the Valley.

'If y' say.' The brownie refused to argue. He scratched at the end of his long nose. 'Bread and butter would be welcome.'

'All right.' Mya checked the meadow was clear before stepping out into the open. The sickle moon was giving a little light between the thin clouds. They made their way in silence; too wary to make any noise until they reached the fenced garden of Mya's cottage. Wind chimes dangled from wooden posts, nailed in with iron. Old, worn horseshoes were hanging here and there.

'Can you pass?' Mya asked.

'It'll feel a little prickly but iron isn't so bad for brownies and we can tolerate touching it.'

Mya opened the gate and let him through, firmly bolting it behind them. She hurried to the door, worried Jack may have woken and found her gone. Only when she'd hung up her cloak did she realise the brownie hadn't followed her inside.

'You can–'

'Nah!' the brownie halted her with a warning finger. 'Never invite a Fey into your home unless you are sure you can trust 'em! Once you invite me in, I'll be able to come and go as I please!'

Mya hesitated, torn between good manners and protecting her safety and Jack's. For some reason she'd instantly taken to the little brownie, but it could easily be an act on his part. Once they had been the most helpful and benign of all the fey, living with humans and helping them in their daily lives. Occasionally a brownie would turn on a bad or greedy master and they would become as evil as they had once been good; but Mya had no intention of keeping the little creature.

'I'm Mya,' she told it. 'What's *your* name?'

'Hey, you know I can't be giving you my real name.' He waggled a finger. 'You can call me Feather.'

'Well, Feather.' Mya decided. 'You can come in, but... if you want to come in again you must have the courtesy to stop at the door and knock. I don't want a fey slave to do my chores for me so as soon as I've seen to Jack, I'll make you a set of clothes to free you.'

Feather tipped his wide head to one side. 'A strange vallier indeed! I'll accept those terms; only... the Valley is an extremely unsafe place for a brownie. Would you take my labour in exchange for a little food and a place to shelter? I saw you had a small barn…'

'I also have a house and plenty of room for such a little guest. You are most welcome, Feather.'

He gave a bow, making her laugh. 'Well, Mya. Hold off on the new set of clothes for now and we have a bargain.'

Mya busied herself grinding up the bark with her pestle and mortar whilst Feather ate his bread and butter with a dab of honey. She'd found him a wooden eggcup to drink from which she filled with mead. Without being asked Feather got the fire going and swung the kettle over it to boil up water for the willow. Mya's eyes were stinging with tiredness by the time they had it ready and she climbed up into the attic with Feather waiting anxiously at the bottom of the ladder.

The candle only had about an inch left but its yellow glow was comforting and strong. She stroked Jack's damp hair from his forehead and reluctantly woke him.

'Is it morning?' The boy asked hoarsely.

'Not yet. Drink this tea down if you can.' She'd added honey both for his throat and to sweeten the bitter bark. He drank down thirstily, then pushed the cup away abruptly when he realised what he was drinking,

'Aunt Mya! We had no willow left; you didn't go out into the woods at night?'

'It's okay.' She shushed him. 'I had help from a friend. He's downstairs and you can meet him when you're feeling better. Drink it all up now.'

He did as he was told and she settled him back under his blanket.

'Would you like to keep the candle?'

He nodded, looking anxious; he knew how much candles cost.

'It's fine.' Mya smiled at him. She kissed him on the forehead then climbed down the ladder.

Feather had tidied everything away.

'You don't have to do that! You're my guest at least for tonight.' Mya gazed guiltily at the table which had never looked so clean.

'Girl, you look so tired and have been kind to an old brownie, it was my pleasure. Now get some sleep yourself; things will change in the morning.'

'I need to make you up a bed.' She glanced around the small room for inspiration. The room served as kitchen, workroom and living space with a small end curtained off for her own bedroom. She had a spare blanket but nothing to serve the brownie as a bed or to give him any privacy.

'I can use the chair by the fire,' Feather said seeing her dilemma. 'It's a better bed than I've had in years.'

'All right; I'll fetch you a blanket but tomorrow I'll try to make you something more suitable.'

'Girl, you really are going to have to learn the rules.' Feather shook his head. 'People don't make things for brownies; it's the other way around. If you go through life giving everything and not pausing to accept anything for yourself or noticing your own needs, you end up with nothing; and greedy friends instead of true ones.'

She puzzled over his words for a moment, then took a blanket from the cupboard and left it on the chair.

'Well good night, Feather.'

'Good night m'lady Mya.'

She drew the heavy curtain across the room and stripping down to her under tunic got into bed. For a while she found it hard to sleep. She listened for any movement of the brownie the other side of the curtain. Finally, tiredness overtook her, and she drifted off with the brownie's words sounding in her head; *things will change in the morning*.

***

Mya woke to the sound of laughter. She quickly put on her dress and pulled the curtain across enough to slip through. Jack was sitting beside the fire, Feather in the chair opposite. The black kettle was steaming merrily, and they had laid the table with boiled eggs, fresh bread rolls and a jar of blackberry jam. The small churn was beside the door already filled with goat's milk and water had been fetched from the outside pump to fill her wash basin.

Feather followed the line of her eyes. 'I didn't want to disturb your privacy and take it into your room.'

'You've done all my morning chores!'

'Well, don't look so upset about it, strange girl.' Feather cocked his wide head.

'He did mine too!' Jack grinned happily. 'Can we keep

him?'

'Feather is a person, not a pet.' She couldn't help but scold. 'You still look pale, Jack, I'm not sure you should be out of bed yet.' She went to feel his forehead, but he moved aside impatiently.

'I feel much better and I was hungry.' He didn't meet her eyes and shifted in his seat before glancing up. 'Thank you for going out to get the willow, Aunt Mya.'

'You're welcome. Well, I guess since you are up you could do a little reading.'

'Reading now, is it?' Feather scratched at his hooked nose. 'Few of your social standing would be bothering with reading and writing.'

'My parents kept a shop,' Mya said in explanation. 'And I intend that Jack get the best apprenticeship he can and not spend his life making a living from mending.'

Feather looked at her thoughtfully for so long she turned away, swallowing and touching a hand to her warm cheek.

'I'm fourteen next week!' Jack told the brownie excitedly. 'And I'll be going to the next Journeyman's fair!'

'Which fair?' Feather asked sharply.

'Trade Pass,' Jack said firmly.

Mya caught the momentary relief in Feather's eyes and wondered what the brownie had feared. He'd suggested she had the Gift; perhaps Jack did too, after all his mother had. Maybe the little fey feared they would strengthen the Ward and he and his kind would be driven out of the Valley again.

There was no way Mya was about to let the boy go anywhere near the capital city, Ayresport, though.

'Well, breakfast's getting cold!' Feather prompted as though he himself wished to change the subject.

She sat at the table, eating rather self-consciously as the others has already had theirs. Jack fetched one of his books and settled back by the fire, snuggling into his blanket.

'Feather,' she asked cautiously. 'Will you stay here and make sure Jack rests and looks after himself whilst I go into Briarton to deliver my mending?'

'Of course, I will,' Feather replied at the same time as Jack protested he didn't need looking after.

'Well, you can help me make myself a little room,' Feather suggested to the boy. 'And I can tell you stories of Piskies and Pookas!'

'And brownies?'

'And brownies.' Feather laughed and gave Mya a wink.

She gathered up her mending, breathing slowly and glancing up several times at Jack and the brownie. Every child of the Valley was taught from an early age about the Fey, how to avoid them, how to escape them and how to defeat them; mostly they were taught how to fear them. Mya's mother had sometimes spoken wistfully of a time when good people would be granted the aid of a benign fey such as a brownie. It was a fey who had killed Mya's parents; a succubus. As she covered her basket of mending with a blanket to keep it dry, she couldn't help probing at the old wound, but much as she hated and dreaded succubae, she couldn't lay blame at the door of the brownie. Maybe he was right; maybe she was a strange girl. Her sister had hated all fey with a passion. Her sister's husband, Hal, had been too drunk most of the time to care either way.

She added two of the small bread rolls to her basket. 'Right, you two behave,' she told the boy and the fey as she swung her cloak around her shoulders.

'Yes, Aunt Mya,' Jack replied dutifully, though he barely looked up from his book.

Feather gave her a solemn nod.

She closed the door slowly, part of her still having doubts. *Too late now, Strange Girl,* she told herself. *It was too late the moment you invited him home like a stray kitten.*

She froze and let out a sigh when she saw the garden and yard. Everything had been swept, weeded, stacked and tidied. Still, she was more than a little grateful; with the brownie's help she'd have time to take on more mending and even go back to making new clothes if she invested in some cloth when they journeyed to Trade Pass.

Briarton was little more than a village and was situated high in the hills at the edge of the Vale. They were mostly shepherds and farmers but boasted a blacksmith, an inn and a healer. A small stockade surrounded the village but some, like Mya, had poorer houses just outside in the meadow. She'd originally come from Ayresport; her grandfather on her mother's side a fisherman and her grandmother a trader's daughter. Her father came from a family of tailors. Her parents had made the journey many miles inland from the harbour city all the way to Trade Pass; a town which traded with the merchants who came down through the mountain pass to the east. They'd made a living as tailors before the Ward had failed; before the fey had found a way in and killed them.

The sun was already more than two hours risen and most of the thin clouds present in the night had tattered away to reveal a pleasant pale blue. Smoke curled upward from behind the high stone walls of the town from the chimney of the bakers and the forge of the smith. She could see in the distance the town's wooden gates were open and two farmers were driving their wagons through to the market. The jingle of the protective bells plaited into the horses' manes reached her on the wind a moment before the smells of the town; wood smoke and human waste. That was one of the few benefits of living out of town, it was easier to breathe.

This time of day the gates were not manned as the Valley had no enemies but the fey. Mya stepped onto the cobbles, feeling every one through her thin-soled shoes. Most of the buildings were built with a sturdy lower level of grey stone and an upper level of wood. The more prosperous were whitewashed, and some even painted in bright colours. Here and there a thatched roof sprouted, but more common were the baked clay tiles. The small market was set up for the morning in the square where the town's largest well stood; but Mya didn't have goods to trade there. Instead, she made her way to the inn whose mending she had most recently taken in. Briarton was a stopping off point between Trade Pass in the east, the farmlands and charcoal burners to the west of the valley and Ayresport in the southwest. Briarton Inn was often full in the summer months, less so in the spring and autumn and empty in the winter, but for local people who liked a drink or two and a bit of company.

The large arched door swung open easily as she pushed and she found the landlord busy stacking cleaned tankards on his shelves. His maid was scrubbing the tables, and she gave Mya a smile as she continued with her work.

'Mya!' The man beamed at her. 'I didn't expect you until tomorrow.'

'It didn't take me as long as I thought.' She lifted the basket onto the bar.

The landlord was a tall, thin man with wispy hair now going to grey. He was a widower of five years and Mya did quite a lot of mending for him and occasionally made something from new. She removed his now repaired clothing and the curtain she'd re-hemmed from the basket. Unlike some of her other customers he never examined her work and she couldn't help appreciate the fact he trusted her. She did however hold up the blue linen shirt she had cut and sewn for him.

'Well, that is fine!' he complimented, taking it from her and running his fingers down the wooden buttons. Did you want coin this time?'

Mya hesitated. Money was tempting as she was saving to give something to Jack when he found his apprenticeship; however, she usually got a much better deal trading for goods from the landlord who got things cheap from the locals.

'Or I have a nice wheel of cheese, a whole shoulder of lamb and a bottle of dandelion wine?'

Mya broke into a smile. She rarely treated herself but the Landlord knew what he could tempt her with.

'This is Jack's fourteenth spring, and he is to go to the Journeyman's fair at Trade Pass next week; I'd like to do something nice for him,' she admitted. 'So, I'll take your trade.'

'Well, now.' He placed his hand firmly on the bar. 'If the boy's to be a young man, he deserves a feast. Leave it with me.' He disappeared down into his cellar and came up some time later with his arms full.

'Joff!' Mya protested.

'Now, now.' The landlord gave a shake of his head. 'You do well by that boy and you take less from me than others might.'

She moved aside the two bread rolls as he placed in the basket a bottle of dandelion wine, two small dark beers, a wheel of cheese, a carefully wrapped leg of lamb and a small jar of preserved cherries.

'I thought you might put those in a cake?' He fumbled in his pocket and brought out a silver coin. 'And this toward his apprenticeship.'

Mya realised her mouth was hanging open and closed it quickly, her eyes stung as, embarrassed, she managed to stop the tears. 'Joff, that's kind of you.'

'Hey, Beth and I, God rest her, never had children to save for. Your Jack is a good lad. I was thinking, if he has no luck finding what he seeks, I'd be willing to take him on here; there are worse trades than brewing and inn keeping and at least he'll be close.'

'I'll tell him.' Mya smiled awkwardly. More than one

townswoman had commented in the past at her working for Joff; that he was a widower and no doubt looking for a wife. He had never shown any such interest in her before though and she told herself she was being paranoid.

'Oh!' she said, recalling herself. 'Did you have any more mending?'

'Nothing for the moment, sorry; but if you have time to call around to Mrs Barnrest on Well Street, her in the white house, she has some alteration needs doing.'

'Her fifth baby.' The young plump maid paused in her scrubbing to roll her eyes. 'It ain't just her daughters growing out of their clothes!'

'Thanks, I'll call around. And thank you again for Jack's gifts.'

'Just ask him to consider my offer; orphan or no I can think of no better lad in Briarton.'

Mya couldn't help feeling a little pride at those words as she left the inn. Jack really was a good lad. In the mornings he helped her with the goat and chickens and then went into town to run errands for the blacksmith. In the afternoon he tended their large garden of vegetables and herbs and spent his evenings practising his reading and writing. Losing both his parents at such a young age had made Jack a somewhat quiet and serious boy, but one determined to make something of himself.

She called at the Blacksmith's to let him know Jack was ill but recovering from his fever, and then crossed through the busy market, pausing at a fabric stall and deciding the prices here were too high; better to wait until Trade Pass. She scanned the crowds for a familiar face and saw him seated on the stony ground of a narrow alley between two tall houses. The old man was wrapped in a threadbare cloak with its hood pulled up over his white hair. He had an unkempt beard and watery blue eyes; his shoeless feet dirty and cracked. A small wooden bowl was placed in front of him and despite the busy market was still empty. A coughing fit racked him and several people turned to scowl at him in disgust. 'Old Flem', the people of Briarton called him and if he had any other name, he never shared it. He had arrived before winter to the dismay of many who tried to drive him out. There were a few though who took pity on the old man who did no harm to any.

'Flem!' Mya called quietly. She fished under the blanket to draw the two bread rolls from her basket.

'Mya!' The old man smiled, breaking into another coughing fit. She watched him with concern whilst he brought himself under control. He took the bread and tucked it under his shirt as though afraid someone would steal it.

'Listen, Flem.' Mya watched his lined and dirty face guiltily. 'Next week Jack and I need to travel to Trade Pass to the Journeyman's fair–'

Old Flem leapt to his feet so swiftly Mya gasped. He grabbed her arm, pinching it fiercely, and she pulled back in fear.

'Mya, don't ya go t' the Journeyman's Fair!' She shrank from his warm sour breath. 'Lord Vallier 'as sent his guard and a Spellward, a woman, a dangerous woman. She'll 'ave your Jack and you'll never see 'im again!'

He let go and Mya stepped away, rubbing awkwardly at her arm where he had hurt her, the heavy basket in the crook of her elbow. Torn between disbelief and dread she didn't flee from the old man's sudden attack but instead asked; 'How would you know who is at the Journeyman's fair? Jack needs to go–'

'Same way as I know that bread y' gave me is brownie made.' He looked right at her with his blue eyes.

Mya froze, her heart racing. How could he know the bread was made by Feather? Unless…

'Yes.' He nodded, glancing around to be sure they were not being observed. 'I know the fey; I have not the Gift but have lived with Spellwards and amongst fey. Mya, you mustn't go to Trade Pass but you can't stay here either. The Lord Vallier is sending out seekers to every town and village to round up those with the Gift. He wants more power.' Old Flem folded inward, becoming a frail old man again right before her eyes. 'Mya don't go. Give me a few days an' I'll see if I can get ya a safe haven.' He shuffled around and stepped into the throng of the market before she could say another word, leaving his bowl behind.

Before she knew it, her feet were hurrying her back toward the town gate. She stopped and groaned inwardly when she realised she'd completely forgotten about Mrs Barnrest. She no longer felt optimistic enough to try for a new customer, however, all the promise of the day had faded and even the contents of her basket felt like no more than a heavy weight to her now. She started walking again, trying not to run back to her cottage.

'It's just nonsense,' she said to the sky as she crossed the meadow.

But what if it isn't?

There was only one person she could think of to ask. A very little person.

***

Outside the cottage door she took in some deep breaths and forced a smile onto her face. Stepping in she found Feather and Jack both lying on the thin mat before the fireplace with an array of counting sticks laid out between them. Jack's skin was a little flushed, but she didn't have the heart to send him up to bed.

'You two look like you're having a busy morning,' she said instead.

'We're practicing bartering and numbers.' Jack got unsteadily to his feet and his eyes fell on the basket; she often brought back something nice in payment from the inn. The smile that broke out on Mya's face then was genuine.

She put her hand under the blanket and drew out the wheel of cheese and placed it on the table.

'Cow's cheese!' Jack's eyes widened, and he placed a hand on his stomach.

'We can take our goat's cheese and eggs into town tomorrow and trade it for flour.' Next, she took out the lamb. 'I'll go out in the shed and see if there are any potatoes left to bake and we can have a feast tonight!'

Jack swallowed, his mouth already tasting the lamb. She put her hand back under the blanket.

'More?' Jack asked aghast.

She pulled out the dandelion wine. 'For our feast tonight.' She smiled. 'And for my two men...' She grabbed up the two small bottles of dark beer. 'Do you like beer, Feather?'

'I would love a taste of beer, kind lady.' The Brownie bowed.

'And then these.' She paused to tease them both, then took out the jar of cherries.

Jack's eyes lit up and Feather's grew large as moons.

'Not all for tonight.' Mya raised a finger. 'If we can get flour tomorrow, I'll make a cake of most of them, however...' She opened the jar and handed two cherries to first Jack and then Feather. She watched them both eat, taking pleasure in their enjoyment.

'Right.' She clapped her hands together. 'Let's get the cottage ready for our feast! Jack, please get the fire going again. Feather, would you help me in the garden?'

'It would be my pleasure,' the brownie agreed.

It didn't take long for the brownie to notice her sudden silence when they went outside.

'Not as happy as you pretend,' Feather stated as they picked from the few withered potatoes they had left. 'What brings this cloud on what should be a glorious day? Do you fear giving up young Jack to his apprenticeship?'

'Feather.' She looked down at the little creature in his old jerkin and weskit. She had only known him a few hours and yet there was no one else she could think of to go to. 'I had a strange warning today. There is an old man, a beggar who I sometimes take food to. He told me I shouldn't take Jack to the Journeyman's Fair. He also said we weren't safe here.'

Feather watched her as she spoke and sighed sadly.

'Kindness is oft repaid in ways we don't expect,' he told her. 'Tell me of this old man.'

Mya described him and Feather's expression remained completely still.

'It is as I thought.' The brownie rubbed at his hooked nose and gave a shake of his wide head. 'Leave it with me, my Strange Girl. I'll look into it.'

Their small feast was a merry one with Feather regaling them with tales of fey escapades and pranks. Jack fell asleep in the chair by the fire with a cup of wine in his hand. Mya carefully took it from him and covered him with a blanket.

'How did you come to have Jack?' Feather asked quietly.

Mya checked Jack really was asleep. 'My family moved from Ayresport to Trade Pass when I was about twelve; father said it was because it was so much cheaper to live there. My sister was sixteen then and not long after married a weaver named Hal. He appeared pleasant enough at first but by the time I was myself sixteen it was obvious he was a drunkard and did nothing to help the family business.' She glanced at Jack again to be sure he wasn't listening. 'My sister lost two children before Jack was safely born. He was only four when the Ward began to fail and no longer protected as far as Trade Pass. My parents… my parents were killed one night by a pair if succubae who flew in through a window.

Hal was by tradition handed the business by my sister who inherited; but within a year he had drunk himself to death on our money. We had nothing but the building and our stock of cloth by the time we'd paid his debts. My sister, Pria, she'd guessed she had the Gift and had herself tested when a Seeker came to the fair. She chose to go to Ayresport to earn her fortune as a Spellward and to send the money to me for Jack. I couldn't manage the shop and Jack alone and unprotected so we sold all, and I bought this cottage.

'Pria sent me letters every week to begin with, though they often arrived all together depending on people travelling from Ayresport to here. Some letters contained vague references to the fact all had not been what she'd expected. Then a steward with an escort of guards turned up here with Pria's pay, a final letter I suspected of being forged as it didn't seem truly her hand, and the news she'd died in service to the Valley.' Mya looked down at her hands. 'I suspected something was wrong but had no one with whom to discuss it. Soon after it became common for anyone who became a Spellward to die young "in service to the Ward". Since then I've tried to steer Jack away from any thoughts of the Gift or wanting to be a Knight or Spellward; I didn't want him anywhere near Ayresport.'

She gazed down at the sleeping boy. He had the dark brown curling hair of his mother and her family, but his eyes were brown like his father's had been. She could see both Pria and Hal in his small nose and rounded smooth cheeks.

'I would do anything to keep him safe,' she murmured.

***

After Mya had woken Jack and ushered him up to bed,

Feather slipped out of the house and under the gate. The hoot of an owl made him freeze, and it was several minutes before he dared to move. The grass in the meadow was taller than he was and hid him well, but there was a lot in the world for a small brownie to fear. Long ago things had been different, nearly every brownie had a home with a human to their mutual benefit. When the indiscriminate Great Ward spell had been cast, all the brownies had been driven out into the forest and hills or up into the high mountain to the east. They'd taken shelter wherever they could, competing with fiercer fey and animals. They had their magic, but theirs was the magic of growing and mending. Feather had lived many years in the unused part of a badger set until he'd been driven out and back toward the Valley. A homeless brownie didn't expect to last long.

He found himself a rabbit trail heading in the right direction so he could make swifter progress. Humans with the Gift could often feel when a fey or magic was near; it was not commonly known some fey had the same Gift. The two men had built a fire, often dangerous in the wild, but not to these men. The brownie approached cautiously, every hair on his body standing upright in expectation of fear. He didn't know what weapons these men would have to guard themselves against fey so he didn't want to show himself too soon.

'Psst!' he tried, wanting to get the attention of the men but nothing else. He found a small stone and threw it with all his strength.

'Psst! Old Flem if that's what y' be calling yourself!'

He waited nervously, the forest around him feeling watchful and somehow heavy. Then the noisy tramp of human feet came toward him.

'Who wishes to speak to me?' A voice called suspiciously.

'Feather. A Brownie!'

'And why would a fey be seeking Old Flem, eh?'

'For the girl, for Mya.'

For a moment there was silence and then a hearty laugh made Feather jump out of his skin.

'So, you're the one taken up with the girl and her nephew?' Old Flem brought his laughter under control. 'Well now, that won't please the Lord Vallier.'

'Well, we ain't particularly interested in pleasing the Lord Vallier.' Feather found himself getting annoyed. 'Now I've heard you both in the woods of late and I want to know what you're up to and what it's got to do with my humans.' He folded his arms determinedly.

'Well, you're a brave fellow talking so to a Spellward!'

Feather's eyes grew wide and his mouth clamped firmly shut. A *Spellward*!

'You're quiet, brownie, has a fox et ya?'

He found his voice though it had none of its previous bravado. 'Why would you warn Mya away from the Journeyman's fair if you work for the Lord Vallier?' Feather feared he'd dropped Mya into an awful lot of trouble. Perhaps these two men were spying out traitors to the Valley.

Another voice called out, softer, younger. 'Let him come. This is the first Wild Fey I've known take up with a human of the inner valley since the Ward.'

'Come along.' Old Flem sounded kinder, more natural. 'On our honour we will not hurt you; be welcome to our camp.'

Feather peered through the dark tunnel of the undergrowth to where an orange glow flickered and twisted shadows. He wanted to go but something rooted his feet to the spot.

'You've scared him with your teasing, Flem,' the younger voice chastised. 'Come brownie, we've left the service of the Lord Vallier and work for another. We come here from the Hall of Pillars.'

Feather almost sat down on the ground, his knees seeming to fold. 'From the Hall?'

'From the Lady of flowers and wind, the queen of rain and sun.'

Feather's muscles felt suddenly light and a wave of dizziness washed through him, it was all the little brownie could do not to burst into tears.

'Be welcome at our fire,' the younger man offered again.

Feather crept forward, spotting the long, worn boots of Old Flem before the rest of him. The old, bent man gestured toward the fire with one hand and trying to keep one eye on him and another on the camp ahead, Feather followed the dancing light.

The younger man was not what Feather had expected from his voice. He was somewhere in his early thirties; however, his face was cut across by a red and ugly scar from his chin to the outside corner of his eye. He had dark-blonde hair, long and tangled, and about two days' growth of stubble. He was dressed in studded leather with a frayed and faded green cloak about his shoulders. There was a long narrow sword at his side and a dagger at his other hip; a bow and quiver lay near him on the ground. The only thing about the man that appeared friendly were his pale green eyes flecked with a dark grey.

'I'm Caelin,' the man introduced.

'Caelin!' Feather sucked in air and glanced back to check Old Flem had not got behind him to trap him. 'I have heard of you!'

'Aye.' Caelin rolled his eyes. 'Most fey have.'

Feather scratched nervously at his hooked nose whilst Old Flem seated himself slowly on the ground. Caelin waited patiently whilst Feather studied him; the brownie couldn't help a little shudder at the weapons.

'This iron is not for Wild Fey.' Caelin pursed his lips in what passed for a smile from the scarred man. 'Not those holding to Her Grace's truce.'

'Here.' Old Flem poured a little ale into a wooden cup and held it out for Feather.

Feather reached out his hands; embarrassed at their shaking. He took a sip of the ale and politely passed the cup back.

'So.' Feather took in a deep breath to steady his nerves. 'Why are you at Briarton? What do you want with my humans?'

'I'll admit my choosing to save the boy is selfish.' The firelight reflected in Caelin's eyes made him seem fierce. 'We need help against the Vallier and his witch of a Spellward, Kasira. I'm looking for an apprentice who is strong in the Gift; I need Jack. If I don't take him, Kasira will.'

'Take him where?' Feather couldn't look away from Caelin's fiery eyes.

'To the Hall of Pillars; to Her Grace of the Dawn Court.'

Feather wanted to protest, he'd only just found a home! Two days ago, he would never have believed he'd find a human as kind as Mya or a boy as clever and gentle as Jack. If they took Jack, he would still have Mya; but if these two renegade Knights were telling the truth, then the seekers the Lord Vallier had sent out would take Mya away too and force her to give her life in servitude to the Ward. He was only a little brownie but he would *never* let that happen if he could help it. Brownies were not meant for living out in the wilds, but if that was where his Mya was going then he would go too.

'I'm not sure Mya will let you take them…'

'Not Mya,' Old Flem mumbled with a sigh. He glared accusingly at his companion. 'Caelin will not have a woman with him.'

'But!' Feather looked from one to the other. 'You can't leave Mya. The Spellwards will get her.'

'We have had this argument, little friend,' Old Flem said sadly.

'I'll travel with no treacherous, faithless woman.' Caelin's eyes did look ugly then.

'She is not!' Feather put his hands on his hips. 'She is kind—'

'Kindness is a weakness or a trap for the unwary.' Caelin cut him off. 'I'll not take the woman.'

'Well then, I'll take her to the Hall myself! But we won't let you have Jack without us!'

'Us?' Caelin sounded amused. 'And what would a little brownie do to stop a Spellward as strong as I?'

'Whatever I had to!' Feather all but shouted, his lip trembling and his eyes stinging. 'You help both my humans or you leave them be!'

Caelin turned away from the fire as though to hide his eyes and the light made his scar look raw and new.

'We will come to the cottage tomorrow and I'll give them their choice. The boy comes with me or he gets taken to Ayresport. I'll not take the woman.'

Old Flem remained silent, looking into the flames.

Feather realised he was shaking and clenched his fists harder. He was too angry and scared to think of anything to say. In truth there was nothing the little brownie could do if either Caelin or the Seekers took Jack.

'Flem, see Feather gets safely back to the cottage,' Caelin

said tiredly.

Feather's eyes narrowed a little; so, there was goodness in this bitter man.

'Come on.' Old Flem got awkwardly to his feet.

They walked back at Feather's pace, the little brownie was all but running. The old man said nothing until they got to the meadow.

'He doesn't mean to be cruel.' Old Flem broke the silence. 'He taught a woman once, and she betrayed him.'

'One woman is not all women.' Feather snapped impatiently. 'And my Mya is a rare woman.'

Old Flem raised his eyes to look over the meadow. 'I don't disagree, brownie, but Caelin is as stubborn as stone. He doesn't even trust Her Grace, not really.' Old Flem scratched at his beard. 'All is not lost yet; there are other forces that might move a stone where an old man and a feather cannot. I'll watch you to the gate.'

Feather accepted his dismissal and hurried through the long grass. He crawled under the gate and ran across the yard. This was the time of night brownies traditionally did all their work whilst a household slept, however he had spent so much of the day with Mya and Jack he felt too tired to work even with the aid of his magic; especially after his escapade into the woods. Nothing had gone quite to tradition since he had met Mya. Feather used a simple spell on the door latch and let himself in.

The cottage already smelt comfortingly familiar and Feather couldn't help feeling sad. Perhaps he shouldn't have been so quick to believe luck had blessed him. Still, he didn't have to lose his humans and go back to being alone; not yet. He took a moment to listen to Mya's soft breathing and Jack restlessly moving in his bed upstairs, then padded over to the big cabinet against the far wall. Jack and he had made a small room for him in the cabinet's bottom with a strap nailed into the door so he could open it easily. Feather hopped in and sitting on his little bed made of a towel mattress and a cut-off strip of blanket he shut the door behind him. Tired as he was, he took another hour to fall asleep whilst he racked his brain as to what could possibly move stone.

Chapter Two

Mya woke to find the living area empty, but glancing out the window she saw Feather standing on a stool milking the goat. She decided not to wake Jack but let him sleep on and recover some of his strength. She lay the empty bottles that remained from their feast in her basket and carefully placed as many eggs as they could spare in there also to take into town to trade. Anxiety made knots of her stomach as she thought of the old man's warning. Feather had promised to look into things but what if he only found Old Flem's words were true?

She heard the clatter of the bucket handle, wood on wood, and pulled the door open.

'Good morning, my girl.' Feather was wiping his broad hands on his trouser legs where he'd splashed a little milk. 'You look like you had less sleep than me.'

'Feather, what am I to do about the seekers and the Trade fair?'

The little brownie sighed and looked down at his worn leather shoes. 'Mya, my dear girl, what the old man warned you is true; but don't you fret! He'll be coming here soon with another man, one who wishes to help Jack. Let's get this milk in the churn and I'll tell you what I know.'

Mya gave a nod, breathing a little easier. She took up the heavy bucket and tipped the contents into the churn whilst Feather retrieved the milking stool.

'I went out into the woods last night.' He placed the stool in the corner and reluctantly came to the table to explain to Mya what had happened.

'I've heard of Caelin!' Mya exclaimed. 'He's a knight of the Vallier's court in Ayresport who became its most powerful Spellward and protector. But...' She looked at Feather in confusion. 'Did he not leave Ayresport for some controversial reason and get killed by the fey about six years ago?'

'No.' Feather raised a stubby finger. 'Not killed. Amongst the fey he is known as "Caelin the Traitor." It's rumoured he turned against the Lord Vallier; that the ugly scar he carries on his face was a parting gift from the Spellward, Kasira.'

'The Valley's darling,' Mya breathed. Everyone knew tales of the beautiful young woman, strong in the gift, who now valiantly guarded the Lord Vallier and gave her life energy to protect the Valley.

'Aye, the very 'darling' who is out hunting those with the Gift to force them back to Ayresport.'

Mya gave a shake of her head. 'So, this Caelin the Traitor wants me to give him Jack to save him from the Valley's greatest heroine?'

Feather scratched at his nose. 'Well, when you put it like that it doesn't sound good.'

Mya stood up and paced around the table. 'If Jack goes to Ayresport, he will die like his mother; but I can't let Caelin the Traitor have him! What would he want with a boy with the Gift anyway?'

'He wishes to take an apprentice.'

'An apprentice! What would he apprentice in? Traitoring? Running away?'

'Well, actuall–'

'Oh, Feather!' She threw herself into a chair. 'What should I do?'

'Mya.' The brownie looked up at her with his small black eyes. 'You realise it isn't just Jack who's in danger? If Seekers from Ayresport come here and find you have the Gift, they will try to take you too.'

In her concern for Jack Mya had barely thought of herself and Feather's words stung.

'We wouldn't be safe anywhere in the Valley,' she realised. 'If we stay, we'll be taken to Ayresport. If we go to Trade Pass or anywhere else, we'll just have to move again and again. If we left the Valley, we would be in danger from the fey.'

'Caelin could protect you from the fey.' Feather watched her carefully. 'If he trained you and Jack, you could then protect yourselves.'

'I'd probably be safer with the fey than Caelin the Traitor!'

Feather scratched at his nose. 'You would only have to travel with Caelin for a while; just until you reach my people. Then we can keep you safe.'

'Brownies you mean?' she asked in confusion.

'Wild Fey; and her Grace, Nemeth of flowers and spring.'

'But wouldn't fey hurt us?'

'Not those of the court of Queen Nemeth at the Hall of Pillars.'

Mya felt a twinge of guilt, she couldn't find it in herself to believe Feather. She'd never heard of either wild fey or any queen. To her fey were fey, and most hated humans. There was only one way she could think of to get herself and Jack to safety and that was to go beyond Trade Pass and through the mountains out of the Valley.

'Mya, Nemeth is–'

The ladder rattled as Jack started his sleepy descent.

'I'll warm some milk.' Mya shot a warning glance to Feather to end their conversation for the moment.

'You should have woken me.' Jack protested as he reached the floor.

'You haven't long recovered; you need your sleep.' Mya tipped goat's milk into the kettle and swung it over the fire. She fetched the last of yesterday's bread and the cheese Joff had given them.

'What were you talking about?' Jack tore off some bread. 'It sounded serious.'

Mya hesitated. In less than a week Jack would go for an apprenticeship and be considered a young man able to make his own choices; she should tell him everything. She couldn't help her instinct to protect him though and save him the worry now churning in her stomach.

'Jack, there'll be a man visiting us today. He's looking for an apprentice and he would like you to consider his offer.'

'What trade?'

Mya looked at Feather. She had no idea what trade Caelin the Traitor considered himself in.

Feather gave a helpless shrug. 'Jack should know everything.'

Mya nodded, knowing Feather was right. She poured them all some warm milk and then told Jack all she knew including the nature of his mother's death. He took it all in silently, a frown on his face. When she finished speaking, he remained silent and Mya refrained from trying to force a response, knowing the boy would come to it in his own time.

'You told me my Mother died a heroine, defending the Valley.'

'And she did.' Mya touched his arm. 'Without Spellwards we would all be prey to the… to the less friendly fey. I suspected something wasn't right from your mother's letters, I think my parents did too, that's the real reason they left Ayresport. Old Flem and Feather have confirmed my suspicions. Those with the Gift die young in service to the Valley.'

'Can I be excused?' Jack looked up at her.

Mya's heart was in her mouth. Jack had always been a sensible and practical boy but he also loved his tales of heroes and adventure. She'd always tried to steer him away from his mother's fate but she wondered now if he had secretly hoped he'd be found to have the Gift at the Trade Fair and whisked off to a life of luxury and renown.

'Of course,' she said sadly. 'But please don't go far; I'm not sure when our visitors will come.'

Jack nodded and cutting himself a slice of cheese slipped from the chair and out the door.

'Try not to worry,' Feather offered.

Mya couldn't even bring herself to look at the brownie but busied herself clearing the table.

'For what it's worth.' Feather rubbed at his nose. 'I'll go with you, or stay; whatever happens, I'm at your service.'

'Thank you.' Mya managed a polite smile. 'I'll not have time to go to market now today so would you help me boil and pickle these eggs?'

'Of course.' Feather gave a little bow but the worry lines didn't leave his face.

***

Jack returned just before midday, breathless from running. He burst in through the door and announced, 'Aunt Mya, they are coming! Old Flem and another man.'

Mya's heart gave a jolt, but she tried not to let Jack see her fear. 'Feather can you get the kettle boiling please? Jack you had best tidy yourself up.'

She kicked herself mentally at how daft a thing it had been to say; it didn't matter what impression Jack made if she had no intention of letting Caelin have him. Even so, she bound up her hair and removed her work apron. The knock at the door made her jump; it was polite and soft making Mya decide at once it had been Old Flem. She was uncomfortable at the idea of letting either man into her home; but if they really were here to help Jack, then the least she could do was show some manners. Jack came hurrying back down the ladder, jumping the last part. Mya exchanged a glance with Feather and then opened the door.

For a moment she didn't recognise Old Flem as he was standing tall and straight; taller than her. In the past he had always been stooped and crook-backed.

'Mya.' He gave a slight bow; his voice strong and somehow younger than it had been. 'May I introduce to you Caelin, Knight of the Hall.'

Mya looked at Caelin only briefly, shyness stepping in. He had the appearance of a traitor with his ugly scar, stubbled chin and tangled mane of hair. He was dressed in greys and browns with a green cloak over his studded shirt. She spotted the sword at his side and froze.

'Leave that outside and you may come in,' she said, opening the door wider and moving back into the cottage. It surprised her when the man complied.

Feather had set out cups and Jack was standing at the head of the table as if to show he was indeed a man now. Mya introduced them and Jack didn't hesitate to shake both their hands.

'You've met Feather.' Mya looked toward the brownie.

'We have.' Old Flem smiled kindly.

'Please sit.' Jack invited and Mya felt a mixture of pride and humour.

They sat in awkward silence as Mya poured them all tea from the kettle and arranging her long skirt, sat down to join them.

'You know of the situation?' Old Flem asked Jack.

'I do.' Jack nodded looking the old man straight in the eye. 'Why were you pretending to be a beggar in Briarton? You are neither as old as you made out or as ill. You haven't coughed once.'

Old Flem gave an amused snort of a laugh and Caelin raised an eyebrow.

'Well, you certainly speak your mind.' Old Flem said.

Mya bristled protectively.

'I was spying,' Old Flem admitted, humour making his blue eyes sparkle. 'Caelin sent me in to look for potential apprentices and allies; both were few and far between. Of those we found we were to decide on who was the strongest candidate for Caelin's apprentice; your going to the Journeyman's Fair made us hasten that decision.'

'Jack was the strongest candidate?' Feather guessed.

'No.' Old Flem shook his head. Caelin stiffened; his face darkening. 'You are the strongest here in the Gift, Mya.'

Mya stared at the old man in shock. Well, there was no doubt about it then; she had to get herself away from the Valley. Aware Caelin had already refused to take her she decided to save herself the embarrassment of further rejection.

'Well, I have no intention of being taken to Ayresport and being used to widen the Ward. I don't want to chase brownies from their homes. As I see it, I have two choices. I leave the Valley through the mountain pass to the Kingdom of the Horse Lords or I go with Feather to this Hall of his on our own.'

Caelin's eyes narrowed, and he gazed at her intently. She couldn't tell what emotion hid behind his still face.

'Mya, no!' Jack gasped. He turned to Caelin and said firmly, 'I'm not going with you unless Mya comes too. I go where she goes.'

'Me too!' Feather gave a firm nod and folded his arms against his barrel chest.

Caelin glared at them all in annoyance. 'This is no childish game. There is more at stake here than you could possibly understand. We need human allies with the Gift. Strong in the Gift. If I have to do this alone I will, but alone I'll…' His nostrils flared, and he clenched his jaw. 'Dying I don't care about,' he finished softly. 'But failing is another matter. You have no idea.'

'If you enlightened us, we would have an idea.' Mya kept her voice just as soft.

For the second time Caelin looked at her with his strange guarded expression.

'I can tell you some.' Feather turned to the Spellward, daring him to stop him. 'I can tell you about the Wild Fey and the Dark Fey.'

All the stiffness fell from Caelin and he visibly sagged, nodding to give his agreement.

'Well.' Feather shuffled in his chair. 'The fey of the Valley, isolated as we were, for years had little to do with the Royal Courts of the Seelie and Unseelie Gentry far over the mountains. We became wild, ungoverned; just looking out for ourselves and surviving day to day. Most of us preferred it that way, away from the fighting and the dangerous games of the Courts. Then one day one of the royalty of the Unseelie Court arrived at the Valley to set up court and demand fealty. She was beautiful and powerful and she seduced and enchanted many.'

Mya saw Caelin flinch at those words.

'It didn't take long for her true nature to come out and she surrounded herself with the cruel and sadistic. Those of her court became known as the Dark Fey, those eluding it, the Wild Fey. Many tried to flee her court and were hunted down. Attacks on humans became a sport but humans countered. Those with the Gift that had once lived humble lives amongst the common folk as healers and entertainers were invited to Ayresport to create a great work of magic; the Ward.

As you know the fey were driven from the valley up into the mountains and forests in the north. The Dark Fey's court was broken up, and it was believed their terrible queen fled back to her Unseelie kin.'

'Believed?' Mya at once picked up on the brownie's meaning.

'I was a knight in my prime when the Ward went up and it saved us.' Old Flem gave an amused shake of his head as though his being young were an impossible thing.

'You're a knight?' Jack sat up.

Old Flem stood and gave a low bow. 'Ben Flame, once Knight of Ayresport at your service!'

'Ben Flame!' Jack leapt up, his eyes wide as he looked at Mya and then back at the old man. 'You slew the beast of Beacon Hill! And you saved the lady Kasira from the hobgoblins and brought her safely to Ayresport where she used her power to stop the Ward from crumbling completely!'

'Worst mistake I ever made, boy.' Ben glanced at Caelin who got to his feet and went to stand looking out the window. Ben raised a hand to silently bid the others wait.

Mya found herself watching Caelin; his shoulders were tense and she could see the muscles of his jaw working.

'I heeded the Vallier's call as many with the Gift did.' Caelin spoke so quietly Mya had to strain to hear him. He didn't turn around but continued to gaze out the window. 'I was a newly made Knight but from a minor family of no consequence; I wanted to be a hero. I was strong in the Gift and had a good reputation as a Knight so Renvart himself took me on to train me; the Lord Vallier's sorcerer and the architect of the Ward. Renvart had already found the Ward was not permanent and needed constant feeding. Renvart did his best, and we all helped but it took so much power...' Caelin breathed in deeply in a silent sigh. 'We put out a call for new apprentices to join us and did so every year since; but one came who betrayed us all.'

Mya waited but Caelin didn't speak.

'I brought Kasira to Ayresport,' Ben said eventually. 'She was like sunlight on flowers and everyone...' He glanced at Caelin. 'Everyone loved her. Renvart was a cautious man and only he and Caelin knew the full truth of the Ward and how to work the spell. Kasira she... she learnt the secret of the Ward. Renvart was her first victim. When he was giving his energy to the Ward, she forced or tricked him into giving all he had and sending him to his death.'

'But Kasira is the hero of the Valley!' Jack protested.

'And I the traitor!' Caelin snorted bitterly. 'Though in a way—'

'In a way nothing!' Ben snapped and Mya got the impression this was part of an old argument. 'Kasira had fed several of the strongest Spellwards to the Ward before Caelin caught her. She tried to seduce him to her cause but despite the love he bore her Caelin *is* a good man and he tried to stop her. She accused Caelin of being the traitor and everyone believed her. All but me who knew Caelin well. He is the most noble of knights.'

Caelin snorted.

'When Caelin escaped Kasira, she sent us out to hunt him down. With planning and a little luck, it was I who found him, but he was already with an unexpected ally. The fey.'

'Our Lady,' Feather said reverently.

'Yes.' Ben's face broke into a wide smile. 'We cast a glamour and feigned Caelin's death. I took his 'body' back to Ayresport and even Kasira didn't see through the deception.'

'My sister wrote of Caelin's disappearance.' Mya frowned

as she recalled the words of the letter. 'It said nothing of traitors.' Mya watched Caelin's back. 'How is it the fey name you Caelin the Traitor but the people of the Valley don't?'

'It was all hushed up to hide the truth behind Caelin and Kasira's "altercation",' Ben supplied. 'It was commonly believed he'd fled after Kasira had ended their relationship to start an affair with the Vallier, and he'd gone away to die of a broken heart or was killed by the fey.'

Caelin growled. 'As if any woman were worth that.'

Ben winced and smiled at Mya apologetically. 'Anyway; we went for a while to Astol so Caelin could heal. When we came back to the Valley, I settled in a place called Ashgrove but Caelin couldn't find peace. He went travelling beyond Trade Pass into the lands of the Horse lords looking for… well, that's Cae's story. Recently he came back and dragged me out of my cups and back to Astol to seek help to take back the Valley from Kasira. It became obvious we had no chance against Kasira without the help of at least one powerful spellward.'

Jack leant forward in his chair, moving his cup aside. 'So why go to the fey and why would they help?'

Caelin turned around and stepped back to the table, his face fierce. 'Because Kasira *is* fey!'

'She's the Queen of the Dark Fey!' Mya realised.

Caelin's eyes narrowed, and he tilted his head a little as he regarded her, but sat back down slowly. 'Yes, she is.'

'But how could she get inside the Ward?' Jack asked.

'Because I invited her,' Ben admitted sheepishly.

'Invited?' Feather cocked his wide head.

'Ben!' Caelin chastised; then looking hard at the other three he commanded, 'That goes no further than this room. The Ward works in many ways like a home; some fey can come in if you invite them.'

'Like brownies,' Feather breathed.

'She had the Gift, so you invited her to go with you to Ayresport.' Mya turned to Ben, her heart clenching in sympathy for the old man.

'I did Mya. It was a trick, the whole thing. She was never in danger; she never needed rescuing. What she wanted was an old fool of a knight like me wanting to relive the glories of my youth.'

And a young man who would fall in love with her and reveal all the secrets of the Ward, Mya thought but had the kindness not to say aloud. Then it came to her with a shock and she gasped aloud. 'Kasira killed my sister!'

Ben and Caelin exchanged glances. Mya instinctively placed her hand protectively over Jack's.

'She did,' Ben said sadly.

'You could have stopped her!' Jack shouted. 'You could have saved my mother!'

Both men flinched at the hurt in the boy's voice and Caelin's response was surprisingly gentle. 'I tried, Jack, I give you my word. Kasira's powers are great and her greatest ability of all is to evoke love and adoration. The only reason

I saw through her was because of something she failed to consider. My love for her was not born of enchantment but was genuine; true love sees through enchantment. You already know the result of my trying to stop her.' His hand went self-consciously to the large scar on his face and Mya realised with horror the woman he'd loved had caused the ugly injury. 'The only amends I can make for your mother, Jack, is to keep *you* safe.'

'Well.' Jack drew himself up. 'If you want to make amends, you must save my aunt from the same death as my mother. You have to let her come with us.'

Ben tried to hide his smile but Caelin didn't look at all amused. Mya dared not look at Caelin; knowing her fate rested in his hands but too polite and shy to make demands of him. Caelin closed his eyes, then looking down at the table he spoke. 'Despite all I am still a Knight and as such I cannot stand idly by whilst a lady's life is in danger.' He looked up at Mya then and she struggled to hold his green-eyed gaze. 'Whatever your nature might prove to be there is no doubt of your danger; 'Sira will use you or kill you. I'll not teach you how to use your Gift, but I'll take you as far as the Hall of Pillars if that's your wish; you can decide from there where you wish to go.'

Mya took in a deep breath and again held Caelin's eyes. 'Thank you, sir. I understand now why you don't trust me and I can't hold that against you. I'll make no demands of you other than you take care of my nephew and keep him as safe as you can. Will you tell me what your plans are for Jack and more about this Hall and the fey there? I think we both need to know just a little more before we commit ourselves.'

Ben raised a surprised and approving eyebrow whilst

both Jack and Feather looked on seriously.

Caelin nodded. 'I intend to go back and kill Kasira.' The slightest flaring of his nostrils and tensing of his throat gave away the pain behind those words.

He still loves her!

'I need someone stronger in the Gift than I if I'm to have any hope of defeating her.' Caelin turned to Jack. 'Confronting Kasira will be perilous and it will endanger your life, I'll not lie to you about that. But I'll not take you with me to Ayresport if I don't feel you could survive. I'll teach you all I can of both the Knightly arts and Spellwarding, but it will take months of hard work and dedication. Are you willing to take on such a challenge?'

'I am.' Jack nodded firmly.

Mya's muscles tensed and she sat very still. 'Sir, if it will take months then many more with the Gift will die. I'm guessing when all are gone the Ward will fall and fail and it will leave the Valley to the mercy of the Dark Fey?'

Caelin nodded and there was sadness in his expression. 'We will not be in time to save all, but it is not as bad as you fear. This is where the Hall of Pillars comes in. It's a sanctuary, a place of peace and healing. It's also apart in time from the Valley and the rest of this realm. Whilst time passes quickly there, it lingers here. A year there is no more than a month in time for the Valley.'

'Her Grace is powerful and a great healer,' Ben said.

'If she is so powerful could she not stop Kasira, sir?' Mya asked the elder Knight.

'Please, Mya, there is no need to call me "Sir".'

'It's your title and you've earned it.' Mya said.

'And I also have a name. Ben. Anyway, to answer your question; if she ever left there and entered this Realm, she could never go back.'

'I see.' Mya frowned. There was a lot to think about logically; but her heart had only one answer. She placed her hand on Jack's again and turned to Feather. The small brownie nodded and offered his hand to Mya. 'We'll do it.' Mya said firmly.

Caelin sat back in his chair and looked at her steadily. 'Good.' He nodded. 'But I must have your promise you'll not seek to learn to use your Gift whilst under my protection.'

'You have my word,' Mya replied seriously and at once.

He regarded her unblinking, his eyes hard as though trying to read her thoughts. 'What plans have you made to leave for Trade Pass?'

'I have travel rations put aside,' Mya told him. 'The goat and chickens were to go to Emily and Stephen's farm for the three weeks we're away. We were set to leave four days from now.'

'The house?'

'Locked up.' Mya shrugged.

'Very well. Do everything as planned and tell no one anything different. If Kasira and her Seekers come asking at Briarton, they must think nothing is amiss so we can get a head start. If she thinks for a moment you've fled, she'll know people other than myself have discovered the truth and we'll run out of time. It will take about a week to get to the Hall so your supplies should suffice.'

Mya nodded. 'I'll trade at the market tomorrow as I normally would.'

Caelin grunted his approval. 'Ben will go back into town as we need to keep an eye on things there. I'll be at my camp; Feather, you know where that is if you need me.'

The brownie nodded.

'When do you take your animals to your neighbour's farm?' Caelin asked.

'They are bringing their wagon the day before we leave to collect them.'

'Very well, then three nights from now Ben and I will come for you.'

Mya nodded, realising her heart was beating fast and her hands were clenched. 'You have until then to change your mind,' Caelin added almost kindly and Mya thought she saw a glimpse of who this man had been before the bitterness and anger had set in.

'We'll be ready,' she told him.

'Come, Ben.' Caelin stood and the other's all got up automatically as manners and courtesy stepped in.

'If you need me, seek me in the town.' Ben looked from Jack to Mya. 'Until three nights hence, my Lady.'

Mya blushed, knowing she was no Lady in the courtly

sense.

'Jack, Feather.' Ben nodded his head at the two of them and then followed his fellow Knight out through the door.

'Mya!' Jack said as he slumped back in his chair. 'I'm going to be a Knight and a Spellward!'

Mya couldn't help smiling though dread kept her serious. 'Just remember, Jack, you will be training to defeat a powerful and dangerous Fey even Renvart and Caelin couldn't stop.'

'I know, Aunt May.' Jack nodded solemnly. 'I'll work very hard.'

'And we start now!' Feather announced. The brownie hopped down from the chair. 'Fey lessons!'

***

The three days passed far too quickly for Mya even with help from Feather and Jack. They took up what they could from the garden to take to market as well as their fresh cheese and eggs; luckily their plans to go to Trade Pass made such behaviour normal. She brought rough flour to make travel bread, oats and dried meat. They set the house as though securing it and intending to return and Mya felt a pang of fear she might never come back here. Her neighbours came for the animals as planned and she pushed away her concern, reminding herself they would be well looked after for the milk and eggs they gave.

Finally, they finished stowing everything in their packs and Mya drew in a sharp breath at how heavy hers was when she lifted it. She wanted to cry but refused for Jack's sake. As the day faded, they sat about the table eating mushroom omelettes and drinking the last of the hot milk. There was little conversation and Jack fidgeted and swung his legs unable to be still.

'Let's get these plates cleaned and stored away.' Feather looked up at Mya and she nodded. As they finished up Feather said to her with some awe in his voice; 'You know, you never once so much as hinted of changing your mind about this since you agreed to it.'

Mya thought about it for a moment. She was afraid, and she hated the idea of Jack going to Ayresport but the boy was entitled to make that choice for himself. She thought of her sister being fed to the Ward by Kasira and all those others like herself with the Gift who might be made to share that fate.

'This is the right thing to do,' Mya told the brownie. 'But maybe not the sensible thing.'

Feather laughed with her. 'I'm the luckiest of brownie's having found the very best of humans.'

'Oh, I don't know about that!' Mya blushed and then started as the door rattled with a knock.

Jack at once leapt to his feet and went to open it.

'No!' Feather gasped. 'Don't open it Jack.'

The boy stopped in his tracks looking at Feather in consternation. 'But–'

Feather held a finger to his lips to shush him.

The door rattled again and Mya's heart flipped over in her chest.

'It isn't Caelin or Ben.' Mya breathed.

'It isn't human.' Feather hissed.

Jack shrank back away from the door.

Mya pointed to the table and Jack stepped back to snatch up the bread knife lying there.

'Can it come in?' Jack asked Feather, eyes wide.

Feather shook his head helplessly. 'It depends what it is.'

The door rattled again.

Mya watched the door handle. It was of iron so most fey couldn't touch it; but then again whatever it was had found a way through the garden fence, filled with nails and hung with charms. She was glad the animals had already been taken safely away. She gasped as the handle began to lower slowly.

There was an anguished shriek and the sound of heavy boots pattering swiftly away. When the door shook again, some moments later, it was with a firm double-tap much higher on the wood. Mya knew at once it was the two knights. She sprang forward past Jack and wrenched it open.

'Mya! Are you all safe?' Ben placed a protective hand on her arm.

She nodded, unable to find her voice for a moment then moved aside to let them in.

'What was it?' Jack asked, still holding the knife but lowering it.

'A Powrie,' Caelin told him, looking thoughtfully at the

knife. 'We're going to have to find you something a little better than that.'

Jack blushed.

'Was it a coincidence?' Mya asked the knights. 'I've had the odd thing stolen, and the animals frightened from time to time but never a blatant visit like this.'

Caelin and Ben looked at each other.

'It's unlikely to be a coincidence,' Caelin admitted. 'Are you ready to go?'

'We need to finish securing the shutters,' she replied, springing to do so at once. Jack helped and Ben gave each a shake to be sure they held firm.

'That's it then.' Mya turned to Caelin who was watching her with his guarded expression again. Mya tried to ignore it and remember it wasn't personal; if someone had done to her what they had done to him, she imagined she would find it hard to trust anyone too.

'You're efficient,' Caelin remarked, not quite allowing it to be a compliment.

Mya couldn't look at him; instead she braced herself and picked up her large backpack.

'My Lady!' Ben cried in alarm and leapt forward to take it from her. 'I'll take that for you.'

'Thank you, sir.' She let the breath out of her lungs and her muscles relaxed, but she couldn't help feeling a little guilty.

Jack hefted his own pack onto his shoulders and Mya took a last look around the house.

'My Lady?' Ben prompted politely.

'Let's go.' She smiled up at the old knight.

Chapter Three

Mya's heart kept telling her to look behind her at her home, but her mind kept her steady and she focused on what was ahead. The sky had darkened to a deep blue and only the barest wisp of cloud obscured the silver stars. Two crows were squabbling in their harsh voices somewhere in the meadow but other than the wind all else was silent. Mya had put on her sturdiest boots and most practical skirt. The dampness of the meadow soon soaked into her skirt, making the fabric heavy, and she wished she could wear trousers like the men.

A soft snort gave away the two horses waiting just under the trees. Both were brown and of better breeding than anything Mya had seen before. They weren't as large as working horses but had a similar build. Ben placed her pack on the back of one with a white sock and a white stripe down its nose.

'Do they have names?' She asked in a whisper as Caelin gestured to Jack to give him his pack.

'This is Asher.' Ben rubbed at his gelding's muscled shoulder. 'Caelin calls his "Horse."'

He said it in such a way Mya assumed it was a joke between the two of them; the glare Caelin gave his fellow Knight confirmed it.

'It will be easier to walk through this part of the forest.' Caelin frowned, his eyes travelling over Mya's attire. 'But you might like a lift, Feather?'

'Oh!' The brownie started. 'Well yes, it would make it easier for me to keep up.'

Caelin dipped to one knee and placed his forearm against the ground. Feather hesitantly stepped onto his arm, holding onto the Knight's shoulder to steady himself and wincing a little at the buzz of the chainmail beneath his feet. Caelin stood slowly and allowed the brownie to step across onto Horse's saddle.

'Be as silent as you can.' Caelin warned Mya and Jack. 'Most fey won't bother a party such as ours but the one's that will, well, they will be the ones we least want to meet. We won't go too far tonight, we need to put some distance between us and Briarton and then we can travel by day. There's an abandoned charcoal burner's hut about three miles west, that's where we're headed.'

Jack nodded; pupils large in the darkness. The Spellward didn't wait for Mya's response but took Horse's halter and started into the deeper part of the forest. Ben indicated for Mya to go ahead of him and she felt a mixture of self-consciousness and reassurance he'd be walking behind her. Jack stepped in ahead of her and close to Horse's stirrup; Mya wondered if her nephew had taken to a little hero worship of Caelin. He certainly wasn't a fairy-tale figure to look at, well not anymore thanks to Kasira, but even she had seen hints of a man that might be easy to admire in other ways.

She held her skirt in one fisted hand to keep it from snagging on the undergrowth, concentrating on where she was stepping and trusting the two knights to watch the forest for danger. When they came close to the brook Caelin turned left and followed its course at a distance before coming to a barely used path. He held up his hand for them to halt and walked forward a short way alone. Mya's imagination went to the dark shape she had seen below the water the night she had met Feather. Then she wondered where the powrie was. It was one of the fey with no fear of iron; they were known to arm themselves with it and favoured heavy hobnail boots. The two knights had done something to scare it off but she couldn't help worrying it still lurked near. Caelin came back, exchanged a look with Ben and then they continued.

Mya heard the brook before she saw it; it was narrow here and someone had built a small crossing out of fallen wood. Caelin led Horse across; Feather looking anxiously down at the water. They had to go in single file and Mya searched every possible hiding place with her eyes. She shivered. The wood was slimy with wet moss and her heartbeat quickened. The water was only shallow but that meant nothing to fey who lived by magic. Once safely across, it was some time before she stopped being aware of the brook being behind her, like some icy fingers reaching out to run down her back.

Deeper they went into the forest growing huge and dense on the north side of the Valley. Mya knew it climbed slowly until it reached the mountains where it covered their knees like a blanket. There, it was said, paths and trails led through them unlike the impassable mountains to the south; but each trail was the territory of fey and each worse than the next, so the tales told.

It was hard to guess the time with only glimpses of stars between the leaves and thickening cloud. Barely any light seeped in between the tree trunks and Mya soon found her eyes aching from straining to see. She winced at every sound; almost waiting to be chastised for each miss-step although even the knights and the horses snapped twigs and crunched undergrowth. Twice she heard a fox bark and once laughter that turned her knees to jelly.

'Go on, my Lady,' Ben said reassuringly behind her. 'It's only a boggart having its fun; it'll do no more harm than try to scare us.'

'It's doing a good job!' Feather confided.

Jack chuckled and Mya was glad her nephew was dealing with their night journey so well.

'Here we are.' Caelin halted.

Mya opened her mouth to take in some deep breaths and wrapped her arms around herself.

She could just make out the dark shape of a hut with a lean-to stacked with wood. They led the horses behind the building and the knights unburdened them.

'Feather, go on in the house with your humans,' Caelin instructed the brownie as he helped him down. 'I'm going to set a minor Ward about the horses and it will feel unpleasant to you if you stay too near.'

'Understood.' Feather nodded at once and joined Mya. Jack had already gone to the charcoal burner's hut and was gingerly opening the door.

'Looks clear!' He announced.

'A moment!' Caelin commanded. He picked up a long,

fallen twig and said one swift word. A green glow like a firefly flowered from the end of the twig and then became a dancing flame. 'I left wood ready in the fireplace and a lantern on the table. Be sure the house is empty still and sing out if it isn't.'

'Yes, Sir,' Jack responded seriously, taking the twig from Caelin with some awe.

Mya and Feather waited behind Jack as he walked back to the door; a glance behind reassured Mya both knights were watching the boy, and she wondered if they were testing him, taking his measure. Mya touched her skirt where she'd stowed a small, sharp vegetable knife in a hidden pocket.

Jack paused in the doorway to peer carefully around the hut, then stepped in to light the small lantern, placing his feet tentatively. Mya scanned every shadow but could find nothing amiss. It smelt damp and unused and thick dust lay over everything. She spotted footprints on the floor; Jack's small ones and larger ones she guessed must be Caelin's. There were tiny paw prints too and droppings declaring the culprits to be only mice; she could see nothing suggesting the presence of fey.

'It's clear, come in!' Jack told them brightly as he bent to light the tinder set in the fireplace.

'I wish Caelin had brought me here in advance.' Feather shook his head as he stepped over the threshold. 'I could have had this place habitable.'

'It's only for a few hours,' Mya said, though her own heart had sunk at the sight of the place.

'It's the last roof we'll have over our heads for a few days so make the most of it.' Ben ducked under the door and came in. 'Cae will stay out with the horses; he doesn't like to be indoors.'

'Do you think he would like tea if I made it?' Mya asked spotting an old kettle.

'It's a nice thought, Mya and generous of you,' Ben said and she could see he was mulling over how to word what he was thinking. 'But Caelin, well, he is suspicious of kindness. We should probably all try to get to sleep, anyway.'

She agreed, although she frowned at his reply.

'Well, I'm gonna tuck myself down by the door here so you can all sleep safe.' Ben unrolled his blanket and gave it a shake.

Mya didn't like the appearance of the musty old bed and it was too warm a spring night to sleep next to the fire; neither did she want to lie on the dirty and dusty floor. She caught Feather's eye, and they both laughed when they saw each other's expressions. Jack and Ben looked at them in puzzlement.

'Five minutes.' Feather grinned. 'And just a little touch of brownie magic.'

He spotted a broom in the corner almost buried in cobwebs. Grasping it firmly he gave it a swish, then released it. Mya gasped as the broom carried on sweeping vigorously across the flagstones and Jack leapt aside with a startled laugh as it sped toward him. With a wide grin Feather touched a dustpan and brush and they went to work on the table and chairs, skimming past Jack so he had to jump quickly over them.

'Water,' Feather murmured, looking to the door.

Ben held up his hand, 'I don't want to spoil your fun now, but there is no well here and I'll not be happy letting you wander far on your own.'

'There was a rain barrel.' Feather looked up at him hopefully with his small dark eyes.

'Be quick!' Ben agreed.

'I'm a brownie!' Feather's smile widened. He snatched the bedding and Jack had to duck as the kettle came flying off the shelf to follow him out the door. Mya laughed as the broom tapped impatiently at the knight's boots to get him to move aside. With an amused shake of his head Ben did so.

'I had no idea this was how brownies got things done!' Mya exclaimed in awe.

'He's showing off for you.' Ben chuckled. 'They wouldn't normally expend all their magic in one go like this and it's unheard of they would let a human see them work.'

Feather stepped back in with a pile of wet bedding larger than himself and the kettle following obediently behind. Ben closed the door firmly and dropped the bar across it. The broom chased Jack around the table making him laugh so much he was out of breath; then it put itself away in the corner. In the meantime, Feather was holding each piece of bedding before the fire and with a whoosh of steam it dried them. Mya couldn't help her instinct to assist and she took the sheets and blanket from the brownie and set about making the bed. The mattress was still damp and musty but the bedding was now deliciously warm and clean. When Mya turned to look the dustpan was tipping its final load into the fireplace and then joined the brush and broom reclining in the corner.

'Have we quite finished?' Ben asked, holding out his blanket ready to lay it out again.

'All done, Sir Knight.' Feather gave a small bow.

'Good.' Ben feigned a scowl. 'You three will have to get used to a bit of dirt.'

'Will I learn things like that?' Jack asked Feather.

'Something like.' The brownie nodded with a glance at Ben who was settling down to sleep. 'My Lady, will you take the bed?'

Mya couldn't help a twinge of guilt at having the only bed, but Ben was smiling as he placed his blanket on the floor and Jack was already settling before the fire near to Feather.

'Thank you, I will. Don't stay up too late you two; I have a feeling we will have an early start and a long day tomorrow.'

'Okay, Aunt Mya.'

Mya went over to the bed and slipped off her boots. Despite the brownie's cleaning she still felt uncomfortable sleeping in someone else's bed so she lay on top of it and pulled her own blanket over her. Today had been frightening, but fun too and she tried not to let her mind wander into her fears to keep her awake worrying. Soaking in the bedding's warmth, she closed her eyes.

***

Feather listened to his human's breathing as they slept. Ben's was loud and slightly rattling but not quite a snore. Jack's whistled a little on the exhale whilst Mya's was hard to make out at all. He shook his head a little at himself, at his showing off his magic and wondering what had possessed him to do it. Despite cohabiting with humans, brownies were by nature solitary and hated to be watched whilst working. Humans spying on a brownie would break the contract between them, but then his arrangement with Mya had differed from the start. Strange girl indeed. Forcing his eyes closed he shut out the hypnotic glow of the burning logs, now an orange smoulder. He would have to get used to human sleeping patterns for a while.

He sat bolt upright as something rustled in the hut's corner. He held his breath and strained to listen, trying to sense the presence of fey. His heartbeat marked out the seconds as the silence stretched. *Just mice*, he told himself; but it was several minutes before he relaxed and lay back down on the corner of blanket Mya had given him to use back in their cottage. For a moment his sharp ears thought they picked out movement outside, but he dismissed it as his imagination or just the horses in the wood shelter. He'd been in worse situations than this, many times before, and worse places, much worse. He tried not to think of them but reminded himself that he was with two knights, one of them a spellward, and his two lovely humans. In fact, when he thought about it, this was ironically one of the safest places he had been in for a long time. Smiling, he settled himself to sleep.

***

Mya woke to the sound of the door opening as Ben quietly slipped out of the hut. The kettle was boiling gently over the fire and Feather was setting out the table for breakfast. Long fingers of weak sunlight spilled between the shutters and Mya almost fancied she could smell the morning. She looked around the room and wondered for the first time who had lived here and what had become of them. There were few possessions and all of them practical; a man then and single. Three horseshoes leant up against the brick of the chimney on a shelf above the fireplace. There was something else there that was out of place and her eyes kept coming back to it; a withered and long dead posy of flowers.

Jack gave a loud and drawn out yawn and stretched under his blanket.

'Well, good morning to you too!' Feather looked up from what he was doing.

Ben came back in and seeing they were all awake went eagerly to the table. There were only two chairs, and he politely declined to sit on either.

'Oh, you go ahead!' Mya told him. 'I need to go outside a moment, anyway.'

'What do you need?' The old knight asked. 'I'll fetch it for you. It's still not safe alone in the forest in daylight.'

Mya blushed. How awkward! This was something she'd never considered when agreeing on their journey. 'I, um, I need to…'

'Oh!' Ben's eyes widened and his cheeks reddened beneath his whiskery beard. 'Your pardon! You must go out. Please don't go far though, stay within calling distance.'

'Of course,' she murmured, hastily leaving. She made her way out to the back of the hut and was relieved to find tall ferns grew up close. Checking Caelin was nowhere in sight she hastily did what she needed to. She passed the water barrel on her way back and stopped. There was little left in it after Feather's magical performance last night and even if there had been clean water, she had nowhere private to wash or change her clothes. With a sigh, she went back into the hut and found someone had poured the tea and Jack was sitting on the bed eating a pickled egg and some bread. She sat on the slightly wonky chair opposite Ben and picked up a slice of bread.

'Will Caelin not be joining us?' she asked, noticing the absence of a fifth cup.

'No, he's broken his fast and is scouting ahead a little way.' Ben told her. 'He won't be long so we had best get ourselves ready.'

Mya nodded as she took in another long sip of her tea. Feather had put chamomile and fennel in it. She wasn't particularly hungry but it might be a long while before they ate again today so she made herself eat the bread.

'Any sign of our powrie friend last night?' Feather asked.

Ben shook his head and swallowed what he was eating. 'No. Caelin said a wolf came close and watched him for a while, but no sign of any fey.'

'A wolf? This close to Briarton?' Mya exclaimed in surprise.

'A lone and hungry wolf would be drawn to the farms.' Ben gave a shrug. 'Between the fey and your farmers, it probably won't last long.'

Oh, poor thing!

The knight took another huge swig of tea, emptying the cup. 'Thanks brownie.' He rolled up his blanket and shrugged himself into his chainmail. The others took the hint and hurried to clean up and pack everything away. When Caelin knocked politely and opened the door, they were all ready and waiting. The spellward looked around in quiet approval.

'Time to go.'

It was a beautiful morning. The few clouds that had haunted the night sky had moved on to leave a serene blue. It was cool in the shade of the trees, but where they grew more thinly the sun was blessedly warm. A multitude of birds sang challengingly to each other and Mya soon forgot her fears. The horses plodded on steadily and Caelin led them confidently along the same narrow trail that had brought them to the abandoned charcoal burner's hut. They stopped for a while beneath the spreading branches of a large beech tree. Old shells and fallen twigs littered the otherwise bare ground around its roots and its wide canopy screened out all but the tiniest thread of the sun.

Not long after, the path they followed took them to a stream where they watered the horses and filled their flasks. Ben and Caelin took turns keeping watch and Mya slipped off on her own again. When she got back Caelin asked, 'Do you have something to protect yourself with?'

'I have a steel knife.'

'No charms?'

'Not with Feather with us.'

'Fair point,' he said to her surprise. He went to Horse and dug into one of his saddlebags. 'Take this.'

Mya opened her hand and he dropped a small flat stone onto her palm; it had a hole in it. 'Thank you!'

Caelin shrugged and led Horse back onto the path to continue their journey with Feather once again ensconced on the saddle. Ben gave her a quick grin as she passed him. She couldn't resist trying the stone and holding it up to her eye she surveyed the forest.

'Do you see any fey?' Jack asked curiously.

'Only Feather!' She laughed.

'Sir.' Jack called almost timidly as he caught up with the spellward to walk at his accustomed place behind him. 'When can I start learning to defend myself? I want to help.'

'Soon,' Caelin replied without looking around. 'On your Gift anyway. There is somewhere we will stop in two days to get you a sword but in the meantime, I guess Ben can teach you a few basics with a sturdy stick.'

Mya frowned, where would he get a sword from in the forest? Surely there were no villages or blacksmiths out here so far beyond the Ward? Perhaps they were heading for one of the villages between Briarton and Ayresport; but when she glanced up at the sky to gauge where the sun was, she saw they were still headed north.

***

It wasn't long before Mya's legs and feet ached but she dared not admit it and risk Caelin's scorn. She trudged on doggedly in silence, no longer enjoying the wild beauty of the forest but concentrating only on where she placed her feet. When evening began to set in and the gloom beneath the trees deepened, she watched Caelin's back, willing him to stop. None of the others had spoken for a long time either; this certainly wasn't how such journeys were described in the hero tales of Jack's books.

Caelin glanced back over his shoulder. 'Ben, keep an eye out for somewhere we can defend for the night. I don't want to travel on in the dark if we can help it.'

Behind her Ben didn't reply and she could only assume he'd nodded his agreement. She took more notice of the surrounding forest again, wondering what the knights would consider a place to defend. The trees here were mostly hazel, alder, oak and beech and where the light reached through the canopy tall ferns and nettles crowded upward. Bees were becoming fewer as flowers closed their petals for the night but midges still danced above the forest flora. The ground rose and fell gradually with only the smallest of hills but always getting gently higher the further north they travelled.

Caelin stopped Horse and bent a little to look to his left. 'This will have to do.' He glanced back at Ben and then led Horse off the path.

Mya glanced around, breathing faster. She shivered, noticing for the first time the temperature had dropped. Caelin came to a halt and at first Mya looked around in consternation, wondering what was defensible about this overgrown spot; then she realised they were standing beside a rowan tree.

'Are you okay here?' Caelin asked Feather who was

sitting slumped on Horse's saddle.

'Aye, I'm good.' Feather nodded his wide head. ''Tis witches and enchanters who can't stand rowan. I quite like them.'

They unburdened the horses and Caelin tethered them so they could get to the long grass between the nettles. Finding ground clear and comfortable enough even to sit on was a challenge, but they eventually settled as night sank upon them. There was enough light for them to still read each other's expressions. Jack sat hunched over his pack, head bowed. Digging into her pack Mya unwrapped the last of the cherry cake she'd made to celebrate Jack's apprentice year. She passed it around and as they chewed on it, everyone's mood lifted and they began to talk.

'This is the first time I've really slept outdoors,' Jack said. 'Whenever we went to Trade Pass, we stopped in barns or inns.'

Mya had always hated stopping at farms to exchange a few pennies or a few hours labour for a roof for the night. It was common practice in the Valley but she'd always feared the embarrassment of being turned down and the danger of then spending the night out in the open. She and Jack had never been turned down thankfully, but then she guessed a young woman and a boy probably seemed harmless enough to most people.

'Cae here prefers the stars to a roof.' Ben grinned. 'But then he's little more than a common hedge knight!'

'As are you, old man.' Caelin raised an eyebrow. 'I love to breathe the night air. Walls are too suffocating.'

Mya took the opportunity to study him. As always, it was hard to tell what the spellward was feeling beneath his guarded expression and she wondered if he would have been more himself had it just been Jack along with them. The scar was frightening to look at, but only in that she couldn't help imagine the pain and shock such a wound must have caused. His green eyes were large in the near darkness and she realised his right eye was pulled slightly down by the scar which gave him an expression of scowling even when he wasn't. He turned, and she dropped her eyes quickly to her hands.

'What of you, Mya?' Ben asked. 'Do you like the open?'

'I love to be outside at night.' She drew in a deep breath and gazed up through the trees. 'Somehow the air seems new at night, like it's only you breathing it; like it's been born from the dew. The world seems larger but not in a scary way, more like you could just run and run and never come to the end. Sounds are sharper and smells clearer, and it makes me feel as though I've just awakened into the world and have only just realised I have all my senses. And I love the wind at night, sometimes it feels like a gentle kiss or a touch to reassure me I'm not alone.'

Ben gave a small cough to clear his throat and Mya glanced up, blushing furiously when she realised they were all watching at her.

'I'm just being silly though.' She wished the ground would swallow her up. What had possessed her to say such a daft thing out loud?

'It isn't silly,' Caelin said quietly. 'It isn't silly at all.' He stood up and went over to the horses.

'Well, come on then,' Ben prompted. 'We should try to get some sleep. Caelin will take first watch. You're a night fellow, Feather, will you take a turn after him?'

'Of course!' Feather replied at once. 'You might just as well make the most of a night owl like me.'

'Jack and I should help too,' Mya offered.

'We'll see,' Ben replied diplomatically.

Mya spread her blanket out as well as she could, stinging her wrist on a nettle in the process. She refrained from rubbing it but put her wrist to her mouth to try to sooth it with her tongue. Keeping her boots on she wrapped herself up and wriggled a little to find a comfortable position amongst the roots and stones. Eventually tiredness won out, and she fell asleep.

***

Feather was awake before Caelin came over to him, stalking as silently as any cat. He'd squeezed himself in between the roots of the rowan and the spellward leaned against it. 'Not much to report. That wolf is still following us, perhaps hoping to get a chance at the horses. I sensed a gnoll nearby, but he was alone and minded his own business.'

'Let's hope he doesn't have friends.' Feather gave an involuntary shudder.

'Yes, I'll be surprised if we go through another night without being challenged. Word will be out that we're in the forest.'

'You think Kasira will have heard?' Feather sat up in

alarm.

'It's possible.' Caelin nodded. 'But I have our route planned to both throw off the scent and get a little help on the way. There's no need to alarm the others.'

'Okay,' he agreed, although he found his heart was racing. 'Would you help me up into that branch? I'll be able to keep a better eye out from there.'

Caelin offered his arm and Feather stepped on, feeling again the buzz of the chainmail through his shoes. He hopped across onto the branch and settled himself where he could turn to see almost three hundred and sixty degrees around him.

'I'm good,' he told Caelin.

The spellward nodded and moved stealthily across their camp to fetch his blanket from Horse and settle himself to sleep.

Feather felt lonely with no one left to talk to, which he knew was ironic since he'd only recently *not* been alone. It had been far from an easy life being a brownie without a home. When he'd first been driven out of the Valley, he'd escaped from one near disastrous scrape to another. His first reprieve came when he found a hobb who took him in; Bertram. Hobbs were not dissimilar to brownies except they liked to live away from human buildings. They were healers by nature and just as happy to help a bird or and animal as a deserving human. Bertram had a house built in the bole of a lightning-struck tree about a mile from a small village called Willowford. The hobb had taught him how to forage for food and how to use his mending and hastening magic to make things grow. He'd also taught him several tricks to evade the Dark Fey and the predatory Wild Fey.

When Feather had been ready to make his own way, Bertram had arranged for him to take over the old part of a badger set, Bertram having healed several generations of badgers there. Feather had many happy years there with Bertram as a close neighbour until the boggarts had arrived. There had been five of them, all a third again larger than himself. He'd never understood how humans could think they were related to brownies or hobbs, you'd as well say a kelpie was a pony. He had only a moment's warning, hearing their voices as they sauntered into the badgers' set. He'd dropped his cup, still full, ignoring the liquid that spilt over his soft woven rabbit fur rug. He'd run for the way out, darting into a side tunnel just in time as the first of the brutes had come into view. He'd gone straight to Bertram to warn him, only to find the hobb missing and his tree home smashed and fouled.

He stayed away for days, hiding in the hollow of a mouldering log with the woodlice and slugs. When he'd crept back, he found to his dismay the boggarts had taken up residence in his home. With nothing but the clothes on his back he'd set out into the forest once again, praying he might find his friend Bertram somewhere safe and well. Instead, he had found his humans. The thought almost made him smile but for the anxiety he still felt for Bertram's fate. Boggarts were cruel and dirty, but not usually murderous, but then they were also usually solitary like hobbs and brownies. Nothing had been as it should be since the coming of Kasira and the invention of the Ward.

He looked towards where Caelin slept and wondered what the whole of the young knight's plan was. What of the Ward if he defeated Kasira and saved the Gifted humans?

What would it mean for Wild Fey such as himself?

A twig snapped off to his right, tearing him out of his reverie. His vision wasn't bad at night but not exceptional, after all brownies were not hunters or predators. He strained his eyes to see if anything moved beyond their camp.

'Snap!'

He twisted around on his branch, heart pounding. The sound had woken Horse and his head rose up, ears swivelling. Feather stood carefully to see further.

'Snap!'

This time off to his left. He was about to call out and wake Caelin when a high-pitched giggle halted him.

'Stupid pixie!' He hissed, grinding his teeth in annoyance. 'Go away!'

A stone came whistling toward him out of the dark and he ducked just in time.

'We have a Spellward with us!' He warned.

Caelin stirred and woke as if summoned, sitting up with his sword hilt in his hand.

'Pixie,' Feather grumbled in explanation.

They both listened for several minutes. When they heard nothing Caelin sighed and settled himself again. Feather sat himself back down and continued to watch.

**

When Mya woke, she found Feather sleeping close to her on his bit of blanket, snoring softly. It wasn't quite dawn but a pale pink light was seeping through the trees and painting the foliage in soft hues. Birds were singing in sporadic bursts of delightful melody, making her heart tingle. A yellow butterfly dipped low over the nettles and danced away erratically and she watched its flight for a moment until her body reminded her of its needs.

Sitting up as quietly as she could she looked around to see Ben was keeping watch over their camp. Giving him an embarrassed smile, she got up and crept away into the forest to find somewhere private. It was okay for the others, all they needed do was step behind a convenient tree! She found some bushes and made a quick survey with the looking-stone. No sign of any fey; however, as she stood up and straightened her clothes she froze. A few yards away the wolf stood facing her. It was large but lean and mostly white with light-grey markings. It looked straight at her with an expression that made it seem almost as startled as she felt. It took a step back without taking its eyes off her.

'Hello,' Mya whispered. 'Hello there, wolf.'

It tipped its head a little to one side, ears tilting toward her. She realised she should probably be afraid, but the wolf didn't seem in the least frightening and she wished she had food to give it; it looked thin beneath its coat of fur.

'Mya?' Ben called anxiously.

The wolf turned and ran, vanishing into the sunbeams as though it were some enchanted creature itself made of light.

'I'm okay!' She called. She hesitated, scouring the forest

a moment longer, before returning to the others.

'I'm sorry,' Ben said awkwardly as she got back to the camp.

'It's okay,' she told the knight. 'I'm glad you're looking out for me.'

The others were all up and about and Caelin had allowed Feather to make a fire to cook up some of their fresh food that was starting to go off and to brew some nettle tea. The Spellward had taken Jack aside and was showing him how to brush down the horses. In no time at all they were packing away their camp and getting ready to move on. Mya almost fancied her feet began to ache in protest at the thought of more walking. When no one was looking she took some travel bread out of her pack and slipped it into her pocket with her knife.

'We need to try to make good time today,' Caelin said as he walked Horse around to take them back toward the forest track. 'We'll be crossing one of the tributaries of the River Ayre, the Wither, and it's not a good river to be near after dark. There's an old barrow close to the ford inhabited by an ogre and he and I are not friends.'

Ben gave a snort.

'However, it's the way we must go. Jack, when we stop for a rest around midday, I'll teach you how to summon your gift and one basic spell of defence.'

Jack's face broke into a grin and it warmed Mya's heart to see, although she feared all too much Caelin had hastened Jack's lessons because he would need to defend himself very, very soon.

Chapter Four

A grove of oaks provided them with a place to stop and rest for lunch. One of the eldest trees had fallen leaving a large gap in the forest canopy letting in the warm spring sun. They shared out their food rations and gave the horses some carrots and a handful of oats to make up for the meagre grazing. Ben had cut two staves of hazel as they were walking and gave one to Jack. Whilst the knight showed him how to hold it like a sword and some simple blocking, Mya slipped away into the forest.

Using the stone, she scanned the lush green undergrowth to check for any fey, though it wasn't really them she was looking for.

'Wolf!' She called under her breath. Then a little louder. 'Wolf?'

She sucked in air in surprise when a pale broad head shot up from the ferns to her right.

'Here!' Putting her hand in her pocket she took out the bread and held it out. The wolf's muzzle lifted as it scented the air but it made no move to stand or come toward her. Worried Ben might already be concerned for her, she threw the bread, and it landed with a swish somewhere in the ferns. The wolf stood gingerly, creeping forward a step at a time; it darted in and snatching up the bread turned and ran. It had a black tip to its otherwise cream and grey tail.

Smiling, Mya made her way back to the others.

Ben was still swinging his stick at Jack who was fending him off clumsily but with a serious look of concentration on his face. Caelin raised his eyes at Mya's approach and called out to them.

'My turn, Jack. Let's take a little walk.'

Jack tuned to look hesitantly at Mya and she forced a smile to let Jack know it was okay. Inside though, she couldn't help feeling both a little hurt and a little angry. She'd said she would abide by Caelin's wish not to teach her, there was no need for him to be sneaking off to teach Jack in secret.

Ben had the good grace to look a little embarrassed.

'I could teach you,' Feather said.

She stared at the brownie in horror. 'No, Feather! Thank you, but no. That would be betraying Caelin's trust as much as if I followed him and Jack.'

'You promised not to learn from *him*; you said nothing of learning a little brownie magic if your Gift will bend that way.'

Ben blew out air and shrugged as if to say it was nothing to do with him.

'Maybe when we get to the Hall,' Mya conceded. 'But not when I'm travelling under Caelin's protection, it would feel like a betrayal.'

Feather gave a shake of his head and looked at Ben.

'Well, um, perhaps we can teach you something that isn't magic?'

'Sling!' Feather brightened. 'Mya, let me teach you how to use a sling.'

'That sounds okay.' She turned to Ben for reassurance.

'It would be a good weapon for you to start with,' the knight said eagerly. 'Do you have a sling brownie?'

Feather reached into the inside of his jacket and slowly pulled one out, looking at it thoughtfully before holding it up. 'I do. A good friend gave this to me and taught me to use it. Bertram was his name.'

'Well now, it's your turn to teach a friend.' Ben smiled warmly. 'Let's set up a target. I don't expect we have long.' He drained the dregs of his cup and placed it on the slowly decaying trunk of the fallen oak then moved back out of the way.

Feather held out his slingshot and Mya took it carefully, mindful of the fact this small weapon meant a lot to the brownie.

'Right,' Feather began. 'Wrap this loop around your wrist and let the cord fall through the space between your thumb and finger, lying against your palm.'

Mya did so. It was obviously made for a creature smaller than herself but it slipped easily over her own hand.

'Now hold the knot at the other end between your thumb and finger.'

Mya nodded, following the instructions. Feather took a small bolt out of his pocket and handed it to her.

'Put this in the leather pouch there. Yes, that's it. Now, when you're ready swing the sling forward fast, moving from your shoulder. Release the knot as you swing forward. When you're ready…'

Mya swallowed, glancing at the others and taking in a deep breath. She swung her arm; the sling making an almost pleasant whining hum through the air.

'Let go!'

She did and the small bolt flew over the cup and vanished into the forest.

'Not bad!' Ben exclaimed. 'You had a good release, and you weren't far off with your aim. Give an overhead shot a go.'

Her shot had actually disappointed Mya though she supposed she couldn't expect to be any good on her first try, and probably shouldn't be so hard on herself.

'Hold it the same way,' Feather encouraged. 'And start as you did but this time as you swing you raise your arm so you're circling the sling above your head, this time the movement comes more from your elbow. Try to add the strength of your arm as you swing to release.'

Mya nodded, prepared herself, and taking in a deep breath swung her arm. She let the air out of her lungs at the same time as she released the knot between her finger and thumb; the small bolt hit the tree trunk only an inch below the cup.

'Oh! Well done, my girl!' Feather clasped his hands together.

'Looks like I will have to make you a sling.'

They turned to see Caelin standing behind them with Jack. Her nephew was all but glowing and she guessed his lesson had gone well; she was shocked at the little stab of jealousy deep in her stomach.

'I'll make one.' Feather drew himself up.

Caelin gave a slight bow, ignoring the brownie's defensive tone and remaining polite. 'As you wish. Are we ready to go?'

They weren't but hurried to be so. As they left the oak grove Mya couldn't help a glance behind her, it was foolish, but she really hoped the wolf was still following.

As before Caelin kept them going at a steady pace along the overgrown trail. A knot of apprehension gripped Mya as the afternoon wore on, she couldn't help thinking of Caelin's warning of the river and the barrow ogre. Jack was still full of energy after his lesson and he and Feather conversed frequently, their conversation even going to what it was like to live with badgers. Above them the clouds gathered and thickened and the warmth of the sun faded.

Caelin halted and raised his hand. Feather and Jack ceased their chatter immediately.

'We are not far from the river,' the spellward explained. He stilled, his eyes growing distant and his head tilted as he listened. Mya realised she was holding her breath and made herself breathe. 'Let's get off the path,' Caelin decided.

Mya glanced behind at Ben for reassurance, but the knight's expression was grim.

They skirted the trunks of the larger trees where the forest floor was clearer and it was easier to walk. Mya found her hand slipping into her pocket and she held the small knife, its handle reassuring against her palm. Her skirt kept snagging on the undergrowth and when she tore it away from a grasping bramble, it ripped a little. A mocking giggle sounded from somewhere above them.

'We should turn our clothes inside out,' Ben growled. 'That will get rid of the little pests!'

'And me with them.' Feather shuddered.

'That affects you too?' Jack asked in surprise.

'It would drive me crazy.' The brownie winced. 'Don't ask me why, but I cannot bear to see clothing inside out; it's just so… so wrong!'

'It's only pixies,' Caelin said without turning. 'But something guarded the ford so be wary.'

That sobered them all immediately and Mya wondered what it was Caelin had seen or sensed. For the first time she wished she could use her Gift so she had a better idea of what was going on. With a sigh, she realised she should ask.

'Sir, what was at the ford?'

Caelin turned his head a little over his shoulder to speak, showing all of his vivid scar. 'It was a Barghest, Mya.'

Ben gave a low whistle. 'Well, I'm glad we didn't have to tangle with that!'

'Hmm.' Caelin reached up and rubbed Horse's neck. 'Avoiding it hasn't helped us any; the only other safe crossing over the Wither takes us a little too close to the barrow.'

'Not necessarily the lesser of two evils,' Ben complained.

'The difference is the ogre is here because it's his home and loathe him or not he's Wild Fey. That barghest was Dark Fey.'

'We are hunted already?' Ben asked in consternation.

'I at least am hunted,' Caelin said. 'Too many Fey have now seen I'm alive for it to still be secret and Kasira will be in a hurry to change my circumstances; she'll want to know what I'm up to. The sooner we disappear the better.'

Mya walked closer behind Jack as her protective instinct kicked in; she also felt a little safer herself closer to the large horse. She knew Ben and his Asher were right behind her but it was easier to be reassured by something visible. When they came to the river again even her hair seemed to prickle with nerves. None of them had spoken for a long time and she jumped when Caelin spoke. 'The way seems to be clear.'

Tentatively they crossed over the water on a simple planked bridge with wide gaps. The water flowing beneath was fast, dark and deep and Mya almost tripped up staring down between the wood. Horse stumbled, one of his hooves missing the plank and slipping. He recovered himself quickly and Mya felt light-headed with relief when her feet touched solid ground. Caelin quickly checked Horse's leg for injury and, seeming happy, ushered them on at speed.

'Why would that bridge not have a fey living there?' Jack asked Feather under his breath. 'If I was a fey, I'd wait around at bridges knowing people would have to go there to cross.'

'And the ogre knows fey would think to haunt the bridge hoping to catch a stray human.' Feather replied. 'For most fey hanging around a bridge is as dangerous as it is for any human. We are not so different in a lot of ways, Jack.'

Jack remained silent whilst he took this in. Mya looked at Caelin's back, watching for any sign of what the spellward was thinking. She glanced behind her at Ben and he smiled at her reassuringly. She liked the old knight but couldn't help still feeling a little shy around him.

Caelin hissed in warning and pulled down on Horse's head to stop him quickly. Mya's heart raced as the spellward drew his sword and Ben stepped up behind her.

'Cae?' Ben drew his own sword.

Mya stood on tiptoe to see over Horse's back.

Then she heard it; the snap and crunch of undergrowth being trampled and pushed aside. Something was coming with no fear of being detected. Feather drew out his sling and looked at Mya, his brown eyes wide but his expression determined. Horse shied; scenting something he really didn't like and Caelin had to hold tight to the reins in his left hand. When she saw it Mya couldn't help a cry of dismay. The creature was easily three times the size of the knights with skin a greyish-green. It was dressed in a patchwork of rags and animal skins and it carried a large pitted club in one hand. In the other something wriggled and squirmed and, as the ogre put it to its over-large mouth to bite down, Mya realised it was a pixie. She stifled a scream but turned and retched.

Trying hard to block the image from her mind she fought the nausea but couldn't bring herself to look up.

'Brinsten.' Caelin greeted the ogre.

'Spellward.' It growled. 'I heard you were back from the dead. Were you trying to sneak through my land without seeking my permission?'

'Actually, I was seeking to avoid the Barghest following me.'

Mya dared to look up in time to see the momentary fear on the ogre's bulbous face.

'Barghest.' The ogre scoffed. 'It would have to pay tribute like everyone else. What have you got me?' Its eyes fell on Mya and she shuddered.

'A sword in your belly, ogre, if you think you can touch a hair on this lady's head!' Ben bristled.

Mya shrank to the old knight's side as fear clutched at her stomach. She didn't even want to imagine what the ogre might want with her. Even Ben let out a grunt of disgust and turned away as the ogre stuffed the rest of the now, thankfully dead, pixie in his mouth and chewed away with its mouth open.

'Brinsten, don't make trouble for yourself.' Caelin warned quietly. 'I'll pay a tithe out of respect; your land, your rule. We have some provisions with us and–'

'I want the woman!'

Feather stood up on Horse's saddle to protest but Caelin remained silent and still and Mya's heart pounded. She knew

Caelin had never wanted her along but did he really hate women that much? A strange tickling sensation danced within her chest and she realised with shock she was sensing her nephew calling up his Gift. Jack stood as though frozen, one hand over his heart and his head bowed in concentration.

'No, Jack!' She hissed. 'Leave it to Caelin.'

The spellward gave the barest shake of his head, his eyes not leaving the ogre. 'Brinsten are you really in such a hurry to die? If it's a fight you want, take my tithe and make your fight with the barghest.'

The ogre hesitated and glanced past them at the forest behind.

'We are two of us knights and two of us spellwards, think about that ogre.' Caelin continued in his level manner, giving nothing of his emotions away.

Mya held her breath as the ogre continued to square up to Caelin. Then it seemed to deflate and, grumbling, relented. 'What food 'ave y' got?'

Caelin turned a little, not quite looking over his shoulder, but Mya took his cue. 'We have a jar of pickled eggs?'

'More!' The ogre demanded.

'Well.' Mya steeled herself, making her hands into fists to stop them from shaking. 'All the rest is travel rations. We have travel bread and dried beef?'

None of the others corrected her omissions from her inventory.

The ogre didn't look pleased, but she made herself hold its gaze, it had very human eyes in its warty green face. 'I want both!'

'You may have both.' She gave a polite nod and searched through the bags on the horses. Jack kept looking between her and the ogre, but Caelin's gaze never left Brinsten. She handed the jar of pickled eggs to Ben and, moving their supplies about to free up a bag to put it in, took out roughly a quarter of their dried beef and less of the bread. Ben sheathed his sword to take it all from her and she smiled at him gratefully, more than a little glad they hadn't left her to approach the ogre.

Feather remained standing on the saddle as Ben walked toward Brinsten. Mya stood close beside Jack and managed to refrain from reaching for his hand as though he were still a child.

Ben stopped a few paces away from the ogre and all but threw the goods down. 'Brinsten,' he acknowledged curtly and then turned and strode back.

The ogre growled but leapt forward at once to snatch up his gifts.

Caelin sheathed his sword and stepped back to take Horse's head. 'Goodbye, ogre,' he dismissed as he led them away into the forest. Feather quickly sat down and Ben took up position protectively between Mya and the ogre. It watched them as it went, its eyes lingering on Mya in a way that made her skin crawl.

'If I see you again, Spellward!' It threw one last threat at them. 'I'll want more than a few scraps!'

Caelin didn't respond but took them northward out of the Wither river valley.

***

Evening was drawing on before Caelin allowed them to stop. He didn't seem inclined to give Jack a lesson and the young man had the sense not to ask. Both knights stepped away to discuss something in hushed tones as Mya shared out some of their reduced supplies, slipping some strips of dried beef into her pocket.

'Aunt Mya, how did you know I was going to cast a spell with my Gift?' Jack asked her.

She glanced at Feather, but the subdued brownie hadn't reacted.

'I'm not sure really,' she replied cautiously, touching the base of her throat. 'I just felt it.'

'Inside your ribcage?' Jack's brown eyes widened in surprise. 'Like there was a little bird trapped in there?'

'Yes,' Mya whispered.

'That's how it feels when you call it.' Jack lowered his voice even more. 'You imagine it like a tickling sensation in the centre of your chest and you feed it until–'

'Jack!' She stopped him in alarm. 'You mustn't teach me!'

Jack's expression went from hurt to a touch of fear when he realised his error. They both looked quickly toward the knights but they were still deep in their own conversation.

'I'm sorry.' Jack winced. 'I guess I'm just used to you being the one I share things with.'

A lump formed in Mya's throat. She knew as her young nephew grew, he would find his own friends and hopefully a nice wife, but it was good to hear she hadn't lost their close bond yet. 'Thank you, Jack. Maybe one day you'll be able to talk to me freely about your lessons, just not when we are under Caelin's protection. I need to slip away for a moment, I won't go far.'

Both Feather and Jack looked up at her with wide eyes, but neither protested, after all she didn't really have any choice. She slipped away between the trees to where some bushes grew thickly. Once she'd finished, she took out her hollow stone and checked again for fey. Glancing back at the camp to make sure it was still in sight she moved a little further out into the forest and called softly.

'Wolf!'

She listened for a moment but heard nothing except distant birdsong, the creaking of trees and the buzz of insects.

'Wolf!'

A huge shape lurched out in front of her from behind a tree, its warty hand flexing to grasp at her wrist.

'Got ya!'

Mya screamed.

A flash of white came from behind her, almost bowling her over. With a growl the wolf's jaws clamped down on the ogre's arm and Brinsten let out his own cry of pain. Mya fumbled in her pocket for her tiny knife, tangled in with the strips of meat. The ogre lashed out with his club, hitting the wolf with a horrible thud.

'You leave him!' Mya darted forward slashing at the ogre's arm.

The wolf let go its grip and took two limping steps back whilst Brinsten recoiled from Mya's attack. Then a commotion behind them heralded the arrival of the two knights and Jack.

'Ogre!' Caelin pulled Mya roughly behind him. 'I warned you.'

With a roar the ogre swept his club up toward Caelin's head but the knight stepped back and flexing his fingers set loose a spell. The club sprouted leaves and split into soft vines hanging limply from Brinsten's hand. The ogre dropped it in disgust and swung a fist, the air before Caelin shimmered and with a howl the ogre slammed it into a shield of ice.

Mya backed away to give them space but edged toward the wolf rather than the safety of Ben and Jack. Its hackles were up and its lips curled to show its teeth; all its attention on the ogre.

Caelin drew his sword, his expression making even Mya quail. He thrust it toward Brinsten who dodged aside and flailed his arm to protect his belly. A red welt opened in the ogre's forearm spraying blood, Caelin's strike so quick it was like magic. Enraged Brinsten launched himself at the knight, unmindful of the steel blade. Mya heard Jack gasp and Caelin disappeared from her view. Ben stepped anxiously forward his own sword held at the ready but hesitating to step in.

With a crack like ice breaking a rock, the ogre went flying back to hit the tree with such force it shook and several leaves came spiralling down. For a moment Mya stood frozen and all of them stared at the ogre that lay unmoving. Then Mya realised Caelin wasn't moving either.

'Sir!' She sprang forward to kneel beside the knight. 'Caelin?'

Caelin twitched and stirred, Mya's muscles weakened as relief flowed through her.

'Sir, are you hurt?'

Caelin opened his eyes and blinked rapidly as though the dappled forest light hurt his eyes.

'That spell he cast would have felled the strongest of spellwards,' Ben said softly beside her. 'He'll have a hellish headache. Jack, help me get him back to camp.'

'Is the ogre dead?' Jack asked in awe.

'He is.' Ben knelt and got an arm under Caelin to lift him to his feet. Mya stood aside and the old knight grunted with the effort. 'We best hurry,' Ben prompted them. 'We'll be vulnerable out here without Caelin's Gift and there are those who would've felt that spell. The dangerous and the curious will be gathering.'

Mya picked up Caelin's dropped sword and searched for the wolf, it was still with them, head and tail hung low. 'Come my *good* wolf,' she encouraged. 'Are you hurt badly? Let's get you some food. Come, Wolf.'

She turned to follow after Ben and Jack who were supporting Caelin between them and when she glanced around, it heartened her to see Wolf was following them. Then with a thought like a blow she realised who was missing.

'Where's Feather?'

***

Feather had leapt up at once on hearing Mya's scream, grabbing for his sling. Caelin and Ben had raced straight past him with a terrified Jack on their heels. Then something made the hair on the back of Feather's neck stand up and he turned in time to spot a fey sneaking into their camp. The Powrie went straight for the horses.

'Hey!' Feather shouted, fumbling to place a bolt in his sling. 'Not so fast fellow!'

The powrie pulled a face that would have curdled milk but it wasn't something that would halt a worldly old fey like Feather. He whirled the sling above his head and let the bolt fly. The powrie dove behind Jack's discarded pack and it ground its teeth and chattered like an angry squirrel. It was up on its feet in an instant, twirling its iron mace. Feather flinched, the thought of being impaled by the metal making his teeth hurt. His fingers dug into his pouch and found another obsidian bolt.

'What do you want here, Powrie?' Feather demanded.

The powrie tapped the cloth on its head and winked with a hideous smile. The cap it wore was a dull brown and Feather's eyes widened in realisation. Powries were one of the few fey who had an immunity to iron but as always there was a price to pay; in the powries' case it was a price in blood. A fresh murder kept a powrie's hat bright and scarlet, the longer it went without causing a death, the duller its hat and the weaker the creature. This one looked in dire need of a kill. With a twinge of guilt Feather wished he'd gone on after the others and left the powrie to the horses.

The powrie raised its mace and charged, its hobnail boots thudding across the forest floor and inside Feather's head. He didn't have enough time to get much momentum and power behind his shot but it hit the powrie square on its crooked nose. The powrie faltered but still came on, blood dripping down its face. The much smaller brownie had no choice, he ran, darting sideways into the undergrowth. Feather knew there was no chance of outrunning the larger fey and hiding was impossible with it so close on his heels. His pride shied from running toward where the knights had gone but he couldn't think of a better plan.

Then he felt it; the tang of magic from the Gift. There was no doubt in his mind Caelin had let loose a spell and that meant a whole heap of trouble. The powrie's boots still came pounding behind him along with the rasping of its breath. He didn't dare turn, but instead picked every narrow way he could under low growing brambles in the hope of slowing it down. There was only one way in which a tiny brownie had an advantage over a murderous Redacap; magic. Powries had traded in magic for their blood curse allowing them to touch iron.

It was hard for Feather to concentrate when he could all but feel the powries vile breath on the back of his neck, but he reached out with his inner power and a tree root twisted up to trip the powrie. It cursed, but Feather didn't look around or pause and soon enough the iron boots came thudding behind him again. Feather turned back toward the horses, scared to go too far into the deep wood and praying the others would be back soon. He reached out into the sap of a bramble and as he passed through it sprouted rapidly to form a thick barrier that snared and snagged the powrie.

'Damned house rat!' It yelled after him.

Feather stumbled over onto his knees in shock as he felt the rebound of a powerful spell let off not far away. For a confused moment he thought the powrie had somehow attacked him with magic after all. Then he scrambled up with his palms and knees smarting and threw all his energy into a last burst back to the horses.

'Feather!'

Relief flooded through him at the sound of Mya's voice but it was short lived. Her voice was full of fear.

'Here!' He gasped.

He saw her above the undergrowth searching for him and froze as the muzzle of a grey and white wolf was thrust toward him. It sniffed at him, its eyes seeming too intelligent.

'Wolf! He's a friend.' Mya hurried over. 'Oh Feather, you had me so worried! Are you hurt?'

'Just lost a little skin.' He pressed his palms together. 'That powrie came for the horses. What happened to you?' He tried to see past her.

'Brinsten attacked me. Caelin killed him but casting his magic has... well he's barely conscious.'

Feather closed his eyes in sympathy. 'There's a high price for a killing spell. Listen, that powrie is still near and even he will be trouble without Caelin to protect us. We best get moving fast.'

'Ben says there's somewhere we can get to before nightfall if we hurry.'

Feather nodded and went quickly to the horses. Ben already had Caelin secured in Horse's saddle. He picked Feather up and placed him amongst the baggage on Asher.

'Right, we don't stop.' Ben addressed them all. 'Not for anything. If night catches us out in the open without Caelin...'

'Jack, keep Caelin on Horse.' Mya stepped determinedly forward and took Asher's head. 'Ben, you'd better lead the way.'

Chapter Five

The forest darkened quickly; the temperature falling so even at their fast pace Mya was chilled. Wolf had ranged ahead several times, always circling back to check on them. Now he stayed close to Mya with his head lowered and she feared he was still hurting after the blow the ogre had given him. She glanced back to see Jack followed close behind. Caelin had managed to stay in his saddle but his skin still had a grey hue and his eyes were barely open. She wondered how much willpower it was taking the man to remain even as conscious as he was. She tried not to blame herself but she knew she should never have gone so far from their camp to find Wolf.

Ben strode ahead, he'd barely said a word but had kept up his relentless pace. She wondered where he was heading that he believed was safe. She glanced at Feather but decided against asking the brownie who was being introspective himself. Her heart gave a lurch as a pheasant startled ahead of them and shot upward with an angry cackle. Wolf watched it but there was nothing but tiredness in his eyes.

'Will we make it?' Jack called out from behind.

Shadow's deepened and songbirds ended their singing one by one. There was barely a glimmer of silver light through the trees from the west where the sun had vanished already behind the distant mountains.

'Well, well, well!'

Ben drew his sword and Wolf growled up at the branches above them, hackles rising. Jack held out a hand to steady Caelin as Horse stopped abruptly. It was a woman's voice. Mya looked up but couldn't see anyone. Then a green and brown shape, unmistakably female, detached itself from the tree and came sliding down a vine to land silently amongst them. She had short glossy black hair and eyes of a deep, dark green. Her clothing was so tight it almost appeared painted on and made of leaves. Every movement was slow, deliberate, elegant and seductive with seemingly no effort at all. There was a quiver and bow at her back and a long silver knife at her hip. She looked Jack up and down in a way that made the boy blush and Mya bristle.

'Lissa!' Ben sheathed his sword and hurried back toward them with such relief on his face Mya's own eyes threaten to water. The sinuous woman threw her arms around the old man and he hugged her back.

'Old bear.' She smiled into his shoulder.

'Were you looking for us?'

'Half the Valley will be!' She chastised him playfully but her eyes showed concern as she pulled away from Ben to peer at Caelin. 'That spell was *fierce*. So angry.' She turned to Mya, raising an eyebrow. Mya took a moment to study the half-fey's face, and she realised the forest-clad woman was much younger than herself.

'I'm Mya.' She touched a hand to her chest. 'This is Jack, this is Feather, and this is Wolf.'

Lissa raised a perfect eyebrow. 'You travel with a Wolf?'

'We haven't figured that out yet.' Ben admitted. 'I'll leave that to you, or your father. Everyone, this is Lissa, she's a dryad.'

'Half dryad.' She smiled showing small white teeth. 'Half druid!' Her eyes fell on Caelin again and with barely a pause she moved fluidly ahead. 'Let's get a move on. I can get some protection from the forest but we're a way from The Grove yet.'

'Ashgrove!' Feather said with some awe as they started after the young woman.

'You know where she's taking us?' Mya asked.

'I've heard of it but never been.' Feather told her. 'It's a town surrounded by a high wall and a moat coaxed from the river Hart. It protects a dryad grove and its chief is a druid. Humans live there who abide in harmony with the forest and the fey. We're past the reaches of the Ward now my girl, even as it was at its full strength. We're on the edges of the Valley as it's marked on the maps of Men.'

'But we're still such a way from the mountains!'

'Not such a way.' Ben glanced back over his shoulder. 'Maybe four days' travel.'

Mya tried to recall maps she'd seen of the Valley. Five rivers came down from the mountains to the north, each one joining the huge river Ayre. Each river made a small valley of its own through the mountains, most of which were thickly forested. There'd been nothing on the maps of villages or groves. She wondered how much else was unknown to the average folk of the Valley.

A stone shot out from the undergrowth, hitting Asher and making him start and shy. Feather clung to the saddle and Wolf let out a low growl.

'Keep going!' Ben commanded, though he loosed his sword an inch.

Mya sucked in air as she sensed her nephew draw up his Gift defensively, it was as though her heart had pins and needles.

Something tittered out in the darkness.

'Hobgoblin.' Feather ground his teeth. 'A pest but not too much of a problem if he's on his own.'

Mya didn't bother to ask how much of a problem it would be if it wasn't alone, and there was still the powrie and barghest to consider.

A low whistle came from ahead and Lissa responded in a higher tone.

'Scouts!' She told them cheerfully.

Two men stepped out of the eerie twilight shadows. Both were dressed in brown and green and armed with both bows and axes. The elder of the two had a neatly trimmed beard with just a touch of grey.

'Lissa,' he greeted respectfully. 'We've secured the road as far as Ashgrove.'

The younger man looked over Lissa's companions and smiled at Mya shyly. Beside her Feather gave a groan.

'Feather?'

The brownie had his eyes tight shut and was gripping the front of the saddle with his fingers.

'Are you unwell?'

'Your pardon!' The young man called out. 'I didn't know you travelled with a brownie!'

He handed his bow to the other man and quickly took off his jacket, turning it so it was the right way around.

'Better?'

Feather opened one eye, then the other and nodded, though to Mya he still appeared off colour. She had never understood why turning clothes inside out had such a strong effect on fey.

'Let's get inside the walls,' the elder man said sternly.

There was barely enough light left now by which to see and Mya's tension eased when both men took up position at the rear of their group. Her muscles ached, and it seemed her feet caught on every stone and root. Then through the trees she spotted the warm glow of firelight, even Asher picked up his head.

'Ashgrove!' Lissa spun about to face them. 'The Tree City!'

City? Mya wondered.

They broke through the trees and out into a small stretch of cleared land, she heard the water of the river singing. On its opposite bank stood a high wall of grey stone on the top of which were set a few braziers like miniature suns in the night to her tired eyes. Lissa led them to a bridge on the other side of which stood a gate strengthened with strips of iron. Four men stood guard but let them through with no more than curious glances.

Mya looked anxiously at Feather as they passed through the gate but the little brownie bore the proximity of so much iron well. Wolf on the other hand gave a whine and turned to slink away.

'No, Wolf!' Mya called it in alarm. 'You can't go back out there on your own, it isn't safe. Stay with me, I won't let anyone hurt you.'

Wolf froze and looked up at her with his intelligent eyes, seeming unable to choose.

Lissa stepped lightly up to it and it didn't flinch as she placed a hand on his broad head. 'Be welcome. Stay tonight in the Grove with the Dryads where no man may touch you.'

Mya's eyes widened when Wolf followed at the Dryad's heels and she looked from the animal to Lissa, her heart giving a momentary, painful squeeze.

***

When Lissa had said 'city', Mya had pictured something like Trade Pass, but Ashgrove was nothing like it. Many homes stood within the walls but each was as unique as one tree from another. Some were made of stone, others of logs and some even woven from withies and hung from the high branches. Gardens surrounded all those set upon the ground with a respectful distance between each. There was no road as such, more a worn trail between the young ferns and tall grasses. Light spilt out from some of the homes and she caught the occasional voice, but most were silent and restful.

The bearded man took his leave, but the younger stayed

with them.

'I'll walk you to the inn then take your wolf on to the Grove,' Lissa told them. 'I don't think it would be fair to make him go in.'

'I wouldn't make him do anything,' Mya replied defensively.

'Will they have beds free do you think?' Jack asked hopefully. 'And maybe a hot meal?'

Lissa laughed, reminding Mya of a blackbird's warble. 'I'm sure they'll oblige. We get a few travellers this early in the Spring, but not many.'

They heard the inn before they saw it as someone was playing a lively tune with a fiddle. Conversation spilled through the windows along with the lamplight and the pressure in Mya's chest eased, although the knot in her stomach remained.

'I'll get Adam,' the young man offered gallantly with a smile at both Lissa and Mya.

Ben stood at Horse's side and gave Caelin's arm a squeeze. 'Just a little longer, Cae.'

When the door swung open again a portly man with a balding head bustled out; Mya guessed he must be somewhere near sixty.

'Sir Ben!' He shook hands enthusiastically with the knight. 'And Sir Caelin.' The inn keep's brow furrowed in concern. 'Well, let's get you all settled.' He pushed the door open and hollered in, 'Meg!' He let the door swing back and turned to take Horse's head. 'I'll get these beasts to the stable, you go on in and Meg will sort you out. There's another of your kind abides here, master brownie, but good-natured fey are more than welcome within.'

'Thank you.' Feather gave a small bow and stood to let Jack lift him down.

'I'll take the wolf on to the Grove and join you in a bit,' Lissa said. 'No one is allowed in the Grove without my mother's permission so he won't be bothered by anyone.'

Ben helped Caelin down from his saddle and it took both him and Jack to support him into the inn whilst Adam led away the horses. Inside the inn was relatively full with an assortment of men, some women and even two hobbs.

A young woman in a low-cut dress hurried over, drying her hands on her apron.

'Sirs, my Lady.' She gave a clumsy curtsey. 'You look like you want your rooms first before dinner? We're not very full upstairs so I can spare you three?'

'Three is fine, Meg.' Ben shifted to keep a better grip of Caelin.

Meg watched Caelin wide-eyed, her shoulder drawn in defensively, and Mya couldn't help but notice her fear. She wouldn't have been surprised if poor Meg had been on the wrong end of Caelin's temper at some point.

'This way.' She ushered them in although the knights had obviously stayed here before.

The stairs were near the door and wide enough for both

Jack and Ben to support Caelin; however, they came up to Feather's knees in height so the brownie had to pull himself up each one.

'Can I help you?' Mya asked anxiously.

'I'll manage, my girl,' Feather puffed. 'Anyway, it wouldn't be seemly for me to be carried about by a lady.'

'I'll put you in the best room,' Meg told Mya proudly as they got to the top. 'Here's the keys for rooms two and three just here.' She handed them to Jack. 'This way my Lady.'

Mya followed her to the end of the corridor and then turned right at the end along another. A single solid door nestled in the whitewashed wall to the left and taking a large bronze key from her pocket Meg opened it. 'Have you got anything you'd like brought up from the stable?'

'Oh, I have my pack; I should have thought of bringing it.'

'No, no.' Meg smiled at her. 'You're the guest. I'll pop it up for you when I get a moment. There's clean wash water on the stand. The dryads told us to be expecting you. I'll be but a moment.' She took a candle down from a lamp on the wall and going into the room lit others for Mya before leaving with another smile.

Mya gazed about her with growing delight. The room was large with a wide window set with leaded glass. The bed was big enough to sleep four people with heavy curtains tied to the posts. The bedding looked invitingly clean and comfortable and she sat on it, the mattress gave temptingly under her. There was a dark wood dressing table on which stood a bowl and a jug of simple clay. On a table before the window was a vase generously filled with dried lavender, heather and other wild flowers, giving the room a musky smell. Mya had never stayed in such a luxurious place in all her life.

She got up and went over to the window to gaze out. It was hard to make anything out in the darkness beyond the surrounding trees. Murmuring came from the common room below, dulled by the thick-woven rugs.

'My Lady?' The door opened a little and then Meg stepped in with her backpack. 'Shall I close the shutters for you?'

Mya hesitated; the night outside was tantalising from the safety of the inn. There was the faintest hint of stars as though they shyly watched her back between the new leaves. She realised Meg was still patiently waiting and smiling at the woman said, 'Yes please.'

Meg gave a nod and pulled them across. 'What's it like, my Lady?' Meg turned and asked hesitantly as though afraid she was overstepping. 'Being down in the Valley?'

'Mya, my name's Mya. I'm not a Lady, just a tailor.'

'Begging your pardon, miss, but you are a Lady. You have such gentle manners.'

Mya couldn't think what to say to that, she felt both flattered and embarrassed. 'The… the Valley is okay, I guess. People are a little fearful of the failing Ward.'

'The Dryads and the Druid keep us safe here.' Meg smiled happily and then a little concern crossed her face. 'Though it's not good to go outside the walls on your own.

There are Dark Fey out there and not all the Wild Fey are as nice as hobs and brownies. Will you stay here?'

'No, we…' Mya stopped herself, not sure how much of their plans she should give away. Actually, when she thought about it, staying here or maybe even coming back here wouldn't be such a bad option. 'We're just visiting so Caelin can recover.'

A cloud seemed to fall over Meg's face at the mention of the spellward's name, but she pulled herself out of whatever had upset her and cheerfully asked, 'Are you ready to come down to eat?'

'Oh, I'm starving!'

'Come on then,' Meg grinned.

Ben, Jack and Feather were already waiting for her seated around a table in a quiet corner away from the bustle of the room. The fiddler had gone but an elderly woman with long silver hair now played a harp beside the fire. Feather had a small tankard in front of him brimming over with foam from a dark beer. Both Jack and Ben had larger versions both of which had already been partially drained. Feather's chair had been made especially for smaller customers with the seat very high and the spokes making a ladder down one side.

'I thought we could share this.' Lissa swaggered over and draped herself in the chair beside Mya. In her hands she held two ornate glasses and a long-stemmed bottle. 'Elderflower wine, you like?'

Mya liked very much, but she restrained her enthusiasm, still not sure if she liked this sensuous woman. 'Yes please,' she said politely.

'We have Venison or lamb with some slightly ancient root vegetables.' Meg offered.

'Venison please!' Mya asked at once. Venison was a luxury she and Jack could rarely afford; the hunters in Briarton more commonly caught rabbit and pheasant to sell in the market. Then her stomach gave a lurch when she realised she had no idea how much she'd have to pay for hers and Jack's meals or their rooms. She was too embarrassed to ask anyone but Feather and she didn't want to ask him in front of the others.

Lissa poured wine generously into her glass and she picked it up. 'This is beautiful!' Mya said aloud.

'We have some fine craftsmen in Ashgrove,' Lissa said proudly. 'You won't find better in Ayresport.'

'Have you ever been there?' Jack asked curiously.

'I won't go in *that* city.' She glowered. 'Or any other in the Valley.'

'Here we go!' Adam and Meg arrived, balancing plates in their arms. She wasn't surprised Jack had opted for venison too whilst Ben had chosen lamb; Feather had a smaller plate of roasted and wrinkled vegetables.

'I'll warm some broth for Sir Caelin when you are ready to take it up. Liss!' Adam tossed an apple and Lissa snatched it out of the air as quick as a cat.

Mya's stomach churned in anticipation as she looked at the steaming meat drizzled in a dark red gravy. 'Are you not hungry?' she asked Lissa in concern.

'Dryads don't eat flesh and I ate earlier before I came out looking for you. Go ahead. You look famished, don't worry about me.'

Mya picked up her fork and was soon absorbed in the rich savoury flavours. She picked up the wine and took a sip; it was tart at first but mellowed on her tongue and she fancied she could taste gooseberry and elderflower.

'Good?' Lissa grinned.

Mya couldn't help smile back and nodded as she took another sip. Her stomach and taste buds hadn't been this contented since Jack's birthday feast.

Her nephew was first to finish eating. 'Can I take the broth up to Caelin now?' he asked Ben.

'If you wish. Just catch Adam's attention. If Caelin seems deep asleep don't wake him though, it would be best to let him rest.'

'Can I take some beer up too? For me?' he asked Mya.

She couldn't find it in her heart to say no; Jack asked for so little. 'Go on.' She smiled.

Ben handed the boy the key and Jack sprang away with surprising energy.

'He seems devoted to Caelin, and to you,' Lissa commented speculatively.

'He's a good lad,' Ben agreed.

111

'If you'll excuse me,' Feather said, standing on the highest spokes of his chair. 'I want to have a catch up with those two hobbs.'

'Of course,' Ben said.

Lissa poured more wine into Mya's glass.

'Will you go straight on tomorrow?' Lissa asked the knight.

'That depends on how well Cae recovers.' Ben sighed. 'It doesn't matter how much of a hurry we are in, going up into the mountains without a spellward at full strength, would be suicide.'

Lissa ran her finger around the top of her glass. 'What if I came with you?'

Ben sat back in his chair. 'Now, Lissa, you know Cae won't have you with us.'

'He's taking Mya.' She pouted.

'Mya doesn't wind him up like you do! Anyway, why would you want to come?'

She swirled her glass. 'Seriously? Kasira is a big threat to us all, and leaf and tree only know what plot she'll concoct with the Lord Vallier. It's in the interest of Ashgrove that Caelin get to Astol.'

'How do you know–'

Lissa laughed like a bubbling fountain. 'My father is *The Druid* and I'm a daughter of the Grove; we are not foolish. Her Grace is the only one strong enough to shelter Caelin for any length of time. Despite his anger and grief, Caelin is too intelligent to rush head first to Ayresport. When he came through here in the winter, we guessed he was seeking something in the north of the Valley. Jack has the Gift, so that all adds up, but you...' She narrowed her eyes at Mya and searched her face. 'You have the Gift but he would *never* teach a woman. Never.'

'We refused to let him have Jack unless he also took me to somewhere safe from Kasira,' Mya told her.

'Really?' Lissa looked her up and down. 'Well, you've got iron in you, human, there's more to you than I thought. You know I might actually get to like you.'

Mya wasn't sure which way to take that but Lissa poured the rest of the wine in their glasses and waved the bottle in the air. 'Innkeeper!' she yelled. Mya watched the fey with wide eyes, her mouth slightly open.

'Ladies!' Adam bustled over and uncorking another bottle placed it on the table for them and took away the empty.

'I think I may just leave you ladies to it.' Ben shifted in his seat. 'I'd best see how Cae is doing anyway and let Jack get off to sleep.'

Lissa leapt up and flung her arms around his neck to plant a kiss on his whiskery cheek. 'Goodnight, Sir Flame.'

'Night, Lissa.' He shook his head with a smile. 'Good night, Mya; don't let her get you into any trouble!'

'Me?' Lissa retorted.

Mya played with the stem of her glass and scratched at her cheek with one nail. She glanced up and saw Lissa was looking at her speculatively with her green eyes.

'At first glance you don't seem like the sort to go charging off through the forest,' Lissa said. 'Did you say you're a tailor?'

'Yes.' She took a sip of her wine. 'My family's trade.'

'Not your husbands?'

'No husband.'

'No husband?' Lissa sat back in her chair and arched an eyebrow. 'So, Jack's father ...?'

'Oh, no!' Mya sat up. 'Jack is my nephew!

Lissa laughed contritely. 'Oh, I am sorry. The two of you look so alike. So; how much of your coming here was to follow Caelin?'

The wine made Mya's mouth work before she had time to think.

'Why would I want to follow Caelin for any reason other than the safety of myself and my nephew? He has *some* good qualities, I suppose, but why would any woman with some self-respect follow after a man who hates women so much?'

'Why indeed.'

Mya froze at the quiet tone of the usually flamboyant woman and realised her error.

'Oh, I...'

'Hey!' Lissa touched Mya's arm, springing back at once into the lively woman she had been before. 'Adam keeps some great apple brandy!'

Anxiety pressed against Mya's ribs from the inside. 'But we haven't finished the wine and I don't know if I can afford all this!'

'That's taken care of, sweetling, you're a guest of the Grove! We're the ones who provide Adam with all his Brandy and wine.' She grinned. 'Come on, try some brandy with me and we'll take the wine to the Grove and you can meet the dryads.'

'I thought no one was allowed in the Grove?'

'No *man* is allowed, but a woman is on invitation. Are you up for it?'

'I'd love to see it.' Mya agreed.

'Come on.'

When they stepped outside the inn, the cold night air hit Mya and sent goose pimples across her skin. She hadn't realised quite how much she'd drunk until they started walking. Twice she blundered into low twigs and Lissa took her hand to both guide and steady her. Outside of the walls of Ashgrove the forest had been a frightening and inhospitable place; in here, even in the darkness, Mya began to see its beauty. She could smell the soft earth and the fallen leaves and a freshness to the breeze. There was the barest of whispers where the leaves caressed and her long skirt swished about her ankles. Lissa made not a sound but her hand was warm and reassuring.

A silvery light glimmered between the trees and at first Mya thought it might be the moon or the stars but it shifted and moved in the strangest of ways.

'Fireflies!' Lissa squeezed her hand, seeming to read her thoughts. 'They allow no fire in the Grove. The dryads of the Grove are hamadryads, bound to the lives of their trees. Others have come to dwell here also of course.'

'Your mother, is she a hamadryad?'

'She is. My father built Ashgrove to protect her.'

The sound of panpipes and laughter teased them in bursts as the wind herded it around the trees. Mya slowed her steps, her eyes searching the shadows to see if anyone was watching them. She'd expected some kind of wall or fence to mark the boundaries of the Grove; instead there was a thick hedge of holly. As they drew close, the branches bent and lifted forming an arched corridor through which they could pass. Within were the ash trees both ancient and sapling. It was too early yet in the spring for these sleepy trees to be in full leaf but by the light of the fireflies Mya could see the black buds at the end of new shoots. The bark of the trees was a dark grey that the fireflies made silver; the fine lattice pattern of fissures and ridges reminded Mya of an old person's skin.

Mya stopped in her tracks as she spied the figures moving or languishing upon the verdant green grass. Several pagodas, made from delicate withies and painted white, sheltered colourful cushions on which dryads rested. Some were up and dancing and she saw it was a satyr who played the pipes for them. He had dark curly fur running up his hoofed legs as far as mid-stomach; two small horns peeped through its unruly mop of hair. The dryads themselves were clad in anything from nothing at all to sheer flowing dresses; she realised what she had first thought of as scandalous about Lissa's attire was in fact the young woman trying to conform to human standards.

'The Uisinn Grove.' Lissa breathed in deeply. 'Come and see this!'

Still keeping hold of Mya's hand, she took her to a sapling, about their height. 'This one is mine.' Lissa ran one finger affectionately up a branch thinner than an arrow shaft.

'Lissa!' A high clear voice called out.

'Melody!' Lissa's face lit up as a dryad with long flowing brown hair and a green knee-length shift came almost skipping toward them.

'You've brought us a human.' Melody looked Mya up and down curiously.

'This is Mya, she's from the Valley.'

'Oh, how awful for you,' Melody commiserated. She appeared to be about thirteen but Mya guessed she must be much older. 'Do you dance?'

'I have brought her to meet my mother.' Lissa quickly came to Mya's rescue. 'I'll join you shortly.'

Melody appeared satisfied and raced off back to the dancing.

'Did you really bring me to meet your mother?'

'I thought you'd prefer that to dancing.' Lissa replied.

'She's the leader of the Grove and she likes to meet anyone of any interest. Don't worry she's much more sensible than the younger dryads; wise even.'

Lissa led her across to one of the pagodas where a dryad with hair as black as a raven's and dressed in a surprisingly solid blue dress sat contemplating. She was attended by two young girls and Mya saw they were human.

'Mother.' Lissa greeted her somewhat stiffly. After the way Lissa had spoken about her mother Mya was surprised by the formality between them.

'Unalissa,' the dryad greeted. 'It is good of you to visit the Grove.'

'This is Mya who travels with Sir Caelin and Sir Ben. She's from the Valley but has a brownie. I thought you would like to meet her.'

'Be welcome, be seated,' the dryad invited warmly.

Mya complied hesitantly.

Lissa took the cork out of the wine bottle, swallowed some and then handed it to Mya. 'I'll be back soon.' She sauntered away with her hips swaying.

'It isn't easy for her,' the dryad said in her rich deep voice, drawing Mya out of her daydream. 'Neither human nor dryad and belonging to neither world. My name is Seska.' Mya found herself transfixed by her gaze. 'So, why are you here?'

'To escape from Kasira and see Jack safely to Astol.' She repeated what she'd told Lissa.

'No.' Seska shook her head slowly, her smile was kind but there was also a twinkle of amusement in her eyes. 'Look deeper. Why are you here?'

Confused Mya thought about it. 'Because I was afraid of what would happen to me and Jack if we stayed in the Valley?'

'If you have to ask me if that is the reason then it isn't the answer.' Seska brushed the back of Mya's hand with her fingertips. 'You are from the Valley but have a brownie who has followed you from your home; that tells me a lot about you. Lissa is a lonely girl. Human women do not trust her and human men want her company for the wrong reason. Did you know dryads value chastity as one of their highest virtues? They will choose one man and die rather than succumb to another. I worry for Lissa with her human blood.'

Seska's gaze was unrelenting, as though trying to draw something out of Mya. Mya shifted her position and pulled at the collar of her blouse.

'There is a goblet there.' The dryad pointed. 'Please feel free to finish your wine. I must go to see my husband. It was nice to meet you, Mya.'

'Oh, it was nice to meet you too!' Mya scrambled to her feet.

'Don't change that heart of yours, young human, feed it and make it stronger.' Seska beckoned to the two small girls and swept away as lightly as a snow flurry over the grass.

Mya sat down slowly on the colourful cushions and putting the wine bottle to her lips took a long sip before remembering herself and picking up the goblet. It was all right for someone like Lissa to act all wild but there was such a thing as manners. She nodded to herself. Then with startling sadness she recalled Seska's words and realised she *was* jealous. She was jealous of Lissa's seeming freedom, jealous of her confidence and jealous of her easy beauty.

'Hey, I didn't mean to neglect you!' Lissa draped herself against the delicate pagoda. 'You look worn out; I shouldn't have kept you out so late!'

'Oh, I wanted to! It's a long time since I've been able to just… to just… to do things just for me.'

'Let's get you back to your room and the warm.' Lissa offered her hand and pulled her to her feet.

They made their way back to the inn in companionable silence. Lissa pushed the door, and it swung open easily. It surprised Mya it hadn't been locked, but then she remembered where she was. Truly this would be a great place to settle one day if she could.

'Well, goodnight then.' Lissa shocked Mya with a swift kiss on her lips. The half dryad laughed at her expression. 'I'll see you tomorrow.'

Mya watched her go and shook her head to wake herself up. As quietly as she could she made her way up the creaking wooden stairs and took her key out of the pocket in her skirt to open the door. Despite her earlier recollection of the fact she was guarded by wall, moat, dryad and druid, she locked it securely behind her. Stripping down to her shift she clambered gratefully into the huge bed, her feet burrowing into the soft mattress. As she contemplated the fact this was probably the nicest bed she had ever slept in, she fell asleep.

Chapter Six

Mya groaned as she slowly surfaced into the waking world.

'Good night, was it?'

She sat up quickly which made her head pound. 'Feather!'

He chuckled. 'The others are down having their breakfast. I thought I'd just nip in and check on you.'

'How's Caelin?'

'He's recovering. He's almost himself physically but his Gift is slow in restoring. A kill spell is not a good thing, especially for one with a noble heart.'

'Does he blame me?' she asked timidly.

'No, girl.' Feather hopped down from the chair. 'He blames himself for not dealing with Brinsten sooner. Caelin and Ben are of the old knights; those that live by rules of chivalry and honour. They respect the laws of both fey and men and so he allowed Brinsten the right to his "territory," to live as was his nature.'

Mya thought about it and much as she had disliked the ogre, she couldn't disagree it'd had a right to live.

'I'll leave you to your privacy.' Feather bowed. 'I've left you some food should you feel up to it.'

Despite the fuzziness in her head and the churning of

her stomach, the idea of food made Mya ravenous. As soon as her door closed, she scrambled out of bed then stopped; hadn't she locked the door last night? But then a door was nothing to a brownie who had been invited in.

She found a covered plate on the table and lifting it found eggs, bacon, mushrooms and fried potato. There was also a glass of apple juice. Ignoring the slight queasiness in her stomach she made short work of it, savouring especially the warm runny yolks. Feeling a little better she did as good a job as she could of tidying herself up, deliberating between wearing her one skirt suitable for travelling again, or something less sturdy. She opted for a long blue one, somewhat creased but considerably less dirty and torn. She picked up her food tray to take down, then remembered herself and left it, although she hesitated and glanced back at it before walking from the room.

The others were still seated around one of the large wooden tables when she got to the main room. There were two other smaller groups still in the inn speaking together in subdued tones. She couldn't see any sign of Lissa and frowned to herself, wondering at her feeling of disappointment.

'Well, I'm surprised to see you so early and looking so well after a night with Lissa!' Adam the innkeeper bustled past her carrying a tray to one of the other tables.

Mya's cheeks flushed, and she hurried to join the others. Jack was almost bouncing in his chair, whilst Caelin's eyes looked puffy and the paleness of his skin made his scar all the more vivid.

Ben greeted her. 'Good morning, my Lady.' He'd

trimmed his beard shorter against his jaw and it made him look younger.

'Sir, how do you do?' She asked Caelin politely.

'Well enough to be on our way soon,' he replied.

Ben gave a cough to discreetly express his disagreement.

Caelin glanced at his fellow knight but refrained from arguing. 'We'll spend today procuring supplies and readying ourselves for entering the mountain passes. There's a good blacksmith here so I'll have a sword made for Jack. Mya, you might want to remind Feather about the sling he said he'd make you.'

Mya blinked at him, her mouth slightly ajar, she'd been sure Caelin would make excuses to leave her behind here rather than let her go on with them. 'I have mending to do,' she told him. 'And I want to sew one of my skirts into trousers. If any of you have anything you'd like me to repair please leave it up in my room.'

She looked around at them all, sagging a little when none of them seemed the slightest bit scandalised at her suggesting she wear trousers.

'That's kind of you, Mya, thank you,' Ben said.

'We are to meet with The Druid at noon,' Caelin told Mya. 'You should be there too. Apparently Seska wishes him to meet you as well.'

There was the slightest hint of accusation in his voice but Mya dismissed it as her imagination.

'If you'll excuse me, I'm for the blacksmith.' Caelin

stood, pushing his chair back and striding away.

'Should I go with him?' Jack asked anxiously, clearly excited about getting his own sword.

'Leave him for the moment,' Ben said with a sigh. 'Whatever's in his head he's best left to work through it on his own.'

'Would it be all right if I explored a bit then?' Jack asked Mya and Ben.

'Of course; I won't keep you shut in whilst I'm sewing,' Mya told him.

***

Feather sat on the inn's kitchen step deep in thought. A bee hummed as it went from flower to flower in the large herb garden, quickly joined by another. Already the day was warm, and the sun pierced the trees with golden shafts giving a tantalising promise of the summer to come. He'd spoken with the hobbs who were visiting the inn and had been disappointed they'd no news of his old friend, Bertram. More worrying still was the news they had of the wilds to the north; of the mountain path they must now take through the Hart valley. The hobbs had said gangs of Dark Fey, evicted from Kasira's court when the Ward spell was cast, still roamed the upper valley. It was just his luck when he'd thought he'd found safety, he'd been sharply thrown back into living in danger.

He breathed the scents of the garden in deeply, catching also the wood smoke and alcohol smell of the inn. The hobbs had said there were several houses without a brownie and he'd find himself a good home here if he asked around;

but Feather had found himself bound not to a home but to a family. As though to reinforce his thoughts Jack appeared along the path with his youthful lope, so different from the conserved wariness of the knights. Somehow sensing someone watched him, Jack turned around and halted at once to wave.

'Feather! I'm going exploring, do you want to come?'

He found himself caught up in the boy's enthusiasm and he responded by slipping off the step onto his feet.

'I guess I can't see the Grove,' Jack stated as the brownie fell in beside him. The boy automatically shortened his stride and slowed his pace.

Feather sighed at the hopeful tone in the boy's voice. Jack wasn't the first human male to daydream about finding his way to a dryad grove and he wouldn't be the last.

'Lissa seems really interesting,' Jack went on.

Feather gave an inward groan. This wasn't the job for a brownie!

'She is a nice young woman,' he said carefully. 'But also a fey, and you have to be careful to be aware of the rules of each race and kind. If you treat her like a human, you might… well you might make an error.'

Jack took the information in solemnly. 'Is she a warrior? I've heard of both dryads and nymphs who are.'

'Yes, she is a follower of the Huntress. There are other dryads of the Huntress here who are not hamadryads and tied to their trees. They guard Ashgrove along with the human scouts. The dryads of the Grove, Seska's kin, are followers of the Healer.'

'I thought about being a healer.' Jack waved a fly away from his nose. 'The one at Briarton must be the richest man in the town! Aunt Mya and I would never have had to worry if I'd been able to apprentice with him, but I'm only an orphan of tailors.'

'No one is ever "only" anything, my boy,' Feather told him. 'Before the Ward those with the Gift often became healers as did the old sorcerers to the court like Renvart who invented the Ward. But once the Ward became the reason for training those with the Gift, and the creation of the Spellwards, healing magic became a low priority.'

'How old are you, Feather?'

Feather almost choked in surprise at the sudden change of course. 'The innocent impertinence of youth.' He smiled and shook his head. 'You would think me old no doubt, but fey don't measure age, we are what we are.'

'Don't you have a Birthday?' Jack asked in shock.

'No, my lad, I don't.'

Jack frowned to himself.

'My boy the years do not mark who or what you are, your deeds do. This is your apprentice year, traditionally making you a man, but it's not the day or the year that makes it so, that will be something for you to earn.'

'Like my Knighthood.' Jack gave one firm nod.

'Hmm, yes,' Feather agreed. 'But there is more even than

that. There will be training and ceremonies to make you a knight, in the eyes of tradition, but what makes you a knight in your heart and soul may be a different thing.'

'I want to be a true night, like Caelin and Ben!'

'They are both good examples, and bad examples too.' Feather gave a snort of amusement. 'Caelin has as knightly a heart as you could find and it is determinedly stubborn. Honour, loyalty, love, they all fight to tear him apart.' Feather looked up at Jack's silence and saw the hurt on the boy's face and sighed. There were worse heroes to have than Caelin he supposed.

'He'll be a good teacher for you Jack, but keep your mind open as there will be things you need to learn for yourself which cannot be taught by another.'

Jack nodded silently.

'Look, my boy! It's the holly hedge.'

'Is the Grove behind there?' He asked wide-eyed. 'I wish I could see it; are you allowed to?'

Feather stepped closer to the dark green, spiky bushes. He held his hand out palm outward and cocked his head to one side as he sent a little of his growing magic toward the holly to persuade it to part. Nothing happened.

'No, not even a brownie can enter without invitation, not so much as a rabbit gets in, I expect that Seska doesn't know of it. There's a small market here if it interests you?' Feather suggested.

Jack lit up with renewed enthusiasm. 'I have the coins

for my apprenticeship Mya saved for me, I could get things for our journey. Perhaps...' He faltered uncertainly. 'Perhaps I could get things I need from the blacksmith's too, some armour or such like.'

'I'm not sure you should spend your apprenticeship money, young Jack. I'm not wholly certain how these things work but do you not give a fee over to your master for your keep and tools until you begin to earn a return for him?'

Jack fidgeted and avoided Feather's gaze. 'I hadn't really thought of that with this all being so sudden and different. I didn't think of it as an apprenticeship as much as Caelin saving us so I can fight for the Valley. I guess I should offer him the money though.'

Feather looked up at Jack, it was hard for the little brownie to see the boy's face when he himself was only two feet tall and twisting his neck to try to keep eye contact. Jack had said it so calmly; the fact he was going to learn from Caelin in order to face possible death in return. Mya was mostly very self-contained but in her he'd seen bursts of fear, anger and joy. This boy was so quiet and well-mannered for his age Feather couldn't help feeling a little concern.

'Why is it you agreed to go with Caelin?'

'Why, to save Aunt Mya of course! But I must admit, being a knight and spellward are really exciting.' Jack frowned, staring down at the path. 'When I was very young, I wanted to be a spellward like my mother. I knew I couldn't be a knight as I'm only a tailor's grandson. When mother died, I hated her for going away to Ayresport. It didn't seem noble and romantic dying in some silly accident with magic. I ... when Aunt Mya and you told me the truth about what happened...' Jack rubbed at his nose to try to hide the fact he was getting upset and cleared his throat to steady his voice. 'I was angry at Mya at first for hiding it from me but I know she was only trying to protect me.'

'And she was never really sure, until recently she only had her suspicions,' Feather added.

'Yeah.' Jack gave a loud sigh. 'I barely remember my mother sometimes. Mya kind of became my mum and a friend all in one. Part of me wants to race off to Ayresport to avenge my mother, but when I see the vengeance in Sir Caelin's eyes sometimes... that kind of fury frightens me.'

'A betrayed heart never heals whilst the mind torments it,' Feather said quietly.

They were heading back into a more populated part of Ashgrove where the houses stood closer together and the gardens were smaller. Feather spotted the coloured awnings of the market stalls further along the path and the smoke from the furnace of the blacksmith. Jack brightened again and unconsciously touched the purse sewn securely to his belt.

Still just a boy, the brownie smiled to himself.

'Look, Caelin is still with the smith!'

Feather squinted to see where the boy was pointing and could just make out the upright and tense figure of the knight. Jack checked himself from speeding up, politely remembering the brownie's much shorter legs. Caelin spotted them almost at once and waited patiently without a word. The clang of the blacksmith working on his anvil drowned out the distant chatter of the small market. Feather had never been to a market before, it looked dangerously full of large people with clumsy feet, and he regretted suggesting it to Jack. The iron in the blacksmiths was like a headache trying to worm through his skin, but he bore it as all brownies did.

Jack swallowed and cleared his throat, his fingers tangled together before him. 'Sir, I didn't think of it until now, but I have an apprentice fee saved up, well Mya saved it, and, well, it's only right I give it to you.'

Caelin stiffened even more. He glanced down at Feather then held the boy's gaze as he replied. 'It would not be right for me to take Mya's money, or yours. Those with the Gift may have once paid an apprentice fee to become healers or magicians before the Ward was made, but that's no longer so. Knights don't pay for their training but are taken on from noble families as pages to learn their craft. With that said.' His shoulders moved with a silent sigh. 'My means are limited, outcast as I am, and I cannot equip you as I'd wish but for the kindness of our hosts. Much as it niggles at my pride, it would be wise for you to use some of your money to better equip yourself. You're not used to armour, and wearing it would both be added discomfort for your friend, Feather, and would slow us greatly on our journey. There is a man here who makes good leather for the Ashgrove rangers, we should pay him a visit.'

Steam rose from within the smithy and the smith stepped out with his clothes damp from his work.

'As good as new!' He announced holding up a sword for Caelin's inspection.

'My thanks.' Caelin slipped his sword back in its sheath.

'This the boy?' The smith raised a dark eyebrow and measured Jack with his eyes. 'Doesn't look like he could lift a stick!'

Jack started indignantly but the smith's laugh soon reassured him it was meant in fun.

'You'll soon build muscle when Sir Cae here has you practising.' He turned to Caelin and said more seriously, 'It will be ready by nightfall.'

'Good.' Caelin gave him a curt nod. 'Come, Jack, let's see what we can find you.'

***

Mya set aside her sewing and carefully slid her precious needles into a small piece of leather which she kept in a wooden box with her thread. She'd sat in the chair beneath the window to get as much light as she could for her work and the sun moved all too quickly across the sky. She locked the room up and slipped her key into the pocket of her skirt and hurried down the stairs to the common room of the inn. Both Ben and Lissa were there waiting, and the room was almost as busy as it had been the previous evening.

'Have you seen Jack?' She looked around, her eyebrows drawn together in a frown.

'He'll be fine within the walls.' Lissa dismissed her concerns. 'Shall we get off then?'

Mya had been more concerned Jack might miss their meeting with The Druid than that he'd gotten into any trouble; after all, no one had actually told them where to meet him. She gave a mental sigh and told herself she needed to trust the boy–the young man–to be responsible for himself.

'I'm ready,' Mya agreed.

Lissa seemed more serious again this morning but as they made their way through Ashgrove, she pointed out different houses and trees, telling Mya a little of the history of her forest city. They headed toward the centre and the holly hedge surrounding the Dryad Grove, but skirted around it to where the forest became thick and overgrown. There were a few small wooden huts set between the brambles and ivy, but for the most part this was the most uninhabited area of Ashgrove Mya had seen. The sky opened up above them as they stepped into a natural clearing made by a large pond. Almost all its surface was green with algae and pond weeds. Small thin reeds made its edges shaggy and unkempt but with a wild beauty that caught Mya's imagination. The sun was bright on the water between the plant life and turned the yellow celandines to gold. She spied a long, low cottage, tucked just inside the trees to their left. A large black crow on the thatched gable gave a loud caw.

'That's Elder Crow letting my father know he has guests.' Lissa smiled.

The door to the cottage swung open and Mya was startled until her mind resolved what she was seeing. At first it had appeared to be a stag dressed in a hedge, but she realised it was in fact a man. He wore a headdress made from a pair of elegantly sweeping antlers and a cloak of hide and ivy. In his hand was a staff made of a still living branch bearing new leaves. As they drew closer, Mya saw a similarity in the shape of the man's face and Lissa's. They both had a small chin spreading to a wider jaw and high cheekbones almost like a cat. Unlike Lissa's sleek black hair, his was a long and curling steel-grey.

'Sir Ben, daughter.' The man greeted them formally. 'And this must be Mya?'

There was a merriness to his voice and his eyes that warmed Mya to him at once.

'I am,' she replied, not sure whether to give a curtsy or hold out her hand. She ended up doing neither and chastised herself that he'd think her rude. 'I am very pleased to meet you.' she added quickly.

'Sir Caelin and the others are within.' The Druid gestured with a strong-looking tanned and calloused hand. 'I am Glonell; please join us.'

They followed him within and Mya was surprised at how bright the inside of the cottage was despite the shadow of the trees. There were four windows in the main living area and the back door stood open wide. A large fox was curled up on the threshold in a patch of sunlight. The interior was crowded with furniture carved from tree stumps using the roots and all. The table in the centre had been formed from the upturned base of a huge tree, the roots snaking out darkly in tantalising shapes and patterns to support one long flat carved table top.

'This is beautiful!' Mya couldn't help reaching out a hand to touch the black wood.

'Thank you, please sit.'

Mya glanced at Caelin who'd been watching her and he quickly looked away. Feather was perched on a tall stool with a narrow high back, carved to look like wooden flames, and she took a seat beside him. Her own chair was just as naturally ornate, but surprisingly comfortable. Jack, who sat between Feather and Caelin, held a parcel of cloth in his lap which he clutched possessively.

'Rosehip tea?' Glonell offered his guests. It wasn't a particular favourite of Mya's, but she accepted politely.

'Well, then.' Glonell sat, arranging his strange cloak as he did so. 'You are here as guests of the Grove, and very welcome are you, but there's a quest bringing you through here that affects us all. Seska has concerns about the reasons behind your chosen path, Sir Caelin, but the result you seek is one desirous to us. We all would like to see the demise of Kasira, and her hold over the Lord Vallier and the Valley relinquished. It's for that reason, despite your presence being a danger, we have allowed you into our walls. But there is a price.'

Lissa looked down at her lap almost guiltily whilst Caelin's face grew hard.

'Speak your terms,' Ben said steadily.

'Lissa, tell them what the scouts have seen.'

She nodded and spoke with a seriousness Mya had not seen in her before. 'As you know you were followed here. The Powrie we've chased away, but the Barghest has gone north ahead of you. There's also a pack of hobgoblin gathered to the south of here, some twenty so the scouts have counted. They can only guess at your intentions but your allies are few. When you leave here and set out north, then it will become clear you are making for the Hall of Pillars, in Astol.'

'As I've said, your quest is of great importance to all the Wild Fey and free folk of the Grove.' The druid leaned forward toward the knights and lowered his horns. 'Sir Caelin, I doubt there'll be another Spellward in years, if ever, who'd go up against Kasira. We can't let you and your apprentice leave here unprotected, and we would like to assist you. You cannot deny your company was left vulnerable once you had cast a kill spell. Had you been further from the Grove… well.' Glonell spread his hands emphatically.

Mya could see Caelin's jaw tighten, but he gave the barest nod of his head in agreement.

'Once young Jack here is trained and you leave Astol, that will be a different matter. In the meantime, I'd like to send one magic user and two of my scouts with you.'

Caelin tilted his head to shake it. 'So large a party would never slip north without notice. We are already more than I would have wished to take.'

'Never the less, I think you would be wise to take my offer. You're hunted, as you know, and a follower of the huntress would be invaluable to you in avoiding your pursuers.'

'The Huntress?' Caelin sat back and looked from Lissa's cocky grin to the stern face of the druid. 'The last thing I want is…' He checked himself, but Mya could easily guess his feelings. The very last thing he would want was another woman with him, especially one who flirted as naturally as breathing.

'She is my daughter and the daughter of Seska.' The druid seemed suddenly much less friendly. His horned hood no longer awkward and comical, but instead sharp and dangerous. 'Would you insult us by refusing such a great gift?'

'You would risk her safety to protect us?' Ben chose a more tactful and gentlemanly approach. 'That is indeed a huge gift.'

'It would be a bigger risk to us all if I didn't send my best.' Glonell settled back in his chair. 'There's more than just your pride and survival to think of; this is far more important than revenge, Sir Caelin.'

'Now that I will not bite my tongue for!' Caelin's face grew red although he held his voice in check and didn't raise it. 'This is not about revenge.'

Glonell didn't blink, and the knight held his gaze without flinching. The druid nodded.

'As you say. So, this is a quest in which all those opposing Kasira would be wise in supporting and seeing through. We will supply you for your journey and I will add a horse for your apprentice—'

'A horse!' Jack sat up unable to conceal his excitement.

'A knight needs a horse. You, Sir Caelin, will accept my help.'

Caelin looked down at his hands folded in his lap. He slowly moistened his lower lip and chewed at the skin just inside it. He scratched at the stubble on his cheek before glancing up at the druid. Mya's chest muscles constricted in sympathy. At the end of the day the spellward was beholden to no one; though she guessed Nemeth of the Hall of Pillars had some claim to his loyalty. Caelin had said what he intended was for the good of all of them, fey included, but she didn't doubt Glonell had touched a raw nerve with the accusation about revenge.

Caelin nodded reluctantly. 'When I put my own feelings aside, I can see you're right, druid. I will happily take your scouts.' He turned and looked hard at Lissa. 'But you I'll only take if I have your word you'll respect my authority on this quest as far as Astol, and you'll behave appropriately.'

'I'll be going as a representative of the Grove and the Huntress,' Lissa retorted sharply as though stung. 'I take those duties seriously.'

But as Caelin turned back to the druid, she rolled her eyes and grinned at Mya completely belying her words.

'You've made the right choice.' Glonell nodded to himself. 'Let Lissa know what supplies you need and we'll do our best to oblige you. Will you be leaving tomorrow?'

Caelin nodded. 'That is my intention.'

'In the early hours my scouts and huntresses of the Grove will go out and clear the forest of enemies. They'll head out in all directions not just north. It may give you a small reprieve but Kasira and the more intelligent of her Dark Fey will no doubt have already guessed your best hope for shelter, if you leave here, will be Astol. I fear she'll not allow you to live if she can help it.'

Caelin's hand went to the scar on his face. 'I know that well.'

'I'll leave you to make your preparations.' Glonell stood to dismiss them. 'I have spells of my own to work on tonight.

You will find allies amongst bird and beast for a while.'

'Our thanks to you,' Ben said with genuine warmth. 'It's good to know we're not alone in this.'

'I'll walk with you back to the inn,' Lissa told Mya enthusiastically.

Jack was also bursting with excitement and as soon as they stepped outside the cottage, he showed Mya his parcel. 'Aunt Mya, I have a set of leather armour and my sword will be ready by tonight! Lissa! I can't believe your father is giving me a horse!'

The half-fey laughed delightedly. 'Well, we can't have you riding the wolf!'

'Have you seen him at all, Wolf I mean?' Mya felt guilty she hadn't checked on him.

'He's in the Grove and seems happy enough, though Melody got upset when he caught and ate a rabbit! My mother says he doesn't behave right for a wild wolf but he's not domesticated either.'

'Perhaps he should stay here. I'd hate to think of him all alone in the forest with the barghest and powrie on the prowl.'

'He can take better care of himself than you or I, I would think.' Lissa gave her a playful nudge with her arm. 'But my Mother will not keep any animal captive and I have a feeling your Wolf will seek the freedom of the forest before long.'

***

When they got back to the inn, they found Caelin had slipped away and Ben gave an apologetic shrug. The older knight helped Jack into his leathers as the boy insisted on trying it all on again to show his Aunt and Lissa. He had brown padded trousers and a leather tunic with bronze rings, allowing a small amount of protection from arrows or a sword. A thick belt circled his waist from which hung his empty scabbard and leather guards were buckled to his forearms.

Mya smiled at him proudly; he looked now very much a young man and knight's page.

'Oh, and we got this for you!' Feather fumbled inside his jacket and brought out a sling and a pouch of small pellets. 'Elf-shot.'

Mya took the sling and opened the little pouch to look at the small black obsidian spheres. 'Thank you,' she said. Her heart lifted even as her stomach clenched into a knot. It was a stark reminder of what was waiting for them outside the walls of Ashgrove.

'Right then,' Lissa said. 'Let's sort out what food supplies we need for us and the horses. The sooner we get done the sooner I can get Adam sorting us out a proper leaving feast for tonight.'

Chapter Seven

Mya woke in the early hours; the slightest of grey light slipping through the shutters in sharp shafts. The inn was almost silent, but a distant creak suggested someone else was up and about. Outside the wind shushed in the trees and an occasional bird sung a few tentative notes and then ceased. She shivered, not from cold, but from a foreboding something was happening in the world.

Deciding there was no point trying to get back to sleep, she got up and picked up her newly made trousers. They were double layered as, from her previous experience of the forest, she guessed they were likely to get snagged or even torn. She'd made a belt out of left-over fabric plaited together and she tied it in a firm knot about her waist. The trousers themselves were comfortable enough, but she felt strangely naked without a long skirt.

Somewhere in the distance a hunting horn sounded; long and deep. She opened the shutters and the chill air stung her face. She couldn't see far through the trees but the sky was taking on a pink hue as the sun rose and she decided it was late enough to try the common room. Her bags had already been packed the night before in anticipation of their leaving today. She left them where they stood, and going out into the hall, locked the room carefully behind her.

The corridor was empty and only one lamp still burned, the stub of a candle within barely giving any light. Only one window led into the hall high above the stairs and she kept one hand to the wall in case she misjudged the steps in the dark. As she opened the door to the common room, the fatty smell of pork, and toasted bread, greeted her. A subdued conversation trailed off at her interruption. Tentatively she stepped in and found the only occupants to be Feather and the two hobbs who often frequented the inn.

'My girl!' Feather exclaimed in surprise. He gave a bow to his companions as a polite farewell and, slipping down from the chair, came over. 'You're awake early.'

'I couldn't sleep,' she confessed. 'How about you? Are you up late or early?'

Feather gave a chuckle. 'Both I think! Adam is still abed but I've been helping the inn's brownie set up breakfast. What can I get you, my girl?'

Mya hesitated in answering. She was hungry but there was a little knot of apprehension in her stomach. The journey from Briarton to Ashgrove had been dangerous enough and Ashgrove to Astol would be considerably more so. 'Maybe just some toasted bread and eggs for now.' She settled on something plain.

'I'll get you some chamomile tea to go with it, unless you would prefer a brandy?'

Mya laughed and some of the tension in her stomach melted away. 'I'm not nervous of continuing our journey! Tea would be lovely.'

She sat at one of the tables as Feather went off to the kitchen and smiled shyly at the two hobbs. All three of them looked up as the door to the rooms opened and Ben stepped in.

'Good morning, Mya.' He yawned as he joined her. 'Caelin and Jack are just fetching the horses then they'll be in for breakfast. Are you all ready to go on?' He sounded concerned. 'I don't mean to insult your bravery or your love for Jack, but you know you can stay here and be safe?'

Mya shook her head at once. 'I mean to go with Jack and see this through as far as *he* will let me.'

Feather burst backwards out of the kitchen door balancing a tray larger than himself in his hands. On the tray was a plate of eggs and another of toasted bread, a small teapot and two mugs.

'I see I must get another mug.' He raised an eyebrow.

'Here, let me.' Ben leapt up and took the tray from Feather who disappeared into the kitchen. He came back out with a third mug and a square of butter on a small saucer. Ben laid the eggs and bread before Mya who felt awkward being served by the old knight when it should have been the other way around.

'Dig in.' He prompted her.

'I have sausages, fried bread, bacon and eggs if that'd suit you?' Feather asked Ben.

'Sounds good!' Ben patted his stomach.

Mya ate awkwardly until Feather returned with Ben's food and then she was able to eat more comfortably with the knight occupied with his own breakfast. Feather had brought out a slice of fried bread which he nibbled on himself.

'Did you hear the hunt go out?' The brownie asked.

Ben wiped his mouth with the back of his sleeve and quickly swallowed what he'd been chewing.

'I did. The horns called at least thrice so they caught sight of something they were hunting. Let's hope one was the barghest. Caelin wishes to leave before the Hunt returns, to give us the best start, so we may not learn of it.'

'Will Lissa not know?' Mya asked.

'Lissa didn't join the Hunt,' Feather told her. 'She stayed at the Grove last night to pray for blessings for our quest.'

Mya couldn't imagine the half-fey praying rather than going out on a wild ride. It seemed Lissa was far from easy to understand.

The outside doors swung open and Jack came almost skipping in, mist followed about his feet as though clinging to him.

'I'm famished!' He exclaimed. 'Oh, Caelin says he'll see you all outside in about half an hour!'

'I'd better hurry with your breakfast then!' Feather hopped down from his chair.

'Is Caelin not eating?' Mya asked in concern.

'You know him.' Ben gave a loud snort of a sigh. 'I'll take him out some bacon in a slice of bread.'

'Aunt Mya.' Jack sat in the chair next to her, his eyes sparkling. 'My horse is black and white like a magpie!'

'Does it have a name?'

'The scouts said they call her lucky but I can change her name if I wish now she's mine. I haven't decided yet.'

'As long as you don't call her Horse!' Ben gave a shake of his head. 'I'll grab food for Cae and then take my things out. Don't be late!'

'We won't.' Jack replied.

***

Mya shouldered her pack and, leaving her key in the lock, went down to the inn door and peered outside. There was still a little low mist snared around the tree roots. Her trousers felt odd against her legs and she glanced around at the others, running her hand down her thigh. She felt oddly vulnerable, but no one even looked at her clothing. The supplies they'd been given had already been safely packed onto their three horses and Ben took her bag and secured it to Asher's back. She stepped gingerly up to Jack's mare. The horse was more black than white with three white legs which made her look as though she'd lost a stocking. Her tail was black but her mane was mottled, as was her neck, and she had a small white blaze down her face. Mya stroked the long, soft nose whilst Jack lifted Feather up onto the saddle.

'Good morning.' Lissa called out as cheerful as a starling. The mist parted as she and two scouts joined them. 'Your scouts are Morgan and Ferris.'

She indicated the two men who followed behind her on foot. They were both dressed in greens and grey but one had a deerskin jacket and the other a thin leather jerkin. Both carried bows with a sword and long knives at their sides and large packs and a quiver on their backs. The one in the deerskin Lissa had pointed to as Morgan; he was the younger and had brown hair and a beard cut close to his face with traces of ginger. Ferris had dark curly hair and was clean shaven; he was short and stocky. Lissa had also dressed like a scout and had all her supplies in a pack on her back that appeared far too large for her small frame.

'Sirs, my lady.' Ferris nodded politely. 'Would you like me to take point?'

Caelin looked the man up and down and Mya bristled at the knight's disdainful attitude toward the Ashgrove scout, even though she didn't know Ferris. 'If you would. We'll head out north and then cut back south-west about three miles past the turning to the route to Astol. A small bluff but it might pay off.'

'Very good.' Ferris gave another bob of his head.

Morgan was looking over the rest of them and when he caught Mya's eye, he chanced a friendly smile. Mya returned it politely and then turned to check her bag on Asher's back.

'All set?' Ben asked Mya and Jack.

'Ready!' Jack straightened himself up to his full height.

'On we go,' Feather agreed.

They left Ashgrove through the south gate through which they'd first entered and skirted around the large forest settlement rather than take the north gate. They'd gone less than a mile when Lissa called back to Mya.

'Looks like your friend is coming with us!'

Mya looked to where the half-fey indicated with her head but it was several minutes before she caught sight of grey fur.

'Wolf!' she said with delight. She straightened her back and lifted her shoulders, breathing more easily.

The mist cleared quickly as the sun became stronger and there was neither sight nor sound of any fey or of the dryads who had gone out on the hunt. Mostly they travelled in silence though Jack and Feather sometimes exchanged a quiet sentence or two. Caelin allowed them to stop to rest and eat just after midday and the two scouts swapped places; Morgan taking the lead to check the way ahead. Mya hadn't seen Wolf for some time despite taking him some food out from the others for him, but Lissa who'd gone with her for safety, assured her he wasn't far away.

'He's certainly taken a liking to you,' Lissa said as they re-joined the others. 'Perhaps he is lonely not having a pack and for some reason thinks we will make a possible replacement.'

'You shouldn't encourage it,' Ferris reproached. 'Like as not it will turn on you and eat you or at the least try for the horses.'

'I'm not so sure.' Lissa mused. 'It's like it thinks it's human.'

'Well, if it will fight for us like it did against the ogre, I'm all for encouraging it!' Ben announced.

'Time to move on.' Was all they got from Caelin.

'Will we carry on with my training now you are better?' Jack asked hurrying to walk behind the knight and pulling his mare up behind him.

'Tonight, we will,' Caelin agreed.

***

Caelin was true to his word and took Jack away from the others as they set camp that night. They'd settled on a hill populated mostly by hazel with seemingly little protection from fey. Mya watched the two new men in their group, they seemed nice enough, but she couldn't think of any polite small talk or bring herself to interrupt their conversation. Lissa resumed her playfully flirty behaviour with all of them as soon as Caelin was out of earshot.

'So, who is doing your work for you tonight?' Morgan grinned at the half-fey.

'Elder Crow until night sets in completely.' She leaned nonchalantly against one of the trees. 'Then Mother Owl; though you'll have to catch her a mouse to make up for her loss of hunting time.'

'I hope she isn't too hungry.' Feather joined in.

'Your ears are rather long brownie.' Lissa looked at him with mock seriousness. 'She may mistake you for a rabbit.'

'Are the birds tame?' Mya asked in interest.

'About as tame as Lissa.' Morgan chuckled.

Lissa scowled and then blew the man a kiss.

'Most animals will do a dryad or a druid a favour or two.' Ferris drew the conversation back to seriousness. 'In return for a healing, some food or some other bargaining piece. Some of them, like Elder Crow and Mother Owl, find they like the deal and strike up something more permanent. We should make the most of them for the next couple of days whilst we have them, but not get complacent.'

'Speaking of which.' Lissa, who always seemed to Mya to be the most observant of them, all pointed over Mya's shoulder. She turned to see Wolf had crept close to the camp.

'Do you think he might have been a dryad or druid's, um, helper?' Mya asked as she slowly moved over to their supplies to take out a portion of the cooked chicken they'd been given in Ashgrove. Wolf took a few steps closer, mouth open in anticipation of catching it. She threw it and he caught it with a snap and had it devoured in less than a second. Ferris's eyes narrowed and his brows drew down in a frown when she took a second and larger piece of meat from their supplies to toss to the animal.

'It's possible I suppose.' Lissa shrugged. 'Though it would make me wonder what happened to that druid or dryad for the wolf to now be wandering the wilds looking for a new companion.'

'I'm still not happy encouraging it.' Ferris grumbled.

Instead of running back into the undergrowth the grey wolf sat back on its haunches watching them all. When no one showed any signs of trying to approach it lay down but remained alert to every sound and movement.

All of them got on with setting up and securing the camp for the night. Mya turned her gaze to where Caelin and Jack had gone. Despite her promise not to learn how to use her Gift whilst travelling with Caelin, she couldn't help her curiosity at how Jack's lessons were going.

'I can probably teach you, you know.' Lissa sat down close to her.

'No!' Mya said in alarm. 'I mean, not now whilst we're travelling. Maybe one day.'

'Do you think you want to learn to use it?' Feather asked. 'In years past it was a great thing to have and a blessing to a family and even a community. Now it's a burden and a danger to have. Dormant your Gift might go unnoticed. Whilst Kasira lives though, if she finds you know how to use your Gift and are opposing her, she will hunt you and either throw you to the Ward or just kill you.'

'But if I taught her, she would be better able to defend herself against Dark Fey and any Spellward who is under Kasira's sway.' Lissa argued. 'And she can help us against Kasira herself; after all she has the stronger potential according to Ben.'

'How does he know?' Mya asked curiously, glancing toward the knight to be sure she hadn't been heard. 'I didn't think he had the Gift himself?'

'He doesn't.' Lissa lowered her voice, all playfulness gone. 'The poor man was made a Seeker, looking for those with potential for the Gift to recruit them to Ayresport. Of course, at the time, he thought himself on another noble quest to save the Valley.'

'That's when he found and rescued Kasira.'

'And saw someone incredibly strong in the Gift.' Lissa nodded. 'Had he not been a man, or bedazzled by her glamour, he might have wondered why someone so strong in the Gift needed rescuing at all. Poor Ben still feels guilt over that and all those he recruited to Ayresport. He spent quite some time in Ashgrove whilst Caelin was healing and plotting in Astol, and was in a sorry state, drinking and… well,' Lissa diplomatically didn't elaborate. 'But my parents got him back to himself. To cut a long story short, Mya, he's trained to see and read auras. Someone with the Gift has a purple aura. The darker and brighter the stronger the Gift.'

'So, there isn't any way I can really hide it.' Mya looked from Lissa to Feather. She swallowed. 'My choices seem to be to cower away in Astol or Ashgrove hoping Caelin and Jack defeat Kasira; or come out into the open and learn to use it so I can protect myself and help against her.'

'That's about the size of it.' Lissa nodded. 'I know what I'd choose.'

'Yes, well, I'd rather Mya was safely sheltered in Astol or Ayresport,' Feather said. 'Jack too for that matter; but then again I know what I would do too,' he finished with a sigh. He looked up at Mya with his dark brown eyes.

'What I want to do, and the right thing to do, seem to amount to the same thing,' she told him. 'But I've made my promise to Caelin and I can't begin to learn from any of you until we reach Astol. I guess it gives me time to decide.'

'What are you three up to?'

Mya jumped guiltily as Ben strode over having finished his conversation with the two scouts.

'Nothing but mischief!' Lissa flashed him a grin.

'Why is it I think you're not joking?' Ben narrowed his eyes and shook his head. 'Ferris, Morgan and Myself will take the watches tonight, you'd better get some sleep while you can. Whatever the Hunt chased away last night will no doubt come creeping back tonight. Tomorrow won't be such an easy journey.'

'Well, that's something to look forward to.' Lissa pouted at him. 'You're becoming as grumpy as Cae!'

'I've earned the right to be grumpy!' Ben retorted, but belied his words with a grin. 'Go on, try to get some rest.'

Mya settled into her blanket, looking around and seeing Wolf had crept around the camp to be closer to her; it made her feel safer. She couldn't bring herself to relax, though, until Caelin and Jack returned. Jack was almost glowing with excitement and instead of laying his blanket near her he remained with the knights. Mya told herself it was as it should be; but she couldn't help feeling a little hurt.

***

Over the next two days they made their way further northward through the awakening forest. The sky clouded over, but with some trees still only budding, patches of dull light found their way down to them and it remained quite mild. Of fey they met few and most of them Wild, not Dark, and they were offered no more opposition than the occasional taunt or thrown stone. Wolf remained with them, staying closer but never within touching distance as he had done when Mya had been attacked. On the second night Mya had been allowed a turn at keeping watch over the camp and she'd sat there wide eyed and nerves on edge, jumping at every sound. If Wolf took no notice, she guessed it was nothing to fear, but if he turned his head to listen, she remained on guard almost holding her breath until he settled again. The hours seemed to stretch further ahead of her until Caelin quietly got up from his blanket and took over so she could sleep.

Steady drizzle set in on their fourth day from Ashgrove, turning into larger drops as it collected in the trees above. The already limited conversation of the group filtered out to the occasional observation of fey or animal tracks. The terrain became steeper, and it wasn't long before Mya sighted the start of the mountains looming over the trees. She'd travelled a little in her life, but she'd never gone close to the mountains before.

'They make you feel rather insignificant, don't they?' Lissa caught her looking up at them instead of watching where she was going. 'Older than the oldest tree but slowly growing, changing and moving like an ancient living thing. These mountains were here when the Huntress and the Healer were young and they are both immortals. It makes me dizzy wondering about such a great expanse of time. We'll be following a pass cut through by the river Vine shortly and you'll be able to touch the grey rock of the mountain's feet.'

'Are we far from the pass?' Feather asked.

'About two miles at a guess.' Lissa turned and placed a hand on Jack's horse's shoulder. He'd settled on calling it Magpie. 'I'll be surprised if we reach there unchallenged.'

Mya pulled herself out of her daydreaming and renewed her attention to the surrounding forest. They'd gone perhaps another quarter mile when Ferris appeared on the narrow track ahead of them and made a signal with his hand she didn't understand. The others understood it all too well, Morgan and Lissa both nocked arrows to their bows and the knights drew their swords.

'Hobgoblin.' Ferris told them under his breath as they caught up. 'Our friend the powrie is with them with a nice bright-red cap. They've built themselves a little stockade to block the pass.'

'Hobgoblins don't build,' Caelin stated. 'You saw no one else with them? No humans or other fey?'

'Not in the time I observed them.' Ferris gave a shake of his head.

'Jack.' Caelin called abruptly. 'Come ahead with me a little way; we'll see if we can sense anything powerful at the pass.'

Jack gave a quick glance in Mya's direction then scurried after the spellward.

Mya had to force herself not to protest and folded her arms across her body anxiously. Feather had his sling out and Lissa had circled around to take up position behind them all and was scanning the forest. Mya searched the undergrowth with her eyes for Wolf but he'd vanished. Her anxiety built until she was almost dizzy and she slipped her hand down to the pocket she had sewn in her trousers to grasp her knife. She'd practised a little with her slingshot but the touch of strong iron was far more reassuring.

Caelin and Jack appeared on the path, the boy looking pale and serious. Caelin didn't wait but barked out orders at once.

'Whatever might have been there it's just the goblins and powrie now so this is the best time to strike. Lissa, you and I will weaken their stockade; Ferris and Morgan I want you to keep them busy with arrows. Once we've broken a way through, Ben, Jack and I will make a charge which the rest of you can cover with arrows and shot. Mya, keep hold of the horses until we are ready for them and try to keep out of the way!'

Chapter Eight

Mya fumbled at Magpie's reins as everyone else set off at once.

'Steady, my girl,' Feather said from the saddle although the brownie's voice was itself shaky.

Drawing in a long breath Mya pulled firmly and Magpie started forward without protest. She almost had to run to keep up with the others. The mountains now dominated the sky, overshadowing the forest and bringing an early end to the day. She tried to see through the trees ahead, her heart pounding so hard she thought it might break her ribs. The others stopped and Magpie bumped into her shoulder. She barely noticed the bruising impact.

'Listen for Sir Caelin,' Feather whispered. 'Do what he says at once.'

Mya nodded curtly without turning, still trying to guess what was happening beyond the screening trees. Lissa was alert and ready like a cat that had sighted its prey and was waiting for the right moment to jump. Mya wished she could be as excited as the half-fey at the prospect of a fight. Caelin beckoned Lissa to him and she stood between the spellward and Jack. Slowly they stalked forward and Ben indicated for Mya to keep up.

'On my mark,' Caelin said softly. 'Ferris, Morgan and Feather shoot at anything sticking its head up. Mya, you too if you think you can. Jack, you try the growing spell to weaken the left side, you Lissa the right. I'll break us a way through the centre. As soon as a way opens, we'll charge it. Mount up.'

Jack scurried back to Mya, and she lifted Feather down so her nephew could scramble up into the saddle; she was surprised at how heavy the small brownie was. Clumsily, Jack urged Magpie level with the knights and Mya took out her sling and shots. Caelin barely waited for the boy before he was moving again and Mya followed Feather around to the left of the group, trying to keep pace through the undergrowth. The trees thinned out all too soon, and bare craggy rock thrust out of the earth trimmed with scraggy mosses and small tenacious ferns. Mya spotted the stockade at once, a pile of stone and hastily chopped wood filling the path ahead like a dam. An angry squawk told them their presence was known.

'Now.'

Missiles came whizzing up over the barricade and Mya flinched aside behind the scant shelter of a spindly ash. The scouts and Lissa were already firing off arrows and the whine of a swiftly whirled sling told her Feather also hadn't hesitated. Not skilled enough to worry too much about a target, Mya put a bolt to her own sling and spun it clumsily; releasing it too soon so it flew off harmlessly across the face of the barricade. Lissa paused and focused hard on her arrow which took on a green glow. She shot it into the wood of the barricade which at once sprouted new leaves and twisted like live snakes so rocks tumbled. As Mya placed her second bolt, she saw the centre of the barricade was behaving in much the same way; the left side stood stubbornly resilient.

With a thud a stone bolt bounced off Ben's armour and Asher shied, trying to turn and pull back into the trees. The hobgoblin who had launched it paid for its boldness and was hurled back off the barricade with an arrow from Ferris through its chest.

'Shot!' Morgan congratulated.

'We're just wasting arrows.' Ferris shook his head with a glance at Caelin.

Jack sat stiff and hunched, his face growing red with effort but still nothing was happening to the left of the barricade. In the centre a huge branch erupted upward, hurling rock like an angry giant flailing an arm as it tried to rise from the earth. Lissa spun on her heels and shot another glowing arrow into the barricade on the left, and again the wood sprouted. Jack sagged, his face reddened and his eyes watered.

Morgan cried out as a bolt hit him in the shoulder and he staggered back. Blood welled through the cloth but he straightened at once and grimacing with the pain took another shot. Mya noticed he only had three arrows left; if they didn't break the barricade soon, they'd have nothing to stop the hobgoblins coming out into the open and shooting them at will. She wished with all her heart she could reach out with her own Gift and pull the barricade down.

She called out. 'Jack! Don't give up!'

Jack's shoulders rose as he took a deep breath and focused back on the barricade.

The hobgoblins had abandoned the now unstable centre and had moved to the closest edge, rallying to counter attack. Risking arrows, a dozen leapt up and hurled their bolts at once. One struck Horse who reared and tried to run; another grazed Mya's cheek both bruising and cutting. Ferris was bowled backward as one struck him directly in the forehead and the others whistled past slicing the undergrowth.

Undeterred, Feather, who was already whirling his sling, loosed and took out a hobgoblin in return; both the injured Morgan and Lissa also reducing their enemy's numbers. Jack gave a cry of triumph but swayed on his feet and as Mya raised a shocked hand to the blood on her face more of the wood in the barricade sprouted new growth and unravelled. The hobgoblins squealed and chittered as the barricade collapsed; wood washed away by the small river it bestrode.

'Now!' Caelin cried out, making Mya jump and Horse sprang forward at once. Ben was tight to his flank on Asher, and Jack hesitated only a heartbeat before urging Magpie after the others.

Morgan hauled Ferris to his feet and Lissa grabbed the older man's last arrow from his quiver to use herself.

'Come on!' She yelled over her shoulder to Mya without looking to see if she followed.

Feather peered up at Mya anxiously, but she hid her terror and forced her legs after the others. Some of the hobgoblins had tumbled down their side of the barricade and were already recovering to turn on them. They varied in size and shape but were all at least three times the size of Feather. Their skin was a brownish-green hue, their bodies squat and limbs long. On all of them their features were exaggerated; mouths as wide as their heads or grotesquely long and drooping and filled with pointed teeth. Noses bulbous or unnaturally elongated; eyes all stretched and narrow or goggling from their faces. Lissa and Feather both took out two of their number and the two knights bowled still more over, sweeping down with their swords as they headed for the growing gap in the barricade. Jack didn't engage with the fey, holding firm to Magpie's neck and trying to keep up.

Mya realised at once that in focusing on taking the barricade the knights would leave the rest of them behind with the surviving hobgoblins. Morgan was hampered by the injured Ferris and held is bow uselessly in his other free hand. Poor Feather was struggling to keep up, especially as he still shot from his sling as they ran. Lissa slung her bow across her body with lithe ease and drew her long knife from its sheath. She launched herself at the first two hobgoblins rushing them, moving aside from their lunges and then darting in swiftly to cut them with such speed and grace she made it a dance. Another of the creatures skirted around to come at Morgan and Ferris but Feather knocked it flat on its back with a bolt.

Mya scrunched her sling in her left hand and drew out her own small kitchen knife. The gap in the barricade seemed an age in distance and from beyond it came the sounds of fighting. Fear for Jack overrode all else and the first hobgoblin that grabbed for her got a slash of the poisonous iron across its palm and deep into its reaching fingers. Its yowls of pain were cut off abruptly as Wolf came racing past her in a blur of white and grey, seizing it in its jaws and shaking the hobgoblin like a rabbit. Mya caught up with the two scouts and shadowed Ferris' left and vulnerable side. Four hobgoblins now lay strewn and bloodied in Lissa's wake and a fifth lay fighting swift growing ivy binding itself about its neck. Wolf pinned another and tore out its throat.

Five hobgoblins remained, and they bunched together to head them off.

'Here!' Mya slipped her arm around Ferris' back to take the man's weight. Morgan gave a nod and let go of his companion to catch up with Lissa. Mya staggered under the sudden weight of the much larger man, her grip awkward with the knife still in her right hand. Feather caught up to her but Wolf flowed past going straight for the hobgoblins. Mya sucked in air as she saw one raise a bronze sword, but the wolf somehow understood and went for a fey armed only with its claws and teeth instead. Morgan tossed his bow to his left hand and drawing his sword engaged the armed goblin, one of its fellows darting in to try to outnumber the man. Mya could do nothing but watch and feel frustratingly useless as Lissa danced up to draw away the other two.

'My last bolt,' Feather said as he whizzed his sling above his head. 'I have more on Asher.'

Wolf had killed his hobgoblin and turned to leap at the one with the sword from behind, causing Morgan to step back in shock and surprise. Feather cursed under his breath as his bolt only hit one of the other hobgoblins in the shoulder. Mya had her own bolts in a pouch at her waist but couldn't even get to them to pass to Feather without dropping Ferris. Lissa cried out as one of the hobgoblins slashed at her thigh, leaving a line of red; but she didn't falter and thrust her own bronze sword into its stomach. Morgan finished the last of them and grabbed Lissa's arm.

He called over his shoulder to the rest of them. 'Come on!'

Wolf waited until Mya had caught up before loping at her side, his muzzle and chest stained with blood. Ferris gave a low groan and, shaking his head, revived himself a bit more. Most of his weight lifted from her shoulders so she was able to increase to a hobbled run.

The breach in the barricade was littered with rock and still sprouting wood making it difficult to negotiate. Mya couldn't turn to check on Feather's progress without yanking Ferris around with her, so she could only hope the little brownie was still with them. She could hear the knights were still fighting and braced herself for what she might see as they came around the barricade.

The first thing she spotted was Magpie, his saddle frighteningly empty. She stifled a cry but movement drew her eye, the two knights and Jack were standing back to back to fight off a swarm of the smaller foe. There was blood on Jack's face.

'Here!' She pushed herself out from under Ferris's arm, and grabbing her pouch turned and threw it to Feather who was puffing and red faced as he ran to catch them up. The brownie caught the pouch and readied his sling shot without even pausing. Lissa and Morgan were cautiously looking to join the fighting; Ferris scowling as he reached around for his quiver only to remember it was empty. Wolf was looking back at Mya expectantly, tongue lolling.

'Come on!' Mya told the wolf, gritting her teeth and gripping her small knife so hard her nails bit into the muscle of her thumb. With no thought of strategy, she ran straight at the hobgoblins menacing Jack; fear and fury pumping adrenaline through her body and overwhelming her mind. Her ears buzzed and her vision blurred almost red. She sliced down at one of the green-skinned fey at the same time as Wolf leapt and clasped his jaws around one's head. A bolt whizzed by and Lissa and Morgan fell in to either side. The hobgoblin shrieked and gibbered at the burning touch of her iron, and bile rose to her throat as she stabbed more purposefully into its chest. Another turned, long black nails clawing at her, but she kicked it in the head twice as it goggled at her in stunned surprise. Blood splattered from its broken skin and it crumpled. Wolf barged into her as it went for another, his fur course through the fabric of her trousers. Something moved to her right, and she spun, knife out.

'Whoa!' Lissa jumped back.

Mya blinked and shook her head, trying to clear the fog from her mind. She realised Caelin was speaking.

'I could do with grabbing some of my arrows back.' Ferris had replied to whatever the knight had said.

Mya looked around and saw to her shock the fighting was over, the hobgoblins lying mostly unmoving, though some twitched and groaned.

'We need to press on.' Caelin's eyes flickered up toward the sun.

'I'll grab what I can and catch up!' Morgan was away before anyone could protest.

Without warning nausea swept up from Mya's stomach and she vomited, barely moving her feet in time to avoid it. Embarrassed and shocked, tears rolled down her cheeks.

'Aunt Mya!' Jack cried out in consternation.

'Let's get you some water.' Lissa put a comforting arm around her shoulder. 'And some of us have wounds need tending.' She shot a scolding look at Caelin.

'We don't have time to hang about,' Caelin said, concerned rather than angry. 'We don't want to be caught here when night sets in.'

'Five minutes.' Lissa promised him. 'We'll move faster for it in the long run.'

Caelin nodded.

Mya tried to go to Jack, to see how badly injured he was but Lissa held her firmly and pulled her toward Asher. She took out a flask and handed it to her. Mya took a sip, and was startled into wakefulness when she found it was strong apple brandy and not water.

'Better?'

Mya nodded, wiping her eyes with the back of her hand.

'You did really well, my Lady.' Ben joined them and squeezed Mya's shoulder. 'Remind me never to upset you!'

Mya wasn't sure whether to feel hurt, worried or pleased at his comment.

'Your leg?' Ben asked Lissa.

'Needs binding.' The half-fey rummaged in her bag for some strips of cloth and a small pot of salve. 'But nothing serious. You two?'

'I'm good,' Ben reassured her.

Mya nodded. She was all right although her knees felt like they had no bones left in them and her body shook. 'Jack!' She turned around to look for her nephew. He was with Magpie, bringing the horse back over to the rest of them. He'd washed the blood off his face in the river and Mya saw to her relief it was a small cut and not deep.

Morgan came running back to join them, several arrows grasped in his fist.

'Anything?' Ben asked.

The scout shook his head.

'Are we ready?' Caelin asked impatiently.

Lissa finished tying the cloth she had wound about her leg. 'Ready.'

'Lissa, you'd better ride on Asher with Mya for a bit,' Caelin instructed. Jack had already lifted Feather onto Magpie's back. 'Ferris, you take my horse, and Jack you had best ride too. Morgan watch our backs. I'll take the lead for a while.'

Ferris made to protest but Caelin was in no mood to be contradicted again.

'You may have a concussion and we can't risk you slowing us down.'

Mya could see Ferris wasn't happy, but the man climbed up into Horse's saddle.

'Right, let's close some distance between us and Astol,' Caelin said under his breath as he took the lead and headed along the path westward.

The narrow and overgrown trail followed the merry river, bending with it between the dark mountains. The trees here were mostly small and stunted, although some ancient giants had found enough soil to grow, their roots spilling over the path. Brambles and tall bracken often barred their way, and the trail narrowed or disappeared under the undergrowth as though used only by small fey and animals. Several times they had to leave the path and walk through the shallow river instead.

Wolf stayed with them, his presence making the horses nervous. He remained shy and wary, not letting anyone get too close, but not even Ferris complained any more about the animal coming with them. Daylight had almost gone from the sky and the temperature plummeted so Mya still shivered, but this time from cold. She found herself glad she shared Asher with Lissa as the half-fey's back was warm where she held onto her.

Nearly all of them, including the horses, started as some stones skittered down from the cliff above on their side of the river.

'Are we spied on?' Ben asked, his hand going to his sword.

'Undoubtedly.' Caelin sighed tiredly.

All of them scoured the mountainside and the path behind and ahead with their eyes.

Ferris gave a shake of his head. 'Nothing.'

'It's our Powrie friend.' Caelin told them. 'He seems to be alone but he may have allies up ahead.'

'Maybe his only friends were those we already dealt with,' Ben suggested.

'We can hope.' Caelin's voice was flat and almost emotionless.

He stalked forward again and the rest of them followed.

It was only minutes later the remnants of daylight seeped away like the last grains in a sand timer. Mya's heart pumped faster, and she moved closer to Lissa. Bird song ceased but for the raucous challenge of a distant crow. The river became a black hole in the narrow landscape, its rippling flow loud between the mute mountains. The horse's hooves clipped and thudded where the bare bones of the rock protruded through the mossy undergrowth. She wanted to ask Lissa if she knew if there was a safe place they were stopping for the night, but she didn't dare speak and give her fear away. Her legs were stiff and aching after their earlier encounter with the hobgoblins, and her unaccustomed riding.

Caelin stopped and Lissa pulled up Asher. No one said a word and Mya strained all her senses to see or hear what had caused the Spellward to halt. She stretched to look over Lissa's shoulder. Caelin indicated with his hand and he left the trail to force his way up the steep slope of the mountain.

Lissa whispered. 'Time to walk.'

Mya awkwardly pulled her leg over Asher's back and slipped to the ground, stretching up onto her toes to loosen her muscles. The others dismounted also, and they led the horses up at an angle.

A prickly slow-berry bush snagged at Mya's clothes and scratched her bare hand. Lissa interposed herself between the bush and Asher, protecting the horse from the thorns as they squeezed through. Wolf slipped past them to range ahead and then dropped back to walk within touching distance of Mya.

The foliage opened up and Mya found herself on a small ledge before a gaping maw of a cave. The others had stopped outside whilst Caelin took a few cautious steps into the blackness.

Feather whispered from down near her boots. 'Testing for fey.'

'And bears!' Lissa added.

There wasn't room on the ledge for all of them, so all Mya could do was wait and listen.

After what felt like an age, Caelin came back out, his face grim.

'The Wicca Furze-hogge, Mutzlepaw, lived here.'

'Lived?' Lissa's voice was loud in alarm.

'The place is ransacked but there is no sign of her.'

'Those hobgoblins!' Lissa all but spat. 'If we hadn't already killed them–'

Caelin shushed her with a raised hand. 'We'll shelter here for the night. Feather, I'll cast a Ward so you'll have to hang back for a moment. I'll invite you in as soon as it's set.'

'I'll wait with you, Feather,' Jack offered at once.

Mya had expected some dank and dark rocky hole and was instead pleasantly surprised. There was a large double door woven out of withies and hung with small brass bells on red ribbons. Rushes scented with dried lavender were strewn across the floor but had been kicked about and spoilt by trampled food and smashed jars of ointments and liquids. Shelves had been pulled down and the straw-stuffed bed shredded. Morgan had up-righted a table and lit two candles he'd found in the bedlam. The horses they'd left just inside the doors snuffled in the rushes for anything edible.

'Let's straighten this out.' Lissa's mouth was set in a firm line, all sign of the playful, flirty fey Mya had first met was gone. Tired as she was Mya nodded and set to helping at once. It surprised her when Ben and the two Ashgrove scouts also joined in, righting and trying to fix furniture.

'Who is the Wicca Furze-Hogge?' Mya asked curiously.

In the entrance to the cave Caelin was concentrating on setting his Ward.

'She's an Earth-Fey,' Lissa explained as she tied up the broom and began sweeping the rushes. 'Her name is Mutzlepaw, and she's a witch; not of the Hag variety, a hedge-witch, a healer. She's quite shy and solitary but she'll… she used to help anyone. Sometimes she would make a rare trip down to Ashgrove to trade her potions and cures; often people would travel from Ashgrove to do the same.'

Mya found a sack. From the musty, earthy smell, it had probably contained potatoes. She began carefully dropping the broken jars into it.

'Wash your hands thoroughly after,' Lissa warned.

Caelin called out into the night, making Mya jump. 'Feather of the brownies, welcome be you, enter may you!'

'A little formal.' Lissa said under her breath with a raised eyebrow.

Feather and Jack came in, much to Mya's relief, and Caelin closed and latched the withy door.

'Oh!' Feather exclaimed, looking around in dismay.

'I understand your sentiments but you should all get some rest,' Caelin told them. 'The Ward should keep us safe, but I used a lot of power which will leave us vulnerable tomorrow.'

'Should we set watches still tonight?' Ben asked.

'Yes, one of us should remain awake. I'll take first watch.'

'No,' Ben said with surprising firmness. 'You should most definitely sleep and try to regain your strength, we'll need you tomorrow.'

'Let me watch,' Feather said. 'I won't be able to sleep until I've finished cleaning up here, anyway. I can doze on one of the horses tomorrow.'

'We'll need your powers too, brownie.' Caelin shook his head.

'Well let me take a watch.' Mya spoke up at once, jumping at the chance to be of more use.

'Very well. Feather, when you've finished what you must for your peace of mind wake Mya.'

Feather nodded.

They settled as best they could on the floor of the cave after tending to the horses and giving them a little feed. Feather moved about the cave as silently as a brownie was able, tidying and mending what he could. As much as he knew he should preserve his magic he couldn't help use a little to fix the things beyond the work of hands. Caelin stirred and Feather started guiltily; but the knight slept on. There were only three hedge-witches of Wild Fey kind in the Valley and so Feather had heard of the Wicca Furze-Hogge, though he'd never met her. If the hobgoblins had killed her, then it would be a great loss to them all. He'd not seen any blood anywhere in the cave which had been encouraging.

Goosebumps prickled his arms, and he turned to look hard at the withy doors. The two thick but stumpy candles still burned on the tables and shadows danced against the thin brown twigs. Wolf padded forward with only the lightest of footfalls on the stone floor, ears alert. The horses twitched and stirred. Feather reached for the broom.

Something hit the door with a soft splat and some of the bells rang faintly.

Feather looked at Wolf who stared back at him with an expression clearly saying, 'what was that?'

Then something harder, sharper, hit the door and it shook a little setting the bells to ringing louder. Caelin sat bolt upright and scrambled quickly to his feet. Lissa and Ferris woke more slowly sitting up to see what was going on. The others, exhausted from the trials of the day, still slept.

'Feather?' Caelin asked.

'Fey; we know no more than that.'

'We?' Caelin queried.

'The wolf and I.' Feather gave a shrug.

They listened in frozen anticipation. Just when Feather thought whatever it was had gone, something huge landed against the doors, bending them inward momentarily and setting the bells to ringing madly.

'What's happening?' Ben stumbled up out of his blanket and the others roused themselves in a panic. Wolf began a low growl deep in his throat.

Outside something laughed hysterically.

'Powrie!' Feather exclaimed angrily. 'That cursed Redcap!'

'It can't get in through the Ward.' Caelin reassured them.

Something thudded against the doors again and Feather jumped despite Caelin's words.

A high and unnatural voice called through the door. 'Won't you come out and play little brownie? Little humans?'

Feather shuddered.

'Why don't you try and come in here!' Morgan retorted.

'Shhhh!' Caelin scolded the other man. 'You'll encourage it.'

Mad laughter warbled through the night followed by another soft, wet splat.

'It can't get to us.' Caelin repeated. 'Try to sleep.'

'Sleep!' Morgan said incredulously. 'With that thing making a racket?'

'That's its purpose.' Feather looked around at them all. Mya's eyes were wide in the candlelight. Jack blinked at him blearily. 'It can't hurt us in here so he'll rob us of peace and sleep so we are more vulnerable tomorrow.'

'Perhaps we should just go out and get him?' Ben suggested.

'And he'll lead you a merry dance keeping you running about all night and those of us with magic will waste more power.'

'The brownie is right.' Caelin sighed. 'We must try to sleep.'

Taking his own advice, the spellward walked back to his blanket and lay down. The others also tried to settle as the door bounced inward with another thud and a fit of manic giggling.

'Ooohh little humans come out and play! I won't hurt ye! Come out of your shell brave spellward! He he!'

The voice made Feather queasy, and he was glad when Wolf sat back on his haunches seeming determined to sit the watch with him. Behind them he heard Morgan fidgeting in his blanket with obvious annoyance.

'Shall I fetch my other friends if you won't play?'

Everyone in the cave became very still; all no doubt contemplating the same thing that was running through

Feather's mind. Did the powrie really have other friends and if so who or *what* were they?

'Ooh please come and play?' The Dark Fey's voice was childishly pleading.

Thud.

'I don't want to have to play with the barghest, he's no fun. He'd like to play with you though!'

Icy fingers walked up Feather's spine. Was it a bluff to scare them into wakefulness or was the barghest really somewhere near?

The voice was suddenly deeper, fierce and grating. 'Play with me!'

Wolf growled getting back to all fours.

'Pleeeeease! Oh won–' the voice was cut off and turned into a panicked screech of fear and pain. Caelin got rapidly back to his feet.

Wolf whined.

Silence lay heavy on their ears.

'Another trick?' Morgan asked uncertainly.

'I can't feel anything.' Lissa looked from Caelin to Feather.

They waited.

Feather almost jumped out of his skin when a different voice yelled in to them. 'Oi y' scallywigses! Ain't y' gonna let me in me own 'ome?'

Lissa leapt to her feet, hope on her face. 'Is that really Mutzlepaw?'

They hesitated some more, no one willing to believe it.

'Oi y' blockheeds! I can smell y's all! I smells a dryad an' some 'umans an' ... blessed moon 'ave y' got a farmyard in me 'ome? Let me in right now!'

'Sounds like her.' Lissa winced.

'Be prepared.' Caelin strode forward and unlatched the door. 'Mutzlepaw the Wicca Furze-Hogge; welcome be you, enter may you.'

'I should thinks so too!'

Caelin stepped back as the doors swung inward. The chill of the night flowed in and the gap between the withies showed nothing but darkness. Then a hunched and distorted figure hobbled awkwardly in.

'Weeell have some manners an' help me then! I used me best walking stick to skewer y' powrie!'

'Mutzlepaw!' Lissa bounded forward to hug the smaller fey. Her arms went around her carefully as her head and back were covered in spines like a hedgehog. She wore a skirt of rags and an apron the strings of which vanished under her spines. Her arms and hands were almost, but not quite, human-looking; the fingers were long and narrow and edged with black nails. Her face was not as elongated as a hedgehog's and her nose also was almost human. Her small black eyes were animal-like and their expression hard to fathom. She stood almost four feet tall although her hunch made it less.

'Oh, bless y'!' She blinked rapidly as she looked around her cave. 'Y' have set much t' rights!'

'That was mostly Feather,' Lissa admitted, introducing him. Caelin closed and barred the doors.

Feather smiled at the other fey, though his head was still taking in the news. Had this old hedge witch really killed his nemesis the powrie with a walking stick? Part of him was disappointed he hadn't been given the opportunity to do the job himself.

'Hello my fine fellow.'

To Feather's amazement the fey laid a hand momentarily on Wolf's broad head in a blessing and it didn't flinch away or avoid the contact.

'Your pardon, Mother, for our intrusion.' Caelin found his tongue and his courtesy. 'We needed a place of safety. Were you here when the hobgoblins attacked? You weren't hurt?'

'Please, sit down.' Ferris pulled out a mended chair and threw his own blanket across it to make it more comfortable.

'Thank ye, young man.' Mutzlepaw hopped up and settled herself, snagging the blanket a little with her spines. The others gathered around her, Mya shyly, Jack curious and eager. Feather tried to keep half an ear on the door whilst the hedge-witch spoke.

'I 'eard their ruckus as they was a-coming up the valley. I dint 'ave much time but they sounded like a big rabble o' ruffians. Not bein' sure o' me chances I scarpered quick as these ole legs could get me higher up the mountain path. 'Twas clear they were just out f' mischief as they didn't seem t' look for me. Then me' marrow froze as He came a looking for 'em, an a scolding 'em in his cold dead voice t' be getting back down t' man some barricade.'

'Who, Mother?' Morgan asked almost in a whisper.

'It were a barghest.' Mutzlepaw also dropped her voice. 'None other than Rashmin his self!'

Feather spun around from his vigil on the door and gave all his attention to the hedge-witch. Rashmin was a name he knew and dreaded. Rashmin was one of Kasira's captains from the court of the Dark Fey. He realised he should have put two and two together when Caelin had first made them aware a barghest followed them; but his mind had steered well away from such a dreadful thought. He looked at the Spellward but the knight's face was still and composed, giving nothing away.

'I took a peek at me 'ome, could'na help me'self, an' saw the state of it.' Mutzlepaw gave a sad shake of her head. 'But you's 'ave done me a kindness an' done much for me. I was tore between checking this barricade they gabbled of, an' warning the trow village up above the Stair. I picked them as the greater need. I came back home as y' see and found that rascally fellow tormentin' ye, an' so busy feelin' pleased with 'imself he never checked ahind 'im.'

'He has plagued us a good while,' Ben said. 'You did us a good turn tonight, Mother.'

'It was dangerous for you to come back though,' Caelin scolded gently. 'Even for one of your gifts and skill. You would have done better to stay with the trows or go on to the shelter of Astol.'

'A home is a home, Spellward; it is long since you had one or you would understand.'

Hurt flashed so briefly across Caelin's face before he controlled it Feather wondered if anyone else had seen it.

'Oh, but you *must* come with us!' Lissa exclaimed. 'It won't be safe for you here.'

'Our fight with the hobgoblins will have given our destination away to Kasira.' Ben agreed. 'The barghest will still be near and she'll send other's, if not to stop us then to wait for us. Only Her Grace and Astol can shelter any Wild Fey safely; this valley will become an extremely dangerous place.'

Caelin hung his head, his shoulder's rising and falling in a silent sigh. 'I didn't consider the consequences to this small valley. Mother, please come with us and help me persuade the trows they must come too.'

'Aye, 'tis a bind we are in.' Mutzlepaw nodded. 'But Sir Ben has the truth of it. Very well; for the sake of the little folks above the stair I'll come with ye and seek sanctuary with Her Grace.'

The scouts, including Lissa, looked delighted as did Ben. Mya was chewing on her bottom lip and Jack watched the elderly earth-fey with wide eyes. Over Caelin a sadness settled that added shadows to his ravaged face. The brownie's heart swelled with pity.

'Come on then!' Ben clapped his hands together. 'Let's have another try at this sleep.'

Morgan helped Mutzlepaw up and lent his arm to aid her to her restored mattress. The others all settled back to their blankets and Wolf, seeing all was well, eventually curled on the floor with his nose in his long tail. Feather stood for a long while leaning against the broom, listening to the night outside with his thoughts far away.

Chapter Nine

Mya yawned and covered it quickly with her hand. Feather had generously left it until only three hours before dawn before waking her. Miraculously, after the events the day before and here in the cave, she'd managed to get some sleep. Despite the Ward and the death of the powrie her nerves had remained somewhat on edge, and her sense of relief grew as grey light seeped through the gaps in the withy doors. Mutzlepaw was the first to wake behind her, and the old fey limped across to her shelves to shake her head at her ruined and depleted stores.

'Help me make breakfast will ya' girl?'

Mya got awkwardly to her feet, her muscles still stiff and protesting. She stared at the earth-fey, transfixed by her strange appearance and odd little movements. She looked away quickly, her cheeks warming, as Mutzlepaw glanced up and caught her eyes.

'Haven't see'd many fey, have ya valley girl?' Mutzlepaw blinked at her.

'No ma'am.' Mya cringed guiltily.

Mutzlepaw passed her some roots, tubers and dried mushrooms. She bustled off to the back of the cave, and moving a smallish rock, gave a delighted exclamation. Reaching into a deep hole she drew out something wrapped in cloth that turned out to be a wheel of goat's cheese.

By now the others were waking.

'Fetch me some water in that bucket, will you?' the hedge-witch said to no one in particular.

Caelin picked up the bucket. 'Ferris, let's take a look outside and check how things are.'

Ferris shook off any remnants of sleepiness at once and went to unbolt the doors. He had a dark bruise edged with green and yellow across his forehead. Wolf slipped out behind them.

'Can I help?' Feather asked.

'Pound these seeds 'ere in the mortar,' Mutzlepaw instructed. 'We'll make some loaves.'

Mya set to peeling the roots and tubers, not entirely sure to which plant each belonged. Caelin and Ferris returned to say there was no sign of any fey in the valley, other than the powrie still lying dead on the ledge.

'It must have taken some force to drive that stick through it,' Ferris said, looking at Mutzlepaw wonderingly.

Feather mixed his seed paste with a little water and tipped the mixture in lines on the stones of Mutzlepaw's stove where they hissed. The hedge-witch dropped all the roots and tubers into a pot of boiling water and asked Mya to keep an eye on it whilst she herself disappeared outside. The hedge-witch called out two names loudly, twice, then came in and busied herself selecting items to place in what looked like two sets of miniature saddle bags.

Mya took the opportunity to quietly confer with Feather. 'A trow village was mentioned last night. I've heard they are good, but sometimes tricksey fey?'

'They do no harm to humans but those that harm them first, if that's what you mean by good,' Feather replied, turning his small flattish loaves. 'But yes, they love to play pranks and take much joy in music and dancing.'

'I spent some time in their company,' Ben said a little sheepishly. 'When I left Cae in Astol. They brew a strong liquor from flowers and are jolly folk to be with.'

'Aye an' y' spent too much time in a trow cup, Sir Knight!' Mutzlepaw scolded as she dropped her bags down by the door. 'Are them roots soft yet?'

Mya squeezed one up against the side of the large pan and it split into white pulp. 'It is.'

The fey took over, draining all the water and mashing up the remaining contents with the goat's cheese and some herbs. Feather took the loaves off the stone griddle and they all gathered as best they could around Mutzlepaw's table; the females of the group being ushered into using the only chairs. The mashed roots and tubers were a strange mix of sour and sweet and Mya wasn't sure if she liked it, but it was hot and filling and helped to moisten the dry nutty bread. They washed it down with nettle tea sweetened with a little honey.

The strangest sound had several of them leaping to their feet, it was like a giant child laughing huskily and ending in a strangled bleat. For once Mya wasn't alarmed, for she recognised the noise at once. Two goats came trotting into the cave, a nanny and a billy with large curling horns. Mutzlepaw scraped the remains of their breakfast into the bucket and gave it to the goats. Mya slipped half a small loaf into her pack for Wolf for when he returned.

They didn't need prompting by Caelin to finish stowing their things, and Feather cleared away their dishes and cups with help from Jack, whilst Mutzlepaw secured her bags to the goats.

'Are we ready?' Ferris asked.

'We'll go back down to the main track along the river,' Caelin announced. 'We'll be easier to spot and more likely to meet fey, but should make faster progress for all that. We have two full days of travel ahead of us but only one night if we make good time. Morgan and Ferris, take the high road above us to check for ambush but stay within hailing distance; re-join us at the Stair. Ben, watch our back. Lissa, keep an eye on the river.'

Lissa nodded and Mya sighed, her shoulders sagging. She watched Caelin with her jaw clenched; why hadn't he tasked *her* anything?

Outside the sky had clouded over and the day was heavy and dreary with the threat of rain. Mya averted her eyes from the crumpled form of the powrie with its dull brown cap, and the carpet of sticky scarlet spreading out on the stone beneath it. Mutzlepaw pulled free her rowan walking stick, and taking hold of the ropes around the goats' necks led them down the overgrown path from the ledge. Mya couldn't see Wolf and began to worry, but as they came down into the river valley, he ghosted out from the trees and kept pace to their left.

Caelin set a fast pace along the river's winding route amongst the folds of the mountains. Mutzlepaw kept up with her awkward swaying hobble and no sign of weariness. Three times during the morning, where the small valley narrowed,

Ferris and Morgan ended up back on the path with them and for a while they all had to walk in the river itself to avoid sharp jagged boulders over which the horses couldn't climb. They took a short break just after midday and Feather was lifted into a tree to keep watch for them. He'd managed to catch up on a little fitful sleep on Magpie's back. Not long after, rain came down in an incessant drizzle, and in moments they were all soaked through to the bone and feeling thoroughly miserable.

Lissa took in a sharp breath and Mya turned to see what the half-fey was looking at. She strained her eyes to peer at the river through the moving curtain of rain. All she could see were two small rounded rocks, shiny as wet velvet, one with what might have been two birds perched on it and some black bedraggled weed. Then it rose, and she stepped back away from the water, colliding with Magpie.

'Kelpie!' Lissa called out in alarm.

At her cry the shape vanished back under the water, and when Caelin rushed back past Horse there was nothing but the slightest of ripples.

'He aint fool enough to attack such a party as ours.' Mutzlepaw tapped her rowan stick against a rock. 'But best keep out o' the water an' close together.'

'You know this one?' Caelin asked.

'Aye, he is a handsome charmer, that one, an' starved of both sport and victims. He'll make mischief if 'e can without riskin' 'is own self.'

'Then we do as you say,' Caelin said grimly. 'No one goes anywhere alone and we invite no strangers into our company.' He looked sharply at Mya as though he thought she in particular would do such a thing, and she refrained from a scowl until he turned away.

As the afternoon drew on, they heard the rush and thunder of a waterfall. The path moved away from the river and closer against the sheer flank of the mountain. Ferris and Morgan re-joined them again.

'The Stair looks unguarded.' Ferris reported. 'No sign of the Trows, but then they wouldn't be out at this time of day.'

'Very well; guard the summit and have your bows ready,' Caelin replied.

They came out of the sparse trees to the foot of a tall cliff over which the river spilled in white foamy tresses. To the left of it someone had cut a stairway into the wall of the mountain; steep but accessible to horses. It was only wide enough to go in single file and the two Ashgrove scouts sprang quickly up it; Morgan looking away to what lay ahead past the fall and Ferris keeping an eye on the company. Caelin as ever led the way, and Ben and Lissa argued briefly over who would follow last until she gave in to Ben's pleas he be allowed to be a gentleman. Feather remained on Magpie as for him the stairs would have been quite a challenge, and Mya followed just behind to keep him company. Wolf waited, not wanting to be trapped in such close proximity with nowhere to run to. When they had all nearly gained the top, he followed.

At the top of the fall the river had widened the valley, and a small meadow filled with tall grasses and bright yellow dandelions was cut almost neatly in two by the water. Mya recognised sloe bushes, crab apple trees, dog rose and alder as well as brambles and hazel; this would be a rich place indeed in the late summer. Small holes dotted the rock of the mountain on their side of the river as though inhabited by rabbits with claws of steel or diamond. A fragile-looking bridge of wood and rope swung in the wind over the river. There were tree stumps and logs cut and polished into tiny benches and tables and rickety stalls that might form a bedraggled market.

'Do you think they've gone on to Astol already?' Lissa asked Mutzlepaw.

''Tis unlikely they paid me heed.' The fey shook her spiny head. 'Some o' the trow wives might 'ave 'ad sense t' harken, but they feel themselves safe in their mountain caves for the most part.'

Mya looked about at the holes, there were a few creatures amongst the fey who were small enough to get in, but hobgoblins most certainly wouldn't fit.

'Well, we have no time to tarry and speak with them,' Ben said with a wistful sigh. 'Let's be on.'

The valley remained wide for almost three miles before it narrowed back down to a few yards of undergrowth and a barely noticeable path between the mountain and the river. They made only one short stop to rest before Caelin was hurrying them on again. The rain finally ceased, and the sun broke through, but as before evening came quickly. The sun dipped down behind the mountains with only a sharp orange glow like a halo about their edges. Wolf moved in closer to Mya.

They kept going until full dark was upon them; the clouds rolling back in to hide the stars. Reluctantly Caelin stopped where there was a slight overhang in the cliff and the space between it and the river widened.

'This will have to do,' he told them. 'We'll watch in threes keeping an eye in both directions and on the river.'

They settled themselves and their animals, sharing out their food rations but not daring to light a fire. Mya's clothes were still damp, as was her blanket, and she found herself wishing she'd drawn the first watch instead of the last with Morgan and Mutzlepaw; she was too cold and uncomfortable to get to sleep. She hadn't been trying for long when she heard Jack call out to Ben.

'A fire!'

Mya pulled herself up onto her elbow and looked around.

'And music,' Ben added.

'Keep an eye to the river!' Caelin warned his fellow knight. He'd not been on watch but had roused at once. Lissa still guarded the path behind them to the east but glanced back over her shoulder.

'Them be trows.' Mutzlepaw told them. 'Seems some *are* on their way t' Astol.'

'And they don't seem to have much care for their own safety.' Caelin glared angrily in the direction of the noise and dancing light. Mya could see the muscles of his jaw move as he clenched it.

'Ah but I sense no danger here,' Mutzlepaw said, standing up with the aid of her stick.

'Nor I.' Lissa joined in. 'And I for one would feel safer in a larger party. You know how sensitive trows are, they'd be gone in a wink, fires and all, if any danger threatened.'

'We should be resting.' Caelin continued to protest.

'I'd rest better with a warm fire and those little fellows on watch, if they'll have us.' Morgan said.

'I'll go ask,' Mutzlepaw said without waiting for any permission.

'If we go,' Feather warned Mya and Jack. 'Remember your lore about Trows! Do not steal from them, remain well mannered. They will offer food and drink; the drink is potent but will not harm you other than to go straight to your head. The food will also be fine unless you upset or offend them in some way, in which case it will not be as it seems, but rather something nasty and rotten. It would be best to eat and drink only from our own supplies.'

'Caelin doesn't look happy about it,' Mya observed.

'He's concerned for our safety,' Feather replied. 'His over-caution has no doubt saved us, but can be wearing. It's well meant I'm sure.'

Mya couldn't find herself feeling quite as charitable as the brownie, thinking rather that Caelin hated it when he wasn't in complete control of them all.

Mutzlepaw came waddling out of the darkness. 'We be all welcome!' She called out.

They led the horses carefully through the darkness, trying not to get tangled in the bushes or trip over any invisible roots. The distant music of pipe, dulcimer and drum ceased abruptly and Mya strained her eyes in the dark to see the fires still danced and spat.

'Have they fled?' Jack whispered.

'Not yet,' Feather told them. 'But they are cautious.'

They stopped on the edge of the firelight, night blind from looking into the flame. Mutzlepaw raised a hand to bid them all wait. Gradually Mya's eyes adjusted and she noticed movement just outside the orange glow of light. All at once the music struck up again and small figures came forward into the open, some already dancing. They were about twice Feather's height and varied in shape and feature as much as one human from another. All suffered from some deformity, from a squint to a humped back, a club-foot to boils. They were dressed in rags or plain spun flax with hair mostly brown and long. More than two-thirds were female and many of them children.

Two hurried forward with squeals of delight to take hold of Ben's outstretched hands.

'Sirbeen!' They called him in high pitched voices and words so fast they were hard to catch. 'Sirbeen dancedance!'

'Steady, my ladies!' Ben laughed as he allowed himself to be dragged into a stumbling and out of time reel.

'Come, Morgan!' Lissa flashed her fellow scout a playful grin, and he whisked her into the dance without hesitation.

'I'll help you hobble the horses,' Ferris told Caelin. Jack, wishing to stay in the spellward's good graces, hurried to assist them.

Mutzlepaw moved away to join a group of old trow matrons she appeared to know well. A cluster of shy fey, who seemed to be older children, approached Mya and Feather. They offered them a tray of berries and a flask of liquid.

'Oh, no thank you we have eaten,' Feather said quickly to save them both. 'But we will have a little sip if it's honey berry juice?'

'Yesyes!' One of the little ones bobbed enthusiastically, smiling to show broken and black teeth.

Feather took the leather flask and drank a little, then passed it up to Mya with a smile and a nod. She drew a little into her mouth tentatively, just enough to wet the tip of her tongue. It was sweet and sticky like honey with the mild tang of elderflower. There was a sharpness too of barely ripe berries that stopped it being cloying.

'Thank you.' She gave a slight curtsey. The little trows were delighted by this and chattered away to her all at once and so fast she couldn't make out a thing.

'Let me tell you some brownie stories.' Feather quieted them. The trow children snatched at the smaller brownie's clothing and led him to a quiet area on the edge of the light of one of the fires away from the dancing, and the prancing musicians. Seeing her looking lost Ben excused himself from his lady trow friends to come to her rescue.

'Will you join the dance, my lady?' He asked with a bow.

'Oh, but I don't really dance!' Mya said in alarm. 'It's many years since I did so.'

'Trust me, my lady,' Ben said, warmth and kindness in his whiskery old face. 'Let me lead you and I'll not let you falter.'

Shyly Mya placed her hand on his outstretched arm and he led her to the centre of the circle of fires. The trow tune was still lively, but Ben took her left hand and placed his other against her back and attempted a fast-paced waltz. At first her feet stumbled, but Ben held her firmly and as soon as she relaxed and began to laugh, both at herself and the trow's lilted tune, her feet found their own way. The flickering firelight sped by and the old knight's eyes twinkled with merriment. Many of the other fey had joined in, trying to dance in the same manner with mixed success. With a laugh Lissa twirled past them and back into a similar hold with Morgan though he lacked Ben's posture. The trow musicians changed their tune to better suit but Ben stopped sharply, Mya almost colliding with him. Mya looked around to see what had caught Ben's attention, and she was in time to catch Caelin pushing Lissa away none too gently.

'I don't dance, madam, just leave it!'

Lissa's merry smile crumpled, and blushing scarlet she turned and ran off away from the firelight.

Ben started forward but Mya stopped him. 'I'll go.'

Mya was all but blind from the brightness of the fire but she could hear the river to her right and she held her hand in front of her to ward off grasping branches.

'Lissa!'

She cursed Caelin for his insensitivity.

'Please, Lissa, where are you?' She called out into the darkness. The river was unnaturally loud and the music of the trows far away. Her eyes adjusted and above the trees a few stars glimmered.

'Are you lost, dear heart?'

Mya froze, sucking in air sharply, her heart hammered. She turned to see the silhouette of a man not a yard away from her. He was tall and broad shouldered with a narrowed waist and hips. Long dark hair flowed across his shoulders and back. He took a step forward and Mya's heart skipped; he had an unnatural beauty that would sear any woman's soul.

'Let me help you.' He held out a long, slim hand.

Mya's lungs ached, and she realised she'd not taken a breath. She knew this seeming man was a fey, but she couldn't take her eyes off him nor stop the rapid beating of her heart.

'Come with me, pretty lady.' He held out his hand invitingly.

A branch came swinging out from nowhere striking the kelpie; Lissa grunted with the effort. 'Get away!'

The spell broke and Mya stepped back, mortified and ashamed she'd allowed it to bewitch her for even a moment. The kelpie hissed, its perfect features marred by anger. Lissa raised her hands and blue fire crackled like captured lightning between her fingertips.

'Get back to the water, kelpie!' Lissa challenged.

'Why not let me have her?' The kelpie said in its smooth rich voice. 'Let me have the little mortal maid as a plaything, I'll not give her pain. Let me take away your rival.'

'I'm not her rival,' Mya growled. 'Her friendship means more to me than any man!'

'You mean that?' Lissa gasped.

The kelpie took two discreet steps backward. 'You could both come with me?' He threw at them playfully.

'Be gone!' Lissa threatened him again with her burning hands.

The kelpie flashed them a smile that would have melted a heart of ice and withdrew back to his river.

Mya took a moment to slow her breathing, one hand at her throat. She looked up to see Lissa was watching her, her green eyes wide.

'I meant that,' Mya said. 'I wouldn't hurt you for all the Valley.'

The fire died in Lissa's hands and she flung her arms around Mya and squeezed her so tightly she couldn't breathe.

'Lissa.' Mya pulled back to look into the half-fey's green eyes. 'I know you have very strong feelings for Caelin, and I can even understand why, but can you not see he will only ever hurt you? He's too full of resentments, anger and bitterness to allow room for love.'

'But I might be able to–'

'No, don't you dare!' Mya interrupted. 'You can *never* fix or change another person. Only they can do that, and they also have to be willing and ready. Caelin is too in love with his own suffering and self-loathing. Lissa you deserve so much better, please try to believe it.'

'Lissa! Mya!' Caelin's voice rang out sharply and Mya realised the music of the trows had ceased.

'We're here!' Lissa called, her eyes not leaving Mya's. 'We're fine!'

They made their way back toward the fires and the music started up again. Caelin was waiting for them, anger and concern passed quickly across his face before he hid them.

'This is why I didn't want women—'

'Not now!' Mya snapped at him, putting her arm through Lissa's. 'Enough of your bullying! We'll take this watch.'

Her muscles were clenched tightly and her anger heated her skin, but deep in her chest her heart gave a tingling twinge of guilt. She was sure Caelin had meant no harm, but surely, he knew how Lissa felt? They set up their post near the horses and goats away from the fires. Mya's thoughts drifted to the kelpie and the burn of her anger turned to a flush of embarrassment. She scowled at herself, she might have felt the fey's charm spell, but she hadn't actually fallen for it. She gazed back toward the others, seeing Caelin's sullen shape, cross-legged and hunched over, alone at the edge of the firelight. It was some time before she shook herself and turned away.

***

The music faded soon after midnight and the fires dwindled. The trows began to vanish, and the others made their way back to where Mya and Lissa stood watch. Morgan and Ferris offered to take over and Mya gratefully relinquished; wrapping herself in her now dry blanket. Dawn came all too quickly and Mya woke with an uncomfortable disquiet in her stomach. She'd lost her temper with Caelin. He might very well have deserved it, but it wouldn't make travelling with him any easier.

The only sign of the trows were some burnt patches of earth where the fires had been. Breakfast was hastily eaten cold rations, and Caelin had them under way before the sun had fully appeared in the narrow valley between the mountains. Lissa was cheerful and chattered away to Feather and Jack as they walked, keeping her voice low and soft. Caelin checked their path and the two scouts walked at the rear. Mya found herself often drawn to the sparkling water, wondering what lay beneath the silver ripples of the surface.

Three times they caught up to where Caelin waited and they stopped to rest. As the day wore on, they became more and more quiet, concentrating their energy on walking and watching for danger. A heaviness settled over them and Mya found her anxiety growing. Wolf moved so close to her his fur almost brushed her leg; he was alert and wary with his tail curled almost under himself.

'Do you feel it?' Lissa dropped back to walk just ahead of her, her voice barely a whisper. 'Something bad oppresses the valley.'

The sun faded and looking up Mya saw Caelin waiting for them on a rise in the path, his hand was on his sword hilt.

'What are you thinking?' Morgan called to Lissa, but it was Mutzlepaw who answered.

'Dark Fey.' The hedge-witch hissed. 'A Wight!'

'The Barghest?' Lissa halted, then realised she was holding them up on the narrow path and hurried forward.

'Trouble?' Ben asked Caelin as they caught up.

'Nothing ahead,' the spellward replied. 'But something follows hard on our heels. Go on ahead and pick up our pace, we have about another five miles to go before we reach the gateway.'

'You'll not wait for it alone?' Ben asked in concern.

Caelin shook his head with a wry smile. 'No noble sacrifice would that be, but a foolish suicide buying you only minutes. No, we will be stronger together but I must take the brunt of it.'

Ben nodded and making his way to the front led them on again almost at a run.

'What defence must we use against a Barghest?' Mya asked Feather breathlessly as she hurried to keep up.

'Show no fear,' Feather replied. 'Fear will give it power over you. It's a harbinger of doom. To see it is to foretell your death. Rashmin is different though, he follows no laws of fey but the command of his mistress, Kasira. To defeat it?' Feather shook his small round head. 'I know not.'

How can you not fear something you can't defend yourself from? Mya wondered. She knew Caelin was powerful; but then he'd had to seek her and Jack to get help to go up against Kasira, so he most definitely had his limits. Mutzlepaw's killing of the powrie suggested there was much more to her than there appeared and Lissa had some power too… but still, Mya's heart raced faster and the hairs rose on the back of her neck.

Ben kept up his breakneck pace, and no one found the breath to speak. Early night came swiftly as once again the sun fell behind the mountains. No sound came but from their hurried flight and even the river became a silent black flow of velvet, covering its deep secrets. Wolf gave a low, deep growl in the back of his throat, shoulders hunched and tail tucked low.

'Keep going.' Morgan urged Mya as she stopped to see what had disturbed the animal.

Despite Feather's warning, fear welled up from inside her, tightening the muscles in her chest and throat. She tried to reason with it, but her body refused to accede to logic against the force of imagination and anticipation.

'It's close!' Mutzlepaw announced. 'An' there are others with it!'

'How far?' Morgan called to Ben.

'We have over a mile to go.' The old knight's voice was hoarse.

'We won't make it.' Lissa shook her head, but she sounded undaunted. 'Keep an eye out for somewhere we can defend.'

Mya looked around hopelessly, barely able to see a few feet in any direction. She touched the hilt of her knife, wondering how much protection the small piece of iron would give her.

'Stand!' Caelin cried out.

Lissa was at his side in an instant with an arrow nocked to her bow. Morgan helped Feather down off Magpie and then chased the horses further up the path. Ben took up position beside Lissa and Ferris to their left. Mutzlepaw hopped up onto a rock half fallen into the river, and Morgan moved beside her. Jack stepped up behind Caelin and Mya felt a tickling sensation in the air as he called up his Gift. She took out her sling and joined the others with Wolf snarling, all teeth and bristling fur, at her side.

'Can you cast a Ward to protect us all?' Mya asked Caelin hopefully.

Caelin shook his head. 'Even a small Ward just to circle us would take a huge amount of power. All they would have to do is wait for my strength to fail and we'd be all but helpless.'

She felt them before she saw them, black holes into the night, emanating terror. There was movement without form or sound; creatures that missed the earthly senses to be perceived only in heart and mind. Red glowing eyes appeared and were gone in a blink, first in one place and then another.

'Hold firm.' Caelin's voice was soft and steady, a salve to Mya's fraying nerves. Wolf stopped his growling but kept his defensive posture.

Mutzlepaw chanted under her breath though Mya could see no evidence of whatever magic she wove. There was no sound, nothing to warn of where their enemies might strike from. Blackness leapt out of the night, a formless beast that might have been a dog with burning embers for eyes and a phosphorescent maw of teeth. It tried for Ben's throat but the knight lifted an arm protected by an iron vambrace to block the jaws. The iron screeched as though scored by metal and Ben awkwardly tried to bring his sword around. Caelin was faster, thrusting his sword into emptiness. Lissa called up her ball of blue lightning and was about to assist when Morgan cried out. Another of the Black Dogs had come at them from the shadows to menace the young man who had nothing but a bow and a knife and his leather armour to save himself. Lissa hurled her orb of magic and it caught in the ephemeral creature's 'fur' like a crackling web. It howled and shook its head, backing away, still alight.

Greenish light seeped up from the forest floor in strange wisps lighting everything in a sickly glow. Mya jumped aside from some that started by her feet but Feather's voice came to her.

'Foxfire. Mutzlepaw's.'

Far from being reassuring, the fey-light revealed their full peril. She counted quickly, five Black Dogs in all stalked them.

A fog of light came weaving through the trees breaking apart into the tiny bodies of fireflies; more of Mutzlepaw's magic. The Dogs shrank back but were not long perturbed by the false dawn. Three of them came at once including one who still sparked with Lissa's lightning. One went again for Morgan who tried to guard Mutzlepaw. He raised his knife and slashed out to no avail. The Black Dog went for his throat but Morgan turned so its teeth sank into his shoulder and it tried to shake him like a rag; blood sprayed as his flesh tore.

The second came straight at Caelin who, having learnt from Lissa's success, blocked it with a flash of blinding white light like a small star which shot into the dog's chest and burst there. The third leapt straight over Lissa and came at Jack who had only succeeded in creating a small flame in the palm of his hand. Without thinking Mya pushed Jack out of its path and found herself standing there with teeth and eyes bearing down on her. Her body froze, but the Gift stirred within her; useless without the knowledge of how to use it. Then a white lupine of flesh and blood launched itself upward, hitting the Black Dog full in its head and shoulders and landing in a heap of limbs and snarling jaws. Feather tried to use some of his brownie magic to stir the ivy into snaring the dog; but it wasn't quick enough and couldn't grasp the shifting unsolid form.

Ferris had gone to help Morgan, his long dagger leaving welts in the unrelenting beast that closed up and vanished in seconds. Morgan was weakening quickly, bleeding his life away. Mutzlepaw chanted rapidly, holding up her staff which glowed brightly. It leapt from her hand and skewered the Black Dog, pinning it to the earth. Frantically it scrabbled but although the staff hadn't killed it, it couldn't free itself.

Mya watched helplessly as the other Black Dog tore at Wolf. Jack tentatively moved closer and, darting in, touched the Black Dog with his fiery hand. With a yelp it tore free of Wolf whose white fur was dripping scarlet. Lissa added her blue lightning to the flames caught in the ghostly fur and with a yowl it leapt past them all and vanished with a splash into the river.

Morgan was down, Wolf and Ben injured, yet three Black Dogs remained. Mutzlepaw looked even frailer without her stick and Mya guessed the hedge-witch had used a lot of power already for her spells. If only she had the power to create a Ward to protect them all!

The third Dog had withdrawn from Caelin, its belly glowing red from the inside out where the Spellward's 'star' had lodged as though it were indeed a creature of blood and flesh. The remaining two circled around, hungry eyes on the scarred knight.

'Get Jack away,' he hissed as he called up silver light into each gloved hand.

'No!' Jack whimpered as Caelin took two steps closer toward the circling Dogs.

'Help Ferris get Morgan to safety!' Mya ordered the boy. He stumbled to obey and Mutzlepaw hopped down from her rock to join him.

'Mya!' Feather's small voice called her appealingly, but she and Wolf moved to stand behind Caelin with Lissa and Ben.

The Dogs leapt for Caelin, all three. Lissa called all of her power into a Banishing spell and throwing herself forward, touched two of the Dogs; with a howling whimper both dogs disintegrated.

The remaining Dog had borne Caelin to the ground, and he was struggling to keep its jaws from his throat.

'Ward!' Mya shouted and then filling her lungs again screamed with every ounce of her strength; 'Ward, Caelin, Ward! Save yourself.'

Ben hacked futilely at the Dog with his sword, Lissa tried to call more power as she struggled to stay on her feet but could get no more than a dull glow. Feather had called fire up into his own small brown hands and was running forward to where Caelin lay buried in black squirming shadows. Then Caelin summoned up a Ward, but instead of pushing the Dog back away from him as he had expected, it began to distort and twist; then vanished with the suddenness of a snuffed-out candle flame.

'Cae!' Ben breathed out in surprise. 'You shouldn't be able to perform a Banishing?'

'It was a Ward.' Caelin glanced at Mya. 'Get the others to Astol.'

Ben bent to try to help his fellow knight up with his one good hand but Caelin pulled himself up onto one elbow and said more forcefully. 'Ben, get the others to Astol!'

Drawing back as though stung, Ben went to Lissa and putting an arm under her slender shoulders, half carried, half dragged the young fey along the path after the others who hadn't retreated far.

'How badly are you hurt?' Feather demanded firmly.

'Winded.' Caelin tried to sit up and Mya, unable to stand by, stepped forward to help him. 'Ribs!' The man yelped as she touched him. 'Broken ribs.'

'I can fix them a little,' Feather offered, calling his brownie mending magic to his fingertips.

'No time.' Caelin shook his head stubbornly.

'What happened to no noble sacrifices?' Mya put her hands on her hips. 'Let Feather take a moment to heal you then we can catch up with the others.'

'My Lady is right,' Feather said. 'We are not out of danger yet and we need you.'

'Your "Lady" is right about a few things.' Caelin snorted. 'Did you know casting a Ward whilst touching a summoned creature would banish it?' There was accusation in his tone and his eyes fixed on hers.

'How would I know that? It just made sense for you to use it to save your stubborn hide!'

His eyes widened and his mouth opened for a while before his muscles relaxed and he spoke. 'I've used nearly all of my strength though.' Caelin let her help him gingerly into a sitting position.

'You still have your sword and that mind of yours,' Feather pointed out as he ran his hands gently over the man's ribcage.

'That will do–' Caelin started, but the words halted on his tongue. A sense of dread fell over them so powerful and so sudden it took Mya's breath away. The foxfire was fading, and the fireflies were drifting away, but there was still enough unworldly-seeming light by which to see the thing approaching them. It was twice the size of a man and as black as the dogs had been. Like them its eyes glowed as red as the simmering heart of a volcano and it was covered in fur like a great bear.

'Rashmin.' Caelin named the creature.

'Spellward.' Its voice was strangely honey and tar; deep, drawling and compellingly pleasant. Even so, it set Mya's heart to pounding so fiercely with fear her body shook with each pulse. Wolf let out a whimper somewhere behind her. Feather had appeared to shrink down inside himself but slowly, carefully, he drew himself up and continued healing Caelin's ribs. Mya kept her eyes from straying down to where the brownie was hidden so as not to give him away.

'It is good to see you brought to your knees.' The barghest laughed lazily. 'And hiding behind a woman too!'

Caelin didn't respond, refusing to be stirred into wrath by the taunt. Mya's own tongue had cloven to the roof of her mouth. All she had was the small knife from her kitchen clasped in her locked fist. Even with Feather's healing Caelin was not in a good way, leaving them at the barghest's mercy, and she doubted it had any. She prayed the others would have enough time to get away. Feather took a slow step backward, then another.

'Kasira would have you brought before her so she can make you wish you had died indeed the first time!'

'Then she has her desire already,' Caelin replied. 'Already has she made me wish that a thousand times over.'

'Puny human heart!' The barghest scorned. 'She would also see you twisted and in agony!'

'I am as you see me,' Caelin said. 'Broken and in pain. What else would your mistress wish of me?'

Feather continued to move away; all but invisible in the way of brownies. Caelin was clearly buying them time and Mya thought frantically for a way to use it usefully. She could only come up with one answer. She didn't know how to use it, but she did have power. She herself had sensed it when others called up their Gift and she guessed it must be the same for all magic users. Perhaps if the Dark Fey chieftain thought they were not completely helpless, it might gain them something.

'Your death, ultimately.' The barghest's red eyes swirled like whirlpools of lava. 'Even as you are, I think you would be too much trouble to drag back to Ayresport. I think I may have to break your legs into splinters and cut off your hands...'

Mya couldn't help letting out a small gasp at the grisly threats. She felt inside herself, as Jack had inadvertently told her to do, finding the place that tingled in her sternum like pins and needles. She imagined it to be like a tiny flame and she fed it with nothing else but her thought, her determination and even her fear.

'What's this?' Rashmin appeared to swell and grow larger, filling all of Mya's vision and at once she realised she'd done the wrong thing. 'The little mouse is a spellward? I thought Kasira had eaten you all up!'

Wolf side-stepped around to stand beside her, teeth bared. She wanted *so* much to tell the animal to run away, to save itself, but showing fear was the worst thing she could do in front of the Barghest. Following Caelin's example she didn't move, didn't speak; didn't tear her eyes away from the twin fires in the beast's skull. Time seemed to cease, stretching out each second with the thudding of her terrified heart.

Then a black shape launched itself over Caelin straight at the barghest; one of the Black Dogs attacked its erstwhile master.

Caelin leapt to his feet with no sign of fatigue and called up his own power, and Feather came running up behind them with Mutzlepaw's staff held aloft like a clumsy spear; Wolf circled to attack.

Rashmin grabbed the Black Dog in a bone-cracking embrace; it squirmed and raked at him with its phosphorescent claws and teeth. Feather thrust Mutzlepaw's stick at Mya but she shied back from grasping it.

'Take it!' The small brownie demanded. 'Put your power in it!'

'I can't! I promised—'

'Damn both your prides! If you want to live do as I say! Move the power; open a channel through your arm and hand and force it into the rowan staff!'

Rashmin had flung the Black Dog down and turned on Caelin who hadn't yet attacked. Mya realised the spellward probably had little power left and was holding back. She switched her small knife into her left hand and grasped the smooth walking stick. 'Staff', Feather had called it. A witch's staff she realised, not a walking stick at all. Her power was large and alive inside her as though she'd swallowed some creature whole that strained to burst free. The barghest swiped at Caelin with outstretched claws but he dodged aside and followed through to barely miss the giant man-bear with his sword. Wolf and the Black Dog now came in from two different sides as though they worked as a pack to harry their foe.

Mya opened a channel for her power into her arm and hand and it flowed through her like a tickling numbness. Not knowing truly what to do she had done no more than to 'allow' it in her mind. The staff vibrated and glowed subtly.

'Good! Good!' Feather urged excitedly. 'When you're done, give it to Caelin; you've not his strength to throw it!'

The power emptied out of her as though all her blood had been sucked away. Her vision turned momentarily white, and she swayed, reaching out her hands, although there was nothing to hold on to.

'No, no!' Feather grabbed at her trousers. 'You called up everything you have! Oh, it's my fault!'

But Mya gritted her teeth and forced herself upright. She could barely see and her skull felt as though it were being crushed. Against the nausea she called out to Caelin.

He spun on his feet reacting at once to her cry. Rashmin came at him, both Wolf and the Black Dog snapping at Rashmin's shaggy-furred heels to drag him back. Caelin grabbed the staff as the world rocked violently beneath Mya and she fell clumsily, her shoulder hitting the ground hard. Coldness, a chill beyond the touch of winter, came flying out from the barghest as it cast its spell. The ground at once turned white with frost in a large circle and spread outward. Burning pain seared Mya's skin and her clothing froze, she cried out, agony making her muscles rigid.

Caelin hurled the staff like a spear an instant after Rashmin cast his spell. It hissed like a hot poker in water as it passed through the unfolding cold. Distracted by casting its spell, the barghest reacted just a little too slowly and the staff caught him below the ribs, sinking into his barely solid form. He grabbed at the rowan staff and had barely begun a howl of rage before Caelin thrust his hand at him and cast a Ward as he had for the Black Dog. With an expression of shock Rashmin crumpled inward, then vanished.

The night stood silent and empty, the unnatural frost glistening in the light of the few remaining fireflies. Caelin gagged and then quickly controlled his nausea to survey the path and river. The Black Dog had moved toward Feather and Mya but Wolf barred its way.

'I'll deal with it.' Feather looked Caelin up and down. 'Can you help Mya?'

The Spellward nodded, his skin pale and the scar vivid.

Feather approached the Black Dog that towered over him whilst Caelin got awkwardly to one knee to lift Mya.

'I can stand,' she managed, though her tongue was huge and swollen in her mouth. He lifted her anyway, her clothing breaking free from the clinging frost. He staggered, shifted her into a better hold and then straightened up.

'You saved me from an unbearable and drawn out death,' he said for her alone. 'For that I will always be in your debt. But you also learned to use your gift whilst travelling with me. You betrayed me.' He growled through gritted teeth. 'You broke your word as all women do. Stay away from me when we get to Astol. Stay away from Jack whilst he's with me. I don't want to have to look at you.'

Mya sucked in air, but it caught in her lungs and she couldn't speak. She tried to shake her head, but her muscles were rigid. Her heart thundered in her ears and her cheeks burned. She closed her eyes tightly, unable to bear the expression on Caelin's face. Nausea churned in her stomach and she gratefully gave way to unconsciousness.

***

Feather looked up at the Black Dog that was drooling strings of saliva from its glowing fangs despite the fact it was little more than a ghost.

It growled in a gravelly voice. 'Is our deal done?'

Feather thought over his words carefully. He'd struck a quick bargain with it, if he removed the rowan staff and released it, the Dog would serve him. It had seemed the safest exchange of favours at the time. He knew he had to be wary of what he said as the Black Dog would take any opportunity for revenge.

'Go back to your natural place and serve no more Kasira and the Dark Fey court; harm me not, nor my friends, and I release you.'

'Done.' The Black Dog growled and was away at once into the night.

Hoof beats sounded, swift, echoing between the mountains so it sounded like many and from all directions. Caelin waited just a little ahead of him on the path with Mya in his arms and Wolf at his heels anxiously looking up. The horse came into view and Feather was relieved to see it was Magpie with Jack clinging onto its back.

'Aunt Mya!' He called out, clumsily bringing Magpie to a halt and swinging down off the horse.

'She lives,' Caelin said. 'You should not have come back for us.'

Jack ignored the remark to peer anxiously at his aunt.

'The others?' Feather asked.

'They've reached the Gateway but didn't want to go in without you. I was growing worried and hated that we'd left you, so I just rode back before they could stop me. Morgan... Morgan is dead.'

Feather heard a sharp intake of breath from Caelin but the spellward said nothing. He was visibly sagging under Mya's weight.

'Jack, take your aunt a moment if you can.' Feather took charge. 'Sir Caelin, you'd best hop up onto Magpie and make sure Mya doesn't fall off. Jack, we will need to move fast. Set me up on your shoulder if you don't mind and we'll make faster progress.'

Surprisingly Caelin didn't protest, and he and Jack got Mya up into Magpie's saddle and he climbed on behind. Jack picked up Feather, and he perched a little awkwardly on the boy's shoulder and had to hold to his collar for balance. Jack set out at a jog and the others followed behind, Wolf at the rear. As at the stair, the distant sound of a waterfall grew steadily louder and Feather's spirits lifted as he knew they were coming close. He couldn't bring himself to feel relieved and dared not hope they would make it; but then the whiteness of the fast falling water was before them and the rest of their rag-tag group waiting anxiously.

'Mya! Sir Cae!' Lissa wiped at her tear-streaked face with her fingers. Morgan was laid limply across Asher's back and her other hand rested on his shoulder as though she comforted the dead man.

'Foolish boy!' Mutzlepaw scolded Jack.

'Rashmin?' Ben asked.

'Gone,' Caelin told him. 'Banished, maybe dead. I'm not sure what casting a Ward within a fey does, to be honest.'

Feather shuddered.

'Is Mya hurt?' Lissa's eyes were wide and bright.

'She used all her power.'

Lissa's mouth fell open in astonishment. 'How?'

'Let's get into Astol,' Ben said. 'We can talk later.'

'Good idea!' Feather raised a mossy eyebrow.

Caelin urged Magpie into the river and with a bit of prompting got the horse to walk through the white foam of the fall. They disappeared behind it.

The others followed, Jack holding up his hand and Feather held onto his index finger both to reassure Jack and to help keep his balance. He held his breath as they stepped into the fall; the water was freezing and the pressure of it momentarily immense. Feather closed his eyes and when he opened them, he found himself in a brightly lit meadow. The trees were bronze, red and yellow and bearing the lingering fruit of late Autumn. Bees buzzed around late blooming flowers and two crows noisily announced their presence.

'Welcome to Astol,' Lissa said.

Chapter Ten

Mya became aware of voices and a cold wind brushed lightly against her face. Her heart ached and her face still burned. She didn't want to open her eyes, didn't want to wake up and face the world. She'd broken her word and now she would be excluded from a large part of Jack's life. She faced months of scornful, angry looks, of constant reminders of her supposed betrayal. And she wouldn't be able to tell Jack why, she gasped in air, in case... in case Jack believed it too.

Feather must have noticed her stir, as the brownie softly called her name.

Reluctantly she opened her eyes and looked up at a large beech tree whose spreading branches sheltered her. With a shock she realised the leaves were turning brown, and some fell, twirling and drifting. She sat up to look around at Feather.

'How long have I been asleep?'

'Don't worry, my girl.' Feather reassured her. 'Time is different in Astol. We have missed the summer unfortunately and have walked into autumn.'

Mya gazed around her; they were on the edge of a forest and in the distant south mountains filled the horizon. Wolf was sitting nearby on his haunches and watching her with his intelligent eyes. The horses and two goats grazed nearby and the rest of the company appeared to be resting. All but one.

'Morgan died,' Feather said softly on seeing her looking. 'His wounds were too great, and we didn't get him here in time. We've taken a break to bury him and rest. How is your head, my girl?'

'Fine,' she replied absently, too tired to even cry, although her chest constricted painfully. Morgan had been a nice young man who'd forgiven her shyness and always talked to her anyway. She drew in a breath, searching for Lissa. She finally spotted her perched in one of the trees away from the others.

'Thanks, Feather.' She pushed herself up off the ground, getting unsteadily to her feet.

'You're sure you're okay?' Feather peered up at her, his face lined with puzzlement.

Mya nodded and made her way over to the half-fey. She was a little weak and muzzy as though she'd fought off a bad sickness, but she gritted her teeth and endured it.

'Mya!' Lissa perked up at once, though her eyes were red and puffy. She sniffed and wiped her face. 'You're up already.'

'I feel like I've been asleep for months,' she replied. 'How are you doing?'

Lissa gave a shrug. 'My head's still pounding from using too much power, but I'll live.'

'Time to move on!' Caelin called out.

Lissa sighed and scowled. 'I don't know why he's in such a hurry; we're safe here in Astol, and we have lots of time here.'

'I always thought it was Faerie in which time moved faster, not the other way around,' Mya puzzled.

Lissa's eyes grew huge as she stared at her, then she burst into a tumble of bright laughter. 'Oh, I'm sorry, I don't mean to laugh at you. I forget how you humans are with deceiving yourselves. *This* is the Mortal Realm, Mya, *you* come Faerie; the Valley is in Faerie.'

'No, but...' Mya held her breath. It was ridiculous, yet made an awful kind of sense.

'But?' Lissa raised a perfect eyebrow.

Mya felt as though the ground tilted beneath her. 'If it's true, then why don't we know that?'

'Because the people who do know, don't want you to,' Lissa replied. 'The Lord Vallier and his ancestors enjoy control and power too much.'

'But what of the Horse Lords north of the valley?'

'Centaurs.' Lissa smiled. 'They have human traders who bring goods to Trade Pass but they would not go there themselves.'

Mya reached out to brace herself against the tree. Everything was completely upside down. When she considered it, it made perfect sense. She tried to recall if anyone had ever told her differently, but couldn't remember a single occasion. Had her parents known? Had her sister? Like everyone else in the Valley she'd assumed the Valley belonged to them and the fey were the intruders, enemies.

She gasped as a terrible idea struck her. 'Is that why Kasira wants to destroy the humans in the Valley? To claim it back for the fey?'

'She wants to claim it back for *her*.' A scowl settled on Lissa's lovely face. She hopped down from the tree and Mya recalled Caelin had prompted them to move on with their journey. 'She is a member of the fey Royal Unseelie Court, one of the Gentry, and is looking for a kingdom of her own. The fact humans are not native here and took the land won her a lot of support from those fey who became the Dark Fey.'

'And then Renvart created the Ward.'

'Indeed.' Lissa picked up her bow from where it rested against the tree. 'And they drove out those of us native to the Valley.'

'Do you think Renvart knew? Does Caelin?'

'Yes, and yes.' Lissa glanced over at the knight. 'Though the truth came but lately to our spellward.'

They joined the others and Mya was relived to find Jack was unharmed though low in spirits.

'My Lady.' Ben scrutinised her, looking surprised. 'Would you like to ride Asher a while?'

'Oh, no thank you!' She replied. 'A walk and stretching my muscles will do me the world of good.'

'Extraordinary,' Ben muttered.

Mya wondered what he meant but was soon lost in the landscape of the mortal world. The valley created by the mountains opened out below them, a series of hills and lesser valleys through which silver streams glistened. Small scattered forests glowed russet, dark green, brown and even yellow. The sun was warm and soothing when the wind dropped, and bird song was loud and joyous in her ears. A gravel road crossed their path, and they turned onto it. They came to some ploughed fields, recently harvested, in which crows and smaller birds hopped searching for left-over grains. Scarecrows stood, ignored and lonely-looking, one tilted at a sharp angle as though in mid-fall. Mya could see no sign of any people, but as they came to a rise, she saw a large grey-stone building nestled in a sculpted park. It stood three stories high with decorative turrets and a battlement with crenulations. A huge portico dominated the front of the building with dark polished granite pillars the tops of which were carved to mimic spreading tree branches.

The Hall of Pillars.

Mya wasn't sure what she'd expected, maybe something like Ashgrove, but certainly nothing so *human*.

'There are fey here,' Feather breathed. 'Lots of them.'

Mya looked around but could see no one as they approached the beautiful but daunting building. She was surprised when Caelin stepped off the gravel road and cut across the shorn grass to go around the faux castle.

'Does Nemeth not live here then?' Jack asked.

'She does,' Ben replied. 'But we are not front door visitors.'

Mya turned to Lissa and the half-fey shrugged.

The house was much larger than it had first appeared, going back a long way across the top of the green hill. On reaching the summit, Mya halted in her tracks as she gazed across a large lake surrounded by colourful trees; amethyst, scarlet, azure, deep plum and sunflower-yellow. Dark green fir and elm showed their heads above the others and glossy rhododendron bushes clustered at their feet where the sun broke through. The lake sparkled, laced with lily and drifting duckweed. Steps led up from the lake to the house and a huge fountain in which stone nymphs played. An otter frolicked in the crystal water and paused to watch them curiously, showing no fear of them or Wolf.

At the back of the house there was another portico of stone trees, less deep than at the front. Mya was startled to see the back of the building was wide open like a cave, more pillars standing row upon row within and taking up two stories in height. Each was carved with a unique pattern of ivy, mistletoe, honeysuckle or jasmine; the upper parts of each mimicked every tree Mya could think of. Marble mixed with different hues of granite and tall stone pots contained either small fountains or a riot of trailing flowers spreading upon the flagstone floor. The high ceiling was painted to resemble the sky, pale blue at the entrance and darkening gradually into a starry night in the far depths of the hall. Distant music intertwined with the singing of the fountains and birds flew in and out as though it were in truth a forest and not a simulacrum. A doe peeped shyly at them from behind a tumble of sweet peas, still blooming despite the season. The doe's ears swivelled to Wolf and back and she stepped away out of view.

'It's beautiful.' Lissa breathed.

Movement drew them and Mya realised they were being watched by more than the deer. A seat was set amongst the flowers and from it a woman stood, dressed in a simple robe of blue. She was small and slender, like Lissa, with hair as white as the marble falling straight past her shoulders and then curled in ringlets almost to her knees. Her skin was pale and softly wrinkled; Mya guessed her to be in her eighties and yet her movement as she came out to meet them was that of a girl in her prime. Her eyes were the same deep blue as her dress and showed no age at all.

'Your Grace.' Caelin knelt on one knee and Ben awkwardly did the same. Taking their cue, the rest of the group copied and Wolf tentatively stepped forward.

'Stand, be welcome.' Nemeth's voice was soft as feathers, mirthful as a brook. 'You have attained the first part of your quest, Sir Caelin.'

'I have, your Grace.'

Mya was all but stunned by the reverence and even affection in the spellward's face. So, there *was* a woman in the world the man didn't hate.

'Please, let me introduce those you do not know. This is Jack, a Gifted human of the Valley and his aunt, Mya. This is Ferris, scout of Ashgrove and Lissa, daughter of Seska and the Druid. Our fey companions are Feather, and you know Mutzlepaw?'

'I do.' Nemeth dipped her head daintily in acknowledgement. 'I seem to have also half a village of Trow on my estate. You had best come in and let me know all that has occurred.'

Mya looked around to the horses, wondering what they should do with them and she almost jumped when she saw a diminutive man had hold of the reins. On closer inspection she realized it was in fact a fey, only a little above four feet tall, with bandy legs and elongated arms. He wore a brown suit and a plaid cap and his eyes were a dark yellow colour.

'My spriggan, Dusty Tom, will take care of your animals.'

Mya turned back to find Nemeth's smiling eyes on her.

'And my brownie, Billy Stub-toe, is organising your guest quarters as we speak. Come and take refreshments; tell me your tale.'

They followed her in, Mya dawdling behind the others as she tried to take in everything of the wondrous hall. Wolf moved to her side and absently she placed a hand on his shoulders, massaging the fur with her fingers. The music became louder the deeper they moved into the room but she saw no sign of any musicians. Nemeth took them to where several softly cushioned seats were arranged almost in a circle. Some seats were long enough to allow three or four to sit, or perhaps to allow one person to lie in comfort. Mya sat beside Feather and Jack on one such seat and Wolf sat at her feet.

Caelin recounted what had occurred since his leaving Astol and Mya found herself hardly able to take her eyes from Nemeth. There was something enthralling about her, something compelling about the softly lined face and the deep ageless eyes. The grace of her movement reminded her of Lissa, but whilst the half-fey came across as playful and seductive Nemeth was all dance-like poise.

When Caelin had finished, Nemeth gave a barely perceptible sigh. 'There can be no hiding where you have come, and Kasira will fear your intent. Sooner or later she will test my borders and the way through which you came will in time become impassable.'

'I'm sorry I've brought trouble to your door,' Caelin's said.

Nemeth raised a delicate hand. 'The trouble was already mine, good knight. I will set a stronger watch upon my gateways for the moment; you must go on with your plan. The rooms above the stables are yours, Sir Caelin, for you and your knights; just stay out of Dusty Tom's way. Mutzlepaw do you wish sanctuary, Mother?'

'I do, your Grace.' The old fey bobbed her spiny head.

'Agnes-Two-Straws keeps a cottage down by the lake still,' Nemeth said. 'The two of you are on good terms I believe?'

'We are.' Mutzlepaw pressed her lips together in a tight line. 'But us 'edge-witches do like our own space. I'd camp out in yer woods if you'll permit it?'

'Speak to Agnes.' Nemeth smiled. 'There are caves and follies around the lake, she will show you which are occupied and which might suit.'

'I thank ya' Grace.'

'Lissa and Mya.' She turned her piercing gaze on them both. 'It would not be seemly for the two of you to stay anywhere but under my roof. I am much busy and you will have to look to yourselves, mostly. Feather though.' She turned to the Brownie with a slight frown on her face. 'A brownie without his home and this territory already taken. Billy Stub-toe isn't one to share, I'm afraid.'

Mya's heart sank; she couldn't bear the thought of Feather being sent out into the woods. If it came to that, then she'd insist on going with him.

'Since I have extra work with the horses an' all I could be doing with a hand.' Dusty Tom appeared beside them. 'An' I'm sure a Brunie will be handy in the fields too. There's a cot going spare in the attic of me cottage now the ganconagh is healed and gone.'

From the scowl on the spriggan's face Mya guessed he was glad to be rid of his previous guest. Mya tried to recall what a ganconagh was and thought from some half-remembered tale he was a powerful fey who preyed on women.

'I would be delighted to be of help,' Feather replied.

'Then it is settled.' Nemeth stood and Caelin and Ben quickly got to their feet as well. 'We lay food out for all at sunrise, sunset and noon. If you do not wish to eat at those times, then by all means take supplies back to your rooms. There are rules in Astol, for the benefit of those who are new here I will relate them. Fey or Human, we do no harm here to each other; this is a place of truce, peace and healing. Do not interfere in the work or territory of the native fey, their permission must be sought should you need to for any reason. I will spend time with you when I can but my healing and other works keep me busy and, as full as Astol is, I still enjoy a little privacy. Human visitation is rare but every new moon I have a delivery of goods and news from a human

man who drives from the nearest town some twenty miles away. When he crosses the borders into Astol, you will hear the bell in the east tower toll; all fey must keep out of sight. If you hear the bell toll at any time other than the day after the new moon, then we have an intruding human or there is some other danger. Gather here to seek news if you must, or wish to help, or stay hidden and out of view. Is that clear to all?'

Mya was about to nod when something occurred to her. 'What of Wolf? Where can he stay and what will he eat? If he runs loose in the woods, he will break your rules and hunt!'

'Child,' Nemeth said kindly. 'He knew the rules of this vale the moment he stepped in, as all animals and fey do. The animals native to this mountain vale live as they must, and as their nature intended, but Wolf is not native. Even so, if he must hunt then he must. There is meat sent in my supplies from town which I can increase, but in the meantime, he can survive well enough on what we provide. As for where he will stay that will be up to him. This is a large valley, and he is a free creature.'

Mya nodded, unable to hold the fey's deep blue eyes for long.

'Right, let me show y' t' the stables!' Dusty Tom suggested brightly.

Mya watched as the others followed the sprightly spriggan who bounded more than walked. She swallowed, wrapping her arms about herself. The day seemed suddenly darker, and colder. Caelin's command would mean she wouldn't be able to visit the stables to see Jack, Feather or Ben; she could only hope she'd meet them often at mealtimes. Nemeth picked up a strange object, black and slightly longer than her hand with odd raised bumps painted with coloured shapes. It was neither metal nor wood but shiny and smooth. A tiny red light flashed and was gone in an instant and, like magic, the music ceased.

'This way.' The fey woman smiled. She opened a door and Mya and Lisa followed her through into a small room from which a stairway wound upward. Everything was painted a bright and pure white from the wood of the stairs, the smooth high walls and the smooth boards on the floor. A pale green carpet flowed down the stairs like a weed-filled river and was soft beneath Mya's boots. Upward they wound their way until they reached a landing with a tall narrow window and a deep ledge. Small white pots contained miniature roses twining up the window frame; peach and scarlet.

'This wing is yours to use.' Nemeth told them. 'There are two bedrooms, a bathroom and a reading parlour. You are welcome to explore the grounds but please respect my privacy and that of my other guests by remaining in this part of the house only, and the Hall. You may find things here a little... strange. There is much human magic they call "technology". It is harmless and will not hurt or affect you in any way, its sole purpose is to improve ease of living. You may ask me questions, and Dusty Tom will help you when he isn't busy working. Steer clear of Billy Stub-toe however, as he is a traditional brownie, not like your Feather at all. If you spy on him, call him without very good need or leave these rooms in disarray he will consider it his duty to punish you.'

'Thank you for the warning!' Lissa raised a perfect eyebrow.

'You will meet other guests at supper,' Nemeth continued. 'Let them approach you; some will prefer to be left alone.'

Mya nodded her understanding. She turned to Lissa and her heart eased a little; she was so glad the half-fey had joined them on their journey. She was starting to fear her stay here might be very lonely. She looked around and realised Wolf hadn't come with them.

'I will leave you to settle in.'

'Thank you, your grace.' Mya recalled herself and gave a curtsey, odd and inelegant in trousers.

Nemeth's eyes sparkled with what might have been mirth and then she slipped gracefully away down the stairs.

'Everything here is so simple and beautiful!' Lissa gave a dramatic twirl, arms wide, and Mya laughed.

'Let's explore.' Lissa enthused, taking hold of a doorknob and thrusting open the door.

The first room was a small library with walls lined with shelves of pale pine. There were tapestry chairs of beige with a pattern of thistles and copper coloured cushions. Matching curtains framed the window and Lissa crossed the room to peer down over the estate.

'I've never been in so high a building!' She exclaimed. 'Let's see the other rooms!'

The next room was a bedroom decorated in white, brown and cream. A large bed dominated the space and a dark-wood dressing table stood under the window. Dark varnished doors lined one wall and a long mirror was imbedded in one. Lissa stood unashamedly before it looking herself up and down. 'Goodness I look a mess! Anyone would think I'd been traipsing through the wilds!' She gave Mya a wink and then laughed, grasping the small handle on one of the wooden doors and pulling it all open.

'It's a closet for hanging clothes.' Lissa stared into the dark space wide-eyed. 'Who would have so many?'

The next room was similar though the soft furnishings were of varying greens. Lissa begged Mya like an excited child to let her have this one and Mya relinquished it to her at once. Both of their scant belongings had been left neatly by the bed and they wondered if it had been Dusty Tom or Billy Stub-toe who'd brought it up for them.

They came to the last door and swung it open, both women peering timidly in. The floor was grey, polished flagstones, and the walls shiny tiles of white interspersed with what looked like green marble. On a tall stand stood what Mya guessed to be a basin to fill with water and beside it was something like a seat. In the room's centre was the largest bath Mya had ever seen, made of a material smooth and white with strange metal shapes with ears and long noses set in the side. In the corner was a raised platform surrounded by a glass cage guarding some glistening poles of metal.

'What's this?' Lissa glanced at Mya and then stepped into the room on cautious tip-toes. 'It would take an age to fill this bath! I don't think I'd dare ask the House Brownie to fetch us water, but Nemeth said not to stray from these rooms.' The half-fey's shoulders sagged.

Mya joined her in the room to inspect the strange objects. Cautiously she touched one of the metal animals by the side of the bath; almost the "ears" looked like the spokes of a wheel made for turning. She applied pressure and jumped back with a shriek as it gave way and water came pouring out of the "nose". Steam rose and Lisa touched the forceful stream.

'Human magic.' Lissa breathed. 'But all the water is running away down that hole there.'

'What's this?' Mya spotted a silver chain wrapped around one of the metal animals on the end of which was a white stopper. Mindful of the heat of the water, she placed it in the hole and both women watched in delight as the bath began to fill.

'Let's try these others!' Lissa said excitedly.

The bowl on the tall stand they found spouted water in the same way as the bath, but the low seat had them baffled. Mya lifted what they found to be a lid, and they peered down at a small puddle of water.

'Maybe you wash your feet in it?' Lissa mused.

'If everyone had tiny feet like you.' Mya frowned. There seemed to be a lever, so she gave it a push and both girls sprang back as a captive waterfall gushed around the sides of the bowl. 'Oh, you don't think…'

'What?' Lissa prompted.

'You don't think it might be a privy?' Mya blushed.

'Oh!' Lissa stared at it. 'It might be!' She spun around to look at the last remaining object, the pipes protected behind the glass. Daringly she tugged at the handle and part of the glass cage opened out to allow her to step in. Mya moved closer to study the long tube of metal herself. At the bottom of the tube was a round box from which spokes grew; Lissa turned it, and a downpour fell upon her as though a cloud had released right above her head. Lissa squealed and leapt out, water dripping from her hair and clothes. Mya couldn't help it, she laughed, and quickly Lissa was laughing with her.

'Oh, but we better turn all this water off!' Mya pulled herself together. 'We don't want to waste all the magic!'

The two women switched everything off and taking a pristine green towel from a shelf mopped up the mess they'd made in case Billy Stub-Toe caught them and disapproved.

'I'd better change.' Lissa looked down at herself. She glanced up at the frosted glass of the window. 'It isn't long until sunset. Shall we explore the Hall whilst we wait for supper? My head is still pounding but I'm too excited to sleep.'

Talking of food reminded Mya of how hungry she was. 'I'll take my things to my room and meet you by the stairs,' Mya agreed. As she was going out the door, she spotted a raised panel on the wall with a small round knob on it. She turned it and the room brightened.

'Oh!' Lissa breathed. 'A magic candle!'

They both looked up to a bright light hanging from the centre of the ceiling amongst a small chandelier of cut glass. Mya turned the knob back, and the light faded and went out.

'Come on.' Lissa urged. 'Let's get down to the Hall; I want to see more!'

In many ways the wondrous Hall reminded Mya of the dryad Grove back in Ashgrove, and mindful fey probably overheard them, she asked Lissa to tell her more of their host.

'No, she isn't a dryad,' Lissa told her softly. 'She is one of the Gentry, Royalty of the Seelie Court. She fell in love with a mortal man and chose to abide here with him for a time. He was a healer, a magician of...' She searched for the word. '"Surgery." She wouldn't take him into Fairy and deprive the mortals here of his special Gift. He aged of course and died, and she lingers here to be close to his memory. He had the estate of Astol and the Hall of Pillars built for her.'

'That's so sad, and lovely at the same time.' Mya sighed.

'Oh, look!'

A door into the Hall opened and a procession of fey came trouping out laden with dishes and trays. There were hobs and sprites, tiny flying sylphs and a host of Trows. They lay out their wares on the low table, some of them melting away and others remaining to feast from the fare and socialize with the others. Lissa grabbed Mya's hand and hurried her along to where the table had been set just beneath the portico. She grabbed up a plate and filled it with fruit and cheese falling into easy conversation with one of the sylphs. Mya shyly picked up some bread and lay a slice of cheese across it, eating self-consciously and catching the crumbs on her plate. Torches lined the stairway and the path down to the lake, their flames dancing in the slight wind. Her heart lifted when she saw the rest of their company making their way up the steps to the Hall; only Mutzlepaw wasn't present. Of Wolf she could also see no sign, but she hoped he was nearby.

'Aunt Mya!' Jack beamed. 'Isn't this great!' He looked with open awe at the assembly of fey and then dived at the table with a boy's hunger. Feather greeted her warmly as did Ben and she got a courteous nod from Ferris; but Caelin wouldn't even acknowledge her. Her stomach clenched in a knot of anxiety and she found she wasn't so hungry after all.

'Mya?' Feather asked in concern.

'Oh, I'm just tired,' she reassured him. 'I'm going to take food out to Wolf if he's about, and then I'll get some sleep.'

'You must be exhausted, my girl,' Feather said kindly. 'I wish I was able to enter the house to take care of you, but brownie law forbids it. We belong to buildings, not to people; all but I!'

Mya smiled down at the small fey and warmth filled her heart, taking away some of the ache. 'If you can't come in, then I must make sure I visit you when I can.'

'You see to your wolf and then get yourself some sleep.' Feather gave a firm nod of his head.

Mya took the excuse willingly, and selecting food she thought might best suit Wolf, walked around to the side of the building closest to the sculpted forest. She called him only once before she saw his pale form appear and ghost across the grass. She put the food down for him and stroked his broad head when he'd finished eating, still licking his muzzle.

'Good night, Wolf, we'll go exploring tomorrow if you like?'

He tilted his head, watching her with his intelligent eyes and without warning was away into the night. Mya took the plate back to the table and picked up a cup of elderflower and some more bread to take up to her room with her. Despite the throng of fey around the table to Mya the night was very empty.

***

She awoke slowly and stretched her limbs blissfully in the soft warm bed. The silken light streaming in through the window told her it was at least two hours past dawn and she was glad of her small supply of food. As she nibbled at the bread, she realised for the first time in her life she had nothing to get up for; no chores, no nephew to take care of, no quest to achieve. What was she going to do with her days? What was she going to do with her life? She stared up at the ceiling, her stomach tightening into a knot. In effect she was now a prisoner here in Astol awaiting the deeds of others to decide her fate. She couldn't go back to her own realm of Faerie whilst Kasira lived and hunted those with the Gift. With no training to protect herself should Caelin and Jack fail, she would *never* be able to go back. She sat up, rubbing at her face with her fingers. Caelin had made it clear she was to have no more part in trying to save the Valley. She cringed away from applying to Billy Stub-Toe to help around the house but she wondered if the more amenable spriggan, Tom, would find her useful work to do. In the meantime, she told herself, there was a new place to explore with Lissa and Wolf. She broke into a smile.

The bathroom showed evidence of having been used, and when Mya had finished exulting in the rapture of the captive warm rain, she made a better job of cleaning it than her friend. Her trousers and work blouse greatly needed washing and mending so she took out her sturdy walking skirt and her best blue blouse. She knocked on Lissa's door and getting no response checked the library; it was empty. With a little fluttering of butterflies in her stomach she made herself go down to the hall rather than hide away in her room. At first the floral hall appeared empty, the sound of the fountains loud and merry; then she noticed what she guessed to be an urisk sitting on the edge of a large stone bowl shaped like one half of a clamshell. The bowl was filled with water and tiny fish darted beneath lily pads. The urisk was man-like in its upper body with brown hair thickening into a curly fleece across his lower body and legs. He had cloven hooves like those of a goat and two long horns. His face was long and narrow and a beard followed closely to the line of his jaw. His eyes were totally unhuman and a little scary; yellow with a narrow oval pupil.

'Hello,' Mya said politely.

'Miss.' The urisk bobbed its head.

'Mya!' Lissa came skipping at her with the enthusiasm and playfulness of a spring zephyr. 'Shall we go?'

Mya barely had time to give the urisk a smile of farewell before she was being whisked away.

They took the path around the lake and Lissa marvelled at the age and variety of the trees, touching bark both rough and smooth, leaning her cheek against some as if listening for a heartbeat or a voice. There were caves and tunnels made of smooth lime or rough flint, some containing statues, pools and little streams in secretive alcoves. Wolf soon joined them and they let him take the lead in their exploration. They found two water mills and were welcomed into one by a killmoulis who showed them around and offered them a plait of nutty bread and a flagon of dark beer. Mya had to mind her manners and try not to stare at the fey's strange appearance. It was similar to a brownie, except it had a huge nose taking up most of its head and no mouth at all. It communicated with gestures and ate and drank by snorting things up its nose.

Mya and Lissa spent the good part of a week exploring the expansive estate, discovering small hidden cottages, and some strange tall white totems on which were thin sails like a windmill's. They could see no doors and no earthly use for such structures. Often, they stopped to spy on the knights and their training from a high vantage point amongst the trees and whilst Mya was glad to see Jack doing so well, she felt more strongly the loss of him from her life. They met some mealtimes but Caelin's stern and unrelenting coldness always left a great shadow over any happiness.

Lissa began to spend more time amongst the other fey, especially when she discovered a small dryad grove and was introduced to the nymphs of the lake, and Mya soon found herself and Wolf alone for their daily explorations. In the mornings she would fill her flask with elderflower and put food into her bag, and they would range further from the house and the lake. It wasn't long before she forgot Wolf was an animal and she began to confide in him.

Two weeks passed by and she returned, as had become her custom, to the Hall in time for sunset and the evening gathering at the table. Jack was telling her enthusiastically about all the non-magical things he had been learning and she felt a pang at how quickly he'd learnt not to mention magic to her. In return Mya told him of the places she had seen and the fey she had met.

'I wish I had time to see all that,' Jack said wistfully.

'I wish I could find useful work to repay her Grace or learn some useful skills!' Mya retorted, letting her frustration get the better of her.

'You know the rules of feys,' Feather said almost apologetically. 'If you pay them, you insult them. But if you wish something to occupy yourself maybe we could practice with your sling or get Ferris or Lisa to teach you the bow?'

'Oh, that would be good!' Mya straightened up, a smile growing on her face.

'Have you thought any more about learning to use your Gift?' Lissa had been lingering near, talking with the urisk, and overheard. 'You're not bound by Caelin's decree anymore. Feather and I can teach you if he'll not, and there are other's like Mutzlepaw and even Nemeth who could teach you much.'

Mya's stomach tightened. Pressure built in her chest and throat as she refused to allow tears to release the tension and emotion. 'I don't want to learn,' she said.

'Mya?' Lissa frowned at her, mouth open. 'What's the matter? You don't have to learn but I thought…'

'We would have much more chance of defeating Kasira if you fought with us too!' Jack continued, full of enthusiasm. 'After the way you fought the barghest with no training at all and saved Caelin–'

'I don't want to learn!' She cried louder than she'd meant and the nearby fey all stopped their chattering. Caelin turned to glare at her.

Heat rose to Mya's cheeks and sweat prickled her palms. 'Oh, just please never ask me again!' Turning she fled off toward the forest with Wolf appearing from nowhere to trot at her heels.

The trees shushed and whispered above her in the soft wind and the night was a comfortable cloak around her. The air smelt clean and sharp with the mellow tang of dying Autumn leaves. She wiped the tears angrily from her face and coming to one of her favourite spots; she sat amongst the wrinkled roots of a willow and looked out across the glass-like water.

'Oh, Wolf.' She sighed. He came to sit beside her and leant his weight against her shoulder; he was warm through her blouse and coat. 'Why am I letting that horrid man rule my life and make me feel useless? What was I supposed to do, let the barghest kill us?'

Wolf gave no answer.

'I kept my promise, I never sought to learn from him or trick him into it, but he's taken Jack from me and made me feel like some evil betrayer! Why should I care what he thinks, anyway?'

Silently she searched for the answers to her questions within her heart and mind. She admired him; and yes, she had to admit there was a certain attraction about him, but she pushed that idea quickly from her mind, thinking of Lissa. Another tear broke free and tickled down her cheek.

'Would that I could catch that tear, make a diamond of it, string it to a golden chain and put it about your slender throat to make you smile.'

Mya started and Wolf growled. Both of them peered about the bole of the tree but Mya could see nothing.

'Do not fear, I am no water-horse.' The male voice was rich and smooth as forest earth. 'And here in Astol all hold to the law of no harm.'

He stepped out of the shadows and Mya caught her breath.

The man didn't have the preternatural appearance of the kelpie, but he was undoubtedly fey, and had the heartbreaking beauty of a seducer of their kind. His hair was the colour and sheen of a ripened horse chestnut seed and his eyes amber wells. He had the build of a warrior but the face and manners of a bard.

'Why does my lady weep?' He was all gentle concern and respectful reverence. 'Sorrow should not mar such radiance.'

Wolf gave a low rumble of a growl deep in his chest.

'You try to flatter me, sir,' Mya replied politely. She froze, swallowing and trying not to show her fear on her face, this must be the ganconagh that Dusty Tom mentioned. Even within the bounds of Astol she didn't dare raise the ire of such a powerful fey. Although she was sensible enough to know what he was, her heart still pounded and her muscles turned to water. 'I'm no foolish girl to be tempted by honey.'

'No, you are a woman indeed and might be tempted by warmth and passion?' He raised an eyebrow daring her.

'I am a woman of honour, Sir, and wait for one worthy.' The blood pulsed fast through her veins and she felt dizzy as he sauntered closer. She wondered how much was a spell and how much herself.

The ganconagh smiled genuinely, and seemingly, guilelessly. 'Let me at least sit with you and keep you company.' He indicated the ground by the river with a masculine hand.

Mya knew she should decline such dangerous company but something in her rebelled and thought *why not? After all what would it matter? I am already worthless in Caelin's eyes and I cannot go home. Why not have something for myself? The* ganconagh *is sworn to do no harm by the rules of Astol, so he cannot make me pine away for love of him as fey of his kind are wont to do for amusement.*

Wolf whined beside her.

'Pray be welcome,' she said. 'But you must behave!'

The ganconagh grinned broadly. 'Me, my lady? I never trespass where I am not wanted.' He sat himself a few inches from her as though to keep a proper distance, but his proximity sent electricity through Mya's nerves and he knew it.

'You wander often in the woods alone with your wolf,' he said, his eyes intent on hers. She blushed and dared not look up at him.

'Yes, we enjoy exploring... have you been watching me?' She sat upright feeling a touch of anger and a thrill of fear.

'I often wander in the woods myself but did not wish to intrude,' he replied smoothly. 'But tonight, you seemed in distress and it touched my heart. I could not leave a lady in sorrow.'

'It's nothing.' She shook her head, wishing words could make it so. She knew she didn't wish to confide in this fey man; she wasn't foolish enough to believe he'd really care for her troubles. Long ago she had given up on finding any such true male companion. She'd been courted once, as a girl, by a youth who was clumsy and persistent. She'd been flattered, but hadn't been able to find love for him, and had been honest with him from the start, not wishing to hurt him. Her parent's death and her subsequent work load looking after the shop had put an end to any thoughts of marrying, and when Hal and her sister had both died and left her to raise Jack, he'd become her entire world and focus. She'd thrown up a wall and blocked all advances, blind to any interest and not allowing herself the luxury of romantic fancy. Her best childbearing years she'd given up for her family, and she was long past being a good catch as a wife for any young man. Yet did that mean she had to continue to miss out on romance and passion?

'You are deep in thought for "nothing".' The ganconagh traced a fingertip along the back of her hand and it made her skin sing.

All her life she had been sensible and good; always devoting herself to the needs of her family and Jack. Lately she'd put herself at the mercy of a man who hated women, obeying his whims and accepting his derision as though he'd some right to treat her that way. Just as she had done with Hal and her sister; and latterly, she realised, she had treated herself.

The ganconagh had picked up her hand and played gently with her fingers; she turned to gaze into his dark honey eyes and a thrill ran through her body from head to toe. She didn't notice Wolf had run off into the forest.

'I...' She blushed and found she couldn't find the words. She scolded herself for her shyness. 'I have never had a kiss.' A blush tightened across her throat and chest and she was sure she must appear the colour of a radish.

'What a tragedy! All ladies should be kissed!' The ganconagh leant forward but paused teasingly with his mouth but an inch from hers. 'Does my lady invite me?'

His breath was warm and her muscles seemed to melt. She was afraid but at the same time knew she wanted this.

'Yes.'

The word had barely escaped before his lips were upon hers, soft but firm. All else in the world vanished but for that sweet pressure and the pins and needles feeling buzzing through her muscles.

He pulled back; the air was suddenly cold against her skin and she drew in a sharp breath. For a moment she feared he'd cast a spell after all. He studied her face intently and amazed at her boldness she let him and didn't look away.

'Lonely girl I could worship you with a wholehearted and intense love only the faerun can give. No other could make you feel the way I could make you feel; will you let me?'

He stroked her arm with the back of his fingers.

There was a hidden warning in his words; outside of Astol he could use his magic to seduce a woman against her will and leave her pining often to death for love of him. This was no good and gentle knight, no man of honour but one who could be cruel and heartless. In some ways he was the very opposite of Caelin; but in others just the same. A part of her knew she deserved so much better than this, but the doubtful voice in her head told her this was all there would ever be for the likes of her.

'My lady I am your servant this night,' the ganconagh said sweetly, playing with the curls of her hair which made her scalp tingle. 'Let me show you how beautiful you are.'

'Sir, do not mock, I am no fool and I am no beauty.'

He blinked once and for a moment she thought he might laugh or try to bedazzle her with words. Instead, he took her hand and pulled her up onto her feet.

'Come,' he said, stepping down closer to the still water. They stood side by side looking into the dark mirror-like lake. The night crowned their heads with stars that went on forever and she caught his eyes in his reflection as it looked up at her. He whispered into her hair as he bent to be closer to her. 'No, my dove, look to yourself.'

She saw there in the water a woman with a rounded face but sharp cheekbones, skin the colour of cream and eyes as blue as a forget-me-not. Pale rose flushed her cheeks and her lips were tinged with red. Brown hair, just a shade lighter than the ganconagh's, tumbled about her shoulders in loose curls. She was a head shorter than the fey and just as slender though her hips and chest were noticeably more rounded. With the enhanced light the ganconagh had invoked for them to see by she did appear far from plain.

'You see,' he said, turning her toward him. 'No trickery, I have just allowed you to see with your eyes and not with the scars and hurts of your heart and mind. You have a soul and nature that would fill any ganconagh with longing.' He smiled self depreciatingly. 'As is the nature of my kind I prey on the vain and the unworthy; but sometimes I am tempted by a gentleness I do not myself possess or understand.'

Mya wondered if any of what he spoke was truth or if he had just found the key to open her to him; she guessed she would probably never know. But right then she did want the ganconagh to make her feel she was special and as lovely as the woman she had glimpsed in the lake. Cautious still she told him, 'You may kiss me again, sir.'

He wove his fingers through her hair to cup the back of her head and she lifted her mouth to meet his ...

'Get away from her!'

Steel slithered from a sheath and they whirled about to see Caelin looking down on them from the path with Wolf behind him.

'Step back, ganconagh.' He growled, looking Mya up and down, and she thought she saw relief in his eyes.

The ganconagh dropped his hand from Mya's hair but his other arm still encircled her waist with his palm low against her back.

'You are mistaken, your aid is not needed here, Sir Knight!' The ganconagh's manner was friendly despite Caelin's threat.

Mya's skin was burning; of all the people to come looking for her, Caelin was the very last she would wish to find her! She clenched her fists, breathing hard and unable to look up at his face.

Caelin stepped down the bank and the ganconagh hissed at the steel in his hand. The spellward grabbed Mya's arm, his fingers digging so hard into her arm she cried out as he wrenched her away from the fey.

All friendliness left the ganconagh's face, and a shadow fell over its eyes and over the lake. 'If you treated the lady better, she would not need the company of a ganconagh.'

'Don't lecture *me*!' Caelin spat. 'I do not seduce vulnerable women!'

'Neither do I.' The ganconagh grinned nastily, 'What would be the fun in that?'

'Just stay away from her!' Caelin's face was flushed and Mya assumed it was with anger. He pulled her up the bank and all but dragged her along the path, his bruising grip unrelenting. Wolf followed anxiously at her heels.

'I can't believe you'd be so foolish!' Caelin broke the silence. 'You wouldn't go wandering off in the Valley on your own at night and it is no different here! If your wolf hadn't come to find me…' He didn't finish, he didn't need to; in his eyes and those of anyone with his old-fashioned sense of morality she would have been 'ruined' forever. She tried to look around at Wolf, but Caelin tugged her forward. Part of her felt betrayed by the animal, but at the same time she was amazed at the length he had gone to, to keep her safe.

She refused to speak to Caelin as he marched her all the way to the Hall where Mya saw Feather and Nemeth waiting anxiously. Her cheeks burned, and she was relieved Jack wasn't there. Caelin flung her toward Nemeth and she stumbled but kept her feet.

'What has become of your laws of no harm?' Caelin demanded of Nemeth. 'There is a ganconagh roaming free in your woods be-spelling women!'

'I was not "be-spelled!" Mya rounded on him, her fingernails dug into her palms and blood roared in her ears. 'I *wanted* to be seduced!'

Caelin stared at her aghast and then stubbornly shook his head. 'He has used his arts on you, you–'

'I knew exactly what he was, and I knew exactly what I was doing!' She shouted back, breathing hard. 'Whether you like it or not I am a woman and I have feelings and I have… well I am as human as any man! You make me feel like being a woman is some terrible crime! You make me feel like I have to be some stone doll that cannot think or feel or set a foot out of line lest it damage your sensitive morals or your shattered heart. It isn't my fault Kasira betrayed and hurt you; it isn't Lissa's. I won't let you make me afraid to be a woman anymore. You know, I do wish I hadn't broken my promise and *accidently* learned to call my Gift; I wish I'd just let the barghest kill us all as you would have preferred!'

Without knowing how she had got there she found herself sobbing in Nemeth's slender arms.

Caelin stood frozen and bewildered whilst Feather had his hands on his wide hips and was glaring up at the knight.

'I think we need to talk later,' Nemeth said to Caelin, then she ushered Mya into the Hall and toward the door to her wing. 'Come, little bird, let's get you to bed.' She called out seemingly to thin air, 'Billy, bring me up some hot milk and honey with a large measure of whisky!'

***

Feather and Caelin watched them go and when Caelin looked down, he saw the brownie glaring up at him, arms folded and foot tapping angrily.

'You have some explaining to do,' Feather told the knight. He rarely got mad, but he wished he were big enough to give the man a stout clap about the head.

'What have I done?' Caelin looked perplexed and annoyed. 'All I did was save her honour! Should I have left her then?'

'No.' Feather pursed his lips and shook his head. 'But 'twas you who drove her to run to his false comfort! What have you said to her? She's been quiet and frightened ever since the Barghest.'

Caelin shifted his feet and looked away. 'I may have… look, brownie! She broke her promise to me about not learning to use magic whilst we travelled here. I cannot have someone around me who I can't trust!'

'Can't trust?' Feather looked up at the tall man disbelievingly. 'You need to hear a few things, Spellward! Thrice on our journey here was she offered a chance to learn to use her Gift and thrice she refused. In his excitement and innocence Jack recounted to her what had occurred in his first lesson but she halted him and bade him tell no more! Both I and Lissa offered to teach her how to defend herself but she would not betray her promise to you! When the barghest would have slain us all I had to *make* her use her power to save your hide. If you want someone to blame for that then blame me. Even since then she will not learn for fear of angering you; though she has every right to. Foolish human, you risk us all with your hate and fear!' Feather realised he was breathing hard. He ran two fingers under the collar of his tunic and tried to relax his chest muscles.

Caelin gazed out over the lake, his face momentarily emotionless; then it crumpled. 'Oh, brownie I've done her wrong. I saw my words to her after we fought the barghest were cruel, but I was too stubborn to take them back, afraid as well. Did you see her power? And that untrained. She recovered so quickly, like none I've ever seen. She would indeed make a powerful ally on our quest; or a deadly enemy.'

'She isn't Kasira,' Feather said softly.

'I know it.' Caelin sighed. He turned and walked into the Hall to the soft seats near the back and Feather followed. 'But when all is said and done, I am a coward, brownie.'

'I have watched you these last days.' Feather chose his words carefully. 'I've seen you have no fear of death or pain. You throw yourself into situations as though you were an immortal faerun. You've built a wall about yourself to protect your heart, but it doesn't take away what you feel, does it?'

Caelin sat on one of the seats, putting his head in his hands and sliding his fingers into his long hair to grip it.

'It shields me not in truth,' he said into his hands. 'I hurt every day for Kasira and hate her with an intensity that scares me. I'm not blind, I see the hope in poor Lissa's eyes and the wariness in Mya's.' He looked down at Feather. 'I've been unchivalrous to both; the one to deflect her unwanted affections and the other… the other to stop thoughts of her gentle patience seeping through the prison of my self. I guard myself well from the perils of a beautiful face these days, but from an inner beauty I had not expected, I did not think to guard myself.'

Feather was taken aback but hid it; the last thing he would have guessed was Caelin might have started to feel something for Mya. He thought for a moment and then said, 'I fear your treatment of Mya has caused her to build a wall about herself as high as yours; had there ever been such a chance for the two of you, you have destroyed it.'

'I have more honour than to involve her in such a way in my life.' He smiled depreciatingly. 'There is that much kindness in me still. I think only of doing my duty where Kasira is concerned and a hope to end my torment. Oh brownie, what mess we mortals make of love.'

A rueful laugh escaped from Feather. 'Indeed, Sir Knight. So, what are you going to do about this?'

'The right thing, for once,' Caelin replied.

***

Mya woke with a pounding head and heavy, puffy eyes. Her arm still hurt and she saw small round bruises where Caelin had gripped her. She felt a weight against her leg and was surprised to find Wolf was sleeping on the bed.

'Don't trust me not to run off, eh?' she said, though she smiled a little as Wolf sat up to regard her. She caught her reflection in the mirror; nothing remained of the beautiful maiden in the lake. The figure looking back at her had sore, red eyes, and hair like a crow's nest. With a sigh, she slipped out of bed, and going to the clothes cupboard, selected from her small store her brown woollen tunic and trousers. It was strange to think how she felt more at home in them now than a skirt. She'd have to see if she could work for some cloth in return to make more clothes; the killmoulis might help her with that. She took her things to the bathroom and changed there after a quick bath, feeling it was somehow improper to change in front of the wolf.

She sat on the end of the bed for several minutes before she got up the courage to go down. It was past sunrise, but she'd learnt early on to keep a store of fruit in her room; this morning, however, she had no appetite. When she opened the door to the hall, Wolf streaked past her out into the open and was away toward the forest. She froze when she saw Caelin was there rather than at the stables; he was pacing but on seeing her halted, then came striding over. She tensed, unable to move and expecting a blow or at least a tirade of abuse but to her amazement he flung himself to one knee.

'My Lady, Mya, please forgive me!'

She took two rapid steps back, staring down at him in shock.

'I spoke ill to you after you saved my life; you did nothing wrong, and I was a fearful fool. The chivalrous thing to do would have been to teach you to use the Gift so you can protect yourself and never to have put you in such a position of danger. In denying you your Gift I have left you unsafe. Please, my Lady, will you forgive me?'

She found her heart was pounding, and she folded, then unfolded, her arms. He looked vulnerable, gazing up at her on his knees. Perversely the defensive and implacable Caelin had seemed safer to be around.

She found her voice.

'I forgive you; but you mustn't make me feel I have done something wrong by just being born female anymore!'

'My Lady I will do my best.' He got to his feet and looked down at her. 'Would you allow me teach you to use your Gift?'

Momentarily the idea terrified her; then she realised her fear was born from days of being made to feel it was something forbidden and bad. She wanted to be able to defend herself, even more she needed to be a part of the quest to save the Valley.

'Yes,' she said. 'Yes, I think you had better teach me.'

Chapter Eleven

Mya breathed in deeply and concentrated hard on the power within her; controlling how much she drew upon and stopping when she knew she had enough. Her eyes were closed as she focused internally, but she was aware of both Jack and Caelin just off to her right. The wind moved through the trees with a soft roar that waned and waxed like the waves of the sea. Birds sang brightly and the wind was warm against her face, although it took away the heavy heat of the summer sun.

'Good.' Caelin's voice broke in. 'You're both great at control. Now release it in a harmless spell; practice something complex.'

Mya thought for a moment. She'd learnt growing spells that spurred the flourishing of plants and to repair the cells of damaged flesh. She'd learnt to summon her inner lightning, what Nemeth called 'electricity;' or begin flames in wood by creating heat. Calling fire into her hand was harder, as the heat had to be coaxed from the air itself, and the only fuel was your own power; your Gift. Being no natural flame, it didn't burn the user, but was difficult to shape and control. Then there was shielding, forming your Gift into a solid wall to hold out a magical attack. It took an enormous amount of concentration and energy and the slightest flaw might let through someone else's magic.

She decided to go for a ball of fire. Whilst practising alone she'd found she didn't have to form it in her hand, but could send her power to a point she chose. It was easier to control if kept close, but she'd found as her willpower grew, she could form it further and further away. As yet she hadn't let Caelin see all she was capable of; despite their time together she was still wary her strong Gift caused discomfort and distrust in the knight. He was always courteous and polite, but he was also guarded with her in a way he never was with Jack.

She opened her eyes and chose a spot nearly five yards away near the edge of the lake. From the corner of her eye she saw her nephew working his own spell but she refused to be distracted. It was with reason Caelin had them working together, they needed to get used to the confusion and disturbance of battle situations. Her fireball grew, but as she fed it, she imbued it with a second command to shape its nature. Behind her she sensed Caelin draw on his power and instinctively she held hard to the fireball and drew up a shield behind her. It strained her willpower to hold two spells of different natures; it was like trying to hold up two heavy objects in each hand of differing shape and balance.

'Good,' Caelin encouraged.

She held her shield firm and pushed her final command into the fireball, it sped toward the lake, split into three and plunged hissing into the water.

'Aunt Mya!' Jack exclaimed in surprise and admiration.

'Concentrate!' Caelin warned the young man. 'Let your shields dissipate.'

Mya did so, sensing the power unravel and dissolve harmlessly.

'Do you both still have power left?'

Mya turned to nod at the Spellward. He'd cut his hair a little shorter during the summer months in Astol and his scar appeared less angry against his sun-blessed skin.

'Shield!' Was the only warning he gave as he aimed blue lightning straight at Mya. Quickly she called up her Gift again and blocked his attack.

Caelin stepped back and lowered his hands. 'I'm glad you were honest with me,' he said.

Jack had turned pale and Mya wondered how much power her nephew had held back.

'Enough for today.' Caelin gave a slight bow and graced them with a rare smile. 'Jack I will see you in an hour.'

In the afternoon's Jack spent his time with Caelin and Ben, training to be a knight. In the ten months they'd been in Astol her young nephew had filled out and looked much more like a young man. His shoulders had broadened, and he now stood a good two inches taller than Mya. He'd gained a lot of strength from sword fighting, riding and from his duties as a page. The softness had gone from his face and hair had begun to grow across his jaw and cheeks.

Mya had a slightly easier time, as after her morning lessons with Caelin her day was her own. She spent time with different fey learning as much as she was able. The two hedge-witches, Mutzlepaw and Agnes Two-Straws, taught her about plants and animals. The nymphs in the lake taught her how to swim and told her wild tales about historical fey heroes and heroines. The strange killmoulis who lived in the watermill was often her lunchtime companion. She'd take him treats from the Hall table and help him with his grinding and weaving. In return he gave her cloth and company, never able to tell her his name having no mouth. Mostly it was Wolf who was always at her side and he stood now in the long grass at the forest's edge, waiting for her to finish. The two of them had become almost inseparable, although Wolf had never again come indoors with her to sleep on her bed the way he had the night of the ganconagh.

'Be wary.'

She turned to look at Caelin, puzzled.

'I don't wish to curb your imagination when it comes to using your magic,' the knight went on. 'Your ability to see a use for each spell beyond the basic and ordinary will make you an exceptional spellward one day; but only if you are always careful of your control and mindful of consequence. Renvart had your vision and power and through it he created the Ward which, as you know, is both a blessing and a curse.' Then to her surprise he gave a small smile. 'And from his Ward you have already created a powerful banishing spell without meaning to. Just be careful when you experiment on your own and take small steps you can control.'

'I hear you.' Mya nodded seriously. 'I would hate to do harm and dread the day I may have to harm intentionally.'

Caelin gave a deep sigh. 'I must teach you and Jack the kill spell soon. It won't be a good experience, but you are both nearly ready and it's a necessary evil to know it.'

'I hope I never have to use one.' Mya shuddered, remembering the ogre, Brinsten.

'Yes, we may hope.' He held her eyes with his green ones. 'I'll see you tomorrow.'

Mya eagerly took the dismissal and she and Wolf headed around the lake back to the Hall. She was on speaking terms with nearly all the fey residents of Astol now, however she didn't linger long after making a sandwich of ham and tomato. She threw two boiled eggs and a thick slice of ham to Wolf and then they were on their way around to the side of the house where Lissa had set up an archery range. Feather was already there and the small brownie was swinging his sling to let fly a shot at a straw dummy. Lissa's laugh was like the warble of a thrush when the bolt shaved off the top of the straw dummy's head.

Feather rolled his eyes and gave a shake of his mossy head.

'Hey, that's four shots in five dead on, not bad going,' the half-dryad told him. 'Mya! How is the magic going?'

'Hello, my girl.' Feather greeted her warmly.

'Caelin seems happy with my control and concentration.' She gave a small shrug. 'He wants me and Jack to learn the kill spell soon though.'

Lissa gave a nod of her head, accepting without hesitation the necessity of such a thing; though Feather peered up at her with thoughtful concern.

Mya picked up her bow and Wolf trotted off into the forest. The bow had been given to her by Nemeth and wasn't made of wood but of some stronger, strange, smooth material. It was a light recurve bow, coloured blue and silver, and they had fixed a small sight to it to help with her aim. The arrows were also made of a material she'd never seen in nature, with stiff flights of blue and black. There were two targets set up, one at a hundred feet that Lissa practised on, and another at just sixty. They'd painted rings on the large squares of compacted straw and Mya could now get every arrow to strike within the circles; perhaps half within the centre two.

She stood side on to the target and nocking the arrow lifted the bow; pulling back at the same time with two fingers on the string. She brought her hand back so the string almost touched her chin, and her thumb rested below her jaw. The muscles in her left arm strained to hold the bow steady as she checked her aim and she made herself relax her arm and loosen her grip on the bow, trying to transfer more of the weight of the pull to her back. Lissa had encouraged her to take her time over her aim, and improve her accuracy, though Mya's instinct had always been to loose as soon as the target was where she wanted it in the small round sight. She found her stance automatically now without having to think about how she placed her feet and where her hand came back to her face.

She loosed and smiled to herself when the arrow hit the centre of the target with a satisfying firm thud.

'Look.' Feather interrupted her concentration and both she and Lissa turned to see where the brownie was pointing. Caelin was hurrying up the steps from the lake to meet Nemeth who stood with an agitated sylph at her shoulder.

'That's Roihen!' Lissa exclaimed. 'Nemeth sent her through the gate to take a look at the pass after those new Trow refugees turned up a fortnight ago.'

'Something is amiss,' Feather said.

Lissa nodded. 'Let's find out.'

Nemeth glanced up as they approached but Caelin was engrossed with what the small winged fairy was telling him. It spoke so swiftly it was hard to make out the words and now and then she darted dramatically from one side of Nemeth to the other, her tiny blue wings a whirr.

Caelin gave a sigh and closed his eyes briefly. 'I should have known she'd not give me even a month of Valley time.'

'Kasira?' Lissa guessed.

'The mountain pass along the river Vine is impassable; she has most of her old court of the Wild Fey gathered there.'

'Will they attack us here?' Mya asked in concern.

'In the end.' Caelin nodded. 'When they run out of patience. At the moment I think they merely wait for us or hope to keep us trapped so Kasira can complete her plan. Roihen says she overheard talk of humans with the Gift being rounded up and forced to Ayresport.'

'Surely people must see now she isn't the benevolent heroine they thought?' Mya exclaimed.

Roihen made another mad dash through the air, changing direction sharply like a bluebottle.

'Roihen says people are being told there are some with the Gift in league with the fey, that all must go to Ayresport to prove their loyalty or...' Nemeth looked at Caelin. 'Or be burnt as witches.'

'And so, in fear, all with the Gift will go to Ayresport,' Caelin murmured. 'And be fed to the Ward or trained as Spellwards to fight for her.'

'You have forced her hand.'

'And now she forces mine.' Caelin held the gaze of the white-haired fey. 'I had hoped to give Jack three years, not one.'

'But you have Mya,' Lissa said.

Mya swallowed and shifted her feet as all attention fell on her.

'Mya is doing well, as is Jack, but…' Caelin didn't need to finish his sentence which hung open in the air.

'How much time do you think we will have here?' Feather asked.

'I can hold them off, I think.' Nemeth said. There was a shiver of doubt in her voice.

'But what of all those people being taken to Ayresport?' Mya appealed to Caelin. 'We can't just leave all of them!'

'If you had another two months here, you might still get to Ayresport before the majority of people make their way there from the larger outer towns,' Nemeth said. 'Even if you left this instant, it will be too late for those in the city itself.'

'And we must fight our way through the pass.' Lissa pointed out. 'That won't be easy.'

'There is another way.'

All of them looked at the tall, slender fey, once of the Royal Court.

'It was my understanding there is only one Gate between here and the Valley,' Lissa said.

'Yes, that is all I allow known.' Nemeth gave an enigmatic smile. 'But there is another way. It has dangers of its own but it will allow you to pass out of here without alerting Kasira's followers. You will come out further west in the Valley and nearer to Ayresport.'

'Then that's the way we must take,' Caelin said; though he studied her face as though searching for a clue to some deception.

'Two months then.' Nemeth gave a firm nod. 'I will make preparations for your journey and there are things in the human realm I can get to help you. Human "magic" if you like.'

Caelin's eyes narrowed, and he folded his arms, but gave a nod. 'Two months. Mya, I'll have to extend your magic training to all day.'

'Of course.' She agreed at once though losing some of the free time she had to go walking with Wolf made her heart sink. Suddenly it hit her, this pleasant time in Astol was all but over. She'd begun to feel relaxed and happy, but Kasira again had loomed unwanted into her life to shatter any sense of peace and safety.

'Come on.' Lissa tugged at her arm and broke her out of her reverie. 'You need to start shooting at eighty feet.'

***

The two months went much too quickly, the summer of Astol marching on into autumn as though it raced for winter.

Caelin taught her and Jack how to create a Kill spell but she was horrified when he brought out a cage containing two chickens. He saw her expression but didn't relent.

'You can't learn a Kill spell without killing,' he said. 'Cast it well and it will be quick and without pain. These two are destined for the table tonight if it gives you any consolation.'

Caelin let them out of the cage. They stepped out warily, looking at the humans with their almost reptilian eyes, jerking their heads in a strange seemingly erratic way as they searched the ground for anything edible.

'Jack.' Caelin turned to the young man. 'Why don't you go first?'

Mya saw her nephew swallow. They'd kept chickens themselves for eggs and occasionally wrung the neck of a bird when they needed meat to supplement their diet. She knew Jack wasn't squeamish, but he didn't like having to kill a bird any more than she did. She wondered how much his hesitation was fear of failing and letting down Caelin.

'Okay.' Jack stepped forward and Mya felt him calling up his Gift.

'No!' Caelin stopped Jack as the young man closed his eyes to concentrate internally. 'Never close your eyes to cast a spell, especially not this one! Imagine if your target moved, or another stepped in front? And always look anyone or anything you kill in the eye when you do so, for the sake of your soul, and of your honour.'

Jack nodded, looking embarrassed and Mya felt guilty she hadn't gone first.

Jack built the spell and cast it; at once the chicken folded in on itself mentally and flopped to the floor. Jack staggered back and then collapsed to the ground with his hand flying to his temple and Mya cringed in sympathy of the pain.

'Lay down,' Caelin said gently. 'Well done. That was quick and direct and very well controlled.'

Mya's stomach twisted into a knot as she realised it was her turn. She reminded herself this was no different than choosing a bird for dinner, and taking a deep breath, she called up her Gift. The spell itself was designed to stop the signal from someone's mind to their body, severing control to the heart and lungs almost like snapping a neck. It was meant to be instant and painless, unlike the nastier spells of some of the unseelie fey that had joined the Dark Court of Kasira. She could understand why Caelin was reluctant about who he'd teach; in the wrong hands an evil or callous person might become a very powerful monster. The only defence against such a spell would be a strong magical shield and few people and not all fey had the Gift.

The moment she built the spell she looked into the chicken's orange eye and focused the power with great precision before releasing it. At once her vision blurred, and the world distorted, the ground swimming rapidly away and back. She staggered and retched, but recovered her feet and shaking her head cleared her vision. Her head pounded, but the pain was dull and deep. She looked up to see Caelin staring at her with something close to horror on his face. She looked down and saw Jack was all but clinging to the grass with his eyes tight shut and his face crumpled in pain.

'How are you still standing?' Caelin breathed. 'There should be a price for such a spell; there *must* be a price!' He took a step backward as though she suddenly terrified him.

'No, Caelin! I promise!' She placed both her hands flat over her heart. 'I promise you, I will *never* use my Gift to harm and would only ever use any hurtful spell in dire need to defend those in peril. I promise you.'

Caelin hesitated, then stepped forward to offer his hand.

'I apologise, my lady. I am training you as a tool to defeat Kasira as suits myself and have no right to be upset when you achieve what I ask. How are you feeling?'

'Like I have been drinking with Lissa for a week!'

Caelin surprised her with a laugh and letting go of her hand reached for a flask at his hip. 'Take some slow sips of this. It's a restorative of Nemeth's. I'll get Jack onto his horse and take him back to the stables, then escort you back to the Hall.'

She nodded and taking out the cork took a small tentative sip; it was sweetened with honey and violets to hide the bitter tang of whatever herbs Nemeth used. Wolf nudged her hand with his nose to let her know he was back and she rubbed his broad head between his ears. Caelin had pulled the semi-conscious Jack onto Magpie and turned the horse about to head for the stables.

'Are you all right to walk?' Caelin asked her.

She nodded, but as she did so each step jarred her bones from her feet into her head to rattle her teeth and deepen the throb of her headache.

'Come on.' Caelin sighed. 'No point suffering for pride. Let me help you up on Magpie.'

She didn't argue, and he helped her up behind her nephew.

They walked in silence, Wolf trotting close to Magpie who had long ago stopped being nervous of him. Jack leant against his horse's neck with his eyes tight shut and his fingers twinned through Magpies mane. Mya could understand what Caelin had meant about a price; taking another life should never be an easy thing and the cost to a magic wielder's body and mind *should* be a deterrent to using such power. All that stopped her would be her own conscience.

'Why is my Gift so strong?' She asked Caelin.

He didn't answer at once, his gaze going far away over the gardens. She saw the muscles of his jaw moving.

'We are each born with a different capacity for it. Amongst fey, their type determines their ability to use magic, and the types of spell they can cast. For example, only pure creatures can banish something of evil alignment, but that same pure nature would make a kill spell impossible.'

Mya swallowed, understanding it was her human nature, not her heart, that determined her magical alignment.

'As for strength, that's entirely different.'

'Is it hereditary? My parents never spoke of having it but both myself, my sister and of course Jack have it.'

'It is hereditary.' Caelin replied without looking around. 'If both your parents had the Gift, it would explain why their children and grandchild are so strong. Your Gift is… exceptional; even Renvart couldn't stand on his feet after a kill spell.'

Mya took this in. It was no wonder she had frightened Caelin so much. It explained why her parents had left Ayresport when the Ward was made; they must have realised something was badly wrong and wanted to protect their children. It still didn't explain why she was so strong. Could it be a coincidence? Fate?

'The humans of this Valley…' Caelin began. Mya waited patiently for him to continue. They were almost at the stable and Ben was there talking with Dusty Tom. 'The first who came here were… brought here by force. A raiding party of the Royal Court passed through what we know of as the Gate of Astol looking for humans to… "play" with. They stole away the comeliest women they could find and, I cannot bring myself to call it seducing, that would be too polite a word.' The muscles moved around his jaw as he clenched his teeth. Feather had been right, this man had such high morals he judged both himself and others uncompromisingly. 'The women bore children to the Fey Lords, but they soon tired of their human slaves and children and abandoned them here in the Valley. We are all of us descended from fey "Gentry," Mya, that is where the Gift comes from.'

Mya's eyes widened but she was too exhausted to respond. She had fey blood? All of the people of the Valley did? She held onto Jack a little tighter.

'How did it go?' Ben spotted them and hurried over. His eyes travelled over Mya's face and his shoulders relaxed though he glanced warily at Caelin.

'It's okay.' Caelin gave a shrug and a shake of his head. 'We should be grateful someone much stronger than me is on our side against Kasira.'

Ben opened his mouth, then grinned broadly.

'Ben can you get Jack to his bed and see he gets some broth down?' Caelin asked.

'Oh, I should take care of him!' Mya protested.

'You should take care of yourself,' Caelin scolded. 'Jack will be fine with Ben.'

The older knight lifted Jack down as carefully as he could and Mya shifted forward into Magpie's saddle. Caelin led them around the lake toward the Hall.

'Nemeth would like to test you.' Caelin was the first again to break their silence. 'She wants you to be prepared to fight. Much as I would wish it otherwise, I have no choice but to admit it's you who is our best hope against Nemeth and not myself or even Jack. A magical fight is not like the practise and learning we have been doing. Even a test such as Nemeth wishes will be dangerous; I'll be there to help shield you.'

'As you have since I met you.'

Caelin glanced at her and quickly away. She immediately regretted her honest attempt at thanks.

'We'll give you two days to rest.' He continued. 'But we only have two weeks left until we must return to the Vale.'

'Will she test Jack?'

Caelin nodded. 'But she will go easy on him.'

And not on me, Mya finished silently.

He stopped Magpie and offered his hand to help her down and she gratefully leant her weight against his shoulder. Her skull felt as though it had come apart and the pieces were rubbing together; she dreaded to think what poor Jack was going through.

'Can you make it to your room?'

She nodded.

'Billy stub-toe is still adamant he won't have Feather in his territory but the urisk said he'd sit with you if you need him. Lissa is running an errand for Nemeth but will be back this afternoon.'

Mya was startled when she found herself disappointed he wasn't going to stay with her himself. 'I have my Wolf,' she replied.

'I can help you up the stairs if you like?'

'No, thank you, I'll be fine.' She forced a smile. She headed in through the Hall with Wolf by her side. The hairs on the back of her neck prickled, and she turned back to see Caelin was still standing there. She gave him a polite dismissive wave to let him know she was okay and self-consciously made her way to the door; she glanced back and saw he'd gone. Wolf followed her up the stairs and she let him into her room. Immediately he jumped up onto the bed and lay down. She took a long drink of the water left out for her, and then curling up next to Wolf, she lay her head on his back and closed her eyes.

***

Mya vaguely remembered Lissa coming in when it was dark and forcing her to drink down some thin beef broth. It was salty and strongly seasoned with herbs. When she woke again light was coming in through the drawn curtains turning them almost opaque. Wolf had gone but Lissa was sat at the end of her bed cross-legged and reading a book.

'Mya!' Lissa threw her book down and leapt to the floor as quick as a cat. 'How are you feeling?'

Mya took a moment to take in the state of her body. She was incredibly thirsty and ached from head to toe, but no worse than if she'd pushed herself too far on a long hike with Wolf.

'I'm good.' She smiled. 'Have you heard how Jack's doing?'

'Still sleeping.' Lissa winced. 'Hey, Nemeth has got her supplies in for our journey! Do you want to look?'

Mya pulled herself up on her elbows and reached for the water. 'If it can wait until I've had a long hot bath and something to eat?'

'Of course!' Lissa headed straight for the door. 'If I can shoo the trow wives out of the way I'll make you something nice in the kitchen.'

The half-fey was out the door before Mya was able to get a word in. Stiffly she got up and going to the bathroom ran herself a steaming bath. The heat of the water was delicious and drew out the ache in her bones. She was just beginning to doze when Lissa came bursting into the room.

'I've got you a huge breakfast!' She beamed.

Startled, Mya drew herself down into the water.

'The new horses have arrived at the stables. Nemeth has been incredibly generous.' Lissa sat down on the edge of the bath, totally unaware of Mya's embarrassment. 'I'll let you pick yours first,' she added magnanimously.

'She's giving us horses?'

'We're going to have to move quickly once back in the Valley,' Lissa said more seriously. 'We need to get you and Jack into Ayresport before Kasira realises Caelin is back in the realm.'

'Do you know what the plan is once we're there?'

Lissa shook her head. 'No, if Caelin and Nemeth have made one then they've kept it to themselves.'

'Why has Nemeth gotten herself involved to help us?' Mya wondered.

'Her life is as tied up with the Valley as it is with Astol,' Lissa explained. 'As you know she was of the Seelie Court. They'd heard of what some of the male Gentry had done, and not all of them were of the Unseelie Court mind you! Many years had passed but Nemeth volunteered to be the one to come here and try to rectify the situation, they elected her as Seelie Queen of the Valley. She found the humans of the Valley were happy and settled, but wanted to give them the choice to return to the mortal realm if they so desired. She passed through the gateway to see what had occurred in the mortal Realm and if it would be safe for anyone to return. Whilst there she met and fell in love with a mortal man who was a great healer, what she calls a 'surgeon'. For an immortal to marry a mortal they must give up something, and the guise put on Nemeth was that should she ever return to the Valley and the faerun realm, she wouldn't be able to pass back into Astol ever again. So here she remained with her husband and after when he died. Years flew by in the Valley and sometimes she would get news from the fey straying into Astol. Then Caelin was injured by Kasira and was slowly dying from the poison on her blade. As the one who should have been Queen of the Valley rather than Kasira, Nemeth feels responsible.'

'But couldn't she claim the Valley from Kasira then?'

'No.' Lissa sighed. 'She cannot bring herself yet to leave the home she made with her husband nor give up Astol as a place of sanctuary to fey and humans. There is also the complication that so many generations of humans have called the Valley home and been ruled by the line of Valliers, they would probably never accept a fey queen.'

'But couldn't she pretend to be human like Kasira?'

'For a few years, perhaps, but when she didn't grow old or die…'

'But she has aged.' Mya frowned.

Lissa shook her head. 'A glamour for the sake of her human husband and those humans she knew. In truth she looks younger than you or I. She could abandon Astol to help us, but then Astol would quickly become lawless with no one to protect the humans of the mortal realm from any unseelie or dark fey passing through. If she came back to the Valley, she'd have to either leave a strong warden or close the gate forever.'

Mya thought about it for a moment. If she had been in Nemeth's position, she was pretty sure she'd go rushing to the rescue of the people in the Valley. But then the people of the Valley were her people and Astol was not her home she'd shared with a husband.

'Come on.' Lissa broke into her reverie. 'Let's choose a horse!'

They skirted the lake and found Ferris busy with Dusty Tom at the stables. There were boxes of arrows they were sorting into bundles and tight rolls of quilted fabric. Ferris nodded at them in greeting.

'There's enough here to arm twice our party.'

'You're coming with us?' Mya asked.

Ferris gave a shrug and the smallest of smiles. 'Came this far and the quickest way home seems to be via Ayresport.'

'How is Jack doing?' She glanced up at the small windows in the thatch of the stable building.

'Still sleeping.' Ferris grimaced. 'He ate a good breakfast though. Ben and Cae are out training together; I said I'd stay near the lad.'

'Thank you.'

'Have you picked a horse yet?' Lissa asked her fellow Ashgrove scout.

'Not yet.' He laughed at the concern and warning in Lissa's voice. 'You choose first. I'll be happy with any of them.'

Lissa beamed at him and Mya wondered at the sometimes-childlike nature of the half-fey woman.

Magpie was there in his stall along with two others Nemeth kept for herself. The three new horses looked like they were bred for both endurance and speed. One was a dark brown with an almost black mane and tail, the second was a paler dun with a chocolate mane. The last was grey with a mottling of darker hair almost like marble. Lissa approached it at once, and tactfully, Mya stroked the noses of the other two. Both of them sniffed at her but the dun snuffled at her sleeve and then her hair, looking at her with its deep dark eyes.

'I'll take this one,' Mya said as she continued to gaze at it, her reflection showing in the large pupils.

'Oh, well then I'll have this grey!'

Mya smiled to herself. 'Do they have names?'

'Humans seem to change their horse's names when they change owners.' Feather came in and dropped a box on the floor. 'Dry travelling rations.' He pulled face.

'I'm calling mine Nemesis.' Lissa said decisively.

Feather raised an eyebrow.

'I'll have to think a bit until I know her better,' Mya stroked the dun's nose.

***

When she awoke the morning of her testing, she found she had a nest of butterflies in her stomach and she regretted at once she'd said she'd be ready. She reminded herself she faced her harshest critic every day in Caelin, but Nemeth had remained enigmatic and untouchably distant during her stay and Mya had to admit the Fey Queen daunted her. She took a shower, trying not to think of the fact she would soon be heading to a place where such magics did not exist. For a moment she questioned what on earth she was doing, but it was only a brief moment. Abandoning the people of the Valley to Kasira was just something she couldn't do.

She stood before her now fuller wardrobe and wondered what someone should wear for a magical battle. She decided on a new pair of sturdy brown trousers she'd made with cloth from the killmoulis, and a practical linen blouse. Her walking boots were now on the worn side and leaked in the slightest rain, but they were all she had and Astol didn't have a cobbler. If Billy Stub-toe was the type of brownie to be making shoes he hadn't had any inclination to look at hers.

She forced herself to eat a little bread and honey to quieten her nervous stomach. Jack and Ferris were absent at breakfast but the others she'd travelled there with were present.

'You look terrified, my girl,' Feather said softly. 'From what I've heard of your lessons you have nothing to fear.'

'I don't want to let anyone down,' she told her tiny friend. 'And I don't want to embarrass myself.'

'Mya, you are the last person who would ever let anyone down. Is Caelin still making you feel like you need to berate yourself?'

'No.' She shook her head and smiled. 'No, he's been as encouraging as his humour will allow him to be. It's me setting myself goals of perfection and chastising myself when I don't reach them!'

'It's no bad thing to aim high, my girl; but when you miss, instead of feeling you've failed, adjust your aim from what you have learned and try again.'

'I can't wait to see this!' Lissa came bounding toward her almost dragging Ben, who she'd linked arms with.

'Oh, but... I didn't think you would all be watching!'

'They won't be.' Caelin stepped in. 'We don't need the distraction or the extra worry of someone being harmed by stray magic.'

Lissa pouted at him but he refused to react.

'If you're ready Mya, we'll go around to the east side of the lake out of the way.'

She nodded, finding her tongue didn't want to work.

'Good luck!' Feather called up to her.

'You're going to do great!' Ben added.

Caelin's silence as they made their way around the lake did nothing to calm her nerves. Wolf ran down from the tree line and tried to follow her.

'No, Wolf!' She held up both her hands. 'Today you can't come with me, you might get hurt.'

Wolf sat back on his haunches and watched her walk away. Moments later he'd vanished.

Nemeth was waiting where a stream flowed down from the forest and into the lake. A stone humpbacked bridge spanned it, only four feet in length. She was dressed in a simple long robe of blue with a belt woven from cloth-of-gold.

'Mya.' The fey woman gave a slight bow which Mya returned. 'I set you the task of crossing this stream. I will try to stop you. Caelin will stay near you, but out of your way with his shield up. If he thinks you have had enough or are in danger of being hurt, he will step in. Are you ready for this challenge?'

Mya nodded before she had time to think about her answer.

At once she sensed Nemeth draw up her power, and she knew she wasn't about to give her the time to make the first move or prepare. She drew her own power into a shield at the same time as calling up her first attack spell. She threw a burst of blue lightning like a wide net, not enough to harm but enough to startle and distract. At the same moment she jumped forward and left, landing on the bank of the stream. Nemeth's fireball missed her right shoulder and behind her Caelin put out the flames.

Not waiting for Nemeth to make her next move Mya called up fire in her hands. As it flew toward Nemeth, something rushed up from the stream; a crystal-clear wall of water sprayed her and automatically she flinched away. She heard a hiss of indrawn breath from Caelin, but despite her distraction, she'd held her shield well and the water didn't touch her. The Spellward had never shown her how to use water and Mya realised the fey woman would have unique tricks of her own too. She kept up her strong attack, pulled out an ivy shoot she'd tucked into the back of her belt, and threw it. Infused with her power it grew rapidly as it flew through the air, but Nemeth caught it with fire. Mya followed at once with a ball of her own that split into three to attack the fey woman from above and both sides at once. Two Nemeth deflected, but the third hit her shield raining sparks before dissipating

The ivy continued to grow and continued to burn, splitting into fast expanding tendrils that tried to grasp at Nemeth's shield but fell away. Mya gasped as the earth beneath her feet moved and she instinctively backed away losing the ground she'd gained. Roots broke up out of the earth and came snaking toward her ankles. She'd never considered a need to shield beneath her feet!

It gave her an idea; she could start fire away from herself so might she be able to send one up from the earth under Nemeth's feet? But then if the fey wasn't shielding beneath her she might really hurt the woman. In her hesitation Nemeth took advantage and battered at her shield with a long and ferocious blast of blue-lightning. Mya drew on more power to strengthen her shield, resisting the temptation to close her eyes and flinch away from the blast. Once confident in her shield, she moved forward into Nemeth's attack. She focused on a point a little behind and above the fey woman and started a ball of flame; making it as powerful as she could whilst still holding tight to her shield. Caelin had moved closer, concerned her shield would fold under Nemeth's relentless onslaught. She fed her command into the swirling ball and then released it with a will. The moment she let it go she increased her shield still more, drawing on her still building reserves. She ducked low and rolled into the stream as Nemeth broke off in startled surprise, Mya's fireball battering her shield from behind in a wave of flame. Mya grabbed at the groping edge of her ivy and taking control of it fed it with more power and a new command.

Recovering quickly, Nemeth stretched out her hand and blasted the stream with an icy force, freezing the water. The spell, and therefore the ice, couldn't breach Mya's shield but the water did and it became painfully cold. Caelin drew close in concern but Mya countered with a blast of fire. When she was sure she held the shield and fire steady, she created another fireball behind Nemeth. It was an incredible risk. Controlling two spells, especially the essential shield, was challenging enough and three spells all but reckless. The fireball she made was small, though it worked. Nemeth halted her attack at once to focus purely on her shield as Mya's fireball hit from behind and she continued the blast from her hands. Then Nemeth let out a cry as the ivy Mya had altered to burrow through the earth came up around her feet and ankles inside her shield. Nemeth stepped hastily back and drew on another, deadly spell. Mya recognised the feel and shape of what she was building at once; a kill spell.

Nemeth released it.

Terrified Mya threw all of her power into her shield.

Caelin leapt, bowling Mya over against the bank of the stream and covering her with his own body.

The spell didn't strike and struggling up Mya saw the huge net of ivy withering rapidly into curling black ash.

'What in Hell's name are you doing?' Caelin demanded, scrambling to his feet. 'A kill spell!'

'For the ivy.' Nemeth replied serenely. She sent out a gentle flow of cold across the grass where fire had taken hold. 'Mya's shield was strong enough to hold out a kill spell, though she used a lot of her remaining strength to do so.' Nemeth turned her blue eyes on Mya. 'You made this bank of the stream, child, you win.'

Caelin still glowered at Nemeth but Mya looked down at her hands and realised she was indeed gripping the mud and grass of the stream bank. Joy seeped into her and at the same time her knees turned weak and boneless. Nemeth allowed her shield to dissipate and held out a hand to help Mya onto her feet and up the small bank. She was dripping water from head to toe but hardly noticed.

'Your attack from multiple directions was exemplary.' Nemeth gave a small elegant bow with her head. 'And controlling three spells with a fourth wild and released was risky but clever. Be sure never to become complacent and always hold your shield tight.'

'I will,' Mya replied solemnly.

'You were also exceptionally steadfast against blasting spells, you barely flinched or turned your eyes away from me. However… your fear of the kill spell let you down.' Her eyes glanced over to Caelin and then back to Mya. 'Your shield would have protected you, but at that point you lost faith in it and panicked. I could have slipped in with a knife or an arrow whilst you huddled away.'

Mya blushed, but when she looked up, she noticed Nemeth sway a little on her feet.

'My Lady, you are ill!'

'Even I am hard pressed to remain upright after a kill spell.' The fey woman did look pale and as fragile as a snowdrop. 'I made a mistake as well. You frightened me into defending myself as strongly and quickly as I could; it has left me with only a small reserve of strength. Had this been a real battle, and I not been fast enough to strike you with a physical weapon, you might have finished me with ease.'

Mya was horrified at the prospect and Nemeth read it on her face.

'And that will be where Kasira will find your weakness. If you hesitate out of mercy, she will kill you, with no qualm or conscience.'

A white horse came trotting rider-less across the bridge and Mya recognised it as one of Nemeth's. The one Mya had chosen followed behind led by Dusty Tom.

'My Lady, let me help you back.' Caelin found his voice as his manners stepped in.

'I can manage.' She pulled herself up into the tall horse's saddle and gave a weak smile. 'Mya will need you and you have things to discuss. I will rest two days and then test Jack.'

Not waiting for a reply, she rode back toward the Hall.

Caelin hopped up out of the stream; he appeared even more thoughtful than usual, eyes cast down with a deep frown on his face. Mya's head was pounding, and she was seeing bright lights in front of her eyes. The Hall looked a long way away.

'How do you feel about your test?' Caelin helped her into the saddle and took her horse's head.

'I... I felt I defended myself well enough and thought of ways to keep ahead on my attack and even learned from Nemeth, but she was right. As soon as I sensed the signature of a kill spell, I panicked.'

'No.' Caelin said quietly. '*You* didn't panic, *I* did.' After a while he continued. 'You learn quickly and adapt. You've seen my weakness and Kasira knows it as well. Don't let her learn yours.'

Mya considered her weaknesses and found she had many, and then there it was plain before her, her biggest weakness was self-doubt.

Caelin helped her down off her horse at the Hall. Ben, Feather and Lissa were all waiting anxiously for her.

'How did it go?' Lissa at once bounded forward to put an arm around her and take her away from Caelin.

'I did okay.'

'She did very well.' Caelin corrected. 'Mya, if you'll excuse me, I'll tell Jack how you did and fetch him some soup from the kitchens.'

'Oh! Tell him I'll come by the stables as soon as I'm well enough!'

Caelin nodded and led the dun horse away.

'Well, tell us all about it then.' Ben prompted. 'I wish we could've watched from closer.'

'You watched?' Mya turned her head too quickly and a wave of dizziness swept over her.

'From the top of the steps here.' Lissa looked at her with concern.

'Go on, my girl,' Feather said. 'There is hot soup and bread waiting for you in your room and some of Nemeth's restorative. You can go over it with us tomorrow.'

'I really would like to lie down,' she replied apologetically.

'Come on, then.' Lissa steered her into the Hall. 'let's get you to your room.'

***

When the day of Jack's test came Mya found herself more anxious than she'd been for her own. Her stomach was in knots and she'd been unable to force down any breakfast. Jack had looked determined although she'd noticed his hands shaking a little. She'd been forbidden from discussing her own test with Jack or sharing any tactics and both of them had respected that rule; however, Mya's stomach was churning in turmoil and she could barely breathe at the thought Nemeth might try a Kill spell against Jack's shields. *Another weakness to hide from Kasira.*

Ben, Feather and Lissa all waited with her at the top of the steps leading from the Hall to the lake. Ben lifted Feather up onto his shoulder so he could better see, and several other fey joined them to watch. Mya realised she was pacing and forced herself to stop. Caelin, Jack and Nemeth were tiny figures in the distance and much too far away for her to sense what spells they might be conjuring. Her heart leapt as a bright light flared up around the three figures. Jack had tried a blinding spell but Nemeth was replying with flame.

'Oh, I can't watch!' Lissa announced, although she continued to do so with her arm linked through Ben's.

Radiance scintillated and danced; flames seared and Mya held her breath. Then everything stilled, and she strained her eyes to see what had become of the three small shapes. She saw Dusty Tom was leading in the horses and it seemed an age before Jack got into his saddle and Caelin led him back. Nemeth rode back ahead of them on her white mare and Mya tried to read her face. The fey woman smiled at them as she got closer and relief flooded through Mya.

'He did well.' Nemeth told them.

'Did he win?' Lissa asked excitedly.

Nemeth's smile faded a little. 'He did not.'

Mya's heart plummeted.

'Do not despair.' Nemeth tried to reassure them. 'He learnt much and showed great control and sense in reserving his power. He is very young yet, remember.'

Dusty Tom had somehow caught up and took the mare's head as Nemeth dismounted and walked sedately into the Hall.

'She barley looks tired!' Lissa said in dismay.

'I'm sure she is more fatigued than she lets on,' Feather said.

Mya found she couldn't wait any longer and hurried down to meet Jack and Caelin.

'Jack!' She called and to her delight the boy looked up and straightened in his saddle. 'Jack would you like me to take you back to the stable and sit with you a while?'

Jack took in a breath and concentrated on his words. 'I would like that very much, Aunt Mya.'

Chapter Twelve

Mya placed a bowl of thick stew and a slab of bread and butter quietly on the bedside table and sat carefully on the bed. It was strange to be in Jack's room in the stables, for so many months a domain of men and all but forbidden to her. Feather passed her the mug of dark beer he'd carried and she placed it beside the bowl. Jack stirred, his nostrils flaring a little at the rich aroma of the food.

'Oh, I'm starving!' Jack announced before his eyes were even open, and sitting up he reached for the bowl. Sopping up juices with the bread he stuffed it into his mouth.

'Feeling better then?' Feather raised an eyebrow.

Jack washed down the bread with the bitter beer before replying. 'I still feel like I've just recovered from a bad fever, but at least my brain isn't trying to burst out of my skull. Being just a knight would have been less physically demanding than being a spellward!'

'Many wish for magic, but few are willing to pay the price,' Feather said. It reminded Mya at once of Caelin's fear that her price seemed to be but small. She wondered about Kasira, would the fey woman be left weak and vulnerable after a kill spell, or be able to fight on like her?

'I'm glad I'm both.' Jack dunked another piece of bread. 'Being a magic user takes a lot of discipline of the mind, but being a knight disciplines the body and heart.'

'You have a lot of admiration for Caelin,' Feather said.

Jack nodded as he chewed at his food. 'Of course! He is a proper noble knight. Don't worry though, I remember what you said back in Ashgrove. I didn't really understand at the time but now I do. Ben is a good man too and he isn't afraid to have fun or get something wrong; I think I would like to be something in between.'

Mya glanced down at Feather and the brownie smiled back. The brownie may have been overlooked by Jack as a role model, but his subtle and wise influence was there to see.

'We're meeting tomorrow to make our plans to face Kasira,' Mya said.

'I'll be there,' Jack replied. 'I'll take a little walk this afternoon to clear my head. I can't believe we only have a week left here. I expected to be at least two years older before I had to face Kasira.'

'It was always a gamble coming here.' Feather sighed. 'Unfortunately, Kasira's spies were too many and the Valley too much in her control. If we wait to improve our chances the cost in lives would be huge.'

'We?' Mya looked round at the brownie. 'You're coming with us then?'

'Of course, I am!' Feather puffed out his chest indignantly. 'I need a home and I won't get one of those until we sort all this business and my humans can settle down!'

'But where would we settle?' Jack turned to Mya.

'I don't know yet, Jack,' she replied honestly.

***

Feather walked cautiously into the hall, his skin prickled and he peered into every shadow and hiding place. He could almost feel Billy Stub-Toe glaring at him from some dark corner. They'd taken a somewhat subdued breakfast and then gathered at the back of the Great Hall beneath the painted stars. Wolf followed them in and sat just outside the circle of cushioned seats. Mya was fidgeting with her hands in her lap, but there was a determined tilt to her chin. Jack had dressed in his light armour of toughened leather with a thin plate buckled to his shoulders, chest and spine. He'd not worn his sword though, and as the other two knights wore only leather over linen Feather guessed they were being considerate of any fey in the Hall. Lissa, Ferris and Mya were all dressed in scouting clothes and Feather nodded to himself; it was good they were all taking this meeting formally and seriously.

Nemeth didn't keep them waiting but was present almost the instant they'd gathered, indicating with a small hand they should all sit. Feather hopped up onto a chair beside Mya. He had to admit his own nerves were a little edgy, this meeting would make the prospect of their facing Kasira all the more real.

'Well, then.' Nemeth looked around at them all and included the brownie in her gaze. 'Your aim is to reveal the truth about Kasira and free the Valley. If you went intending to kill her, then you would make yourselves the enemies of the Valley and her the martyr. However, she will not stand down nor yield the Valley easily and killing her ultimately might be the only way you all survive.'

Caelin clenched his jaw and wouldn't meet the fey woman's eyes. The brownie noticed the wolf was avidly watching Mya, and a shiver ran down his spine as though someone walked over his grave.

'Shall we start with how to get to Ayresport?' Nemeth suggested. 'As I said, there is another gateway, but it exists under the ground. There are tunnels beneath the mountains further east following an underground river and plunging into a pool. Through the curtain of that waterfall you may reach the Valley.'

'I get the impression it won't be simple.' Ben leant forward and rubbed at his beard.

Nemeth gave a small smile. 'The tunnels are inhabited by fey, Wild Fey. You will have to deal with duergers, knockers, gnomes and many other fey of earth variety. There are also some water fey who dwell in the River Black's darkness. They will be a challenge, but not one you cannot overcome as long as you are careful; don't throw away your quest with complacency. They are outside of Astol and therefore not under my rule, remember that. From the tunnels to Ayresport are wild meadow and farms where some of you may be recognised, so you must either be faster than any that spy on you, or those of you that are less well known must go ahead of the others.' She looked at Caelin.

'I've been thinking long on this,' the knight said uneasily. 'Our best option would be to send Mya and Jack on ahead under the guise they are answering the summons. Ferris, you should be unknown in Ayresport and could go with them. Lissa you can't go—'

She opened her mouth to protest at once.

'You are fey.' Caelin silenced her sternly. 'Would you cause Mya and Jack's capture? No; you must wait with me and Ben. Jack, Ferris and Mya, you must spy out our way and see how things stand. We'll hide as close to the city as we dare and try to avoid being seen. Feather.' Caelin turned to look carefully at the brownie. 'You can be our go-between to pass messages, news and plans. No one would expect a brownie in the heart of Ayresport and if you don't use your magic and are very careful, you shouldn't be detected.'

Feather nodded. 'And do I go ahead with Mya and Jack or stay back with you?'

Caelin took in a deep breath and let it out slowly. 'That's the bit I'm not sure of. Much as I'd like to send you ahead to spy out the school of spellwards, if they found you with Mya and Jack it would jeopardise everything. However, it would be hugely helpful if you would go ahead of the rest of us and find us a safe way into the city.'

It didn't take Feather a moment to understand what was needed of him. 'Then I must make my way alone.'

'No Feather!' Mya protested in alarm.

'Now my girl.' Feather raised a finger. 'It must be done. If any of us can find a way into the city, and out again, it's a brownie. Do you and Jack really want to deal with Kasira without Caelin?'

'No,' Mya replied quietly and bowed her head.

'Now I suggest I get as close to the city as I can with Mya, Jack and Ferris, remaining hidden, perhaps amongst their supplies. Then I'll slip away at night and search for a way in. The animals will know though I won't dare use magic to charm them.'

'It will be generations for most animals of the city since they last knew a brownie, or any fey,' Nemeth warned him.

Feather nodded grimly. 'But it will be the easiest way.'

'Wolf might help.' Mya brightened.

'Wolf is like to get shot if he strays too near people,' Ferris said, not unkindly. 'It might be best for him to stay here.'

Feather saw the distress on Mya's face at the idea of Wolf being hurt, but she looked equally unhappy at the idea of leaving him behind and he wondered how hard she would try. The wolf itself still sat upright with his ears and bright eyes alert, seeming to listen to everything they said.

'What about Kasira herself?' Lissa asked. 'Do we have a plan for how to reveal her secret?'

'It's already known to many on the outskirts of the Valley, those of us who live with the fey and still have to deal with the Dark Fey,' Ferris pointed out. 'What if we were to destroy the Ward and let her Dark Fey back in? It's risky but the Spellwards would fight off the fey and surely Kasira's true nature would have to come out?'

'Your idea has merit,' Caelin conceded. 'However, it would be too great a risk. The Dark Fey might not target the city and the Spellwards, but try easier targets amongst the people. There may also be some benign Wild Fey who try to go back to their homes only to be harmed by terrified humans who no longer know the difference between fey.

Kasira would send the Spellwards out in response, to be slaughtered all the more quickly by her Dark Fey, instead of feeding them to the Ward whilst still appearing to be the good protector of the Valley. The only thing we would gain is a postponement of all those with the Gift being sent to Ayresport.'

Ferris nodded as Caelin spoke.

'There is no obvious solution,' Nemeth stated. 'But you must get her to reveal the truth somehow, or risk forever being branded enemies of the Valley.'

'I'd be willing to pay that price,' Ben mused. 'After all being outcasts in Astol or Ashgrove would be no bad thing.'

'If it turns out to be the only way, then we must take it,' Caelin agreed. 'But the truth being known would be preferable. It's not just Kasira who's deceived the people of the Vale, but the Lord Vallier as well. How many still know our history and that this Valley belongs to the fey I'm not sure, but I've never heard tell of it anywhere but in the northern woods and mountains amongst those who chose to live outside the Ward. I fear we must look for an opportunity, wait and watch.'

'But not too long,' Nemeth cautioned quietly.

Caelin nodded. 'Not too long.'

Silence stretched out as each of them considered what lay before them. Feather tried not to let his thoughts wander. There were already several things creeping into his mind about what might go wrong without him searching or worrying for them. He gave a shake of his head at the irony of a little house brownie who fate had chased along to be here, a world away from the life he'd once had.

'I have brought in equipment for you.' Nemeth broke into their thoughts. 'See Dusty Tom this afternoon and he will outfit you with what you need. If anyone queries the strange make of anything, tell them you bought it at Trade Pass when you visited there for the journeyman's fair. Ayresport trade's mainly by sea with the Merren Islands rather than the Horse Lords I believe?'

'That's so,' Ben nodded.

'I will give you a parting feast at sunset and then direct you to the tunnels myself at dawn.'

They took it as their dismissal though all of them were slow to leave. Feather hopped down off the chair and Mya waited for him, Wolf standing at her side.

'Do you fancy some target practice?' she asked.

'Sounds good.' His forced smile turned into a genuine one as he looked up at his human.

***

After their noon meal all of them made their way down to the stables to where Dusty Tom had been storing their supplies. He and Feather had already put together saddlebags for each of them containing travel rations, rope, basic healing supplies, and a small amount of hard pellets Dusty Tom said was for the horses when they travelled underground. There were two small axes, which Ben and Ferris took, and flints for those that didn't use magic. They each had a strange sleeping blanket, padded and lined with a waxy material Mya had never seen before, they were patterned like the fallen leaves of a forest floor. There were obsidian and iron bolts for Feather, and arrows for the archers. They were all gifted with clothing too, and sturdy boots that came to mid-shin. Mya was presented with two sets of green trousers with pockets all the way up the sides, four beige linen blouses and a sturdy leather jacket.

'Lanterns,' Dusty Tom said, holding out two long black tubes that widened slightly at one end where a small round window of glass was set. 'You press this button here.' He did so and a wide beam of light sprang out.

Lissa gasped. 'Does it use much power?'

'It won't work by your magic.' Dusty Tom shook his head. 'There are magic cells inside.' He unscrewed the end and tipped out another smaller tube that was blue and red. 'These are the cells, they must go in with this small button facing toward the glass. There are spares in your saddle bags to save you using up your own energy in the tunnel, but use them sparingly and take fire torches with you also as these won't last all the way! Well,' the spriggan finished, wiping his hands down the front of his trousers. 'That's it! You're all ready to go.'

Mya looked down at the pile of cloth and objects she held in her arms. She was better supplied than she'd been when she'd set out on her journey from the cottage a year ago, just weeks in Valley time. Was she more ready though? *Yes,* she thought. *Yes, I am.*

***

Sleep evaded Mya that night, and she gazed up through the gap in her curtains at the narrow moon. They'd had a cheerful gathering outside the Hall and many of Astol's fey came to say farewell. The ganconagh had shown himself briefly but Wolf had growled at it and Nemeth herself had steered the fey man aside. He'd been gone before Caelin had turned to look in her direction. She still had no ill will toward the fey man, but she hadn't wanted any trouble on their last night in Astol. She still hadn't decided what to do with Wolf. Ferris was right, he couldn't go with them to the farms, and definitely not to Ayresport. Astol was safe but there were no other wolves and she hated the idea of leaving him alone. She'd almost decided she would leave it up to Wolf himself, but that wasn't particularly responsible. She realised she was just making excuses; she didn't want to part with him, but she had to for his sake. It would just be a matter of where.

She must have dropped off because when she opened her eyes again there was soft pre-dawn light leaking through the curtains. She heard Lissa moving about and softly singing to herself. She hugged her pillow for a few minutes, making the most of her last moments of comfort and luxury. Then with a groan she threw off the bedding and went to see if the bathroom was free. She lingered under the hot flow of water from the shower and wondered if she'd be able to make something like it back in the Valley. She'd packed all of her things the night before so she took only moments to dress. The trousers were comfortable but were heavy against her legs with all the pockets crammed with useful items, like her sewing things. Her small kitchen knife was in a pocket at her thigh and she'd shaken her head at her reluctance at leaving it behind; it was almost all she had left of her old life.

She knocked at Lissa's door and pushed it open, catching the half-fey straightening the curtains. She looked around with a start.

'I was going to be daring and leave the room in a mess!' She laughed. 'But even though I might not come back, I was still too scared to upset Billy Stub-Toe!'

Neither of them had seen the house's brownie the whole time they'd stayed, and he remained a remote and mysterious threat.

'Are you ready then?' Mya asked.

Lissa took in a deep breath. 'Let's do this.'

They made their way down to the stables, a light mist hung over the lake which was as still and quiet as a painting. The air was almost biting in its freshness and Mya shivered. They heard subdued voices coming from the stables and Feather pushed the doors open. Ferris led out his horse and Dusty Tom brought out both Mya and Lisa's, saddled and bridled.

'Oh, bless you, Tom!' Lissa bent and kissed the spriggan on the forehead.

'Well now, Tom likes to be useful!' The crooked little fey blushed. 'Shall we get your saddlebags on and secure as many arrows as we can?'

'That would be lovely,' Mya agreed.

She stepped into the warmth of the stable and found Jack, Ben and Caelin were all preparing their horses. All three of the men were dressed in their leather armour with light steel plate across their shoulders, upper arms, chests and spine. It was designed to allow the movement needed by a spellward whilst giving some of the protection needed for a knight.

Mya's heart skipped a beat. 'Sir Caelin, if Jack goes into the city dressed like that, they'll guess he's been training as a spellward rather than as an ordinary knight.'

Caelin froze. 'You're right and I hadn't considered that.' The muscles of his jaw clenched and a deep frown shadowed his eyes, but Mya understood him well enough to know his anger was directed at himself, he wouldn't tolerate his own imperfections. 'Jack you must leave your armour with me when we reach the farmlands.'

Jack's face fell, but he nodded.

Dusty Tom left Feather to help Mya and Lissa, and then saddled Nemeth's horse.

'Have you given yours a name yet?' Lissa asked.

'Not yet.' Mya frowned. So far, the mare had been patient and complying and not shown much interest or personality. Lissa's Nemesis, on the other hand, was feisty and a little naughty and had taken a dislike to Magpie, even kicking out once for no apparent reason.

Ferris was walking his horse, leading it at a fast walk in a big oval between the stables and the lake.

'Are we all ready?'

Mya looked up at Caelin's question and saw everyone had finished and were standing about waiting. Dusty Tom had hold of Nemeth's mare's halter and Feather had been lifted to sit on Magpie's saddle. Without waiting for a response Caelin led his horse toward the house and they followed.

'I will miss it here.' Lissa chattered to Ben. 'The luxuries of the Hall with its human magic, the safety of the grounds. But it's good to be doing something and facing a challenge again.'

'I'm too old to be a hedge knight.' Ben groaned. 'I should be retired with a fortune in rescued treasure and a young buxom wife to take care of me in my old age!'

'More like your young wife will run off with your treasure and leave you broken-hearted and destitute!' Dusty Tom laughed. 'And you'd only spend your money on Trow liquor!'

'True enough.' Ben shook his head.

Nemeth was waiting, looking like a statue of marble beside the water with the mists snared about her feet. She'd dressed in a full, pale blue, skirt and blouse with long tan boots.

'We have a little way to go,' she said as Dusty Tom let go the horse's head and the fey woman urged it forward with a gentle nudge of her legs. She led them around the lake past the house and into the forest where Mya had spent so many happy hours exploring with Wolf. She glanced back over her shoulder and saw Dusty Tom still watching them from the steps to the Hall. He raised a hand to wave and Mya waved back.

The light between the trees was gentle and turned the dying leaves to gold and plum. Beech nuts and acorns crunched beneath the horse's hooves as they followed the narrow trail leading up and away from the lake toward the hills in which the valley of Astol nestled. Lissa hummed to herself and Feather and Jack talked about which animals would gather the autumn harvest ready to hide away for the winter. Even Nemeth laughed when Ben declared he wished he were a bear and allowed to sleep in occasionally.

With barely a sound Wolf pushed out through the russet bracken and fell in beside Mya's horse. Her heart gave a leap and she knew then she wouldn't be able to force him to stay in Astol. As selfish as it was of her, the animal had become a part of her heart and she couldn't bear the idea of leaving him behind. Guiltily, she glanced back toward Ferris but the man was focused on the land around him and not on the wolf.

***

They kept up a steady pace through until mid-day where Nemeth turned from the path and led them upward through the trees. The forest thinned as they reached the summit of one of the hills. It was warm under the sun but the wind whispering in the long grass was cutting. Mya shaded her eyes and looked back the way they'd come but the Hall was no longer visible. They lay out a blanket and had a pleasant picnic and even Caelin attempted to smile and join in a little with their conversations. They packed away slowly and Mya guessed all of them were feeling less excited about their journey and more apprehensive of their task ahead.

Nemeth took them back down the slope of the hill on the opposite side to which they'd climbed and then descended into a small gully. They followed the water upstream for nearly two miles and the surrounding landscape became increasingly rockier and barren of trees. The hills rose to either side, and here and there the water had cut away shallow caves. Nemeth halted her mare and swung down from the saddle landing with a small splash in the clear water.

'We are here,' she said.

To Mya the place where they stood looked unremarkable, the walls of the gully rough and ordinary; the stream busy and oblivious. There was no ominous foreboding, no tingle of power or expectation. Just the other side of a jutting knee of harder rock that bent the course of the water, a cleft just wide enough to squeeze a horse through stood darkly, at first glance seeming no deeper than the other small caves they'd passed. They all dismounted and Caelin walked forward to stand with the faerun queen.

'It is narrow for no more than three yards,' she told him. 'It winds down steeply at first but is then level for much of the way. You will come to a river, it is quite fierce! You must follow it downstream and it will take you out to the Valley. It is a day and a night's journey, though you may lose track of time. The horses will not like it.'

Caelin nodded and drew in a deep breath. 'Thank you, my Lady, I hope you will hear from us soon.'

With no more ceremony than that Caelin took hold of his horses' head and pulled it toward the cleft. Mya let out a cry of surprised protest but Ben placed a firm hand on her shoulder. 'Come on,' he said.

Ferris took one of the torches out of his saddlebags and followed behind the spellward, his horse seeming happy to follow behind the other. Jack came next with Feather still perched on Magpie's saddle.

Steeling herself, Mya took a firm hold of her horse's halter and pulled her around toward the gap in the rock. She paused before Nemeth to give a small curtsey.

'Thank you, my lady,' she said.

Nemeth gazed back at her with her penetrating pale-blue eyes. 'Remember your lesson's child, remember to guard your weaknesses.'

Mya swallowed and nodded, then tugging hard at her horse's head to force it forward, she crept into the dark.

Chapter Thirteen

Warmth away from the wind was the first thing Mya noticed as her senses adjusted. Caelin had called a blue glow in the palm of his hand and behind him Ferris held the bright beam of one of Nemeth's magic torches. Between them and her, Jack and Magpie were only black silhouettes. Behind Mya, Lissa trod silently with a small will-o'-the-wisp bobbing above her shoulder, Ben brought up the rear and Mya heard his heavy tread. Her horse snorted unhappily into her shoulder and she fell back a little to walk beside it, rather than half dragging it, and it stopped fighting against her. Wolf was a pale ghost, his fur tinged with blue and yellow from their guiding lights, who walked cautiously with his tail low just in front of her having followed her in. She contemplated calling up light of her own or digging out a torch, but now she was getting used to the darkness and more confident in the straight smooth tunnel, she decided she was better to preserve her night vision and go without.

The tunnel smelt damp and silty though there was no sound or sight of water. As Nemeth had warned, the floor plunged steeply downward, and the horses became increasingly more nervous and distressed.

'I can do a little spell to calm the animals,' Feather suggested, his voice seeming strangely flat in the darkness.

'Oh yes, please.' Lissa said at once. 'I don't like seeing them so unhappy.'

Mya felt the tingling sensation of power being called and a soft glow formed around Feather. All of a sudden, she scented new grass and imagined a breeze, and her own heart eased and slowed its beat. The horses relaxed and Wolf's tail lifted.

Down and down they followed the narrow way and Mya's knees ached from bracing herself against the slope. She had no idea how far they'd gone but Caelin's blue orb faded and he changed it for one of Nemeth's torches. Eventually the floor evened out and opened into a wider cavern.

'We'll take a rest here,' Caelin said and Mya's legs sagged with relief.

They settled the horses in pairs and took out some cold rations. The floor was slightly damp and quickly soaked through Mya's trousers but she rested her legs gratefully. She called up an orb of light making it as bright as possible and sending it up toward the roof of the passage to maximise its reach. Before and behind, the tunnel faded into a blackness that, from her safe bubble of light, appeared impenetrable and daunting. Around her conversation was subdued and Wolf sat on his haunches close, but not touching her.

She started as somewhere ahead there came three firm knocks like a pick chipping stone. Immediately they all hushed and Wolf's fur bristled.

'Knockers.' Ferris whispered.

Mya's ears strained in the silence but they heard nothing more.

'Let's move on,' Caelin said. 'Mya, subdue your light a little but follow behind me and keep it going as long as you can without straining your power. Jack bring my horse, there should be room enough to lead two abreast and I want to keep my hands free.'

Mya stood and brushed the silty mud from her trousers whilst withdrawing a little of her energy from the orb of light. Ferris passed his torch to Feather so he could lead his horse and keep his sword hand free. Mya tried to recall all she knew of knockers as she took hold of her horse's halter and followed behind Caelin, keeping her light above and behind his shoulder. From what she remembered knockers were small earth fey, extremely reclusive, and hated to be observed. Occasionally one would cause mischief or trouble, especially to any human who stole from them or tried to spy on them, but mostly they were not malicious. There were plenty of fey in the dark places beneath the earth who would cause them harm, however, and the knockers had warned them they were coming to inhabited places.

Water oozed upward through the ground, seeped in silent drips down the walls and fell with a 'plop' from above. Soon a small stream cut a shallow channel winding across their path from left to right and back. Somewhere far behind them a knocker drummed out five times, paused and then clanged again thrice. Mya's horse shied a little at the sound and she stepped closer to its head to take a firmer hold and stroke its nose soothingly. Her own heart was fluttering, and she was tiring from concentrating so long on drawing power and feeding it steadily into the light. She wondered what would become of them if something attacked them. The way was still too narrow for the horses to turn easily so flight would be almost impossible back the way they had come. All at once the tunnel grew more oppressive in her mind and the walls seemed to close in. It was difficult to keep her breathing steady. Beyond the edge of her light the blackness was an impenetrable wall, and without meaning to she increased the brightness of her orb to chase it back.

'Be careful to save your power,' Caelin said, glancing back over his shoulder but not meeting her eyes. She saw the tension in his shoulders and his hand stayed close to his sword hilt. She realised he didn't like it down here any more than she did.

Without warning, the walls ahead fell away, and the light ran across the ground to dissipate into thinner shadow.

'We've reached the river,' Caelin said softly. He stepped forward with such trepidation he might have been traversing a marsh bog and not solid stone. Ferris pushed up past Mya and together the two men edged forward. Mya sent her magic lantern bobbing after them so they could see, and the shadows closed in around her.

'What's happening?' Lissa whispered from further back along the tunnel.

'A moment!' Mya called under her breath.

Caelin turned and gestured for them to follow, and Mya sagged with relief. As glad as she was to be out of the encasing tunnel, vulnerability replaced her claustrophobia as she walked out into the high-roofed and wide river cavern. Stalactites adorned the cave above their heads, dripping water like stone udders, and the river flowed with an eerie silence but for the constant drip of underground rain. Here and there fungi grew in the perpetual dark, almost as colourless as the stone. Their meagre light threw back glitter like gold from the moisture and was dazzling after the darkness of the tunnel.

'It's rather beautiful!' Lissa exclaimed her voice still pitched to a whisper.

Caelin stood with a frown on his face whilst Ferris explored a little further, taking the torch from Feather.

'Looks clear.' The Ashgrove scout gave a shrug of his shoulders.

'We'll go a little further.' Caelin decided. 'I want to get through as quickly as we can so we'll only stop briefly from time to time to rest and eat.'

'Do you want to stick together or shall I scout ahead?' Ferris asked.

'We'll stick together; in fact, I think we shall ride from here whilst we can. Lissa would you take over from Mya for a while?'

'Of course!' The half-fey sprang up onto Nemesis' back and urged her forward to join Caelin. Mya let her spell subside and withdrew her power. Feather's torch had dulled so Ben took out another. Feather stretched out his arms and rolled his shoulders.

The shape of the river cavern varied greatly as they passed through it, but they rode close together even where it was wide enough to have engulfed the inn at Ashgrove. Here and there black crevasses split the rock. Mya shuddered at a creeping sensation there were eyes within watching them. Every sound they made was enhanced and often thrown back at them in a cascade of echoes. Then an urgent hammering struck up almost beneath their feet and it took all of Mya's strength to stop her horse from bolting.

'I really don't like this.' Lissa almost whimpered into Nemesis' mane.

'Are they trying to scare us, or warn us?' Ben looked at Caelin who shrugged in reply.

'Hard to tell with knockers. It might be an idea to leave them some food out.'

'Not a bad plan.' Ferris jumped down off his horse and rummaged for supplies. He left a generous portion on a flattish rock away from the water. The hammering ceased abruptly.

'Let's go on.' Caelin waited for Ferris before urging Horse forward.

As they hurried onward the underground river widened and then deepened. Soon they were splashing through water almost up to the horses' knees, and at the edge of the light ahead of them, they saw it spread across the cavern from wall to wall forming a lake.

'That isn't looking passable.' Ferris' voice was tense with concern.

'I think there's something in that water.' Feather whispered.

'It's a rock fall.' Caelin sent an orb of light bobbing over the eerily still water. 'I think you may be right, Ferris, I don't see a way through.'

'The water must go somewhere else the river would be backed up much further than it is.' Ben dismounted and waded forward to join the spellward. 'Nemeth said nothing of this.'

'It looks recent.' Caelin clenched his jaw. 'Coincidence?'

Ferris snorted. 'A convenient one.'

'Will we have to go back?' Jack asked.

'I think our brownie is correct about the water.' Caelin nodded toward the shallows and Mya gasped when she saw the sharp white of bones picked clean.

'Well I for one don't like the look of that,' Ben exclaimed.

'Even if we got through the water, we can't get through that rock fall.' Caelin worked hard to hide his frustration. 'We have a choice before us of turning back to Astol and fight our way through the Hart Valley, or take one of the side passages we've passed.'

'Not much of a choice.' The old man folded his arms.

'Hey up!' Feather called softly and pointed back behind them. A white glow bobbed in the darkness like a bright candle in a mirrored lantern. Strangely it illuminated nothing beyond itself.

Ben growled in exasperation. 'Jack-o'-lantern, just what we need!'

'Well, as long as we're not daft enough to follow the blighter we should be fine,' Ferris stated.

Ben sprang back with a splash as a wave formed and rippled toward him.

'Get on your horse, Ben,' Caelin said.

Mya sensed Caelin draw up more power. None of them needed telling, they moved the horses away from the lake and the deep flowing river toward the cavern edge and the bobbing Jack-o'-lantern.

'We'll have to go back,' Caelin said through gritted teeth. 'Even should one of those other passages be wide enough for us and the horses and lead to a way out, there's no saying it will take us to the Valley and not back out to Astol or even some other Realm.'

Ben swore and then glanced sheepishly toward Mya.

'The knockers would know,' Feather said thoughtfully.

'They'd never let us see them and trying to catch one would turn the whole lot against us.' Ferris shook his head. 'We'd never get out alive.'

'They might talk to me,' Feather said.

Caelin's eyes narrowed as he sized up the brownie.

'Brownie, no offence, but with that Jack-o'-lantern about, and goodness knows what else, getting lost looking for knockers will be the least of what you face.' Ferris warned.

'I can go with him,' Lissa offered.

Feather shook his head, 'You are too human my dear, I might get away with it but I'm not sure you would.'

'But you can't go on your own!' Mya protested.

'I think I must, my girl.' He peered at her from behind Jack and then tugging at the young man's sleeve asked him to help him down off Magpie.

'We'll give you a day, or as well as we can judge under the earth,' Caelin said. 'Then we must turn back for Astol.'

Jack set Feather down on the slick stone and, to Mya, he looked tiny against the long legs of Magpie. Ferris handed Feather a torch and two magic cells, and Jack passed Feather his small pack which he hefted onto his broad little shoulders.

'Right.' Feather gave a nod of his head. 'I'll see you soon.'

'Are you sure someone can't go with him?' Jack's eyes pleaded with Caelin.

Caelin shook his head. 'If any of us do the knockers will flee.'

'And bring the caves down on us too most like,' Ben added.

'I'll be fine!' Feather forced a smile.

'We'll go back to where we left the offering for the knockers,' Caelin said. 'Meet us there.'

'I will.' Feather nodded.

Caelin nudged his horse forward and Jack reluctantly pulled himself up into Magpie's saddle. Mya turned to look over her shoulder as they headed back the way they'd come. Feather gave her a reassuring wave before switching on his torch and heading for the nearest crevice in the river cavern.

Mya watched as his light disappeared, fighting a compulsion to race after him. Her heart muscles constricted as his light vanished.

They set up a temporary camp and gave the horses some grain from their limited supplies. Lissa called up foxfire to provide them with an eerie green light, and just outside the edges of the darkness, the Jack-o'-lantern bobbed and flickered, not at all perturbed by the fact they didn't follow.

'He's wearing on my nerves,' Ben grumbled.

Anxiety gnawed at Mya's stomach and the silence and pressing blackness outside of their small circle grew heavier and more oppressive. She started with a painful twinge of her heart when a knocker thudded deep in the rock wall behind her.

Tap, tap tap tap tap tap tap tap…

On and on it went until she wanted to scream and the Jack-o'-lantern danced and swayed with no sight of the goblin holding the lamp.

'This is going to be a long wait.' Jack gave a sigh as he sank down onto the floor next to her.

Mya turned around to nod and then noticed someone was missing. She scrambled to her feet. 'Where's Wolf?'

But no one had seen the animal for some time. Mya peered into the darkness, itching to call up a blaze of light

'I don't like this constant knocking,' Caelin said. 'It heralds trouble.'

'Do you think we should get out?' Lissa asked wide eyed.

'But what about Feather?' Jack protested.

'And Wolf!' Mya added.

'Likely the animal has fled to safety,' Ferris said.

Then abruptly the tapping stopped. All of them strained to listen, even the horses had their heads up, eyes showing white.

From somewhere in the distance came the faintest murmur of singing, deep and harsh.

***

Feather tucked his sling into his belt and used both hands to grip the torch that was awkwardly large for his stubby hands. He strained his ears to listen for the knockers, but all he heard was the drip of water and the hammering of his own heart. He trotted as quickly as he dared through the crack in the earth's bones, trying to keep his demeanour determined rather than petrified. He was almost sure, almost, he would have nothing to fear from the knockers, but as Nemeth had reminded them, there were many things living beneath the ground.

The way before him split, and he went a short distance down each passage to listen. Faintly he thought he heard knocking in the tunnel to the right; he contemplated scratching an arrow in the wall, but with a shake of his head, he decided some fey or other would likely mess with any signs he left. Then the knocking started, persistent, continuous and almost frantic.

'Well, that doesn't sound good.' Feather frowned to himself. In a mine such urgent hammering would normally be the forewarning of a rockfall or a tunnel collapse. Unless... no. It was doubtful the knockers would help him find them. After all, what would they want of one small brownie? Still, he followed the sound down the narrowing way, trying to muster up the courage to call out to them but not quite finding his voice.

He was glad he hadn't. As soon as the noisy industry of the knockers ceased, he noticed another sound, a repulsive sound. He fumbled for the switch on the torch and turned it off, plunging himself into blackness.

There were voices, possibly three or four.

They were singing.

Long, long ago, all fey outside of the Gentry spoke in rhyme, but as years passed the old ways slipped away and few now used the outdated mode. Feather shuddered, knowing here in the deeps were creatures long forgotten in the Valley, creatures even the Dark Fey wouldn't want to meet. Their raucous voices sang joyfully of murder and rending, of torturing before eating their victims. Feather found himself rooted to the spot as the hobyah's graphic words froze his blood. He felt sick and had to swallow against the rising nausea. He needed to get out of there. He needed to get out of there right away, but somehow the thought wouldn't reach his body and his legs refused to work. The hobyahs were obviously busy with a victim, he could sneak right away and they'd never even know he'd been there; but it would mean leaving their victim to its awful fate, not to mention abandoning his quest before he'd barely begun.

His leg twitched, then he took the smallest of steps forward, then another. All at once he was scuttling as fast as he silently could, every breath a prayer he wouldn't be caught. The darkness pressed against him but up ahead was the flickering red of fire revealing the entrance to the hobyah's lair. He counted his choices as three. Turn and run, confront the hobyahs and try to save their prisoner, or run on by and continue looking for the knockers and a way out. One choice was heroic but foolish, one was cowardly in the extreme; the third choice was sensible in his situation but made him immensely sad and angry. He weighed up the needs of everyone against his conscience, there was only one choice to make.

He took in a deep breath and hurried past the entrance to the lair, keeping as much in the shadows as he could, and averting his eyes from what lay within. Caelin and the others would have to deal with the hobyahs later if they needed to come back this way.

Then his heart stopped as a low growl sounded behind him. He spun around to see Wolf baring his teeth in a snarl. Feather staggered back and dropped his torch to fumble for his sling. Wolf sprang forward but his leap took him not at Feather but into the hobyah's lair. The hobyahs ceased their singing to shriek and yell curses. Feather ran to peer into the lair putting a shot in his sling as he did so. Wolf had hold of one of the hobyahs in his jaws and was shaking it like a rag. There were two others who hopped and danced on their misshapen legs, trying to get close to Wolf to slash at him with their long, curved claws. They looked almost like dogs, with long muzzled faces, pointed ears, and black hair running down their backs. Wolf dropped his quarry to snap and snarl at the remaining two.

Feather hesitated only a moment before whirling his sling above his head and taking a shot at the nearest hobyah.

The shot glanced off the creature's sharp cheekbone, leaving a line of red, and it whirled around to pin Feather with its black eyes. The injured hobyah rushed at Feather, but Wolf sprang and latched his jaws onto the back of its neck. It shrieked as the Wolf's weight flattened it to the ground, and the grey animal worked its teeth around to get at the hobyah's throat. Feather's fingers found another shot in his pouch and he let fly at the last hobyah as it slashed at Wolf with its long, hooked claws. Feather's shot took it square in the forehead and it toppled backwards, grey fur floating up from the tips of its claws as it stretched to make a last grab at Wolf. Feather ran forward and drawing a small bronze knife from his belt stabbed it down into the hobyah's heart.

He stood looking at it for a moment, contemplating whether he should be sad these might have been the last of this old race if fey. He decided he wasn't sad at all. Turning he found Wolf sitting with his long black-tipped tail curled about his feet watching him. He still couldn't put his finger on it, but despite everything, there was still something about the animal he didn't quite trust. He shook himself, and gave a little bow.

'Thank you.'

Movement caught his ears and looking about he saw a rough frayed sack dumped amongst the rubbish of the cave.

'Hello?' Feather called cautiously. 'I'm going to let you out whoever you are. I'm just a brownie.'

There was no reply, but whatever was in the sack shifted about.

Feather swallowed and glanced at Wolf, he crept forward and sawed at the string holding the sack closed with his tiny knife. The course cloth fell away and the creature inside uncurled to stand up. It was a man; a tiny man smaller even than Feather. His skin was brown and wrinkled, and white hair like a spider's web floated about his head. His eyes were black but reflected what little light there was with the intensity of a diamond.

'A life I owe you, Brownie,' the tiny man said.

'You're a knocker?'

'A knocker I am.' He bobbed his head. 'Yon hobyahs have preyed on us for years.'

'Are there more?' Feather asked.

'All gone now.' The knocker smiled grimly. He glanced at the wolf. 'Hate hobyah's they do.'

'Wolves?'

'Aye, and dogs.'

'Listen, friend, me and my companions need help. We need to get out, to the Valley, back to the realm of the fey. We have horses too, to make things difficult, is there any way through these tunnels to get us there?'

Feather's heart wilted as the knocker shook its head. 'One way only to cross from one place t' t'other. The river it is that crosses the Realms.'

Feather sighed. 'Then we will have to go back.'

'No, no, forward you go! Follow the river.'

'But there is a huge rockfall, it blocks the way.'

'It was, it was, but knockers a tunnel have made! Go into the water and look, look! But beware! The Goram lives there!'

'The Goram?'

'Serpent.'

'Well, I guess it was too much to ask it would be easy!' Feather muttered.

***

Mya strained her eyes, searching the darkness. The long silence had become somehow more unbearable than the clamour of the knockers or the unnatural singing. The Jack-o'-lantern still tormented them, so it was a few moments before she realised the light coming toward them was actually one of Nemeth's torches.

'Feather?' She called out.

Jack got quickly to his feet and Caelin, who'd been standing guard, put his hand to his sword and moved between Mya and the approaching light.

'It's me!' Feather confirmed.

Wolf trotted forward into the eerie green glow and Mya drew in a sharp breath at the blood in his fur.

'Trouble? Are you hurt?' Caelin demanded.

'Trouble, but not hurt!' Feather threw himself down next to Mya and flexed his feet and ankles to take the ache out. He told them about his encounter with the hobyah's. 'It seems they'd been preying on the knockers for years. There are narrow tunnels leading upward and out, but they come out deep in the mountains and not in the realm of the fey. The only way we can go is the way Nemeth and the knockers have directed us, along the river.'

'And what of this Goram?' Ben asked.

'He doesn't sound like a particularly friendly fellow.' Feather winced. 'The knocker says we'd have seven hobyahs to face except the Goram got hungry. Apparently, it's blind, having lived down here in the darkness for years. It's allegedly ten yards long and has a poisonous bite. It hunts by scent and is very sensitive to vibration.'

'And the rock fall?' Ferris asked.

'The knockers tried to kill it by bringing the roof down on it but missed all but the end of its tail, which apparently it broke off to free itself. The river then flooded the tunnels, so they mined through the fall and shored it up. The way out is hidden behind the fallen boulders.'

'And it's big enough to get the horses through?'

'It is.' Feather nodded. 'They had hoped the Goram would take a hint and leave through it.'

Ben sighed. 'I take it we can expect to run into this character. Well, at least we know there's a way out now.'

'Are you ready to get going straight away?' Caelin asked the brownie.

'I reckon the sooner we get back out into open air, the better.' Feather pulled himself up onto his feet. 'But we might want to take precautions. Not much we can do about how we smell, but we might be able to soften our tread. The knockers will help as much as they can, they intend to set up a clangour to misdirect the Goram.'

'Sounds like we've been lucky to avoid it so far.' Lissa said.

'Luck indeed.' Feather nodded. 'The hobyahs were out hunting and the knocker's warnings did much to hide sounds of our being here.'

They tore up two of their blankets to wrap them around their feet and those of the horses. They took a few experimental steps and tied down or bound with cloth anything that rattled or rustled. There was no need for Caelin to warn them not to speak as he led them back toward the rockfall, but despite their precautions, Mya felt a dreadful certainty a confrontation with the Goram was inevitable.

As they led the horses back to the rockfall, Caelin increased the glow of his magic. He held up a hand to halt everyone and handing his reins to Ben, slowly stepped forward alone. Intermittent knocks sounded in the deeps of the underground world and echoed from every crevasse. The spellward reached the water and placed his foot as carefully into the liquid as if he were treading on a sleeping dragon. Nerve-rackingly slowly, he moved out deeper into the lake until it soaked his trousers, darkening them above his knees. He edged around to the left to get around one of the solitary boulders and stood looking intently at something the others couldn't see. Ben opened his mouth to speak but stopped himself and ground his teeth in frustration.

Something moved beneath the lake, bulging its surface and creating the smallest of waves which rippled toward the shore and died before they reached it. It was between Caelin and the others. Mya called her power reflexively but Lissa sucked in air and put her hand on Mya's chest to warn her to be still. Caelin stood as though changed to stone; he didn't even appear to be breathing. Then a white shape rose up out of the water, scaly skin sloughing off droplets of liquid caught brightly in Caelin's light. It snorted, slit nostrils opening and closing, revealing the redness of veins within. Its eyes were filmy and dead-looking, but it turned its head as though searching.

One of the horses gave a whicker of fear and at once the serpent snapped around and dove toward the shore. Lissa let out a shriek at the same time as releasing an unstable fireball too hastily formed. The horses tried to bolt and Mya was yanked off her feet. She hit the rough ground hard and barely missed cracking her head. Her horse tried to drag her, and Ben swore as he fought his own whilst trying to draw his sword. The huge head of the Goram came hurtling down toward them and landed with a splash in the river, soaking them all with its spray. It was a moment before they realised it wasn't moving.

Mya pulled herself up and looked around.

The Goram lay in lumped coils woven in and out of the water; an arrow protruded from one eye. They all turned to look at Ferris who stood with his bow in his hand. He gave a self-deprecating shrug.

'I'd better go catch my horse,' he said.

Caelin waded back toward them. 'Don't go too far, if you don't find it soon, we'll have to do without it.'

'Ride back with me on Asher,' Ben suggested. 'Best you don't go off on your own, anyway.' He handed Horse's reins to Jack.

'Oh, and Ferris!' Caelin called after them. 'Nice shot!'

***

Mya ached from head to toe. Her shoulder throbbed where it had been yanked, and her clothes rubbed against the bruises forming along her hip and thigh. The tunnel through the rockfall had been scary, despite the work of the knockers it hadn't appeared at all stable, and she'd been glad to get to the other side. Ben and Ferris had re-joined them within an hour, the horse having not bolted far once it reached the pitch black away from their artificial light.

'Lucky it didn't break its legs,' Ferris said.

'Well there you go, it's earned its name, Lucky!' Lissa exclaimed.

Mya stroked the neck of her own horse; she still hadn't decided what to call it. Maybe it was too many years of surviving on a smallholding, it was foolish to give a name to something you might have to eat one day. The idea flashed across her mind to call the animal 'Dinner' and she had to stop herself laughing out loud. That was worse than Caelin calling his mount 'Horse'.

With no warning her horse reared, eyes rolling in fear. Mya barely kept her seat as it tried to plunge past the others.

'Gnomes!' Lissa cried out.

Mya called up light, not knowing what to expect. Looking back, she saw at once what had startled her horse, something dark and ugly was burrowing up out of the ground. Mya twisted around in her saddle, unable to take her eyes off what was emerging. It had large knobbly hands with long hardened black nails, red-rimmed goggling eyes, and a face so covered in warts there was no skin between. Loose earth and small rocks fell from above and with it another gnome about half the size of Feather. It landed on Jack's head, burrowing into his hair and slashing at his eyes with its nails. Jack grabbed at it as Lissa rode up alongside and stabbed the frantic thing with her dagger; it fell away but not before its blood spilt down Jack's face.

All around them small eruptions burst from the rock, and stones rained down on them.

'Run!' Caelin called.

They spurred their horses forward, Caelin leading them into the river where the gnomes didn't seem to be emerging. Wolf snapped and growled, then raced ahead to take the lead. Feather had his sling out and the other magic users sent fireballs at any of the creatures leaping from the shore. Mya however, concentrated on keeping her light bright and steady so they could see where they were going. The river protected them a little, but not from the snarling creatures dropping from above. One just missed Mya, its sharp nails scoring down her right leg as it tumbled but failed to grab on. More and more came burrowing from the earth like frenzied ants from a broken nest and nausea churned Mya's stomach.

Caelin held them back from a panicked gallop, afraid one of the horses would stumble. One of the creatures clung to his back where he couldn't reach and he bellowed as it stabbed its horny nails deep into his flesh. Jack made a grab for it but couldn't pull it free until he sent a pulse of electricity through his clenched hand. Caelin stiffened at the touch of the magic, but the gnome fell away like a burned tick.

The horses were becoming frantic as gnomes slashed at their legs and fell from above. Then all at once natural light bloomed before them. Instinctively the horses lengthened their stride, and they let them. Mya felt the tightness of tears in her chest, but she was too terrified still to weep with relief. The brightness of the sun hurt her eyes, blurring her vision, but her horse followed Caelin's lead and they turned left out of the cave, the horses' hooves thudding now on dry stone rather than splashing in water. The spellward halted abruptly and swung his gelding around. Mya felt him build up a huge amount of power and as Ferris passed him, he sent a burst of roaring fire back down the tunnel.

'Get this thing off me!' Ferris growled as he fought a gnome latched to his shoulder and trying to tear at his throat. Ben stabbed it swiftly with his dagger and flung it down.

All of them checked and checked again, making sure they were free of the horrible creatures. Mya couldn't quite shake off the feeling of small grabbing hands and Lissa continued to shudder. Wolf circled back toward them scenting the air suspiciously.

'We're here!' Jack said almost disbelievingly. 'We're back in the Valley!'

Chapter Fourteen

They walked the tired horses down a narrow path following the river through the mountains. Mya was utterly exhausted, but they couldn't drop their guard. Now they were back in the Valley there would be more fey to guard against. It was shockingly warm and Mya remembered it was summer here, and Autumn was long behind them in Astol.

'We should probably rest soon,' Ben grumbled.

'Not until we're further away from those… things!' Lissa said adamantly.

'Aye, it's gonna take strong brandy to wipe that from my mind,' the old knight agreed. 'Lots of strong brandy.'

'I wonder what made them attack us.' Ferris rubbed at the two-day stubble on his cheek. 'Do you think Kasira has them guarding the way and knows of it after all?'

'Probably sheer malevolence,' Feather said. 'Nasty blighters!'

'We'd have a nice big welcoming party here if Kasira knew about it,' Caelin said over his shoulder. 'The fact I returned to the Valley and then back to Astol would have tipped her off I have a plan. She won't take any chances now.'

Caelin's gloomy words left them in silence again until he stopped at dusk to make camp in a wide gorge where they could move away from the river.

'We'll keep watch in pairs,' Caelin told them. 'Jack you'll take first watch with me.'

Jack groaned but Mya envied him despite her weariness, she much preferred to take the first or last watch than have her sleep broken up. Not that getting to sleep was easy; she kept imagining gnomes scuttling over the ground to crawl all over her.

***

Dawn came early and crept in quietly with few birds in the sparsely treed gorge. Mya and Lissa slipped away together with Wolf shadowing them.

'If we go back to Astol, I'm not going through that tunnel.' Lissa declared as she splashed water from the river onto her face and slicked back her short dark hair.

'Me neither.'

'I'm with Ben on finding a good inn and getting drunk. I can't see Caelin letting us though.'

'I guess we can't really risk his being seen.' The thought of a good dinner and some sharp cherry wine set Mya's mouth to watering. 'I don't suppose there's anywhere like Ashgrove this far west in the Valley?'

'You suppose right.' Lissa shook water off her hands and wiped them down her tight trousers. 'There is nowhere else like Ashgrove, but there are small settlements even in this part of the mountains where we would be welcome, and by "we" I mean fey as well as Caelin. You are right though, I think we'll need to avoid any contact with others. Hopefully Kasira will think we're holed up still in Astol and we don't want to change that.' She slipped her arm through Mya's as they made their way back to the others.

'Ready?' Caelin got to his feet.

'Let's get going,' Lissa nodded.

They set out at a steady pace, following the gorge until it flattened out and the mountains lessened in severity. They saw signs of trows but the shy fey kept out of sight. It was only when they reached the forested lower mountains they ran into any trouble. Pixies plagued them with random bursts of laughter, thrown stones and ivy tied tightly across their path. It was no more than a minor irritation but soon frayed all their nerves. A lone gnoll spied on them from the undergrowth, but thought better of bothering them, whilst a gang of hobgoblin braved an attack but were quickly driven away by a strong display of magic.

At night the pixies' taunting didn't cease and the sporadic rustling in the trees and bushes had Wolf on his feet several times growling, it made for very long watches. Once they came upon a flock of sylphs flitting in and out of the sunbeams spearing through the leaves of an ancient beech tree. They were tiny winged ladies no bigger than Mya's little finger and brightly coloured like moon-struck jewels. Lissa slipped away from the others to speak with them though Mya could make out nothing of their answers but a high-pitched humming.

'They have no news of the Valley.' Lissa gave a shake of her head as she left them to their play. 'But they tell me there is a bugbear further down this trail.'

'Caelin rubbed at the bridge of his nose.' That shouldn't be too much to handle, but we'll try to avoid it if we can, chances are it will be Dark Fey.'

'Is it worth me and Lissa taking a scout ahead?' Ferris suggested.

Caelin mulled it over. 'No, I think at this point we'll stick together. We'll keep heading down out of the mountains, try to get our bearings and keep to the forest as long as we can.'

***

They came across two small settlements that day; both ringed about by wooden walls hung with charms and iron. Caelin recognised them both, and they crept by, keeping out of sight.

'They are poor holdings,' he told them. 'Mostly hunters and pig farmers; they would have little to share or trade. I do, however, know where we are now and I might risk a couple of us visiting Adder's Nest to gather news.'

Lissa immediately volunteered but Caelin shook his head. 'You'd be recognised as half-fey and attract too much attention. Ben and I can't go, so it will be between Jack, Ferris and Mya.'

Mya felt a mixture of excitement and apprehension. It would be good to visit another new town in the Valley and replenish their supplies; however, going into a strange place without Caelin and Ben was a little intimidating. She wondered at the town's name; it sounded somewhat dangerous and dark.

Caelin chose Mya and Ferris to go. The scout's experience and skills would be invaluable, and having a woman with him would make him seem less threatening. Mya was a little uncomfortable being on her own with the Ashgrove scout, but if he noticed he didn't mention it.

'We don't look alike but would you be happy if I introduced you as my sister?' he asked.

'That's fine with me,' she replied.

She could see the outer wall of the town through the trees. It was about seven feet in height, the lower half made of stone and the upper of wide wooden stakes. They followed it around for about a quarter mile, the sounds of human habitation reaching them. A man rolled out a deep hearty laugh making Mya smile, and someone was sawing rapidly at wood. As they moved downwind, the sharp scent of human waste caught Mya's throat and made her gag. It was worse than anything she had come across in Briarton or even crowded Trade Pass.

'The smell of civilisation!' Ferris remarked. 'Stick close by me, this is a rough place.'

Mya didn't need telling twice.

They saw the uneven dirt road before they spotted the gates. A man sat lounging in a chair, scratching at his ample belly, but he leapt up on seeing them. His hair was greasy and long, the crown of his head was bald and reddened by the sun.

'Strangers eh?' he said in greeting, hoisting his sagging trousers up a little higher. 'What be you wanting?'

'Just some supplies and a chance to sit down and rest a while out of this fey-infested forest!'

The man looked them both up and down and Mya lifted her chin defiantly holding his gaze.

'Aye, okay.' The man decided. 'But mind we don't hold with any trouble here.'

Ferris raised his eyebrows but kept his opinion to himself. 'Thank you, sir,' he said.

The man watched them as they passed through the wooden gate, held together by strips of iron. Mya's heart sank at what she saw before them. The houses were mostly single-story wooden huts, many in a poor state of repair despite the abundance of timber outside the walls. The roads were pitted with drying puddles and littered with waste. A rat scurried along the side of one building, uncaring of the bright daylight and human presence.

'Come on.' Ferris took her arm. 'There's a trader on the main street from what I remember, and an alehouse of sorts. We'll visit them both but won't hang around.'

Mya didn't like how on edge the scout was one bit.

'You've been here before?'

'Yeah.' He skirted a particularly large pit in the road and nodded affably to an old woman who sat on a bench in front of her home. She didn't so much as twitch and her expression remained sullenly glowering. 'Us Ashgrove scouts learn our way about the whole of the Valley. Lissa hasn't been allowed far though, the Ward would be a problem for her for a start. That's the trader.'

Mya followed his gaze; outside one of the houses several barrels stood, along with a rack displaying bolts of poorly woven cloth. A variety of dead birds and four rabbits were strung from the overhanging roof.

Inside it was dingy, and it took a few moments for Mya's eyes to adjust. There were two customers inside besides themselves, a woman who patiently waited to buy a small sack of flour, and a scrawny tall man who had to stoop to avoid hitting his head on the pots and pans hanging from the rafters. He was engaged in some heated bartering with the trader over a small and worn looking hatchet.

'I don't have a huge supply of coin,' Ferris said under his breath. 'Let's get beans and flour and some of those dried up old potatoes, we can hunt for our own meat in the forest.'

The two men finally came to an agreement, and the customer pushed past them with his hatchet clasped firmly in his fist. The woman placed five dark copper coins on the counter and managed a small smile to Mya as she left.

'Well.' The trader wiped his hands on his grubby apron as he sized them up and tried to decide if he could make any money here or not. 'I haven't seen you before, what can I do for you?'

'Just a few bits to make up our travelling rations,' Ferris said. 'We're on our way to Ayresport.'

'Are you now?' The man raised his eyebrows. 'Not an easy journey these days with the Ward shrinking. Used to protect us here it did, once upon a time.'

'That must have been a bad time when it left you.' Ferris leaned casually against the counter. 'Do you get much trouble from the fey?'

'Not so much within the town. Outside's not good and that's where we have to go to get what we need to live.' He gestured expansively around his shop. 'So, of course, things are harder to get and the prices have to go up, but what can you do?'

'What indeed.' Ferris commiserated. 'Nothing too dangerous out there I hope?'

'There was a dog-mean spriggan ruined one farm about five miles out; ain't been seen in a while though since they drove it off. Mostly just your nuisance sorts. Still, I don't envy you a journey with a young lady to take care of. Urgent business in Ayresport is it?'

'Heard they are desperate for those with the Gift to help with the Ward, my sister here seems to have a touch of it. Rumour is spellwards get worn out fast but in times like this...' Ferris gave a shrug.

The trader narrowed his eyes and looked at Mya appraisingly. 'I guess the rich lifestyle would be worth it to some.'

'You seem to have doubts my friend,' Ferris said casually.

The trader grew reticent and straightened up a little defensively. 'Not for me is all. I guess... well I guess you have little choice with the edict.'

'No.' Ferris hid well the fact they didn't know much about the edict, however Mya thought it might be worth pushing it a bit further as all they had to go on were the overheard conversations of Dark Fey in the Hart Valley.

'Have there been Seekers here in Adders Nest?'

'Aye.' The trader picked at the edge of his counter with a fingernail. 'Took five people and hanged a sixth who refused to go. Look, do yourselves a favour, don't go bragging round here about having this Gift. Seekers made it known they'd pay for anyone handed in to them or information on anyone hiding. You may very well be on your own way t' Ayresport of your own accord, but some here might make a grab for the money if you get my meaning.'

'I do, thank you,' Ferris replied. 'We'll take some goods off you too.'

They paid the extortionate prices and ducked back out into the bright light. They exchanged glances but said nothing of what they'd learned, there were too many people within earshot on the filthy street.

They passed two other traders and a blacksmith before they found the alehouse. A man lay sprawled in the dirt outside mumbling and occasionally raising his voice incoherently. The buzz of conversation was loud through the open door as was the smell of alcohol and body-odour.

'We'll sit and listen in for a while,' Ferris said under his breath.

The inside of this building was as dark as the trader's had been. Although it wasn't long past noon it was still quite crowded. The bar was only a plank across two barrels and a stack of them lined the wall behind the alehouse keeper. They had to squeeze between the mismatched tables and chairs to get there and most conversations stopped the moment they entered. Mya wanted nothing more than to turn and get out of there as soon as possible. She could almost feel the eyes on her.

'Two of your finest,' Ferris said affably.

'We got one ale, and it is what it is.' The man took the lid off a barrel beside him and dipped in a clay tankard, thumping it down on the wood with liquid running down its side. He swiftly followed with a second and held out his hand. 'Ten coppers.'

Ferris opened his mouth to protest, but thought better of it. He dug into the purse on his belt and drew out a silver. The man bit down hard on it, grunted, then dug in his apron for Ferris's change. Mya glanced around and saw most of the occupied tables were the ones in corners and against the walls; it hardly surprised her. She was relieved when Ferris squeezed his way back to a table near the door politely carrying her ale for her.

Mya gazed at her drink dubiously. It was dark and a little cloudy. She took a sip and immediately winced at the bitterness. It had a rather unpleasant aftertaste too.

'Nice?' Ferris raised an eyebrow and a smile of amusement lit his eyes.

'Lovely.' She grimaced.

He chuckled and took a swig himself.

Ferris talked a little of their pretend journey to come, grumbling over the lack of a Ward in these parts. Mya understood at once he was trying to put the others in the room at ease. It didn't take long for the noise of the room to return to its previous volume and Mya winced at the vulgarity of it. She let Ferris's words, now more sporadic with longer gaps between, fade out as she hopped from one conversation to another. One man was cursing and grumbling loudly about the lack of trade coming out of Ayresport; his companion pointed out Adders Nest had little to trade, anyway. A larger group of four were laughing over some prank they'd played on a man who'd seemingly wronged them. One man was complaining to a lady of a dubious nature about the failings of his wife whilst leaning against her ample shoulder. In one corner there was a hushed and hurried conversation between two men who sat on adjacent tables though Mya couldn't make out what they were saying.

Her ears caught the name "Kasira" somewhere in the room. She nodded absently to something Ferris said and tried to pinpoint the conversation.

'... terrified of the Ward failing. They should try living out here for a bit!'

'Aye and what happens when we run out of spellwards? I reckon the Lord Vallier would sacrifice even Kasira to save his hide!'

'Nah, everyone knows she pulls his strings, and more besides! I say let the Ward fail. Them fey as was attacking us in numbers are long gone. Surely it would be better to train all those with the Gift to defend us rather than waste them on the Ward?'

'You don't know Ayresport. Great City? Well, I suppose it is compared to the likes of here, but it's more like its own country. I tell you those that live there don't care a jot about the rest of the Valley. We might just as well be bugs to them. Knights and Spellwards lording it about the place, ladies that look at you like shit in the road if you dare speak to 'em! You wouldn't catch someone from Ayresport drinking ale like this that's for sure!'

'Don't sound like such a bad place to me.'

'Aye, once maybe but now the place is... filled with fear and paranoia. It's a different world I tell you, but not a happy one. I won't be going back there again in a hurry, I'll be heading up to Trade Pass in future, I think!

'Mya?'

'Sorry.' She shook her head, realising she'd become so absorbed in the conversation she'd missed what Ferris had said.

'You finished?' He indicated her ale which she'd barely touched. She looked at his tankard and saw he'd somehow managed to drink all of his.

'Yes, I have!'

'Let's head off.' He stood up and nodding to the alehouse keeper, headed for the door.

As soon as they got outside, Mya took in a deep breath of the cleaner air, but Ferris took her arm and set off in a faster than casual pace. Mya wanted to ask what was wrong, but knew the scout couldn't speak where ears might listen. They made it to the gate and the guard there watched them, but didn't stop them. They followed the rough road for a while before stepping off it into the forest.

'There are Seekers still in Adders Nest!' Ferris explained finally. 'They may not have believed we are planning to go to Ayresport, and I didn't want us to get separated from the others by force. Did you hear those two men plotting to sell them someone?'

Mya shook her head. 'Were they the ones in the corner? I couldn't make them out.'

'Yes, that was them. The trader was right, people here are turning on each other for money, or perhaps just for malice.' They exchanged what they had both heard and Ferris nodded grimly. 'It confirms what little we knew and Caelin has come back none too soon. I'm not sure what he'll think of that chap's opinion of Ayresport, Caelin loved that city, once.'

'Did you know him back then, when he was a knight in the city?'

'No, not at all. I first saw Caelin when Ben brought him to Ashgrove with his face sliced up. I didn't dare speak to him, few did.'

Mya thought she could well imagine the angry and hate filled young man, newly betrayed and broken.

Ferris found his way back to where the others waited with relative ease and they both related all they'd learned.

'We stick with our plan,' Caelin said. 'It sounds like there'll be an influx of "volunteers" and forced recruits filling up the city, so it should be easy enough for Mya and Jack to lose themselves amongst them.'

'I don't like the idea of sending them in alone though,' Ben grumbled.

'Well, you certainly can't go with them, old man!'

Ben was shocked into silence by Caelin's sharp retort.

'We'll head further south, then cut west of Rider's Mead Farm to the edge of the Ward. There was an abandoned shepherd's hut not much further south, if it's still unused we'll split up there.'

Ferris nodded. 'Could also be a good spot to head back to if anything goes wrong.'

'If anything goes wrong, they'll be no heading back.'

Mya scowled at Caelin's return to his old dour nature, but she had to admit, the knight was probably right.

***

They travelled for two more days, coming out of the mountains and staying within the edges of the great forest. Settlements were infrequent, and they completely avoided anything of the size of Adders Nest. They waited until after dusk to turn southward and out into the open meadows of the Ayre Valley. The pixies plaguing them didn't follow them under the open sky, but the lonely screech of an owl drifted after them. The wind drove in thicker clouds and then tattered them away; the temperature dropped and Mya shivered.

'What was that?' Lissa froze in her tracks.

'What?' Ferris demanded.

'I thought I saw... a shadow and movement in the sky.'

'The owl?' Ferris suggested.

'No.' Lissa frowned. 'Bigger than that.'

They scanned the night, and the horses shifted restlessly.

'Let's keep moving,' Caelin said.

Mya watched the spellward's retreating back, his mood hadn't improved in the last couple of days. Mya ran over everything in her mind to see if she could think of anything anyone might have done to annoy him. Lissa dismissed it as Caelin just being himself, and Mya realised having travelled with him, the half-fey's feelings for him had dulled somewhat.

A sudden breeze caught the hair loosened around her face, but it was only when her horse jumped sideways and Lissa let out a shriek, she knew it was no wind.

'Succubae!'

'Mya!' Jack gasped.

Mya grabbed a handful of her horse's mane, her heart in her mouth. Whilst the others called up power or reached for weapons Mya and Jack froze, their eyes locked.

'Could this be them?' Jack said.

Mya shook her head in denial and forced herself to move. She reached her free hand out for Jack's and they both looked up at the scattered stars. Wisps of cloud still passed over them and a three-quarter moon made the edges glow.

Something blocked out the light, turning in a lazy swoop over their heads.

'Two,' Feather said.

'Will they attack?' Jack asked.

Almost in answer, the two shadows alighted as silently as unfurling blossom a few feet away from them. Settling back their leathery wings, they revealed bodies as supple and feminine as any nymph. There was nothing innocent in their nakedness.

'What do you want?' Caelin demanded.

'We were curious.' One of the succubae smiled with false coyness. Her tail curled around in front of her and the end twitched.

'And hungry,' the other added, her grin showing teeth too white between her red lips. 'Humans of power are becoming harder to find outside of the Ward.'

'And ordinary mortals are so dull.' The first pouted.

'So, what are you doing creeping about in the night?'

'Minding our own business,' Caelin retorted.

The first succubus clicked her tongue and gave a little shake of her head. 'Such bad manners!'

'Just be on your way,' Caelin said. 'You'll find us deadly sport.'

The second succubus wet her lips with her pink tongue and looked him up and down. 'There are no spellwards left in the Valley strong enough to defeat us, Kasira has kindly seen to that!'

'Kasira has seen to nothing!' Mya stepped forward and drew up power.

'No Mya!' Feather hissed.

The first succubus took it all in and gave a deep quiet chuckle. 'Well, we had better finish her job for her.'

In an instant both demons were aloft, too fast for Mya's blast of fire. Caelin turned to angrily chastise Mya but Jack growled at him in a way that halted the knight. 'They killed our parents!'

Ferris had an arrow nocked to his bow in an instant and Feather swung his sling-shot at the same time as sending calming energy to Magpie on whose saddle he sat helplessly. Ben and Jack had drawn swords and the younger man thrummed with barely held-back power. Lissa cast globes of light upward but the succubae dove so quickly they gave little extra warning.

'Don't let them touch you.' Lissa yelled needlessly.

Two fireballs preceded the first succubus, barely missing Caelin and scattering all the horses but Magpie. Caelin shielded instinctively and his burst of lightning went wide in his distraction. Jack replied with his own ball of fire but the succubus only laughed and batted it aside with a flick of her long-nailed hand. The second succubus went for Mya, but at the last moment swung aside and her barb-ended tail wrapped about Ferris' arm yanking him upward into the air;

his bow dropped uselessly from his grip. Feather let fly a bolt and it struck the succubus's cheek. Lissa exerted a huge amount of power to send bindweed growing at a tremendous rate to catch at Ferris's leg and anchor him to the earth.

With an eagle-like screech of rage the succubus dropped the struggling man and snatched instead at Lissa. It wrapped itself about the half-fey, arms, legs, tail and wings. Lissa struggled frantically as the demon tried to force her mouth over hers in a deadly kiss to steal away all of her life-force. Both Jack and Mya pummelled at the dark leathery wings with fireballs, scared they would hurt Lissa too; but the Succubus didn't even react.

'It's immune to fire!' Feather yelled.

Wolf sprang forward, catching at the succubus's tail and digging in his paws to try to drag it back. With a snarl it unfurled its wings, and clutching Lissa still with one arm, struck out at Wolf sending him rolling with a yelp across the grass. Lissa freed her knife and, slashing wildly, caught the succubus across the chin and forearm. Instead of dropping her the succubus opened its mouth wide with a hiss to show its long white canines. Wolf sprang back to his feet and leapt, clamping his jaws down on one flapping wing. Ferris had also scrambled up, and limping, grabbed up his bow. Mya formed a lightning spell but hesitated to use it for fear it would do more harm to her friends. Jack didn't hesitate, with a wild cry he leapt up onto the Succubus's back and grabbing a handful of its hair sliced clumsily at its throat with his sword. Blood gushed down its smooth skin, and it dropped Lissa to clasp at the wound in a vain attempt to stem the flow. Lissa stabbed upward pushing her knife between its breasts and it crumpled.

More cautious than its companion, the first succubus had remained in the air, pinning Caelin down with a fierce blast of flame. Aware it was getting nowhere against the spellward's shield it spun to send a blast at Ben who'd remained close by hoping to be able to aid Caelin. The old knight swore and threw himself to the ground, rolling as rapidly as he could away from the heat. Caelin shot blinding blue lightning at the succubus and steam rose off its skin as though he had doused a hot iron in water. It bared its teeth at him in fury and shot upward into the night.

'Has it gone?' Ben pulled himself up onto his elbows and craned his neck to look around at the sky.

'Is anyone hurt?' Caelin called out.

'Nothing bad,' Lissa replied through gritted teeth as Jack helped her out from under the dead succubus.

With the silence of a bat, the first succubus dropped back out of the night. It grabbed Mya's hair, its nails digging into her scalp, and its tail lashed out to knock Jack off his feet. With its free hand it sent a fireball toward Caelin, throwing him backward despite his quick shield. Wolf leapt, grabbing the succubus's arm in his strong jaw and forcing it to release Mya. It slashed at the animal at the same time as lifting upward with its wings; wolf let go plummeting several feet to the ground.

'Wolf!' Mya ran toward his unmoving pale form but halted as the succubus flew at her again.

Ferris loosed an arrow, and it left a jagged tear through one wing close to the demon's waist. Feather's shot hit its shoulder leaving a streak of red. Ben ran at it waving his sword as though scaring off crows from a field. It was Jack again who slew it, grabbing hold of its tail and sending out a kill spell with all of his strength to stop its heart. He fell to the ground at the same time as the succubus.

Mya thought her own heart had stopped. She stared wide-eyed at Jack's crumpled form and then turned to look at Wolf.

'He's okay,' Lissa said breathlessly, crouching next to Jack and lifting a hand to feel for the pulse at his wrist.

'He won't be when he wakes up,' Caelin said grimly. 'Best wrap him in a blanket he'll lose body heat after that spell.'

Seeing Jack would be okay, Mya hurried over to Wolf, tears stinging her eyes and making her almost blind. She stroked his coarse fur and leant her cheek against his ribs to feel any sign of a breath or a heartbeat. Nothing. She sat back, her heart and lungs constricting with the pain of grief.

'Oh, my Wolf!' She sobbed.

Despite the darkness her tears made rainbows that blurred before her eyes and distorted Wolf's shape. She reached out to bury her hand in his fur only to draw it back as though burned. Skin, she'd touched skin! She rubbed at her eyes and her vision cleared, Wolf lay before her as furry as ever. She frowned and gave a slight shake of her head at her foolishness. Not caring what Caelin or anyone else thought, she let herself cry, her heart breaking for the animal who'd had become a closer friend even than Lissa. When she forced her aching eyes open, she gasped. For a moment... for a moment she thought Wolf had contorted into an almost human shape.

'Mya!'

She hadn't heard Feather come up beside her but the little brownie placed a hand on her arm.

'Do you love Wolf?'

'Of course, I do!'

'By the huntress!' Lissa gasped.

'Mya, my girl,' Feather said with as much calmness as he could muster. 'True love can break an enchantment.'

Mya sat up and turned to look at her friend, her head aching and not understanding what he'd said. As her vision cleared, she turned back to Wolf and leapt to her feet almost stepping on Feather. Before her lay not a wolf but a man, naked, bruised and very, very still.

Chapter Fifteen

Mya sat beside Jack in the long grass but saw nothing. She was aware of the others behind her, but she wanted nothing to do with them. In the back of her mind she knew it wasn't any of their faults, but she wallowed in her anger. *How dare he?* Every confidence she'd shared, all their time together exploring Astol, all the while it had been a man not a wolf. Who was he anyway? Some spy of Kasira? Lissa had thought it wonderful, of course she would, whilst Caelin, like her, was fuming at the deceit. Feather had bid them be patient and wait to hear the man's story before they judged him, but Mya was consumed by the unknown invasion of her privacy and betrayal of her trust.

'Mya!'

She became aware Lissa was calling her.

'What?'

'He's waking up.'

She wanted nothing more than to ignore him, but with a sigh she gave in and dawdled over.

It was dark still, daylight a rosy promise beyond the horizon. Ben had placed a blanket over the stranger but she could see he was a tall man. He was thin, but appeared strong, his muscles sinewy rather than bullish. He had a face too narrow to be called handsome with mousey hair shot through with flecks of grey. Lissa was quite clearly taken by him from the way she fussed about him and Mya felt a moment of annoyance. Or, was it jealousy?

'Who are you?' Caelin demanded.

The man's eyes opened and Mya took in a sharp breath. Wolf's eyes, and intelligent. He looked around at them all in bewilderment and then found Mya. For a moment a smile lit his face, but it faded at her expression. She couldn't hold his gaze.

'Who are you?' Caelin demanded again.

Wincing, the stranger pulled himself up awkwardly, his skin blackened with bruises. 'My name...' The words came out clumsily and he touched his tongue. 'I am Ash.' He gazed around at them all, his eyes falling last on Mya. 'I know you.'

'Know me!'

Ben put his arm round her to pull her back.

'Do you remember anything?' Lissa crouched beside him. 'Do you remember being a wolf?'

'I dreamt I was a wolf. Or maybe I was a wolf dreaming I was a man... When I try to reach for my memories, they run away from me like water from a broken pail.'

'Convenient!' Caelin snorted.

Ash assessed the spellward silently. 'I remember I fought at your side.'

'You did that!' Ben agreed. 'Let me get you some of my spare clothes, man, and for goodness' sake let's offer him something to eat!'

Lissa went off at once but neither Mya nor Caelin budged an inch.

'It takes enormous power for an enchantment like the one placed on you,' Feather observed mildly. 'And such things are not done lightly.'

'I understand nothing of enchantments.' Ash gave a shake of his head. 'But of enchantresses...'

'What?' Lissa demanded, handing him a flask of water and a wedge of travel bread. She sat next to him, legs crossed.

'I was, am... I'm a charcoal burner. I lived up in the forest north of Briarton. A woman came to visit me one day, beautiful and seductive, but something in me told me she wasn't what she seemed. I was polite and tried not to encourage her, but she kept returning to visit me. She asked questions about Briarton, casually, as though she wanted to live there. She asked me who I'd seen in my time in the forest, and if I ever had any other visitors. Eventually she tired of my disinterest and offered me money instead. She asked me to tell her if I ever saw two vagabond knights, one a spellward. She wanted me to tell her if they visited Briarton or if anyone there spoke of them or spotted them in their travels between Trade Pass and Ayresport. I'm a simple man, I have no need of riches. I love the forest and the wilds and have all I need there. She wasn't best pleased, she called me a beast, and I was no man to refuse such as her. After that...' He looked up at Mya. 'After there was you, I saw you and I had to follow you.'

Mya's face flushed, as much anger as a blush.

'Did this woman have a name?' Caelin demanded.

'Naksira she called herself. Dark-haired and eyes like a clear blue sky. I see you suspect you know of whom I speak.'

Caelin turned and stalked away. Mya hesitated and then followed him.

'Don't mind them,' Feather said. 'It's been a shock, that's all. Let me find you an ointment for those bruises.'

'I am a stranger to you all,' Ash said quietly, his eyes following Mya. 'I do not begrudge you your suspicion.'

'Come man, not all of us!' Ben patted his shoulder. 'You proved yourself repeatedly wolf or no!'

Feather nodded, remembering the hobyahs with a shudder. 'There's no magic in you. Certainly you didn't change your own shape.'

'Aye, not a trace of the Gift,' Ben confirmed.

'What will you do now?' Lissa asked.

Ash gave a slow shrug. 'Right now, I need to get my head around this and make sense of the missing moments of my life. When last I walked on two legs, the autumn was running toward winter but of what year I couldn't say.'

'We'll give you a moment,' Feather nodded.

Well, this is a tangle and no mistake, Feather trotted through the long grass to check on Jack whose colour had returned a little. He guessed the boy would be in no fit state for at least another day and night. If peace wasn't made between Ash, Caelin, and Mya, it would be an unpleasant wait. He had a pretty good idea what was upsetting the two humans and oddly it was Mya he wasn't sure how to deal with. The two of them had gone off to take care of the horses. If they'd been confiding in each other it would have been something, but as far as Feather could tell they weren't exchanging a word.

'Jack looks a little better,' Feather announced.

'Is he awake?' Ben asked as he approached the brownie.

'Not yet which is probably a mercy. So, what do you make of our present pickle?'

Ben gnawed at his bottom lip. 'For myself I'd be happy to have him along to help us, the more allies we have in this madman's venture the better, but if Caelin and Mya can't see he meant no harm, then animosity will just divide us. It might be better if we sent him on his way back to Briarton and let the lass seek him out later if she has a mind. If there is a later for us of course.'

'Would Ash let himself be sent away?'

'Well… Well I guess we will have to see. Myself I think like you, he'll follow after Mya to protect her if he can.'

Feather nodded. 'We won't be going anywhere far whilst Jack is still out, but let's at least move camp away from these dead succubae, crows are gathering and they'll draw other curious predators.'

'Aye, let's make a push for the edge of the Ward and put at least some danger behind us. I'll go suggest it to Caelin.'

***

Ben rode double with Jack to support him on his old warhorse leaving Ash to ride on Magpie with Feather. Lissa chatted away with Ben and included Ash as much as she could, whilst the others remained mostly silent. Seated behind Ash amongst Jack's supplies Feather couldn't see the once-wolf's face, but he studied him nonetheless. The man rode clumsily and ill at ease though Magpie was a placid horse and needed little control. Ash seemed polite but without the polish of a courtier's manners, the type whose upbringing was rich in pride but not in coin. There was no evidence in his physicality of the profession he claimed, but no knowing how long he'd run as a wolf. In all Feather trusted the man's story; however, he couldn't help a niggle of doubt. After all the man claimed to have withstood all Kasira's attempts at charm and persuasion, which was something the whole of Ayresport had failed to do. Could the man really be so stubbornly principled? He glanced at Caelin and allowed himself a silent chuckle. Yes, humans could be that stubborn. Still…

They came to the edge of the Ward before sunset, several miles closer to Ayresport than where it had stood the last time Caelin had travelled this way. There was little to mark such a significant border, no shimmer of magic, no rainbows or crackling of power, not even a bending of the grass. There was a smell and taste of iron in the air, as though some great battle had spilt gallons of blood fresh upon the earth. Feather shuddered. As immune to iron as brownies were, it was still an unpleasant sensation. Lissa looked pale and drew up her horse.

'That's as close as I can bear.'

'It won't be easy for you even when I invite you through,' Caelin apologised. 'It will allow you passage but not change the nature of the spell. If you wish, you can remain without.'

Lissa shook her head. 'No, I'm going on to Ayresport.'

'Will it remain so unpleasant for the fey all the time they are inside the Ward?' Mya asked in concern.

'Thankfully no,' Caelin replied. 'The Ward itself is like the shell of an egg, and similar in shape, going deep into the ground as well as sheltering from the sky. As you are experiencing yourself, it isn't entirely comfortable to humans never mind fey.'

'I remember when it drew back from Trade Pass, but not much detail of the event, more a memory of the fear. Since then I've always lived and travelled outside of the Ward. I told myself it was the life I was used to, but I think it was the subconscious fear of Ayresport my parents had instilled in me that kept me close to the smaller border towns. Even when my sister left for Ayresport, I made excuses to remain and not move any closer. Part of her feared the city too, or she would never have left Jack with me.'

'Many of us never lived within the Ward.' Ash spoke up. 'Nor accepted the rule of the Lord Vallier. I'm a free man and live within the natural laws of the Valley. Until that witch turned up, none harmed me, and I harmed none.'

'You're not of Ashgrove though.' Lissa frowned.

'My parents are from White Mountain.'

'Oh!' Lissa gasped.

Even Caelin's eyes widened. Mya had heard of White Mountain, everyone had. It had been a prosperous mining town on the northernmost edge of the Valley, producing the stone to build Ayresport, as well as some metals and rarer gems. The Dark Fey had destroyed it, only wraiths walked the empty streets now. The decimation of that once populated town had been the catalyst prompting the invention of the Ward.

'After I was orphaned, I was raised in Wellspring and learnt the truth of the Valley from the Nixies there.'

'So, what brought you to Briarton when you could have made your living at Wellspring and Ashgrove under the guidance of the Dryad and the Druid?' Caelin asked with some suspicion.

'My trade requires I live and work out in the wilds. It's my choice to do so alone. It's also my choice to do my work away from the hamadryads, to whom my burning of even fallen trees, is distressing. Further than that, I don't need to explain myself to you, Sir.'

'If you wish to remain with us further, you will explain yourself!'

'Come now.' Ben held up his hand. 'Lingering here is becoming unbearable for our fey. Let's move on to somewhere more comfortable and then we can sort out once and for all what we wish to do about our friend Wolf-Ash here.'

'For the fey's sake I agree.' Caelin pushed his horse through the invisible barrier of the Ward whereupon he turned about. 'Feather of the Brownies, and Lissa of the Dryads, enter may you, welcome be you.'

Lissa rode forward at once, her eyes wide and her jaw clenched.

'Are you ready?' Ash twisted in his saddle to ask Feather.

Feather drew in a deep breath. 'Go on in, Ash. Let's do it.'

The brownie steeled himself and closed his eyes as Ash urged his nervous horse forward, as though that would keep out the metallic smell and the sensation of standing too close to a tree struck by lightning. Every nerve ending tingled and his mossy hair stood on end. Even his teeth and nails ached as they passed through. Then his ears popped, the pressure around his lungs released, and he drew in a deep breath of clear untainted air.

'Brownie?' Ash looked back over his shoulder in concern.

'I'm well.' He breathed out. 'I go by "Feather." My apologies we've failed to introduce ourselves properly. I guess we felt you already knew us as the wolf. Our leader is Caelin, a spellward and once Knight of Ayresport and consort of Kasira. He was banished and presumed dead once he discovered Kasira was in truth a dark queen of the fey some seven years ago. Ben is also a Knight of Ayresport, but now a poor hedge-knight after choosing to follow Caelin. Ferris is a Scout of Ashgrove as is the half-fey Lissa. Mya… Mya is a young lady of Briarton who is strong in the Gift, as is her nephew Jack. As you've probably gathered, our aim is to enter Ayresport and find a way to expose and defeat Kasira.'

Ash remained silent a while and Feather didn't interrupt. A little ahead of them Caelin consulted with Ferris about where to head for temporary shelter. The two men turned southward and remain far from the main road.

'What is your plan so far?' Ash asked.

'For Mya and Jack to join up as spellwards and gain us information, myself and Ferris are to take lodgings in the city and be sure of an escape route for them. I'm to try to find a way to smuggle Caelin, Lissa and Ben into the city ready to strike at Kasira.'

'Uncomplicated and to the point.' Ash nodded. 'But it leaves Mya and Jack very vulnerable.'

Feather sighed. 'What choice do we have?'

***

They found a small copse of hazel trees in a dip in the landscape at the base of which lay a pond overgrown and clogged with weed. Jack had stirred and Caelin decided it was worth putting the lad through the trauma of waking him up in order to get him to drink some painkillers and restoratives.

'We'll be reaching populated land soon,' Caelin said. 'It'll be harder not to be seen. With the Ward in place we needn't fear fey, so we should travel now at night in order to stay together as long as possible.' He glanced at Ash. 'We must beware of any agents of Kasira's that have been invited through the Ward, however.'

'And there will be spellwards who consider us the enemy,' Ben reminded them. 'And from the sound of it, seekers abroad looking to forcibly recruit. They can both detect power and have ways to spy on the land without actually being able to see us.'

'That's where Lissa and I come in,' Feather said. 'We can set up a spy network of our own.'

Lissa gave a nod. 'I'll make enquiries as to who will help.'

Whilst they settled Jack, Lissa and Feather risked a small amount of magic to send out a call for aid. The first to respond was a blackbird who hopped curiously about Lissa's feet, cocking his head at her.

'He will keep an eye on us here from sun up to sun down if we will feed him,' Lissa said. 'But he is unwilling to travel with us or look ahead.'

'That's a fair bargain,' Feather agreed.

A vixen peered at them from beneath a cluster of bracken and they waited patiently for her to decide about them. At last she loped out into the open and Feather gently touched its mind to impress on it what they needed. The vixen showed Feather an image of cubs not far away, so Feather knew at once she wouldn't be able to range far for them. They agreed for two rabbits she would take over from the blackbird at dusk until dawn, and patrol a little further away than her usual territory if they watched over her cubs.

Feather looked over to where the young man sat regarding Ash wide-eyed, whilst Mya was trying to force more food into him. Jack's skin had an almost green hue and not surprisingly he pushed the bowl of stew away.

'How are you doing my lad?'

'Feather!' Jack managed a genuine smile. 'You're not going to give me a lecture too, are you? I *know* a kill spell should be used rarely, but it *was* dire circumstances.'

'Well, it seemed pretty dire to me,' Feather agreed. Mya opened her mouth to protest but Feather went on quickly. 'However, just be sure it isn't something you come to rely on too much as an option. Had there been other enemies or none of us around, you would have been helpless.'

Jack nodded and Feather guessed he was still too tired and ill to argue much. He just hoped he'd genuinely taken in all of their warnings.

'So, what about Ash then?'

'It is a startling revelation.' Feather looked up at Mya. 'For my part, I believe him about how he came to be a wolf, and he didn't intend to deceive; however, as for his character, I guess that's yet to be proved.'

Mya gazed back at him thoughtfully and then cleared away their food things.

Feather sighed. It was about as much progress as he could expect. Ash's timing couldn't have been worse though the poor soul couldn't have helped it of course. They were about to step up to a dangerous part of their plan and discord was the last thing they needed; it had taken long enough for Caelin and Mya to sort their differences.

***

Ferris returned from scouting and advised they were about two miles away from a small village, a small dairy farm between them and it. Other than that, he'd seen no people or Dark Fey.

'I'd like to continue a while longer together,' Caelin said. 'We're still several miles from the city and I don't want to split up until we must. We'll rest up here until dawn and then be on our way, whether or not Jack is fully recovered, it wouldn't pay to hang around too long in one place.

'Maybe we should try to disguise ourselves and stay in an inn at one of the bigger farmsteads?' Ben suggested.

'You're too well known at the inns.' Caelin shook his head with a disparaging smile. 'And Lissa would stand out too much. No, we must find somewhere either where there are lots of strangers coming and going, or where there are few likely to see us, and nowhere either of us would be known.'

'What about churches?' Mya suggested. 'If we bandage Lissa up a bit, or even all of you, and you act as sick people looking for blessings and alms…'

'Not a bad idea.' Caelin sat up, running the possibility through his mind. 'There's an old church at the fishing village, about three miles north of Ayresport. We can offer to work in return for a little food and the priest's blessing. So then; Mya and Jack you'll enter the city and the training halls of the spellwards. Ferris, you'll go with them as far as you can and then find lodgings in the city. I've saved back what little coin I could to see you through a couple of weeks. Feather, you'll find your own way into the city and try to act as a go-between for Ferris and our apprentice Spellwards. Myself, Lissa and Ben will try to hide out at the church of the fishing village.'

Caelin and Ash regarded each other.

'I would be more use in the city,' Ash said. 'No one will know me unless Kasira herself should stumble across me. If I entered the city separately from the others our association wouldn't be known, and it would give us an extra layer of back up should any of the others be discovered and need help to get out. I'll wait near the city gates at dusk each day until Feather and Ferris make contact, and I'll tell them where I'm staying should anyone need me. I... I would only ask one favour. I have no coin, and nothing but the clothes Ben has kindly lent me. I don't mind sleeping outdoors, but I would rather not starve and I have no skills as a thief!'

'You cannot sleep rough in the city,' Caelin said. 'You'd be arrested and at best thrown out.'

'I have some coin,' Jack offered.

'I also,' Mya said slowly.

'I thank you. I also give you my word I'll pay you back as soon as I am able. Should anything happen to me before that day, let it be known I have coin hidden beneath a flat stone under the water barrel back at my cabin. As far as I'm aware it's still there.'

'Your offer has merit,' Caelin said a little reluctantly. 'Either way, we'll have to trust you to keep our presence and plan a secret, or decide to kill you now. Since I don't wish to kill you here and now, I must choose to trust you.'

'Thanks, I think.'

'Good.' Ben rubbed his hands together. 'I'm glad that's all settled. Right then, I'll take next watch with our friend the blackbird, let's get some rest before we start our night wandering.'

Chapter Sixteen

An anxious knot built up in Mya's stomach as the sun set and they prepared a quick meal. They'd pooled their remaining supplies and money, and Caelin and Ferris divided it based on the needs of the three groups. It had been decided, despite Caelin's reservations, it made sense for Ash to head toward Ayresport first. He would take Feather with him and, whilst the man would camp outside waiting for the guards to open the gates at dawn, Feather would slip away and find his own way inside. If either of them found out anything that might cause them to abandon their plan, they would travel back at once to warn the others.

Ferris, Jack and herself would set out in daylight as would Caelin, Ben and Lissa. The idea of going into the city Mya had heard so much about filled her with dread. Even without the fact they were planning to depose the powerful Queen of the Dark Fey, it was a daunting prospect. She tried to tell herself it would be no different than their occasional trips to Trade Pass, but she knew it wasn't so.

'You're troubled,' Ash said. He didn't look up but continued to tuck the few items they'd given him into a bag as though to remain as unthreatening as possible. It also meant Mya could have pretended not to hear.

'I've never been to Ayresport,' she said finally.

'Nor I.'

When he said nothing more and continued to pack his supplies, she felt compelled to fill the silence.

'I've always taken care of myself and Jack but this is something... unknown.'

'You're a powerful woman, and Jack is not helpless, but if you think when you get there this is something you cannot do, then find me and I'll get you out of the city.' He looked up, and she had to turn away. His eyes were still the wolf's.

'I can't do nothing now I know the truth, and if we fail then who will there be to save the Valley?'

'The valley belongs to the fey.'

She did look at him then, startled by his words. 'You think us humans should leave and hand the Valley over to Kasira?'

He stopped and sat back on his heels thoughtfully. 'It would be one answer, but not the right one. People are here because of the fey. Kasira is here because of the people. The ones who have suffered most are what we call the "Wild Fey," like your Feather. If people left and Kasira remained, they still suffer. If Kasira is defeated but people remained they still suffer unless ...'

'Unless... unless people know the truth. We'd have to not only defeat Kasira, but the Lord Vallier and all those others who have hidden our history and tried to bury the truth.'

Ash nodded. 'Then they have a choice. Like those who live on the edges of the Valley outside the rule of Ayresport. Live in peace with the Wild Fey or leave.'

'Food's up!' Ben called.

Ash stood and walked over to the small cooking fire.

How had the truth been lost? Mya wondered. *How many generations in the Valley had believed this was truly their home and the fey the interlopers?*

***

Feather sopped up the last of the thin vegetable stew with some rough bread and savoured its flavour on his tongue before chewing. He didn't know if he'd get anything to eat at all in the next few days, let alone a hot meal. The others, apart from Lissa, tucked into roast rabbit. Feather wiped out his bowl and then sat patiently waiting. Caelin and Ferris were once again going over the plan and what they should do if any element went wrong. Jack and Ben laughed together, and Lissa stood watch over their camp. Ash sat with quiet self-composure, eating his rabbit with better manners than the old knight. Mya was sparing the man glances whenever she thought no one was looking.

As though he knew he was being watched Ash stood and turned to the brownie in one fluid motion.

'Are you ready?'

Feather pushed his bowl into his small backpack and got to his feet.

'I am.'

At once Feather found himself surrounded as the others wished him good luck and said their farewells. Jack's eyes watered as he tried not to show any emotion, and Mya picked him up to hug him as hard as she dared.

'You be careful!'

'Be careful yourself, Strange Girl!' He lifted a warning finger. 'I will be with you as soon as I can!'

Ash waited patiently, and when Feather joined him they fell into a slow, leisurely stroll, so the small brownie could keep pace.

They covered two miles in companionable silence; the night pleasantly cool and the sky clear and dusted with stars. The wind was strong enough to rustle trees and undergrowth both, and Feather found himself glad of the man's company.

'Would you be offended if I lifted you onto my shoulder for a while?' Ash asked.

'Only my pride.' Feather laughed. 'I take it you wish to make quicker progress and have been too polite to make me walk faster.'

Ash smiled at him showing enough teeth to look wolfish. 'That would be the truth of it.'

'Well, the indignity of being carried seems less than running until I run out of breath, so hoist me up, sir!'

Ash picked him up carefully and let him settle himself on his shoulder. Feather held onto the back of Ash's borrowed shirt to keep his balance. At once Ash strode forward on his long legs and they ate up the miles toward the city. Only twice did they stop on hearing voices. The first time they'd come close to a camp of men which they skirted, the second voices had belonged to a patrol of city guardsmen. There were four, all slouching and silent, none of them taking much notice of the surrounding land. Ash ducked down into the bracken and became so still Feather couldn't even detect his breathing. The men passed on and Ash got to his feet, going on without a word.

It wasn't long before the city stood before them, a dark shadow against the moonlit sea in which a myriad of yellow eyes shone. As they drew closer, Feather's dread grew, for it was vaster than anything he'd imagined. Already from this distance he smelt the taint of human occupancy and the tang of iron. Along the roadside a handful of traders had set up camp, having come too late to be admitted into the city.

'I'll join that camp if I can,' Ash whispered. 'Do you want me to take you closer to the City?'

Feather swallowed. 'No, I best go the rest of the way alone.'

'You have everything you need?'

'Well, an army would be handy if you have one!'

Ash gave a low short laugh. 'I'll have to let you down on that one. I shall try to be near the gates at dusk and at dawn until you can find me to set up a safer meeting place.'

'Then I shall hope to see you tomorrow.'

Ash lifted him down and he stood watching Feather walking away for some time before he turned himself toward the camp.

The night was very dark and the sky open and imposing. Feather gave a little shiver as he hurried toward the towering walls. Tiny trails through the high grass told a tale of mice and rats, and the foxes hunting them. He was surprised at first by the lack of rabbits, but when he thought of how many humans must live within the walls, all wanting feeding, he realised why they were absent. The easiest way for him to find a way in would be for him to cast a spell, as he and Lissa had done to call for aid, the local animals were bound to know any weak spots in the walls. However, the possibility a Spellward or one of Kasira's Dark Fey allies would detect his spell meant it was far too risky an option.

He crept up to the city wall as though it were a sleeping giant. Each stone block in the wall was taller than he and twice as wide as he could reach. All of a sudden, he felt foolish and afraid, what could a tiny fellow like himself hope to do against so big an enemy? He leant his head against the stone and closed his eyes. Maybe he should have hidden in Ash's bag and smuggled himself in that way! He took a deep breath, turned to his right and walked along the wall. It surprised him how little sound came from within the city and wondered if it were down to the strictness of its rules, or the thickness of its walls. He kept glancing behind to be sure nothing was creeping up on him and as he did so the green gleam of an eye made him freeze.

An old dog sat in the grass watching him. It was black and white with a grey muzzle, a missing ear, and one eye closed by a scar. It opened its mouth to loll out its tongue in a pant.

'Well, now!' Feather exclaimed softly. He continued to regard the dog who backed away, legs splayed wide and nose twitching. 'I don't suppose you'd know a way through the wall?'

It cocked its head to listen, but as Feather stepped forward, it scrabbled backward ready to flee. Feather halted, the dog was no threat but probably no help either, its ribs showed through its patchy fur and he felt sorry for it. He took his pack off slowly and reached in for some bread. The dog backed away a little more but halted to sniff when Feather held out the food. He threw it, and the dog came cautiously forward to bolt it down.

Afraid to stay still too long in one place, Feather shrugged his pack back onto his back and continued forward. A soft tread behind him made him turn, and he saw the dog was following him. His heart sank.

'I can't spare you more, my boy. Here, you're not another enchanted man by any chance, are you?'

The dog cocked his head to listen and lolled its tongue back out.

Feather sighed. 'Go on home fellow.'

He trudged on; the dog tagging along. When he stopped, the dog stopped. Eventually he came about the curve of the city wall and the sea was before him. A long silvery carpet of light led across the ripple of the waves to the moon. Feather drew in a deep breath and let his eyes drink in the beautiful sight. The dog nudged at his arm.

'I'm such a fool, I'll regret this,' he told the dog, but dug into his pack for more food, anyway.

The dog spun about with a growl deep in its throat, Feather dropped his pack and grabbed for his sling. Two more dogs edged toward them, hackles high, lips curled back in snarls. Feather's dog circled, head low, putting itself between the dogs and the brownie. Feather put a shot in his sling but the two dogs had already backed away. Slowly and with a last growl they slunk off.

'Well, thanks for that!' Feather hesitantly stroked its shoulder. 'Here, you best have this—'

But before he could pull out any more food, the dog trotted away along the wall.

'Here, hold up!' He hurried after it and, to his amazement, saw it vanish into a thick clump of bracken. When he reached the spot, he found freshly disturbed earth, and getting down on his hands and knees, he pushed through the bracken to find a burrow. He sniffed at the air and studied the tracks. There was no trace of anything but dogs. He took a chance and crawled into the darkness, feeling his way forward with his hands. His hair brushed the tunnel roof and loose earth rained down to trickle down his neck. He hadn't gone far before the tunnel tilted upward, and just as his fingers touched the edge of some brickwork, a cold nose pressed into his face and a wet tongue dragged across his cheek.

'Arrggh, get off!' He pushed past the dog and looked about himself. He was in a building, well, the remains of one anyway. Peering up, he saw they were below ground level in what had once been a cellar. One and a half walls still stood and burnt beams made a skeletal frame.

'Well, boy, I'm in the city.'

The dog wagged its tail.

***

After travelling by night, and hiding out to sleep in the day, Mya found it impossible to do much more than doze. Her thoughts kept going to Feather and worrying how he was doing, then from Feather to Ash. She had to admit he seemed genuine, and also a nice enough person, but she missed Wolf dreadfully and that made her angry.

The sky gradually lightened, and she heard Caelin get up and walk away from their camp. Ferris came back shortly after and she guessed the spellward had relieved him from his watch. She gave up on sleep and got up to pack away her blanket. It wasn't long before they were all up and Mya dawdled through breakfast. There was no putting off this final step of their journey.

Lissa hugged her fiercely and kissed both her and Jack on the mouth before getting tearfully onto her horse. Ben's hug was more reserved and Caelin tentatively shook her hand.

'Try nothing until we are there to back you up.' Caelin gave them a last warning. 'Remember you're there only to gather information and see if you can spot a way to bring out the truth and destroy Kasira.'

'We'll be fine,' Jack replied seriously.

'Come on,' Ferris prompted.

Mya gave a last wave over her shoulder to Lissa, then urged her horse after the others.

They headed directly for the road. It was still early when they reached it, but the sun was well above the horizon and tatters of mist curled toward them from the river Ayre. Mya felt exposed out on the open road and anxiety fluttered from her throat to her stomach. They came to a small hamlet built up around a farmhouse beside the road. There were four small houses, a blacksmith, and a two roomed inn. A group of travellers had gathered to leave and Ferris slowed down to address them.

'Are you headed for Ayresport?'

A man stepped forward and bade his companions be silent. His clothes were well kept, but cheaply tailored, and his long, thick, black beard neatly trimmed.

'We are. Who's asking?'

'My name is Ferris, this is Mya and her nephew Jack, whom I met on the road two days past. I'm a hunter from Adder's Nest. We're heading your way if you'd like to join us? As safe as we are from fey, there's still protection in numbers.'

The man looked them up and down and he relaxed at Mya and Jack's friendly smiles.

'I'm Enrick the trader. This rag tag lot have come with me from Trade Pass, and from Rivertown, along the way. We're about ready to go if you're willing to wait a few moments?'

'Aye, we'll wait.' Ferris nodded.

A young boy brought a pony and wagon around from the farm and Enrick got up beside him. Two late comers stepped out of the inn shouldering heavy looking packs and with them was a young girl in a ragged patchwork dress. Her hair was lank and dark and hung over her face. One man shoved her forward, and she staggered. Mya opened her mouth to protest but Ferris raised a hand to shush her.

'On we go then!' Enrick clucked at the pony and they set off.

Ferris rode up beside the wagon and soon had the trader telling him stories of his journeys through the valley. The man was actually quite interesting, but Mya kept turning her attention back to the bedraggled girl. One of the men accompanying her noticed her interest and showed his teeth in an almost animal snarl, warning her to mind her own business.

'So, these others are just along with you as their guide?' Ferris said as they finished laughing over Enrick's most recent tale. 'You're certainly an experienced traveller.'

'Aye, I take just tuppence a day for advising them on places to stay and safe campsites between inns. Some have travelled with me before, but most are new.'

'You haven't asked us for tuppence.'

Enrick laughed. 'No; but then we are less than half a day from Ayresport and you'd find it easily enough yourselves. So, what brings you here? You have nothing with you to trade.'

'I just fancied a visit to the city and a little more culture than Adder's Nest can provide! Mya and the lad are on their way to join with the spellwards.'

Enrick winced and glanced back at them. 'At least they go of their own choice, and not as the prizes of bounty hunters, like that lass back there. Used to be people had free will in the matter though it's not for the likes of me to say how things should be.'

'No,' Ferris said quietly. 'Can you recommend a good inn for me when we get to Ayresport? Somewhere decent that won't empty my purse in one night!'

Enrick's face broke into a grin. 'I know just the place. Trader's rest, I stay there myself. Rooms are pokey, but clean, an extra five pence gets you a hearty breakfast and supper. It's near the livestock market, so a little on the pungent side, if you get my meaning, hence the lower prices.'

'Sounds reasonable.'

The sound of horses approaching made Ferris turn in his saddle. Mya turned also and saw a group of about a dozen armed men bearing down on them.

'Get off the road!' Enrick shouted.

They scrambled aside, and the horsemen drew up on the road beside them. They wore uniform green cloaks and simple armoured breastplates.

'Who's in charge here?' One soldier demanded.

'That'd be me.' Enrick blurted.

'I recognise you.' The soldier nodded. 'From Trade Pass, yes?'

'That's me!' Enrick grinned nervously. 'Just on my seasonal goods run. These people are keeping me company on the road.'

'Anyone seen a man with a scarred face?'

Enrick gave a puzzled shake of his head.

'Anyone?' The soldier demanded again.

The huddled group all murmured their 'no's'.

'There's a reward for his capture if you do. Bring word to the city guardhouse.' With that the man kicked at his horse and he and his men went pounding away up the road toward the city.

'Well!' Enrick slapped dust off his trousers. 'Someone's upset the Vallier! Let's get going.'

It wasn't long before they caught sight of the city of Ayresport and the sea beyond it. High grey walls spread from the river uphill and then curved back toward the sea. Several buildings towered above the walls, including the castle of the Vallier and the cathedral. One huge spire stood alone toward the far side of the city and Mya guessed it was the spellward's tower.

The gates stood open, the port cullis raised. Men stood stiffly to attention on the walls above and to either side of the gate. They were dressed in a similar fashion to the soldiers they'd met on the road, although they wore cloaks of a rusty brown. They were halted at the gate and Enrick waited patiently as guardsmen rummaged through his wagon. All of them were asked their names, where they came from, and what their business was. Mya couldn't quite determine the expression on the man's face when she said she was volunteering as a spellward, it could have been surprise, possibly pity, but he kept his opinion to himself.

At last they walked through and Mya gazed about in awe.

'Mya!' Jack gasped beside her.

All the buildings were of the same stone as the walls and all had windows made of sparkling glass, some panes so large they filled all the window and not just leaded sections. Covered drains ran alongside each well-kept road, and most buildings had lamps hung outside to light against the night-time. No building stood less than two stories tall and most stretched to four. Even the poorest dwelling in this part of the city surpassed anything built in Trade Pass.

'Mya.' Ferris broke into her reverie. 'Do you want me to escort you and Jack to the Spellward Hall?'

'Oh, yes, please!'

'Enrick, I'll catch up with you at the Trader's Rest shortly.'

'I'll have an ale waiting and tell the inn keep to expect another lodger.' Enrick waved him off good-naturedly.

'It's so big!' Jack breathed.

'It's this way.' Ferris indicated with his head.

They followed the busy main road past shops and a market square. They had to turn off eastward toward the river to skirt around the castle itself that was surrounded by a further wall of stone. After only one wrong turning, they came at last to the home of the Spellwards. Instead of a wall is was surrounded by a high hedge. A tall iron gate closed off the straight path through the gardens to the building nestled below the tower.

'Can I help you?'

A young man in brown robes stood up from his bench in a small stone shelter built beside the gate.

'I'm Mya and this is my nephew, Jack. We've the Gift and have come to join the Spellwards.'

Chapter Seventeen

'Have you been tested?' The young man asked as they dismounted. Ferris stayed on his horse.

'No.' Mya shook her head. 'Both myself and Jack have accidentally done things that make us believe we have it.'

'What things?'

'I boiled a pail of milk just by staring at it when I was angry. Jack has healed injured animals.'

The young man's eyebrows raised in surprise. 'Go on up to the house, follow the path around to the left, and knock at the side door. What about this chap here?'

'We met him on the road and he offered his protection to get us here.'

'You've paid him?'

Mya nodded.

The man flicked his fingers toward the scout. 'Off you go then.'

Ferris glared at the rude dismissal, but turned his horse and left with a nod at Mya. Immediately panic gripped her chest, but she fought it down and forced composure. The young man unlocked the gate and opened it to let them through.

They rode through the immaculate and beautiful garden toward the dark building. The windows were tall and narrow, the glass here leaded and some panes coloured red, yellow, green and blue. Gargoyles leered out from the guttering and several decorative spires mirrored the one looming tower stretching many, many stories, above the rest of the building. It was impossible to see within the dark windows, and the solid front door stood fast and unwelcoming, no sign of any life stirred. When they turned to go around the building, they came face to face with the two bounty hunters who'd brought the young girl to Ayresport. Jack brought Magpie up beside Mya and glared down at the men. They stared smugly back, but shifted hastily off the path when Magpie stepped toward them.

'Bastards.' Jack muttered under his breath.

Mya started in shock, but didn't chastise him.

They dismounted when they came to a small door and Jack knocked firmly. Moments later a woman with her white hair tied back beneath a white cap, and wearing a simple blue dress, opened it.

'Yes?'

'We've come to offer ourselves as spellwards,' Mya said.

'Well, if you truly have the Gift, you are most welcome and much needed.' She looked them both up and down. 'Come on in, I'll get someone to see to the horses.'

They found themselves in a small room with a polished desk, a cabinet full of glasses and two bookcases. Behind the desk was a line of bell pulls and the woman tugged at one.

'Please, take a seat. Can I get you a glass of wine or perhaps a brandy? Have you travelled far?'

'Just a very small brandy please,' Mya said, thinking it might steady her nerves but wanting to keep her wits about her.

A young girl in similar garb to the woman popped her head around the door.

'Berry, please get one of the stable lads around to see to the two horses outside, and let our Lady know we have two more candidates this morning!'

'At once, ma'am.' Berry bobbed a courtesy.

'Have you had many new candidates?' Mya asked casually as the woman poured brandy into two glasses.

'All too few, sadly. We get few volunteers now, what with those nasty false rumours all spellwards die young. There are sometimes accidents with magic of course, but if you're careful and follow your training to the letter, you have nothing to fear.' She smiled kindly at them both and Mya decided the woman believed her own lie. 'A shame they must recruit people more forcefully now, but these are desperate times and once those with the Gift are here and learn the truth, they are happy to stay!'

'I couldn't think of anything I'd rather do than be a spellward and protect the Valley.' Jack said and took a gulp of the brandy. 'We were going to go to an apprentice fair in Trade Pass to get me tested, but when we heard they urgently wanted those with the Gift, we came straight here!'

There was a light knock at the door and Berry popped her head around it again. 'Excuse me, ma'am, Kasira is busy and says to send the new candidates to Hassin for testing, then settle them in if they pass. She'll see them and the new girl, Tealy, after supper.'

'Thank you, Berry.' The woman dismissed her. 'Well then, are you ready for testing?'

Jack stood at once but Mya nodded nervously; they were to meet Kasira so soon?

They were led along a corridor to a double door on which the woman knocked. A low, gravelly voice called out. 'Come in!'

The woman ushered them in and they found themselves in a library with several large comfortable chairs. Mya gazed about in surprise.

'Expected something a little more formal for testing?'

Mya pivoted to see a man sat in one of the chairs. He had a neatly trimmed beard and moustache of a dark-red hue and appeared to be in his late forties. He wore a well-tailored suit the colour of pine needles and placed a delicate cup down on the saucer next to him.

'I'm Hassin, one of the senior spellwards.'

'Mya,' she replied hoarsely and then clearing her throat managed more loudly. 'And my nephew Jack.'

'Welcome to Ayresport.' With a nod at the woman she took her leave and closed the door behind her. 'I don't know what you've heard of testing, but it is a quick and painless process and I see no reason not to do it in comfortable surroundings. Please sit and tell me about yourselves.'

'Our family is from Trade Pass, we're tailors by trade. My parents and sister, Jack's mother, were killed in a raid by succubae. We moved to Briarton when I couldn't keep the shop on my own. We realised we both had the Gift and had intended for Jack to be tested at the next apprentice fair in Trade Pass, but heard those with the Gift were being urgently hunted.' She shrugged. 'We came straight here.'

'And we are glad you did. You both have the Gift.'

'We do?'

He laughed at her surprise, feigned though it was.

'Don't you need to test us?' Jack asked.

Hassin sat back in his chair. 'I'm what's called a "seeker." I can see the aura of power around those with the Gift. Not all seekers have the Gift themselves, but I do. So, you are here to be Spellwards, but do you know what it involves?'

'Protecting the Valley,' Jack replied. 'Giving our power to the Ward to keep it strong.'

'That is a part of it.' Hassin looked at them both intently. 'We each of us give what we can spare every day to hold up the Ward, but that was never what a Spellward was originally for. It's our duty to protect the Valley and its people, and therefore we learn spells of defence and of attack. Mainly our spells are for protection against fey, but they will work against humans too if need be. The main use of the Gift however, its old use, is for healing and for the increase of crops. Originally the Gift was a benign blessing given to the few for the good of many. Only when the Valley was threatened by an incursion of malevolent fey did those with the Gift begin to use it to attack and to kill. Remember that. It was never meant to be a weapon. However, times have changed and our needs have changed. We'll teach you how to protect yourself and how to heal. If you're honourable and suitable, you'll be taught how to use the Gift to fight. How does that sound to you?'

'It sounds fine to me!' Jack said enthusiastically.

Mya nodded. 'And what do you get from us?'

'Your service. You serve the Valley and its people, spending your time and energy in their defence and healing. In return, you get to live in luxury with a generous allowance; but… because of the need to keep up the Ward, you must remain within the city.'

Convenient, Mya thought to herself. Hassin had surprised her, he clearly thought a lot of himself, however he appeared totally genuine. Either he knew nothing of Kasira's duplicity and the murders of spellwards, or he was a very convincing liar. She liked his emphasis on the history of the Gift and that it'd never been meant for violent use.

'What if we decided it isn't for us?' she asked.

'We may yet decide *you* are not what we are looking for.' He leaned forward. 'If that turns out to be the case, then you may go back home, but I have known no one who chose to do so. It can be hard work, but rewarding. Well then, let's get you settled into your rooms and I'll run over what you'll be doing for the next few months.'

He stood and opened the door, gesturing for them to precede him and then led them back along the hall to a large wooden staircase.

'Classrooms and common rooms can be found on the ground floor.' He instructed them. 'Novice quarters are up here on the first floor, the east wing for men, and the west for women. The dining hall for novices is through this door here at the top of the stairs. Servants come and go in the dining room, but only enter novices' rooms every first-day whilst you are at study to clean the room and take your laundry. We do not allow men in the women's quarters and vice versa. The floor above is for senior spellwards and there is no access to novices. You spend six days a week learning, but on the sixth day you get a half day for private study. Seventh-day is yours and you may go into the city, but there is a curfew and you must be back before dark. They serve breakfast at seven, classes begin at eight. We serve the evening meal at dusk. You may walk around the grounds if that's something you enjoy, but only leave the grounds on seventh-day.'

'We have horses.' Jack interrupted. 'I'd like to be able to ride mine and spend time with him.'

'On seventh-day you may, but you will have little time otherwise. The servants will take care of your beasts. Now, there is a lady called Prynarra who will find you in the dining room at breakfast tomorrow morning. She'll assess your training needs and sort out your classes. Jack, wait here for me a moment whilst I take Mya to her room. I'll be back shortly.'

Jack's arms hung loosely at his side and he watched hopelessly as Mya was led away from him. She hadn't considered the two of them would be completely separated within the school, and she couldn't help worry there was something sinister behind it.

'Most rooms are sadly empty these days.' Hassin sighed. 'Those with the Gift are fewer.'

'I was almost put off by rumours spellwards die young sacrificing their powers to keep up the Ward.' She tried to drop in casually. 'How long have you been a spellward?'

'I have served nineteen years.' He glanced down at her. *So; he would have known Caelin and Ben.* 'It's true we lose some to exhaustion, I won't lie to you, but with caution and discipline it can be avoided. There is a certain… pull to the Ward, and it sucks at your energy, but you'll not be allowed near it alone for a long, long time.'

Mya nodded. *How truly blind could these people be?* 'It's reassuring we'll be so closely guarded and taken care of,' she said aloud. 'It's been a little frightening to have this power taking me unawares at the worst times!'

'The fact it has manifested on its own suggests you may be strong.' He chewed at his lower lip, his eyes not leaving hers.

Mya gritted her teeth in consternation at having accidently given that away.

'I can see the aura of the Gift but am not a powerful enough seeker to determine any detail.'

Useful.

'Our stronger Seekers are out looking for people to recruit for our school.'

'There were two bounty hunters we travelled a short way with that had a young girl with them, she looked as though she may have been mistreated and it concerned me.'

They'd stopped outside a door and the dark scowl on Hassin's face made Mya think she'd said too much.

'Yes, she is from an impoverished family who relied on her labour and didn't want her to go. They filled her head with fears she would be ill-used and killed. She'll quickly learn it's lies, and I hope come to trust us. We'll send her family a part of her substantial allowance, and she will have a better life here than ever she could have hoped for at home.'

'I didn't like those bounty hunters.' Mya pushed her luck.

Hassin gave a loud sigh. 'I cannot say I am over fond of those men either, but they are a means to a better end, and one of them has a talent for aura reading. Now then, this is your room.'

He took out a key and, after unlocking the door, handed it to Mya. He pushed the door open and gestured for Mya to go in.

It was a finer room than Mya could have expected for a novice. The main room was divided in two by a wall with a wide arched doorway. The first area contained a fireplace with two comfortable chairs, a small dining table and a desk with an empty bookshelf. Through the arched doorway was a large four posted bed with heavy curtains and another smaller fireplace before which stood a bulbous iron bath. A small kettle was set above the fireplace in the bedroom, and a larger pot for boiling water in the living area. A coal scuttle stood at each fireplace and a stack of wood stood in an alcove in the living room.

'Water can be fetched from a well under the stairs below the ground floor.' Hassin told her. 'You are given an allowance of fuel for the week and you must purchase any more in the city on seventh-day. As well as your weekly allowance as a novice, you'll get a welcome bonus for purchasing necessities for your room. As seventh-day is but two days away we hope you can manage until then?'

'Yes, that will be fine,' Mya murmured.

'In the meantime, you are welcome to bring up teas and snacks from the dining room. We try to discourage drinking alcohol on study days, but you can also take wine from the cellar and note it in the book; we deduct the cost from your weekly allowance.'

Mya nodded.

'If you have questions or need anything for your room, please speak to the housekeeper, Mrs Friend. After your dinner, go with Jack to the small library you met me in, Kasira will join you to welcome you there. Your belongings will be brought up from the stables shortly.'

Mya gave a start and swallowed. 'Thank you.'

Hassin gave a nod and, with a small polite bow, left the room closing the door behind him.

Mya gazed around herself feeling overwhelmed. Even without the subterfuge of being there to spy on Kasira, being here in the school of the spellwards was daunting, and she'd not only brought Jack into it, but had left him alone to fend for himself. Still, there was no point behaving like a helpless girl about it, she was powerful and so was Jack, and their advantage was no one here knew it. Yet.

She moved to the window and checked it had a latch and could be opened. She surveyed the bare stone wall and the ground below where there was nothing but grass to break a fall. The first thing she'd buy in the city would be rope. Telling herself she was being practical rather than paranoid, she then made a careful search of the walls for any spy holes or secret doors, but could find nothing. Taking in a breath she whispered, 'Feather of the brownies enter may you, welcome be you.' She jumped guiltily when someone knocked on the door. As she opened it, she noted as well as the lock, there was a latch on the inside.

'Hello?'

A young boy, neatly dressed in the same blue as the female staff she'd seen, bobbed her a bow as he stood in the doorway struggling to keep a hold of all of her and Jack's baggage.

''Scuse me miss, this is all your stuff from the stables, but I didn't know whose was whose, and didn't like to be going through it.' He tried to bob again and nearly spilled everything out of his arms.

'Oh, let me help you!' Mya ushered him in. 'Just drop it here and I'll sort out what's what.'

'Sure you want me to drop it?' The boy's nostrils flared as he frowned up at her.

'I don't think you could do much else!' She laughed, and he gave her a cautious smile in return. 'You can let go of it on the bed, if that makes you feel better?'

'Oh, gawd miss, I'd be lynched if I stepped in your room!'

'Well drop it there then and I promise I'll take full responsibility. There's nothing in those bags worth anything, anyway.'

The boy hesitated a moment, then bending his knees a little let everything go.

'There, it's all fine, see?' Mya bent to pick out her own bags. 'I'm Mya, what's your name?'

'I'm Reg, Miss.' He peered at her from under his lashes.

'Do you work in the house?'

'Oh, gawd no, Miss. I 'aint suitable for housework. I work in the stables.'

She slowed down her sorting. 'Would you do me a favour? My nephew is rather fond of his horse, Magpie. Would you be able to give the horse a little extra attention? I'll pay you out of my allowance of course.'

'I'd be glad to, Miss.'

'That's very kind, I'm sure you're busy with all the other horses.'

'Oh, not many people keep horses here these days, Miss. You don't need them in the city, and not many spellwards go beyond the walls, and few is sentimental enough to keep hold of their animals long.'

'Oh, I'd hate to lose my horse after what she has been through with me, and Jack would never sell his Magpie. We won't be made to sell them, will we?' Mya was more concerned it would take away a means of escape and independence. She had her doubts they would be able to just walk away should they decide being a spellward 'wasn't for them.'

'Oh no, Miss, I aint heard of anyone being made to do anything; well, not spellwards anyway.'

'You imply people are made to do things?'

Reg stood looking at her wide-eyed and obviously alarmed at what he'd said. 'Well, I only meant us servants get told what to do, Miss, as is right and proper.'

'Oh, please don't be scared of offending me, Reg, I'm only a tailor. More a seamstress these days, actually.'

'Miss...' The boy almost whispered. 'You is a spellward now.'

'Well, that doesn't give me leave to treat anyone badly. I understand if you're wary of me, but I promise you never need fear what you say, or being yourself around me, Reg. I'm grateful for friendship wherever I find it.'

The boy stood looking at her with his mouth open and then with a start remembered where he was.

'Miss I'd best get on. I'm not supposed to hang about in the ladies' wing.'

'Of course, I don't want you getting in trouble. It was nice to meet you, Reg.'

'Thank you, Miss. I promise I'll take extra special care of your horses.'

She gave a nod and closed the door slowly as the stable boy gathered up Jack's belongings. Reg could turn out to be a useful source of information, but she needed to tread lightly and not arouse suspicion so early in her stay. There was no way of knowing who, if anyone, was in league with Kasira. At the thought of the Dark Fey queen, her stomach clenched, already the sky was darkening and it would soon be time to head down to the dining hall for dinner, and from there to their first meeting with Kasira herself.

She tried to distract herself by unpacking what little she had. All of her clothes were rumpled and in need of a clean. With a sinking heart, she realised she had nothing suitable for going down to dinner and meeting Kasira. She picked out the one long skirt she'd not converted into flared riding trousers, and a pretty green blouse, a gift from Nemeth. She hesitated at the door considering whether she'd be best served acting the high and mighty Spellward, or just being herself. She decided on the latter.

She picked up her bucket and headed down the stairs toward the housekeeper's office at the side entrance. She knocked firmly twice and opened the door a little to peer in.

'Mya!' Mrs Friend leapt to her feet. 'What can I do for you?'

'I wondered if you can help me? All of my clothes are spoilt from travelling and I don't want to appear a mess meeting Kasira later. I have little time and I wondered... I know laundry is normally only done on a first-day...'

'Oh, you poor thing, I should have thought of that! Well, there's no time to go into the city now and buy anything, but I can see if Berry can clean up what you have?'

'That would be splendid.' Mya smiled in genuine relief. 'I'm going to take a quick bath. If Berry would be so kind as to bring these up to me, I'd be grateful. I promise I won't make a habit of making extra work for you.'

'Well, you'll be the only one who doesn't then.' Mrs Friend gave a martyred sigh. 'You go ahead and freshen yourself up, leave your clothes with me.'

Mya headed back out to the staircase and opened the door beneath it. She'd expected damp and cold stone steps leading down into a dark cellar, but instead she found carpeted wood and bright oil lamps. She filled her bucket and headed up, tipping water into both the kettle and the large pot. After getting the fires going, she made three more trips to the well before she had enough hot water to fill the bath. On her last trip she paused to peer further up the staircase to the next floor and was surprised to see the stairs ended there. Where was the way up into the tower?

She'd hoped she might bump into Jack, but there was no sign of him or anyone else. The building seemed deserted. Then, as she was rinsing soap out of her hair, she heard voices out in the hallway and the sound of doors closing. She quickly finished and dried herself off, putting on a clean-ish robe whilst she waited for Berry. She was just getting anxious about the time when Berry knocked on the door and called out her name. Mya rushed to open it.

'Oh, Miss!' Berry said breathlessly. 'Sorry to be so long, but I couldn't get the skirt to dry!'

'Don't worry, I appreciate your help at short notice. You're very kind.'

'Not at all, Miss, it's my job. Would you... would you like me to dress your hair?'

Mya raised a hand to touch it self-consciously.

'I wouldn't normally, but it's your first night here and you're meeting Kasira and all... and you have such pretty hair.'

Mya's cheeks tightened with a blush. Pretty was a word she didn't apply to herself. 'I would be *so* grateful. I don't normally do much with it except pin it out of the way.'

'Do you have a comb and pins?' Berry asked. 'I have a few spares I keep in my pinafore.'

'Only a few.' She rummaged in her bags and found a dozen. She handed them to Berry and sat in the chair at the desk. Berry combed through her hair and Mya relaxed at the gentle touch and soothing repetitive strokes.

'Your hair is so thick and glossy.' Berry sighed. 'Mine is as fine as a baby's.'

'Have you worked here long?' Mya asked as Berry curled a lock around her fingers and pinned it.

'Since I was twelve. My mother comes in to do the laundry and she got me the work.'

'Does she do other work in the city the rest of the week?'

'Oh no, Miss. 'Tis only the novices who have their laundry done First-days. The spellwards and Kasira have their laundry done whenever they wish.'

'Still, that's a lot of work to do in one day with all those novices.'

'Oh no, Miss, there are only twelve.'

'So few!' Mya said in genuine shock. 'Even with the call going out for those with the Gift to come forth? And the seekers hunting them out too?'

Berry's hands hovered over Mya's hair and she sensed the girl's hesitation. Did she know more than she wanted to say?

'We haven't had many people come to us in a while. Only recently with the call have a few come in, what with those awful rumours and all.'

'Well, it's a relief to know they're not true.' Mya wished she had a mirror in which she could see the girl's expression.

Berry continued with her hair.

'I'm a bit nervous of meeting the spellwards and Kasira.' Mya eventually broke into Berry's silence. 'They all seem so grand. The building seemed empty today, are they all away?'

'Oh, some of them go down to the hospital to work in the day and do healings. Then there's Petyr and Eddard who specialise in increasing crop yield and go out to the farms. Some attend the council and judgements with the Lord Vallier. They're always working so hard and then, of course, they have to give power to the Ward. Some of them…'

'What?'

Berry stood back. 'Some of them spend a couple of days a week just sleeping to recover their strength. Oh Mya, they so need all you new novices! I have nightmares at night of the Ward failing!'

'Do you know how many spellwards there are?' Mya chanced her luck again.

'There are thirty-two, ten of those are recently trained up from novices. There, I'm finished.'

Mya raised a hand to touch her hair with the tips of her fingers.

'You look lovely.' Berry smiled down at her. 'But you'd better hurry down now before all the best food goes!'

'Thank you so much for today, Berry,' Mya said. 'I shan't forget your kindness.'

Berry blushed but her eyes lit up.

'Well then, off I go!'

They left the room together and Mya purposefully refrained from locking the door. She had nothing worth stealing and nothing that would give her away.

She found Jack anxiously pacing at the top of the stairs. Two young men passed them with curious looks but said nothing.

'Aunt Mya!' His relief was obvious. 'I thought you'd gone in without me.' He was dressed in his best black trousers and a blue shirt, tight across his broadening shoulders. She was relieved his clothing looked clean, but felt a surge of embarrassment at how creased his clothes were. Still, there was little that could be done until they were allowed into the city on seventh-day.

'Miss.' Berry gave a quick curtsey and hurried away.

'We need to find a way of communicating and meeting.' Mya sighed. 'I didn't realise we'd be separated.'

'We can meet for breakfast and lunch at least,' Jack said.

'There are twelve novices and thirty-two spellwards.' She hurriedly whispered what she'd learnt. 'I think Berry may suspect something, but she doesn't trust me enough to say. Come on, we best go in.'

Mya pushed open the doors and tried her best to appear confident. The room was dimly lit with just four oil lamps on the walls and candles on the tables. She was relieved to see there were several tables set out separately and they wouldn't be forced to immediately sit by and converse with strangers. They found an empty table and sat. Mya managed a polite smile to the two men and one woman sat at the table next to them. They appeared to be in their late teens and from their build and appearance hadn't seen the physical labour she and Jack had.

Food was lain out on long tables on one side of the room. As soon as he realised he was to help himself, Jack got up and walked over. Mya followed. There were three large covered dishes, one of which was already empty, one holding slices of lamb, and the third some pork ribs in a sticky red sauce. Mya opted for the lamb, fearful the ribs would be messy to eat, but Jack went straight for the pork. There were plenty of vegetables left warming on racks over candles and

Jack piled them high on his plate. There were decanters of wine and pitchers of water and Mya noted hot water boiling in the huge kettle in the deep fireplace. The array of tea leaves tempted her, but feeling self-conscious in her worn old clothes amongst these well-dressed people, she opted for cold water.

She didn't interrupt Jack until his eating had slowed. She'd taken a cautious glance around the room and had seen no sign of the young girl the bounty hunters had brought here. She caught several of the others in the room looking at her and when she caught their eye she smiled, but no one engaged her.

'I'm looking forward to seventh-day and exploring the city,' she said to Jack.

Jack swallowed his mouthful and nodded. 'Me too. I'd like to ride Magpie down to the sea as well if we get time. I've never seen the sea before.'

Mya caught on at once. It would be the perfect excuse to try to visit the fishing village and find the others at the church if they could. 'Yes, that would be nice, I haven't seen the sea close up either. How's your room?'

'It overlooks the gardens at the rear and I can just see the stables through the trees. I'm almost over the housekeeper's room.'

So, they had put him in a room on the same side as hers but a long way down the corridor. An idea came to Mya as to how she could signal she needed him to meet her, they would just need to sort out some kind of code.

The room had begun to empty and Mya worried they might keep Kasira waiting, but she didn't want to embarrass Jack by making him hurry. Eventually he sat back and put his hands contentedly over his belly.

'Are you ready to go to the library?' Mya asked.

Jack visibly blanched and Mya realised he was as scared at the prospect as she was, but he said, 'I'm ready, Aunt Mya.'

They got up and left the room. Mya was so nervous she felt light-headed and had to hold on to the stair banister. This was no time for her to lose her courage!

A man in his early thirties and an older woman with greying hair passed them in the corridor. The man nodded, and the woman gave them a polite hello. Mya broke into a genuine smile at finally being acknowledged by someone other than the servants.

Then they were at the door of the small library. Mya took a deep breath, and with a glance at Jack, knocked on the door. There was no reply. She tentatively turned the handle and pushed it open. The room was empty. The fire had been lit and two oil lamps stood on small tables. Mya let out the breath she'd been holding, but her stomach remained a tight knot. They entered, and Mya saw someone had set tea things out and water was boiling in a kettle over the fire.

The door opened behind them and Mya's heart flipped over in her chest. She spun around and found herself face to face with the most beautiful woman she'd ever seen. Her hair was as dark as a raven's and tumbled about her bared shoulders in coils. Her eyes were the blue of a summer evening sky, framed by long dark lashes. Her scarlet dress was cut low and tight down to her hips where it flared out into a full skirt. Her smile was genuine and warm, and her aura was compelling; Mya was immediately drawn to the woman despite herself.

'Welcome to Tower Hall. I am Kasira.'

Mya found her voice. 'I'm Mya, and this is my nephew, Jack.'

Jack was staring at Kasira wide-eyed and seemed unable to find his voice.

'Tea?' Kasira offered.

Mya immediately moved to pour it but Kasira raised an elegant hand to stop her. As she moved about the table filling the three cups, Kasira reminded Mya strongly of someone. With a jolt she realised it was Nemeth.

'How are you settling in?' Kasira asked politely.

'My room is lovely.' Mya took the proffered cup and sat down. She glanced at Jack and saw he was still as transfixed as a love-struck boy. She hoped he realised it was the enchantment and would snap out of it. She was fighting her own desire to trust and be enamoured by the fey as it was. Doubts were nibbling at the edges of her resolve; how could this kind and gentle lady be the monster Caelin made her out to be? Was it possible Caelin was the real enemy? She gritted her teeth. She needed to guard herself against the enchantment herself, but she'd keep an open mind until she was certain of the truth.

'I wish I'd thought to buy or make something a little more suitable to wear.' She admitted making conversation. Jack had taken his own tea and sat between Mya and Kasira.

'Ah, of course, you were a tailor before.' Kasira took a dainty sip. 'Did you make that blouse? It's very fine.'

Mya froze, realising her dreadful error. The blouse was from Astol and the material wasn't natural.

'I bought this one in Trade Pass,' she replied quickly. 'It was expensive, but I hoped to copy the cut of it.'

'Well, it looks charming on you, you need not worry about being out of place. It is true spellwards were once only taken from the most influential families of the Valley, but that has not been the case for some time.'

'What about knights?' Jack asked.

Kasira turned her bright smile on the young man. 'Ah, knights are different, mostly because to live as a knight you need money in the first place, for horses and equipment and to feed yourself and your staff. There are a few hedge knights about, I suppose, who take money for deeds. But that goes against the code of a knight, wouldn't you say?'

Jack nodded. 'Yes, it would. Knights are supposed to help those in need, for honour, not reward.'

'Indeed.' Kasira had another delicate sip of her tea and glanced at Mya. Mya had a horrible feeling Kasira knew all about who they were and that they were working with Caelin.

'I always thought I wanted to be a knight,' Jack mused almost to himself. 'But I think being a spellward is just as noble. Will we be able to help in the hospital soon?'

Mya's muscles eased a little at Jack so neatly changing the subject.

'It will be a while before you have learned enough to work there.' Kasira smiled indulgently. 'But when you see Prynarra tomorrow, ask her if you can visit, and I'm sure she will fit it into your schedule.'

'What about the Ward?' Mya asked. 'We hear they badly need us to help keep it, will we give our power soon?'

'Maybe in a week or so. It depends how quickly you learn to call on your power and control its flow. The last thing we want is to rush things and for you to get hurt. All our spellwards are precious to us.'

'There was a young girl who came in with us today.' Jack spoke up. 'I thought she was meeting us here too? Is she okay? She looked rather ill.'

Mya noted for the first time only three cups had been set out on the table.

'She was a little ill.' Concern spread across Kasira's seemingly guileless face. 'She'd had a hard life before she was found and offered the chance to come here. She is a timid little thing and wishes to remain in her room for a while. I am not sure she will be happy here, but she has agreed to give it time. If she goes… well… we will do our best to find her a suitable apprenticeship elsewhere, and will see she is still better off than she was.'

Dread crept like ice through Mya's intestines, after all she had already been through, had the poor young girl already been 'disappeared' by Kasira?

'If she needs friends to help her settle, we'd be happy to be introduced to her,' Jack offered with a glance at Mya.

'That is kind, Jack.' Kasira didn't so much as blink. She finished her tea. 'Well, I shall leave you to relax and talk and have a look around our little library. You are welcome to borrow books for your room but please return them when you are finished with them. I hope you have a good day with Prynarra tomorrow. If you ever need to speak to me, leave a message with Mrs Friend.'

Kasira stood, and Mya and Jack got hastily to their feet. Kasira reached a hand toward Mya and she took it. The fey woman's skin was cool and pleasantly soft.

'Be welcome.' She planted a light kiss on Mya's cheek and then said the same to Jack. 'Make yourselves at home.' She smiled over her shoulder as she swept out of the room and closed the door behind her.

Jack opened his mouth to speak but Mya raised a finger to shush him. They had no way of knowing if anyone listened into their conversation or spied on them in any way.

'She was really lovely,' she said aloud. 'And so beautiful!'

'I've never met a lady like her,' Jack agreed, taking her cue. 'I think I'll love it here even if I can't be a knight.'

'Let's see what books there are,' Mya suggested.

They both made a genuine search through the shelves. There were many tales of romance, war and adventure. There were books on herbs and gardening law, blacksmithing, carpentry and many another occupation. There were a few maps of varying detail and some went beyond the borders of the Valley. Mya's fingers stopped at a section on the history of the Valley. There were only three books. She flicked through the beginning of each and all three seemed to only have conjecture about how people first came to live in the Valley. None said the fey had brought them there. She picked the one that appeared to be the oldest to take up to her room. Jack had picked out a book about the city, containing a few rough sketches of streets and buildings. Mya nodded her approval.

'Well, I guess we'd best get some sleep if we are to be up in time for breakfast,' Mya said. Personally, she didn't expect to get a wink of sleep. She wondered if Ash were waiting still down by the city gate and if Ferris and Feather had met him. She hoped Lissa, Ben and Caelin had found somewhere safe.

Jack gave her a forlorn look, and she knew he didn't relish their separation.

'What about the tea things?' he asked.

'I don't think we're meant to clear them away.' She hesitated. 'But I don't like leaving them.'

'Shall we take them up to the dining room?' Jack suggested. 'We're going that way, anyway.'

'Good idea.'

They cleared everything onto the silver tray and Jack carried it along the hall and up the stairs. Mya opened the door to the dining room; two maids were busy mopping the floor.

'We brought this up from the library.' Jack interrupted them.

The maids exchanged surprised glances.

'Oh, well, leave it on the table there, sir,' one of the maids said.

Jack did so, and they backed out into the hall. Mya glanced around quickly and then gave Jack a hug. He was taller than her now, and she had to stand on tiptoes to whisper. 'If you need me urgently hang clothing over your windowsill and I'll do the same. Take a bucket and we can meet down in the cellar. Be careful.'

She let Jack go and he gave her a solemn nod.

'Well, sleep well, see you in the morning.' Mya steeled herself and turned her back on her nephew to make her way down the hall to her room.

Chapter Eighteen

Feather crept along the wall, trying to keep his feet out of the gutter. He had his sling handy in his belt and a sturdy stick in his hand, which he'd already had to use several times to fend off rats. Despite the lateness of the night, there were still people out in the city streets, and some of them were guards. He was taking a huge risk and there was every chance it was for nothing. Ash and Ferris had said they would try to meet near the gates at dusk, and dusk had long since been and gone. If he had to, he'd hole up here until tomorrow night, there was no way a fey could stroll about the city in broad daylight.

His feet and hips were aching, and he was out of breath by the time he got to the gates. The city was huge to a human, to a little brownie it was beyond vast. He clung to the shadows, assessing the area before him. In front of the gates was a wide, open space, with a well at its centre and wooden scaffolding for market stalls about the edges. A guard house stood to either side of the gate with stairs up onto the walls. Four men stood watch, only one upright and alert and his fellows showing varying degrees of boredom. Streets led off alongside the walls, with the main way directly opposite the gates, and smaller alleys such as the one he now lurked in.

Humans were much fewer now but a drunken trio staggered across the marketplace all shushing each other as they passed the guards. Feather wished he could use his magic to search the area, but he didn't dare, all he had were his eyes. Where in the open square might a man hide to stay out of sight of the guards but still have a good view? An alleyway, such as he himself was in was an obvious answer, but the guard patrols would flush any such person out. He crept forward a little to peer at the buildings and realised several of them were inns with rooms looking out across the marketplace. Would Ash or Ferris be in one of them?

A flare of light drew his attention to the door of one of the inns, a man was standing outside puffing on a pipe. The man took a slow stroll toward the well and leaned against it. The guards watched him for a while but lost interest. The man looked carefully around into the shadows as though searching for someone, and as he turned in Feather's direction, the brownie's heart skipped in relief. He had to stop himself calling out. The marketplace was dark, but for the light from surrounding windows, but it was still frighteningly open. He darted out of his alley and under a market stall. He took a huge risk and stepped out into the rectangle of light from a window briefly, then scuttled back.

Ash stood up and knocked his pipe out against the side of the well, before nonchalantly walking toward the alleyway Feather had come from. When he drew level with the stall, he tripped over his own feet and dropped his bag. As he knelt, he whispered. 'Jump in, my friend.'

Feather didn't need to be asked twice. On hands and knees, he crawled into the bag, and Ash lifted it up to carry it before him.

'I was beginning to fear something had happened to you.' The man admitted. 'I made a few pints last as long as I was able, but I couldn't afford to stay in a market inn any longer.'

'I am grateful you waited as long as you did. Have you seen Ferris?'

'I have. He tells me Mya and Jack were taken into the spellward's school at Tower Hall. He's staying down near the cattle yard.'

'What about you?'

'A dive of a place along the south wall but not too far from the spellwards. How did you get on?'

'Well, I got in.' Feather shifted to let a little more air into the bag. 'The stray dogs have a tunnel under the wall on the north side but it would be too small for a human. It might have been used by smugglers once and filled in. The dogs dug it out again making a den. So, what do we plan? It wouldn't be easy for me to make the distance from here to where we think Caelin is hiding out. That must fall to you or Ferris. If I show you the tunnel will you take me after to this hall of the spellwards?'

'Of course.' Ash nodded. 'Although I'm already pressing my luck wandering about so late, the last thing we need is for guards to ask what I'm up to and what's in my bag! On the other hand, it will need to be night for you to sneak into the Hall and I don't like leaving Mya with no word until tomorrow.'

'Me neither.' Feather sighed. 'I won't ask you to risk—'

'Feather, my friend, any risk I take I do for my own reasons. I am happy to get you to the hall of the spellwards if you are also willing to risk being caught.'

'In a city I stand a better chance with you than alone,' Feather admitted.

'Which way to this smuggler's tunnel of yours?'

As Ash strode through the city, they found more and more of the inns and public houses closing up. Patrons were ushered and sometimes tumbled out into the street, and lamps were extinguished. Twice they passed a patrol of city guards but Ash's easy manner and brief smile rang no alarms with the men.

'This looks like it,' Ash spoke up.

Feather reached up for the edge of the bag and took a peep. The charred carcass of the house stood tucked between buildings against the wall. From his higher position Feather saw the fire had damaged the upper floors of the adjacent houses, and new wood spoke of recent repairs.

'If the tunnel was filled in by city guards, they will probably check it from time to time.' Ash mused. 'If, on the other hand, it was hidden by the smugglers who used to live here, we might have a chance of it staying open. Either way, it's probably being watched. Still, a better option than getting Caelin and the others in through the gate.'

'Could you find out more about it?' Feather asked.

Ash nodded. 'I'll ask about the fire with the pretence of checking how safe the city is from such occurrences. I'm sure Ferris will do a bit of digging too. In the meantime, we need to get the others into the city sooner rather than later. Shall we get on to the Spellward's hall?'

'Yes, please,' Feather agreed.

They had further to go this time and although night was now turning toward morning, and few people were about, Ash kept to his steady unhurried stride. He stuck to the main streets and out in the open, avoiding the narrow alleys and darkened doorways.

'Trouble!' Ash hissed and dropped Feather unceremoniously to the ground. His knee and right hand hit the cobbles hard, and the impact wasn't softened by the bag. He heard scuffling and a grunt, and scrabbled out of the bag to see what was going on. Ash was wrestling with another man and both had knives drawn. The attacker was smaller than Ash, and pitifully thin, but was strong in his desperation. Ash hooked a foot behind the thief's ankle but he didn't quite lose his balance. They disengaged, and the thief tried to dart past Ash and grab the bag. He gave a cry of alarm as Feather slashed at his fingers with his tiny blade. The thief tottered backward, then turned and ran.

'Are you all right?' Ash asked a little breathlessly.

'Just bruised.' Feather winced.

'If he'd asked, I'd have helped him.' Ash gave a shake of his head as he carefully picked up Feather and the bag. 'Let's get going.'

'So, not everything is perfect in the Vallier's great city,' Feather mused.

'Far from it. There's much fear being bred amongst the populace about great hordes of evil fey waiting outside the Ward. Even the word of traders living on the outskirts of the Valley doesn't seem to be enough to dampen such rumours. Spellwards are all but worshipped here, and there is resentment at the outer towns and villages supposedly hiding their people with the Gift for themselves. Someone's done a great job of manipulating public feeling.'

'And I guess since the city's made out to be so safe and so wonderful, few but traders go far enough to experience anything of the world outside the Ward,' Feather guessed.

'The city is isolating itself,' Ash agreed.

The glow of torchlight up ahead heralded a patrol of city guards and Ash decided this time not to risk it. He slipped off the main way and headed partway down a side street before ducking into the gateway of a tin merchant. He waited until the guards had long passed before going back.

'Nearly there,' he said. 'And my inn isn't far on from there.'

'Where can I find you or leave a message if I need you?' Feather asked.

'I read fairly well. We'll find an easily identifiable spot along the hedge of the hall gardens where you can leave me a note. No big fancy words mind.'

'Just as well, I don't know any!' Feather grinned.

'I'll do the same for you. I'll also try to be at our spot after dusk and meet Ferris at his inn after. Right, this is the hedge,' Ash said under his voice.

Feather pulled the rim of the bag down a little. The hedge spread in both directions, perfectly cut and immaculately straight. The only landmark he could see was where it had been allowed to grow up and over the gate and the tiny gatehouse.

'It's a huge plot of land and the hedge curves around all the way to the wall on both sides,' Ash told him. I guess the easiest place to use as a landmark would be where the hedge joins the wall.'

'They obviously have no fear of thieves or spies to choose a hedge rather than a wall.'

Ash strode quickly along the cobbled street.

'I guess only a fool would break into such a place and think they'd get away with stealing.'

'Calling me names, my friend?'

Ash laughed, 'No indeed, I meant no offence. We are both perhaps fools, but you are no thief!'

They reached the edge of the hedge and Ash lowered Feather to the floor.

'The foliage is quite thick almost to the ground.'

'But easy enough to push through,' Feather mused. 'Notice where the main trunks come up from the ground? This third one from the wall splits early and low. Let's leave our messages there. Do you have paper and charcoal?'

'No, but I can get some. You?'

'A little. Here.' He scrabbled about in his pack. He only had one scrap of rough parchment, but he tore it in two and gave half to Ash. 'If you can't wait for me at dusk but need me, wedge a stone in the hedge where the trunk splits, I'll do the same.'

'Good idea,' Ash agreed.

'Now get yourself safely to your inn and I'll see you soon.'

'Good luck to you too.'

'Oh, and Ash.' Feather turned back momentarily as he wormed through the hedge. 'Thank you for your help.'

'You are most welcome.' Ash gave him a small bow.

Feather crawled out onto the lawn, keeping low. The grass was cut so short it barely covered his stubby fingers. He doubted there would be any mole hills, let alone any rabbit burrows, in which he might hide. He took in a deep breath and made a run for it across the grass toward the nearest flower bed. With any luck, if anyone spotted him from the house, they'd think him nothing more than a rabbit. He took a moment to steady his rapidly beating heart and then charged for the next bed. The hall of the spellwards was a great dark shadow with sharp eyes of yellow lamp-light. The false towers looked as spiny as a thorn bush, and the gargoyles appeared to move in his peripheral vision. There was a thrum in the air of magic, and a slight taste of iron and blood from the nearness of the source of the Ward. It made him shudder even though he knew he could pass through it. He wondered what effect it would have on Kasira, living so close to it every day.

His heart sank. There appeared to be nowhere safe for him to hide and no easy way for him to get in without using his brownie magic.

He gritted his teeth and dashed for the cold-looking stone walls. He touched a hand to it and smiled as he sensed no resistance, Mya had welcomed him, if only he could get in!

***

Mya sat on her bed and reached to turn out her lamp, but hesitated. Behind her a cool draught flowed in through the open window. She ran through what they'd learned that day and found it disappointingly little. Tomorrow might be different, tomorrow their tutor would hopefully show them around and she would ask to at least see the Ward. She worried about the young girl who'd come here ahead of them. Perhaps Kasira had been telling the truth and the girl simply needed time alone, but a dreadful fear was dogging her thoughts. What if the girl had not only been forced here, but forcefully given to the Ward?

Mya had stayed up later than she'd intended, reading through the history book. It claimed the Valley had first been settled by a group of families who'd travelled west through what was now known as Trade Pass. The family leading the expedition later founded the line of the Valliers, the rulers, and supposed protectors of the Valley. There was mention the Valley had native fey, who the newcomers mostly lived in peace with. They even named a spriggan as being particularly helpful in starting up their planting. No mention anywhere was given of the royal fey courts, or of the humans of the Valley being their half-breed descendants.

Nothing was said of anyone having the Gift, and the book only glanced over the struggles of the early settlers. It listed bad weather, wild animal attacks and trolls as the main cause of early deaths. There was no mention of illness or disease. The next chapters spoke of how Ayresport had been established as a fishing village and grown into a town. Families had broken away to set up farms of their own, to become hunters, woodcutters and even stone cutters. It was interesting, but told her nothing of what she needed regarding Kasira and how to reveal her for what she was. And what of the Lord Vallier? How much did he comprehend of the truth? If this was the history taught, it was no wonder only those who lived in the wilds with the fey, knew of their origin.

She gasped as something whistled past her ear and hit the wall. She slipped off the bed and keeping low crept across the room to see what it was.

'Elf shot!'

She hurried to the window and peeped over the sill carefully.

'Feather?' She hissed.

A single short bark came from below the window, sounding just like a fox. Mya dared to pull herself up higher and looked directly down. Two dark eyes gleamed up at her.

'Wait!' She whispered.

She peered frantically around the room. Even if she tied her bedding together, she doubted it would be long enough to reach to the ground. With a sinking heart she realised that to let Feather in, she would have to go down and open a door. Water from the well was the best pretext she could think of and she remembered the library had a window. She didn't know the place well enough to guess whether anyone else would be up and about. Their plan had seemed so simple when they were making it and already there were complications. Still, she had to try it.

She listened for a moment with her ear pressed against the door, but couldn't hear anything. She opened it, stepping out into the hall and heading straight for the stairs, trying to keep her demeanour confident rather than stealthy. Most of the candles in the lamps had been extinguished and only one flickered at the top of the stairs. Her shadow danced before her and the walls appeared to move. From the floor above she heard a long and merry laugh, and the low rumble of a man's voice. From the hallway below she heard nothing. She took in a deep breath and started down the stairs, trying not to hurry. The hallway was deserted, and she made her way in the near darkness to the library. She wondered about the other rooms and wished she was brave enough to explore them all, after all, they had advised they were for the use of everyone. There would come a time, she was sure, when she and Jack would have to be bolder in their information gathering.

Heart pounding, she turned the handle of the library door and stepped straight in. The room was in complete darkness but for the orange glow of dying embers in the small fireplace. She felt her way around the table and chairs, and hurrying to the window she let her fingertips find the latch and pushed it open.

'Feather?' She whispered into the night.

'Here!'

She jumped as his voice came from a few inches away. She pulled herself up onto the window ledge and leaned out to reach down for the brownie. He was heavier than she'd expected, but she lifted him and wriggled back into the library.

'My girl, are you and Jack okay?' He asked at once.

'We're fine. We've met Kasira already!' Mya quickly ran through her day and her plans for the next.

'Well Ash and I think we may have a way to get Caelin and the others in, but we must be quick about it,' Feather told her. 'I could see no easy way for me to get in and out of the Hall.'

'You could stay in my room…'

'No, my Girl, I need to pass messages between you and the others and keep my own eyes and ears open.' He considered for a moment. 'Could you invite me into the stables? I should be able to find somewhere to hide there.'

Mya bit at her lip. She didn't dare go out the main door and she didn't want to have to explain herself to Mrs Friend if she was caught in her office at the side entrance. For all she knew, they could lock the Hall up for the night.

She looked at the open window.

Feather read her thoughts. 'If you get caught, it would be even more suspicious than just going out the door.'

'I really don't want to draw attention to myself already when I've found out so little, but I can't leave you with nowhere safe to hide.'

'You and Jack are more important than me, the two of you are the last ones we want caught out. I'll tell you what, let me hide here in the library for today, and if you get a chance go to the stables tomorrow to make the welcome. If you're not able to get in here to see me before sunset tomorrow, I should be able to climb up and let myself out.

The only problem will be I can't close the window behind me.'

Mya reluctantly nodded. 'That will have to do. I feel safer knowing you're down here. This all seems so dauntingly real now. I dread being found out before we're all ready.'

'This was always a risky plan, but we need to ensure people know the truth, rather than see us as evil slayers of the city's heroine. You best get yourself up to bed and try to sleep.'

As if prompted a yawn overtook her. 'I'll do my best to report to you tomorrow. Goodnight, Feather.'

'Goodnight, my girl. Good luck tomorrow.'

Mya slipped back out into the hallway and hurried for the stairs. She had only gone up three when a shadow fell on her. Gasping she looked up to see a man standing at the top of the stairs. He was in his early twenties and dressed in a rich velvet jacket, of a very dark blue, over a black shirt and trousers. His hair was long and dark and his eyes were hidden under heavy brows.

'Well, well,' he said. 'Another recruit and one who likes to be out late. What have you been up to?' He sauntered down the stairs and Mya found herself frozen like a mouse before a snake.

'I… I left my keys in the library earlier and only realised when I tried to lock my room.'

To her consternation he walked around her looking her up and down.

'No need to lock your room at night, I only come in if invited!' He laughed at his own wit. 'I'm Fesla. Come find me if you're lonely.'

With a grin that was probably meant to be friendly, the man stalked off toward the side entrance. Mya didn't wait, but immediately climbed up the stairs two at a time, and rushing to her room closed and locked it behind her.

***

The sound of a door banging woke Mya, and it was a moment before she recalled where she was. The sky through her window was greying, and with a groan she rubbed the sleep from her eyes and got up. Her small fire had long gone out, so she washed quickly in cold water and dressed in the tidiest she had left of her clothes.

She found Jack waiting for her again at the top of the stairs.

'Have you been here long?' She asked and added under her breath, 'Feather is in the library until tonight.'

'Oh, not long,' he replied. 'I didn't sleep too well, how about you?'

'Me neither, I was up late reading that history book from the library. It was interesting but nothing I didn't know already.'

Jack nodded his understanding as they made their way to the dining hall. The room was emptier than it had been the day before. As before food was left out on the long side table and kept warm over candles. She took eggs, bacon and fried bread and sat at the table they'd used before. This time she did make herself some tea, using lemon and mint leaves, in the hope it would wake her up a little.

'Are we late?' Jack asked worriedly as he sat down opposite her with his plate piled high.

'Prynarra isn't here yet, so I don't think so. Maybe we're early.' She looked around, but as before none of the others seemed interested in making eye contact or getting to know the newcomers. It made her uneasy.

She'd almost cleared her plate when an older woman with greying hair walked in. She looked around the room and smiled at Mya. For a moment Mya thought it must be Prynarra, however, the woman walked over to the long table and helped herself to breakfast. She walked back and was about to sit at a table near to them when Mya called out. 'Would you like to join us?'

The woman started, but smiled again and took the chair next to Mya.

'Thank you,' she said. 'I'm Linda.'

'Mya, and this is my nephew, Jack. Is it always this quiet in the mornings?'

'Mostly.' Linda nodded as she picked up her cutlery. 'Most of the novices are youngsters, like Jack here, and seem to prefer a little extra sleep to food.'

'I prefer food.' Jack grinned.

'So I see! I haven't seen you before.'

'Our first day.' Mya told her. 'I'm excited about being shown around but nervous too. Have you been here long?'

'A little over a month. I was surprised they were willing to take me on at my age, but they told me the Gift doesn't dull with years, I just hope my mind is still sharp enough to pick up these new skills!'

'What did you do before?' Mya asked.

'Wife, mother and grandmother. But I've been a midwife for many years and only recently realised my skills in healing were assisted by my Gift. My husband is dead, and my children prosper and don't need me, so I wanted to take a little life back for myself whilst I still had my health.'

Mya nodded. 'What's it like here? You're the first person who's really spoken to us other than Hassin and Kasira, who greeted us.'

Linda finished chewing and Mya guessed she was mulling over her answer. 'There's still a little division over social status. Those from wealthier backgrounds and the Vallier's favoured nobles tend to look down on us tradesmen. Mostly I think it's just everyone's kept so busy, and it's hard to find time to keep up with your old friends, let alone make new ones.'

'But it isn't unpleasant?'

Linda took another mouthful of food. 'It's been a little lonely at times, I suppose, but I've been engrossed in my studies and I'm still glad I came.'

The door opened again and a woman of about Mya's age with blonde hair artfully coiled on her head walked in.

'Ah! Mya and Jack? I'm Prynarra.'

They immediately stood, but the woman made a shooing gesture with her hand.

'No, no, finish your breakfast. Meet me down in Mrs Friend's room when you're ready and fetch yourself a coat as we'll start outside and come back in later.' Without waiting for a reply she vanished out of the door.

'She always leaves me exhausted.' Linda confided.

'Is she one of the spellwards who teach?' Jack asked.

'She is.' Linda nodded. 'She, Hassin and a man called Kristin do most of the teaching.'

Mya was relieved she hadn't named Fesla.

'They're all nice enough, but Prynarra never stops! Hassin can be a little pompous, and Kristin is a bit impatient.'

'Thank you,' Mya said. 'We best get going, maybe we'll catch you at dinner?'

'I'll be here,' Linda smiled.

Mya and Jack fetched their coats from their rooms and hurried to join Prynarra. As soon as they entered the reception room, the Spellward was off out the door and throwing words back at them.

'I was told you want to see the hospital? It's not far and as good a place as any to start. We can chat on the way.'

They didn't have a chance to reply as the woman was already striding off at a challenging speed.

'So, do you both read and write?'

'Very well,' Mya replied, almost running to draw level with her. 'And we know a little of the Valley's geography and history.'

The woman shot her a sharp look, and Mya guessed she knew the Valley's real history.

'Superb! I can get you straight on to your lessons in using your Gift. Did I hear it has materialised on its own? I'd better put you with Hassin.'

Already they were halfway across the gardens and Mya kicked herself, she hadn't asked to go to the stables. She'd have to be sure to insist when they got back.

'He'll be teaching us both at the same time?' Jack sounded relieved.

'Yes, along with four others who are into their eighth month of training. Don't worry about how far ahead they are though, we have few spellwards to spare for teaching and all classes are mixed.'

'How long do most people take to train?' Jack asked.

'Oh, you never stop learning and training.' Prynarra pushed open the gate and waved the robed gatekeeper aside with an imperious hand. 'But until you reach the status of Spellward and take on duties? It varies from person to person, generally between three and five years.'

Mya's eyes widened as she thought of how quickly Caelin had pushed his training on them in Astol. How much had he missed out of what they needed to learn? Yet she'd been able to defeat Nemeth in her challenge. Perhaps the spellwards were just more cautious and thorough, but once again she questioned how much she really knew of Caelin, and whether they could completely trust him.

The sun was still low over the Valley and the heavy clouds made it a dull and dreary day. Several wagons were out making deliveries of fresh foods to the big houses, and downcast servants hurried on errands of their employers. Prynarra led them around to the western sector of the city and, although they didn't go as far as the docks, the area was noisy with the sound of gulls.

When they came to the hospital Mya was shocked to see a huddle of ragged men and women on the street outside. The building was a solid square of large grey stone with barred windows and a tall iron fence. Two men in leathers and lightly studded armour guarded the deep-set doorway.

'It's not open to the city for an hour, so we'll not be too much in the way,' Prynarra explained.

Mya watched in horror as the spellward stepped over the huddled people and 'tutted' as she was forced to step on the edge of a tattered robe.

'Please!' One woman begged, and at once the others stirred and pleaded to be allowed into the hospital.

Mya blushed with embarrassment as she and Jack had to force their way past.

'Will they be allowed in when the hospital opens?' Jack hopped up the steep step into the dark porch. One of the hospital guards opened the door for them and Prynarra nodded her thanks.

'No. These people have no money and we cannot afford to treat everyone who comes. When our paying customers have left, we may let one or two in, if the spellwards have any energy left.' Prynarra saw Mya's expression. 'If we healed everyone who came we'd not have the energy left to maintain the Ward, and the spellwards would become so run down they would be useless! It may sound harsh, but our rules are not without good reason. We sometimes get donations, and those we use to pay for bandages and medicines for the poor, so we do what we can.'

Mya nodded meekly, but she couldn't help thinking the healing Gift shouldn't be just for those able to pay, but instead for those most in need. She wondered if things had always been so, or if this were Kasira's influence. Then she smiled as she recalled she'd first met Feather all that time ago because she couldn't afford the healer's fee and had had to fetch her own willow bark.

As soon as she stepped into the hospital Mya was assailed by the strong smell of vinegar and lemon and she guessed they used them to scrub the floors. There were no carpets, only cold tiles as dark as slate. Tallow candles burned brightly in lamps along the wall. Two women in leather aprons came out of one room, bobbed a curtsy, then continued conferring as they disappeared up some stairs.

'We've two rooms for healing with the Gift and a third for non-magical surgeries. There's a laundry and a kitchen, rooms in the attic for the live-in staff, and a rest room for spellwards. There are four private rooms for the recovery of our more illustrious clients, and four rooms with ten beds in each for our other patients. There's also a cellar room for our charity work.'

Mya winced.

'Any questions yet?' Prynarra spun around to face them.

'How many spellwards work here?' Jack asked.

'There are six who specialise in healing and all the others assist in minor healings on rotation. If you wanted to specialise, it takes much longer to train for this than for defensive magic. It's not only the magic you need to understand, but non-magical healing skills as well. Redda was on night duty, let me check he's awake, and then you can meet him.'

Prynarra bustled up the narrow stairway.

'I don't think we'll find anything sinister here.' Jack scowled. 'Other than the Vallier and spellwards milking the population for every copper.'

'Still, might be worth checking how much Kasira gets involved in the place,' Mya suggested. They quickly hushed as the sound of footsteps echoed in the stairwell.

Prynarra's face appeared around the wall. 'Come on up!'

Without waiting the woman was off up the steps again and with a grin at each other Mya and Jack both ran to the stairs to catch her up. They reached the top in time to see her disappear into a room. They both hesitated in the doorway. Prynarra was perched on the edge of a desk surrounded by three large, dark-wood chairs, cushioned in green velvet. A small cabinet was clustered with decanters of coloured liquids. On a long sofa a man in a tousled blue shirt lay propped up on his elbow. His hair was light brown and long enough to curl, he had about three days' worth of stubble and dark circles under his eyes.

On seeing Mya and Jack he scrambled up and shook both their hands with an enthusiastic warmth.

'Mya, Jack.' His eyes crinkled in a genuine smile. 'Thank you for visiting our hospital.'

'Thank you for taking the time to meet us, you look...'

'A mess!'

'Tired, I was going to say!' Mya corrected him in embarrassment.

'Exhausted, more like.' Prynarra amended. 'When did you last go back to the Hall?'

Redda dismissed her question with a shrug. 'So, are the two of you really interested in specialising in healing? As you can see, we're understaffed and overworked. The duty doesn't appeal to many.'

'It certainly appeals to me,' Mya replied honestly. 'I know it's important to keep the Ward going and defend the Valley from fey, but healing would be more rewarding. I must admit though, I was disappointed not everyone is helped. Back in Briarton we had a greedy old miser of a healer who held debts over so many desperate people's heads, I would love to go back one day and take him down a peg!'

Redda laughed, but Prynarra pursed her lips.

'Well, I hope you get your wish, but as Prynarra has probably explained, we cannot run our hospital on air and we must also eat to get the energy to heal others. As much as I'd love to give my services for free, it's not practical. Perhaps if we had many more with the Gift, we'd be able to venture out to smaller towns and villages and trade our skills for pigs and turnips! But alas, it's not so, and idealists like you and I, Mya, will have to dream of such times.'

Mya smiled back at him. She wondered if he knew of Ashgrove, surely he would love such a place?

'What of you, Jack?' Redda asked.

'I dreamed once of being a knight.' He smiled ruefully. 'But thought the best I would get was a blacksmith's apprentice. Ben Flame was always my hero, but now I can be a spellward, and hopefully be as much a saviour to the Valley as Kasira!'

For a moment Mya thought Redda's eyes had hardened, or had it been her imagination?

'Hassin does some work with metals.' Prynarra told Jack. 'Mostly silver, but if that interests you, I'm sure he'd be happy to show you his work. He has been experimenting with imbuing objects with magical energy.'

'Yes, I'd be interested. In Briarton the blacksmith mostly used me for errands, but he'd begun to show me what he was doing.'

'So, does Kasira specialise in defensive magic, or is she a healer?' Mya tried to ask casually.

'She's too busy to come here,' Prynarra said a little defensively. 'As well as protecting the Ward and running Tower Hall, she assists the Vallier with the running of the city. Lately she's also been working hard at recruiting more novices and has herself ridden out to the Valley borderlands to defend them from Dark Fey. Just recently she killed two succubae out to the northeast.'

Mya restrained herself from glancing at Jack.

'Amazing!' Jack said without the slightest hint of sarcasm.

'It's a shame news of such deeds doesn't seem to reach the outer towns,' Mya told them. 'Many feel abandoned outside of the Ward, and that Ayresport only takes care of itself.'

'Ungrateful peasants!' Prynarra exclaimed. 'Spellwards ar–'

'Working hard,' Redda interrupted quickly. 'To do *all* they can for all the Valley.'

What had the woman really meant to say? Had Prynarra almost admitted the truth that spellwards were indeed dying to keep the Ward going? Might Prynarra be someone Mya could possibly win over to show her the truth about Kasira? And what of Redda? She'd begun to like the man and even suspected he might not like Kasira, but he'd been quick to cover up what was going on.

'So, the sooner you get yourself trained up the better.' Redda grinned at Mya and she forced a smile in return.

'Well, we best get out of your way.' Prynarra stood. 'Make sure you get some proper rest!'

'I'll head back to the Hall in a few hours after Lilly and Rian get here,' Redda promised.

'See you do!'

With that, Prynarra marched from the room without waiting to see if Mya and Jack followed.

'Thank you!' Jack called over his shoulder as they scurried after the disappearing woman.

Prynarra allowed them to take a discreet peep into one of the private recovery rooms, and one of the larger common recovery rooms. As they left the hospital people were being allowed in to be questioned by non-gifted healing assistants. Mya felt thoroughly ashamed as they passed the beggars and couldn't meet anyone's eyes.

'I'm going to try to use some of my allowance to help them,' Jack whispered.

'Me too,' Mya nodded firmly.

On their way back to the hall, Prynarra pointed out some shops she recommended. They took a stroll around the Hall's gardens and were shown an outdoor training area away from the main building. It was a patchwork of burnt, charred ground and over-grown plants. Mya asked to see the stables and Prynarra appeared happy to oblige. Whilst checking on her horse, Mya was able to discreetly make the Welcome for Feather.

They returned to the Hall and were shown the teaching rooms not presently being used.

'This one is where you should come tomorrow to join Hassin's lesson.' Prynarra pointed at a closed door. There was little to distinguish it, so Mya made a count from the library, and noted it was four doors away. 'It would normally be your half day, but Hassin may wish you to stay a little after lunch to get to know you better.'

'That would be fine,' Mya said, although the idea of starting lessons in a room of strangers made her a little queasy. Like Jack, she'd been taught at home by her family.

'Well.' Prynarra clasped her hands together and beamed at them both. 'It's well past lunch and you must be hungry. Is there anything else you need of me today?'

'Well.' Mya looked down at the floor, shifting her weight as a blush burned her cheeks. 'Our allowance. We need better clothes and were hoping to go into the city on seventh-day.'

'See Mrs Friend on Seventh-day morning, she will sort your allowance.'

'Thank you. I don't suppose... would Jack and I be allowed to have a look at the Ward?'

Prynarra gave her such a penetrating gaze Mya feared she'd somehow guessed why they were here.

'Hmm. Well you both seem steady minded and sensible enough, so I should think you'll be safe enough with me, without me worrying about you doing anything daft. Though we could wait until later and see if Kasira has time to take you?'

'Oh, I'm sure we will be safe enough with you,' Mya insisted.

'Very well. Get some lunch quickly and I'll come fetch you from the dining room in a bit.'

***

The dining room was deserted, and little was left out on the side table, but they put together plates of cold cuts, cheese and fruit.

'What do you think?' Jack whispered, glancing around to double check they were alone. 'Did you see how Redda flinched at Ben's name and stopped Prynarra letting something slip?'

'Ben's name?' Mya was startled. 'I thought it was calling Kasira a "saviour" he didn't like.'

They both contemplated the conversation as they ate but Mya couldn't be certain which of them had the right of it.

'Prynarra is confusing too,' Jack spoke up. 'I like her, she's funny without meaning to be, and seems helpful, not to mention her slip that nearly let out the truth.'

'But?'

'She was horrible about those poor people who can't afford healing and thinks people outside the city are worthless peasants!'

'Whether we like her doesn't really matter,' Mya mused. 'What we have to decide is if we can trust her enough to try to reveal the truth about Kasira to her.'

They finished eating in silence, both lost in thought, and Mya jumped when the doors opened.

'Ready?' Prynarra demanded cheerfully. 'Kasira was free after all, and has kindly agreed to go with us!'

Chapter Nineteen

Mya spun in her chair to see the two women waiting in the doorway. Kasira was smiling warmly and Mya felt a tug of compelling attraction, an overwhelming desire to be close to the woman, to confide in her, be protected by her. She was wearing a wine-red blouse and full skirt, and her curling black hair was loose about her shoulders. Mya fought against her need to touch it. She bit hard on her tongue and turned back to Jack; seeing his rapt expression she pressed her foot down on his toes.

'That's so kind!' Mya got to her feet and crossed the room to them. She felt like a half-plucked chicken next to a beautiful swan.

'Oh, not at all,' Kasira demurred. 'It is good to have an opportunity to get to know our new students.'

'This way then!' Prynarra headed off at once.

Kasira gave them both a conspiratorial smile and indicated they should precede her. Cold ants crawled up and down Mya's spine at having the Dark Fey queen walking behind her where she couldn't watch her. Prynarra moved to the top of the stairs, but rather than going down she turned and ascended the next flight to the spellward's floor. Mya rubbed at her chest with one hand, her heart was beating fast and sweat prickled on her back. She had to stop herself constantly glancing at Jack. The difference on this floor was striking. Expensive olive-oil lamps adorned the walls along with ornately framed paintings. Most were portraits of men and women although a few depicted battling spellwards. Along the length of the floor in both directions a thick rug ran in which where the impressions of shoes. Prynarra paid no regard to the damage she might do to the deep and well-kept pile, but strode on, and Mya self-consciously did the same. Jack moved over to walk on the thinner carpet.

Roughly half way down the woman stopped outside an oak door carved with images of trees and nymphs. Ironic that which they'd driven from the city was considered a subject for beautiful art. Prynarra took out a large iron key and unlocked the door. Mya wondered how many of the spellwards had one. Was this a sign Kasira trusted Prynarra?

Prynarra pushed the heavy door open and entered the room. Mya hesitated and followed.

A gasp escaped from her lips.

It was as though she'd walked into another world, and one uncomfortably similar to the Hall of Pillars. At the centre of the room was a spiral staircase of polished metal, around which ran a banister of iron and copper ivy. Six pillars circled the stairs, all of black marble and perfectly straight. At the tops of each were rays of yellow sunlight painted on the raised ceiling. On the walls were murals of forests and above them a cloudy sky through which sylphs peeped. Mya realised this must be the way up to the tower.

She jumped as Kasira spoke beside her. 'Stunning, isn't it?'

'Yes,' she replied. 'Is it a part of the original building?'

'The pillars are original and part of the tower structure,' Kasira told her and reached out an elegant hand to brush fondly at the stone. 'The paintings were added some hundred years ago. The new stairway was a gift to us from the Lord Vallier in return for our services to the Valley.'

'Will we get to meet him?' Jack asked.

'At some point, you will.' Kasira turned her dazzling smile on him. 'Let's go up.'

Mya had to suppress an overwhelming urge to grab Jack's hand and hold it as they headed for the stairs. She fixed a smile on her face and prayed Kasira couldn't sense her fear or hear her heart pounding. As before, Prynarra went ahead, and Kasira insisted on following last. Their steps shook the metal stairway and Mya held tight to the banister. As they climbed above the level of the painted ceiling, the stairs were closed in by whitewashed stone. Now and then the stairs levelled out to a small platform before doors as ornately carved as the first they'd come through.

'What are these rooms?' Jack asked.

'One is the spellward's library.' Prynarra called back over her shoulder. 'Only senior spellwards have access to it. Then there's our viewing room, which is used as a common room, and Kasira's private chambers. At the highest point is the Ward room.'

So, to get to the Ward room someone would have to have a key to the tower and then pass by Kasira's room. That meant they'd have to find one of the senior spellwards to trust and try to get them to witness Kasira feeding someone to the Ward. Or, find some way to get her to reveal she was fey. Mya was so deep in contemplation on how that might be done, she almost walked into Jack when he halted.

'This is the Ward room,' Prynarra announced, and she drew her keys out again, selecting one made of bronze.

'Do all spellwards have keys so they can come up and give power to the Ward whenever they can?' Mya asked.

'Senior spellwards do.' It was Kasira who replied, and Mya could detect no suspicion or coldness in her voice. 'The Ward can be dangerous, and only those who are strong and well trained are trusted to come alone. It is safer that way as you are about to find out.'

A shudder ran through Mya.

Prynarra opened the door, but instead of pushing it inward, it opened out onto the platform and Jack had to step back out of the way. Inside were a set of bare stone steps, bathed in a flickering red light.

'It is not as scary as it looks.' Kasira purred in Mya's ear, making her jump. 'But stay close.'

Mya gritted her teeth and nodded.

Prynarra had already bounced up the steps with her usual enthusiasm, and Jack had hesitated only a moment before following. Mya's skin prickled as she imagined Kasira's eyes on her, or a hand lifting with a knife. She dared not even reach out her senses to warn if Kasira called for power; even that tiniest of uses of the Gift might give away the fact Mya knew much more than she should already. Had they overstepped and tried to find out too much too soon?

As she ascended the steps, the metallic tang of the Ward stung the back of her throat and she coughed. She wondered again how Kasira could bear to be here; Royal Fey were more resilient to iron but certainly not immune. She'd considered somehow using iron to reveal Kasira's true nature, but judging by this, it would take much more to break her enchantment.

As her head reached the height of the Ward room floor, she gasped. Before her stood a red vortex of swirling particles growing wider the higher it rose and vanishing through the vaulted ceiling. It was brighter and more solid at its origin, becoming more transparent the further it moved away. On the floor at its base was a circle of iron filled with wrought patterns and symbols Mya didn't recognize. What was clear though, was to stop the Ward, someone would either have to let it run out of power, or break this heavy metal seal.

She noticed a subtle tugging sensation at the edges of her consciousness, almost a compulsion.

Prynarra had taken Jack's arm to stop him; however, Kasira said to Mya, 'Take a step forward.'

Mya turned and was caught immediately by the Fey Queen's deep blue eyes, it was like looking into a fathomless well in which the sky was reflected. It was hard to see beyond the light playing on their surface, and yet she found herself drawn in.

Kasira smiled, but it was the smile of a predator.

Mya was rooted to the spot, unable to tear her eyes away from those of the fey queen. If she refused her request, she would know Mya didn't trust her and her enchantment didn't hold her completely in its grip, but if she stepped forward, would this achingly beautiful woman feed her to the Ward?

Was their attempt to free the Valley and save those with the Gift over before it had even begun?

With a huge amount of will, Mya tore her eyes away and looked instead at the spinning threads of power spiralling up from the seal. Gritting her teeth, she forced one knee to lift and stepped forward. The pull of the Ward increased significantly, but wasn't forceful, rather it was teasing and tantalising like an itch that was impossible not to scratch. The desire to call up power and let it go was overwhelming.

'Do you feel a strange tugging sensation?' Kasira asked gently. 'Irresistible isn't it?'

'It's like a tickle inside my chest,' Mya replied, stepping back quickly.

'Once you are trained and able to call up your power at will, it is even harder to resist,' Prynarra told them sternly. 'You understand why it is dangerous?'

'Would it suck everything out of you?' Jack asked.

Kasira nodded. 'If you didn't have the strength or discipline to stop.'

'Or someone to protect you,' Prynarra added.

'Come away,' Kasira said, and without waiting turned to the stairs and descended. Mya didn't need to be asked again, but followed immediately, trusting Jack would do the same. She didn't relax until they'd passed through the solid door of the pillar room and back out into the corridor.

'It's been a busy day for you,' Prynarra said. 'We'll finish for today and you can have time for yourselves. Report to

Hassin tomorrow morning, but if you need anything in the meantime, Mrs Friend will pass me any messages.'

Both Mya and Jack thanked her at once.

'I hope you enjoy learning with us,' Kasira said graciously.

'We've learnt a lot already,' Jack replied and Mya had to restrain herself from giving him a warning look.

Kasira gave Jack a delighted smile that would have melted the hardest of hearts.

'Thank you for your time.' Mya gave a quick bob of a curtsey and walked away as quickly as she politely could.

'What do you fancy doing?' Mya asked Jack as they reached the top of the stairs. 'Shall we see if the Library is free?'

'Yeah, sounds good,' Jack agreed. 'Although I'd quite like some fresh air out in the garden.'

'I'm sure we can do both.' Mya resisted the temptation to turn and check if Prynarra and Kasira were still in the hallway watching them. As they reached the bottom of the stairs the young maid, Berry, almost ran into them.

'Berry!' Mya held her hands out to stop a collision.

'Oh, Miss!' Berry said breathlessly. 'Good news! We have another new candidate in the Library. He is just being tested for the Gift, but Mrs Friend is so sure she has asked me to quickly freshen up a room.'

'Who is he?' Mya asked.

'Apparently it's the Lord Vallier's youngest child.'

***

Feather stood up on his tiptoes to stretch and rolled his shoulders. His hiding place between one of the bookcases and the stone wall by the window was extremely cramped and there was no room to sit down. Twice someone had come into the room, taken books on and off the shelves, and quietly gone out again. Then the door burst open and at least two people entered, one a mature sounding woman full of enthusiasm.

'Now wait just in here, young sir, someone will be along shortly.'

There was no reply but Feather could hear someone moving about in the room. He didn't dare move and he cursed silently as his hip ached abominably. It felt like an eternity before the door opened again and he used the sound to hide his movement as he shifted position.

'Ah, so you are Emon? My name is Hassin and I'm a teacher and "seeker" for Kasira. That means I'm able to test if someone has the Gift.'

'Lady Kasira has told me I have the Gift.' The boy sounded very young.

'Did she tell you to come here?'

At the silence Feather guessed the boy was shaking his head. 'She told me I wasn't old enough to come here yet, but I am! I want to be a Spellward and protect Kasira!'

So, old enough to be enamoured by enchantment, Feather thought, *and what does Kasira think she will gain by obtaining this boy?*

'Does your father know you're here?'

'No, Sir.'

'Well, you certainly have the Gift, it's unusual to manifest so strongly in one so young, especially since it runs in families and none of yours have it.'

There was a long pause and Feather wished he knew what was happening. Finally, the boy murmured something.

'Pardon?' Hassin demanded.

'I said the Lady Vallier isn't my mother.'

'A Bastard, eh?' Hassin announced cruelly. 'Who *is* your mother?'

'I was fostered in the city, sir.'

'Your mother?'

The door flew open and Feather shrank back at the forcefulness of the sound.

'Mrs Friend, take the boy up to his room. Emon, my brave man, I will be up to talk to you soon.'

'Yes, Ma'am.'

After some scuffling of feet, the door closed again.

'Who is his mother?' Hassin demanded again.

'I am his mother!'

'You! Bu–'

'Oh Hass, this is no time for jealousy. It was a long time ago I seduced the Lord Vallier in order to control him and the boy has been a useful tool to get him to do what I want. The Vallier has been a little too troublesome of late, so I want the boy under this roof and completely loyal to me.'

'It's not Caelin's then?' Hassin asked sulkily.

Feather's hand flew to his mouth in sudden fear, the woman must be Kasira!

'Now, now, don't be petty my love.'

'Has there been any more sign of that renegade?'

'No. I am still convinced he was responsible for my two succubae; it is as well he does not know how much it has set back my plans.'

There was a chink of glass and liquid was poured.

'Do you have a new plan for killing the other spellwards, my Queen?'

Feather stiffened.

Kasira sighed. 'Without the succubae to drain several in one go, it will be a harder task. It takes too long to feed the humans to the Ward one at a time and there is too much suspicion. I am so close! There are few now left with the Gift, but too many trained spellwards still to just drop the Ward and let my fey take care of them.'

'Then what will we do?'

There was a long silence.

'Everything is nearly in place. I have summoned revenants within the Ward, they will strike at the hospital as soon as I command it. You must deal with your students and feed them to the Ward. I have given you the strongest ones to dispose of, then break the Ward seal. My Boggle captain will help me destroy the others here.'

'How long until your army is all in place?'

'Maybe three days.'

Feather trembled.

'I take it that fool Vallier is panicking?'

'As much as he has hidden the reports of Fey attacks in the Valley from his people, he can't ignore them himself. He is a desperate man, he knows the Ward will eventually fail, and we are running out of spellwards. He is also pathetically eaten up with guilt over the deaths of those with the Gift who were forced here with his knowledge. I fear it might cause him to do something rash.'

'Hence his son.'

'Hence his son. The idiot still does not even suspect the truth of the matter, but he is thinking of dropping the Ward. Too early, and my people will not be in place, giving the spellwards a small chance of holding them off. Just a few more days, my love, and we will rule the Valley and the humans will be the playthings of the fey as it should have been.'

The door opened, and a startled voice said; 'Oh my goodness, I'm so sorry, I thought the room was empty.'

'Oh, don't worry, we were just talking.' Kasira's voice was like honey. 'Do come on in, Linda.'

Someone shuffled into the room and Feather heard glasses being set down on the table.

'Well, I have a new student to greet.' Kasira rose from her chair with a rustle of cloth. 'I will see you later, Hassin.'

'My Lady.'

The door closed. Hassin excused himself and left as well. Linda lingered a while and Feather listened to her soft tread before she too left the room. The small brownie squeezed out from behind the bookcase and sagged to the carpet as his knees buckled.

Three days.

Three days to save the Valley.

Chapter Twenty

Mya and Jack passed the Library slowly, but heard nothing from inside. Mrs Friend was hovering at the end of the hall outside her room in a state of excitement.

She waved a hand at them. 'Come out of the way, quickly.'

'What's happening?' Mya asked.

'Well! The Lord Vallier's illegitimate son has run away from his fosterer and turned up here looking for Kasira, there's going to be trouble over this.'

'Trouble?'

Mrs Friend froze and her expression changed to one of guardedness as she realised she'd probably said too much. 'Well, obviously the Vallier won't be happy. Are you off out?'

'Oh, yes, we wanted to get some fresh air before dinner–'

'Ah, my Lady!' Mrs Friend pushed past them and Mya turned to see Kasira walking serenely along the hall toward them.

'Let's go.' Mya told Jack, and they crossed through the housekeeper's room and out the side door.

'I wonder what that's all about,' Jack said.

'With any luck, Feather will be able to fill us in.' Mya

headed away from the building into the gardens, avoiding the temptation to hang about and observe. They discussed all they'd seen, and what they'd made of the Ward. As daylight faded, they made another attempt at gaining access to the library. Mrs Friend wasn't at her desk and the hallway was empty.

They paused to listen outside the library door, and on hearing nothing, Mya pushed it open. The room was empty. Closing the door behind them, Mya called out anxiously. 'Feather?'

'Oh, my girl!' There was a scraping of wooden buttons and Feather squeezed himself out from behind a bookcase. 'I have such dreadful news.'

Feather related to them all he'd heard whilst Jack kept a hand on the door handle. Mya sat heavily in one of the chairs and gripped the seat so hard with her fingers her knuckles turned white.

'We need to act quickly.' Feather concluded. 'Of those you've met are there any you trust?'

'Redda,' Mya said.

'Prynarra,' Jack said at the same time.

They looked at each other.

'I'm not sure of either,' Mya admitted. 'But it's too soon to make such a judgement.'

'I'll suggest both to Caelin and Ben and find out what they know of the two of them.' Feather sighed. 'I hope they make it into the city tonight, otherwise I have a very long walk to find them.'

'But how do we convince any of them of what Kasira is planning?' Jack asked. 'We need to find a way to prove she's fey.'

'There used to be old tests,' Feather mused. 'Iron, of course, although Kasira seems more than able to hide any dislike for it. It used to be that you'd catch a fey out by speaking in rhyme to one and they can't resist but to rhyme back. I'm not sure she would fall for such an old trick.'

'What if we question Hassin and force the truth out of him?' Jack suggested.

'No.' Feather shook his head. 'That would tip Kasira off straight away. There's a risky plan… we warn of the revenant attack so they're ready to face them at the hospital, and at the same time it would be proof what we say is the truth.'

'But they plan for Hassin to feed the strongest students to the Ward and then destroy it,' Mya pointed out. 'And the main attack is to happen straight after. Surely we need to convince everyone *before* Kasira is ready to attack?'

'Worst-case scenario you and Jack are two of those students and can be ready to stop Hassin,' Feather said. 'But I agree, it would be better to strike before then if we can. As soon as it's dark enough, I'll slip out to find Ash.'

'Will you come back to the library or the stables?'

'As useful as the library has proven, the stables will be safer. Get out there to meet me as soon as you can tomorrow. In the meantime, find out what you can about Emon. If he really is the son of Kasira and the Lord Vallier, we may be able to use him ourselves somehow. We also need to know how human the boy is. If you get the chance, try to glimpse him in a mirror out of the corner of your eye.'

'Would that work on Kasira too?' Jack wondered.

Feather considered for a moment. 'Unlikely, her enchantments are very strong, and her appearance won't be far from truth, anyway. Right, my humans, I had better not linger out in the open any longer and we have work to do.'

'Good luck,' Mya said.

'And to you.' Feather nodded.

Mya and Jack headed up to the dining room in silence, both deep in contemplation. A few other students were already in the room, and Mya guessed Hassin at least, had dismissed his students early because of the arrival of Emon. As she sat down to eat, she paid a little more attention to the others than usual, not hiding her interest or avoiding eye contact. In a few days Kasira intended to kill these people because they were the only hope the Valley had at stopping her and her court of gathered Dark Fey. If she had more time, Mya might have been able to win some of them over, but she knew she stood little chance against Kasira's strong enchantment. She took in a sharp breath when she realised that, in the morning, she and Jack would have to spend time in the presence of the traitor, Hassin.

'You all right?' Jack asked in concern.

'Just thinking about the start of our lesson's tomorrow.' She held her nephew's eyes, and he nodded his understanding.

'It'll be fine, Aunt Mya,' he said with conviction.

Mya smiled despite her fears. Somehow this once awkward boy had become a man right before her eyes.

'Ah, you're here!' Linda stepped into the dining room with a relieved smile on her face. 'Do you mind if I join you again?'

'Of course.'

Linda fetched herself some food and came back to sit with them.

'I guess you've heard all the commotion around the boy who turned up this afternoon?'

'I did hear something.' Mya nodded. 'Is he really the Vallier's son?'

'Apparently so. There were rumours, a few years back, some unnamed woman of noble birth had borne him a child and been paid off to keep it quiet. He married his wife for a political alliance and allegedly she's always been a little frosty; not that it's any kind of excuse. With only daughters I guess he wanted to keep hold of this son, legitimate or not.' Linda shrugged. 'Perhaps the boy coming here will force him to openly claim him.'

Mya had wondered for some time how deeply the Vallier was involved in Kasira's plans. Obviously, she didn't have complete power over him if she'd gone to such extreme lengths to control him. She wondered if the man might make a useful ally, or if he'd be even more afraid to cross Kasira if he was aware of the truth.

They lingered over their meal, Mya reluctant to go back to her room alone. When Linda suggested they take a bottle of wine from the cellar and visit one of the common rooms, she jumped at the chance.

'I didn't realise there were other common rooms other than the library and dining hall.'

'There's a games room, with tables set out for cards and counter games, like Fox and Geese, and a meeting room where people just sit and chat.' Linda told them. 'I guess Prynarra didn't show you what was behind every door downstairs? I was lucky enough to come here on a seventh day when the classrooms weren't in use, so she showed me everything. I rarely go in the common rooms on my own, except the library; I guess I should make more effort to be sociable.'

'Can we go to the games room?' Jack asked. 'I'd like to keep my mind off starting my first lesson tomorrow.'

'Of course!'

As grateful as she was for the distraction, Mya couldn't keep from worrying, and nausea crept into her stomach, growing in intensity. She prayed Feather was on his way to their other friends to pass on their news, and all of them were safe.

'Do you think we should invite the Vallier's son down to join us?' Jack suggested.

'That's a nice idea,' Mya said.

There were two men in their early twenties engrossed in a complicated looking game with counters, they glanced up as they entered, and one nodded in brief greeting. Mya felt a little awkward at their intrusion, but Linda didn't hesitate in crossing the room to sit at a card table by the window.

'I won't be long!' Jack called, and he ducked back out the door.

Linda poured the wine and, finding a pack of cards, shuffled them. The two men had resumed their conversation, they were discussing sea travel, and exploring along the coast past the high mountains cutting off the Valley.

Jack entered the room and Mya saw from his face he'd had no luck.

'He wasn't there,' Jack shrugged. 'Or wasn't answering his door.'

'Oh well, it was a nice idea.' Linda dealt out cards.

'There was a young girl that came here around the same time as us,' Mya said slowly. 'I haven't seen her since.'

'I haven't seen any young girls.' Linda frowned.

Mya and Jack exchanged glances, she had a horrid feeling the young girl would never be seen again.

***

With a pounding heart, Feather hurried across the garden to where the hedge met the wall. He checked the fork of the third bush and found it was empty. He wriggled his way into the scratchy foliage and peered into the street. A man was wheeling a barrow away from him, but nothing else moved within his sight. An anxious hour followed as light faded completely from the city, and Feather considered several times leaving his hiding place to search for Ash and Ferris himself. A pair of city guards passed, and Feather's hope swelled as he spotted a tall man hanging back behind them, only to be dashed when the man came closer and he realised it wasn't one of his friends.

Then the unmistakable figure of Ash strode into view and relief flowed through Feather's muscles. A bag dropped with a slap to the cobbles before the hedge and Feather scrambled in.

'Ash! My news is urgent and not good. Has Caelin made it into the city?'

'Not yet,' Ash replied under his breath. 'Ferris discovered one of the guard patrols takes in the burnt building, they'll not be able to hide there long. We can't get them into an inn until after the city gates open, as it'd be too suspicious them turning up in the middle of the night. They're going to try to get through the smuggler's tunnel in the early hours.'

Feather sighed. 'I guess that will have to do.'

'What's happened?'

Feather told him and Ash swore. 'I guess we'd better come up with something pretty quick.'

'I have a failsafe plan if we come up with nothing better. We use the revenant attack to expose Kasira if there's no better way.'

'But that means Kasira will have everything in place.'

'Exactly what Mya said.' Feather nodded inside the bag. 'I'm open to suggestions.'

'Can Caelin break her enchantment?'

'We would have to ask him,' Feather mused. 'Where are we headed, by the way?'

'The inn nearest the burnt house, I'm afraid. We'll meet Ferris there and wait until it's time to go help Caelin dig his way in.'

Feather spent an uncomfortable time huddled in Ash's bag, barely daring to breathe, whilst around him he felt the vibration of heavily stepping feet. The conversation in the inn had gone from a quiet hum to a raucous buzzing. He cringed back as someone opened the bag, but it was only Ash, who discreetly handed him some bread and cheese. An overwhelming wave of gratitude rushed through Feather, it'd been a long time since he had eaten, and he'd been living on his nerves so much he hadn't realised he was starving. It seemed like an age since he'd enjoyed the hospitality of Ashgrove and the same freedoms as his human friends. He wondered if such a thing would ever be seen in Ayresport where they wouldn't even tolerate many of their own kind. Something of what Mya had told him of her day stirred in his memory and an idea broke through, an idea that might change things for them.

'Time to go.' Ash whispered as he pretended to secure the bag closed and lifted it up.

Even through the bag Feather felt the drop in temperature as they moved outside. The sound of voices faded to be replaced by the steady step of Ash and Ferris.

445

'I've hidden tools in the ruins,' Ferris said. 'Not the best, but all I could afford. I'll pawn them off again tomorrow. How are you doing in there, Feather? Sorry we couldn't get you an ale.'

'Another time.' Feather lifted the flap of the bag a little to peep out.

They reached the burnt-out house and Ferris retrieved his tools whilst Ash kept a lookout.

'I'll go through first,' Feather suggested. 'Start widening it behind me.' He crawled into the dark tunnel and felt his way along with his hands. It didn't take long for his trousers to be soaked through at the knees. His fingers touched cold rough stone, and he realised the tunnel had been made through the wall's foundations rather than under it. The tunnel sloped upward, but he only knew he'd come to its end when bracken tickled his face.

'Feather?'

'Lissa!' Feather sprang up and was immediately grabbed and lifted for a hug and a kiss on the cheek from the half-fey.

'Brownie, good to see you.' Caelin stepped out of the shadows. 'How are Mya and Jack?'

'A lot is happening,' Feather whispered. 'But let's get you into the city first. Ben?'

'Here.' The older man called softly. 'How's the tunnel coming?'

'Ferris is widening it now. Lissa would fit.'

'Go on through with Feather,' Caelin urged. 'If anything happens before we're all through, get away.'

Lissa nodded, and she followed Feather back through the tunnel without a word. Lissa and Feather took over keeping watch for the city guard and Ash was able to help Ferris. It wasn't long before the two knights wriggled through, both filthy from the loosened earth.

'Right, let's fill that back in and get out of here,' Caelin said.

'You need to hear what's happening.' Feather told him everything they'd learned.

Ben cursed and Caelin closed his eyes, drawing in a long deep breath.

'Is Mya okay?' Lissa asked.

'Scared, but she's doing very well,' Feather told her. 'Listen, Caelin, I have an idea but you might not like it. There's a way for you to be near the hospital, possibly even in it, and be free to move about. You'll be able to speak to Mya and Jack yourself and be there for the revenant attack. Dress as paupers and you can make your way straight to the hospital to wait outside now, no need to hide elsewhere until morning.'

'Ayresport doesn't tolerate begging, we'd be thrown out unless things have changed?'

'It seems they have a little,' Feather continued. 'They are not beggars who camp outside the hospital, but the desperate poor who cannot pay. Sometimes the healers can help a few and let them in. The day after tomorrow, the day before we expect the revenant attack, Mya says she and Jack both get an allowance for necessities from the school of the spellwards. They'd intended to use a little anyway to help some poor petitioners at the hospital; let those they help into the hospital be the three of you.'

'That's a good idea, brownie.' Caelin nodded. 'You said there was someone at the hospital Mya thought we might approach?'

'A man called Redda; also, Prynarra, who teaches at the Hall.'

'I know them both, a little.' Caelin chewed at his bottom lip. 'Prynarra and I never particularly got on, as I was too lowly a fellow for her liking, but if we can find a way to persuade her…'

'Something just occurred to me,' Lissa said. 'It might be too simple to work, but get this Prynarra to wear clothing inside out in front of Kasira. She could pass it off as an innocent mistake, but it might be simple enough Kasira wouldn't be guarding against it and might react.'

'Anything is worth a try, and the subtlety might buy us an ally without losing us time. Suggest that to Mya, Feather,' Caelin agreed.

'What of Redda?' Ben asked. 'Bit of an idealist but I always liked him.'

'Me too. We'll take a chance on Redda as well. If either proves false, we'll deal with them along with Kasira. Come on, let's do something about our appearance and be on our way. Ferris, can you keep our gear at your inn for now?'

'Aye, but Ash should take some too in case I'm compromised.'

'There's just one more thing before we split up.' Feather looked up at Caelin and took in a deep breath before speaking. 'There is a boy at Tower Hall that Kasira claims is the son of the Vallier... and herself.'

Caelin froze and visibly paled. 'You've seen this boy?'

'No, but I heard Kasira herself claim the boy's parentage.'

'You think he might make a useful hostage?' Ferris asked.

'She showed no care for the boy when he wasn't in her presence, and it sounded like he isn't aware she's his mother. Rather, she's beguiled him into coming to her at the Hall after causing a rift between him and his father. The boy has the Gift.'

'How old?' Caelin's voice was hoarse.

'Not yet seven.' Feather held the man's gaze and Caelin nodded.

'I recall whispers of some scandal around the Vallier that was quickly hushed up,' Ben said. 'Wasn't it around the time–?'

'He will not make a good hostage for us, but he is a great hostage for Kasira.' Caelin interrupted, glancing again at Feather. He busied himself organising his gear and changing his clothes. Lissa and Ben followed his example.

'I'll get Feather back to the Hall.' Ash offered when they

were all ready. To his surprise Caelin reached out to shake his hand.

'Good luck, Wolf, see you soon.'

Ash nodded and held his bag ready for Feather. They said a few hasty goodbyes, then they were hurrying across the dark city back toward the school of the spellwards.

'What was that between you and Caelin?' Ash asked, eventually.

'Nothing,' Feather mumbled from inside the bag.

'Humph.' Ash snorted, but he didn't press the matter.

***

Mya woke in the early hours of the morning with a blinding headache. After trying in vain to get back to sleep, she slipped out of her room and along the hall to the dining room to see what teas were available. There was nothing medicinal, but she found chamomile and hoped it would be enough to soothe her nerves. She jumped when the door opened and suppressed her instinct to duck and hide. A small boy stood in the doorway momentarily, and on seeing her, froze.

'It's okay,' she called. 'I'm Mya! I couldn't sleep and was just getting some leaves for tea. Would you like some?'

The boy crept in a few steps, his eyes were red, but he wore a determined expression. 'Is there any food left?'

Mya's anger rose. 'Did no one get you any dinner?'

'I... I had tea and cake with Kasira.'

'They clear away everything until breakfast. I've an apple in my room, if you don't tell anyone, we can go to my room and you can have the apple. Shall I make you some tea?'

'Okay.'

'What's your name?' She feigned ignorance.

'Emon.'

'Are you here with your parents?' She asked as they walked towards the women's wing.

Emon shook his head. 'I've come to learn to be a spellward with the Lady Kasira. My father wouldn't let me, but I am old enough to decide for myself.'

'You certainly are,' Mya replied, although in honesty she believed the opposite. 'What of your mother?'

Emon looked down at his feet and kicked at the carpet with the toe of his shoe. 'My mother had to leave me or else my stepmother would have had me killed.'

Mya halted and stared down at the boy in horror. 'Who told you that?'

'My nurse who raised me. She's Kasira's friend. Kasira's been protecting me.'

'That's kind of her,' Mya said through gritted teeth. She knew little of the Lady Vallier and wondered how much truth there was in what the young boy had been told. What a way to grow up!

Mya took a quick glance up and down the hall, then let Emon into her room.

'I'll just get the fire lit. There's the apple on the desk.'

Emon hopped up into the chair and took a bite from the apple at once. 'Where's all your stuff?'

'I've only been here two days.' She glanced around at the bare room. 'I'll be going into the city the day after tomorrow to get a few things.'

'My room is empty too.'

Mya got the fire lit and swung the kettle over it. When she'd made the tea, she suggested Emon sit on the bed and she would tell him a story.

'Now, I'm going to tell you a story about a little brownie called Feather. Do you know what a brownie is?'

Emon nodded, wide eyed.

'Well, Feather is the bravest and kindest of all brownies...'

***

Mya woke with a start. A door had closed out in the hall and she heard footsteps heading away. Her neck ached where she'd fallen asleep awkwardly against the short headboard of the bed. She looked down at the sleeping boy and reluctantly woke him. He groaned and rubbed his eyes.

'Sorry to wake you, sleepyhead,' she said gently. 'It's morning, and you'd better slip back to your room before anyone sees we've broken the rules.'

Emon nodded but moved reluctantly.

'I'll be going down to breakfast soon, why don't you come with me and Jack?'

'Who's Jack?'

'Jack is my nephew. His room is the second from the end on the right. He'd be happy for you to visit him whenever you want company.'

'How old is he?'

'He's fifteen.'

'As old as that?' Emon's eyebrows shot up.

'As old as that.' Mya laughed. 'Come on, you'd better get to your room.'

As short a time as it took Mya to wash in warmed water and change into a clean blouse, Jack and Emon were already waiting for her at the top of the stairs.

'You've met then,' she said.

'Emon came to call on me.' Jack grinned. 'We nearly didn't wait, he's starving!'

'I did wait!' Emon protested.

'Thank you, kind sir.' Mya gave him a quick curtsey. 'Come on, let's go.'

Emon and Jack didn't need to be invited twice, and they hurried down to the dining room. Jack helped Emon get what he wanted from the tall table, and by the time they were seated, Linda had joined them.

'We're going to need to pick a bigger table soon.' The older woman said.

Mya had almost forgotten their impending lesson with Hassin their breakfast was so companionable and fun. Then the door opened and Mrs Friend came rushing in, and on seeing Emon with them, looked horrified.

'Oh! There you are, boy. I was meant to take you up to Kasira's room for breakfast.'

'I'm sorry,' Mya said in alarm. The last thing they needed was to draw any negative attention to themselves at this point. 'He was waiting on the stairs and the poor thing was hungry. I hope I haven't caused you any trouble?'

Mrs Friend sighed. 'No, no harm done I'm sure. Emon, come with me, please.'

Emon reluctantly left his plate of food and took Mrs Friends' offered hand.

'I'll be taking care of Emon.' She narrowed her eyes at Mya meaningfully.

Mya nodded, clenching her jaw a little.

She realised the few others in the room had gone quiet and grew suddenly self-conscious. She wondered how many of the students here knew of Emon's full parentage.

'Well, time to be off for my lesson.' Linda smiled.

Mya immediately lost all of her appetite and pushed her plate away. She regarded Jack.

'Let's go,' he said, although he waited until she stood

before he moved himself.

When they entered the classroom, they found two others already seated and Mya recognised them from the dining room. She wished them a good morning, and they politely replied. They were a young woman, maybe three years older than Jack, with blonde hair plaited and coiled up on her head. The man was about five years older with brown hair and a neat short beard.

'Take a seat for the moment.'

Mya jumped as Hassin walked in behind them

'This is Kyra and Rutger. I've set them some studying and revision for today, so I can spend more time with you. We're just waiting for Hugh and Jessim.' Hassin crossed to his desk and opening a drawer took out a book. Mya took in a deep breath to compose herself and, with a glance at Jack, took a seat. Her pulse raced and she forced herself to calm. She'd only ever wanted a quiet life with a warm home and to find a good future for Jack. She'd never sought power, fame or adventure, so how had she ended up here? A chance meeting with a little brownie called Feather and everything had turned upside down. But then… hadn't she always known something was badly wrong in the Valley? Even before her sister had been murdered, she'd sensed danger hanging over them.

The door opened again and the last two students traipsed in. They were the young men who'd been in the games room the night before.

'Ah, Hugh, Jessim, here's the book. Study it carefully and have a try at the simple growing spell. I'll check how you're doing on First-day.' He handed them the brown leather book.

'Jack and Mya, follow me please, we'll try to get you to call up your Gift.'

They followed him out of the Hall and across the gardens to the practise area. Mya shivered although the morning was mild.

'Ah, good, no one else is here,' Hassin said.

Mya and Jack looked at each other, her nephew's muscles tensed.

'It will be easier for you to concentrate without the distraction of others,' Hassin continued. 'Now, we'll start with me calling up *my* Gift. I want to see if you can sense anything.'

Mya felt it at once when the spellward summoned his power; and he was strong. She had to fight against her natural instinct to call her own and she wondered if that had been his intention. She glanced at Jack who was frowning, and she stared hard at Hassin as though trying to see something.

'Anything?' Hassin asked, looking from one to the other.

Jack shook his head. 'I thought I felt a tingling?'

Mya felt overwhelming pride in her nephew, not at his ability to hide the truth from Hassin, but that he'd taken the initiative to appear the stronger of the two of them. It would be Jack they would consider the potential threat, leaving Mya to take them off guard.

'Yes, that's it!' Hassin pressed his lips together in a smile, his eyes lighting up a little. 'I'll summon my power again.

Concentrate on the feeling and note where it manifests inside your torso. Mya, anything?'

She shook her head, trying to appear upset.

'Well, don't give up, it will happen.'

They spent the morning with Mya pretending to struggle and Jack playing the star pupil. Hassin showed varying degrees of encouragement and frustration, but gave no indication he was anything other than a genuine teacher. Mya found herself hating him all the more, he was training them, only to destroy them, with no sign of remorse or emotion. When she'd had enough of the pretence, she called up a small amount of her power.

'I think I did it!'

'So you have!' Hassin raised an eyebrow. 'Now, like Jack I want you to concentrate on that power, then try to draw on it, and hold it. Reach for as much as you can.'

Mya called on a small amount of her reserves and barely held it, letting a little slip loose as though she was too flighty and undisciplined to keep control. Sparks of static shot through her into the ground.

'Careful!' Hassin cried in alarm, then gave a dramatic sigh to show his opinion of her. 'Well, I guess control will be our priority with you, at least you don't seem to be very strong, so you can't do much damage in the meantime. Right then, let's call it a day and we'll get right back to it on First-day. Well done, that was a good first lesson, but please don't do any more work on calling your power on your own. Go get some dinner and spend the afternoon reflecting on what you've learnt. There are books in the library about the basic uses of the Gift, go take a look. I recommend the one by Alepo. Enjoy your Seventh-day tomorrow.'

Mya and Jack barely had time for a thankyou before Hassin was heading back to the Hall.

Jack breathed out loudly. 'Well, I'm certainly glad that was over!'

'Are you happy to go straight to the stables to look for Feather?' Mya asked.

Jack winced. 'Might that seem suspicious?'

'Yes.' Mya nodded reluctantly. 'You're right. We'll have to wait a little longer to catch up with Feather. Let's go get some lunch, though I have no appetite.'

***

Mya felt grateful, and then guilty, that Linda wasn't there. She didn't have the energy for polite conversation. She picked at some flatbread and cheeses and tried not to be impatient with Jack as he ate his way through strips of beef and leafy greens, smothered in a white mushroom sauce. Finally, Jack put down his fork with his food unfinished.

'Aunt Mya, I'd like to go visit Magpie and your horse to see if we need to get them anything tomorrow.'

'Rusty.'

'Pardon?'

'I'm calling my horse Rusty. Let's go.'

It was hard not to run to the stables, so anxious was Mya

to check Feather was safe and if the others were here in the city yet. She dreaded the stable would be busy, but they found young Reg and the stable master exercising two of the horses in the yard. Another lad was wheeling old straw out to a midden heap. Mya waved to get the stable master's attention and pointed toward the stable. She watched Reg speak to him, and the man gave a nod and wave of assent.

They walked through the stalls, mostly empty, until they found Rusty and Magpie. They checked they were still alone and Mya called for Feather. A moment later they heard a rustling and Feather emerged from a pile of broken tack and old sacks.

'Not the best hiding place,' he said, brushing himself down. 'How are you doing?'

'I'm so glad to see you!' Mya said. 'Are the others safely in the city?'

'They are.' Feather quickly told them their plan. 'So, you are to find them tomorrow and get them into the hospital. Make sure Redda is there, and you can speak to him together. Do you think you'll be able to persuade Prynarra by tomorrow night?'

'We'll do our best.' Jack smiled grimly.

'One more thing. Keep working on your friendship with Emon and keep him close. Luckily, she knows nothing of the two of you, but the boy is a powerful weapon against Caelin.'

'Caelin?' Mya said in surprise.

'Yes. Now, I must hide again until dusk when I'll go to

find Ash. Come look for me again tomorrow after you've finalised plans with Caelin.'

'I can't believe we are really about to do this,' Jack said.

'Believe it, my boy, and believe you can do it. Both of you.'

***

'When should we speak to Prynarra?' Jack asked Mya as they walked back to the Hall.

'I'm tempted to leave it until the last minute in case it goes wrong, but then again, we need to give her time to test if what we say is true. We should try to talk to her either tonight, or first thing tomorrow, before we go to the hospital.'

'Okay. Do you... do you think we'll be able to get rid of her discreetly if she turns on us? We may have to stop her going to Kasira.'

'Let's not tell her any of our plan,' Mya mused. 'Not until we have to. We'll just tell her what we fear and suspect for now; no mention of Caelin.'

'Agreed.'

Mrs Friend was in her room, and they asked her where Prynarra was and were told the trainer had gone into the city. They left a message they'd like to meet with her for some advice, and would be in the library or the games room after dinner. Once in the library they tried to find the books Hassin had recommended, as much to keep themselves busy as to act as was expected of them, Mya dreaded the long night ahead of her alone in her room. There was a sudden commotion in the hallway, a man's deep voice and that of Mrs Friend sounding anxious. Mya nodded to Jack, and they went to the door to peer out.

A tall man, dressed in a fine blue robe with gold trim, was pushing past both Mrs Friend and a spellward Mya recognised as Fesla. He had dark, balding hair and a neat black beard. Two city guards flanked him, neither as tall, although one was almost twice as broad. Both were glancing about, fingers twitchy, but had their hands clear of their swords.

'My Lord!' Mrs Friend protested. 'I really must insist.'

With a start Mya realised this man must be the Lord Vallier. He was younger than she'd expected and certainly less pompous. There was anger in his eyes, but anxiety in the pinch of the muscles between his brows. He glanced at Mya and Jack, but dismissed them and headed toward the stairs.

'I know the way,' he said.

'Your guards stay down here.' Fesla demanded.

When they continued Fesla moved his hands and the two guards froze. They strained to move and call out, but the spellward held them fast.

The Lord Vallier spun around. 'How dare you!'

'I told you, your guards stay down here.' Fesla said.

'My Lord.' Mya stepped out into the hallway and gave a curtsey. 'Would you be willing to wait in the library with your guard whilst we fetch you some tea? Mrs Friend will bring Kasira I'm sure.' She tried hard to convey with her eyes he should follow her, but he was too wound up for such subtleties.

'So I can be fobbed off with more excuses?'

'I had the pleasure of Emon's company at breakfast,' Mya tried. 'I'm sure he considers myself and Jack here as *friends*.'

The Lord Vallier hesitated, and she held his gaze.

'All right.' He let out air from his lungs and his shoulders sagged. 'I'll wait, but not for long.'

Fesla glared at her but Mrs Friend gave her a grateful smile and scurried off up the stairs.

'Would you go to the kitchens and ask if they can bring us some refreshments?' Mya asked Jack.

She could see he was really reluctant to leave her, but he nodded.

With a scowl, Fesla released the two guards, and they sagged, one falling against the wall where he'd been fighting against his invisible bonds.

'That was great,' Mya told Fesla. 'I'd love to learn how to do that sometime.'

'I bet you would, sweetheart. I'll be out here with these two if you need me.'

The guards took the hint and took up a position either side of the door.

'My Lord?' Mya held the library door open wide, and he proceeded her in.

When the door closed behind them, the Vallier's demeanour changed completely. His brown eyes were so dark they were almost black.

'My son was well this morning?'

Mya sat, but the Vallier remained standing.

'He stayed in my room last night, against the rules of the Hall,' Mya admitted. 'He's a brave and determined boy but… people have put ideas in his head to frighten him.'

'What ideas?'

Mya regarded the man carefully. He was perhaps five years her senior and despite being the leader of the humans in the Valley she knew little of him as a person.

'I don't trust you,' she said finally.

The Vallier opened his mouth, his eyes growing large, and sat down heavily in one of the chairs. 'Who are you?'

'My name is Mya. My family was originally from Ayresport but moved to Trade Pass when I was very young. My parents were killed by succubae, and my sister by the Ward. My nephew Jack and I moved to Briarton and came here via Ashgrove to become spellwards.'

'Ashgrove? You've been there?'

'I have. Tell me… why does everyone pretend this is *our* Valley and *we* are not the intruders?'

He looked at her sharply, but she was surprised when he didn't deny it. 'My ancestors decided it would be the best thing to do. We sent a scout out into our home realm and they found it to be far, far ahead in years and a more brutal place than that in which we live. Torture and captivity would have been the best anyone with the Gift could have expected of our native realm. There was also the fear that people there would learn of here and come here to conquer and steal our magics. Families might become divided, as some choose to go, and some to stay.'

'So, you know this Valley belongs to the fey.'

'We were brought here by the fey against our will, and left to survive, it's our Valley now.'

'It's both of our Valleys. It works well in Ashgrove, it could work here too, and then you wouldn't need to feed all your people with the Gift to the Ward.'

He grew pale at that, which told Mya he was very aware of the cost to those with the Gift.

'It worked once until the Dark Queen came to claim the Valley.'

'Indeed.' Mya leaned closer. 'Do you work with the Dark Queen?'

The door opened and both Mya and the Vallier jumped. Jack came in bearing a tray.

'Kasira is coming,' he told them, looking from one to the other.

'Do you?' Mya asked the Vallier again.

'Of course not! Who *are* you?'

'Someone has told Emon your wife will try to kill him.'

The Vallier surged to his feet. 'That's a lie!'

Mya put her finger to her lips, and the door opened again as Mrs Friend announced Kasira. Jack put down his tray to bow and Mya stood to curtsey.

'It was nice to meet you, Lord Vallier,' Mya said. 'My Lady.' She gave a slight bow of her head and she and Jack backed out of the room.

'Wha–'

Mya gave Jack a sharp look to silence him. 'I'm hungry, shall we go to dinner first for once?'

'Oh, Mya.' Mrs friend grabbed her hands as the library door shut. 'Thank you for sorting that out!'

Mya shrugged. 'It was nothing.'

'You have a sensible head and a leader's touch.' Mrs Friend patted her arm. 'There'll be a bottle of our best wine on your table this evening.'

'If... if Emon doesn't leave the hall, he might like to join us for dinner,' Jack said.

'I'll send Berry up to ask if he's hungry. I'm sure My Lady and the Lord Vallier will have lots to discuss before they summon the poor boy.'

For once they were first in the dining room and servants were still placing steaming dishes on the long table. Jack dove on them, taking the best cuts, and Mya couldn't help but laugh.

'Are you Miss Mya?' One of the women asked.

'I am.' Mya shrank back, but the woman held out a bottle of dark red wine.

'Mrs Friend asked me to leave you this.'

'Thank you.' She relaxed and took the bottle. 'We'll save it for when Linda joins us.'

As soon as they were alone Mya quickly related to Jack what had happened in the Library.

'That's great!' Jack exclaimed. 'I thought he was our enemy.'

'Don't trust him yet.' Mya shook her head. 'He's a desperate man, and it seems he's been at least partially complicit in the deaths of those with the Gift. For now, we should leave him out of things, the fewer people involved the less complicated and the less chance someone will give us away.'

The door opened and a group of four students traipsed noisily in, discussing an exciting lesson in attack tactics. Mrs Friend followed shortly after and Mya didn't like the expression on her face.

'I just thought I'd let you know Emon will eat in Kasira's private room this evening,' she said.

'Thank you for telling me.' Mya forced a smile. 'Has the

Vallier gone? I've never met him before.'

'Yes, he's gone.' Mrs Friend pursed her lips. 'You'd have thought he'd try harder.'

'Perhaps he was persuaded the Hall is the best place for Emon?'

'Maybe.' Mrs Friend spun about and marched from the room. Mya and Jack exchanged a glance but couldn't speak.

Linda joined them not long after, and Mya opened the wine they'd been awarded.

'So, what have you done with your half day?' Linda asked as she sat down with her plate. Jack had used her arrival as an excuse to get a second helping, whilst Mya picked at a small bread roll. Mya told of meeting the Vallier but left out any detail.

'Well, that sounds more interesting than my afternoon. I was meant to be studying, but ended up napping! Do you fancy a game of cards this evening?'

'We have to meet with Prynarra for a while but could meet you later?'

'Lovely.' Linda smiled.

***

When Mya and Jack returned to the Library, they found Kyra there looking through the books. They exchanged polite greetings and Mya and Jack settled in the chairs to wait. Mya cursed silently as Prynarra came in and Kyra showed no sign of leaving.

'So how can I help you?' Prynarra asked.

'Well, it was a personal matter,' Mya said.

'Ah.' Prynarra glanced at the other student. 'Shall we go to my classroom?'

Mya nodded, and they followed her out into the hall.

'We're sorry to take up your evening,' Mya said as they entered the other room. 'But this is rather important.'

She took a moment to study the spellward. With her narrow nose and close-set eyes, it would be easy to interpret her expression as condescending; however, the woman had taken the time to meet them on what should have been an evening off. She had also shown considerable care for Redda's wellbeing. Jack positioned himself between Prynarra and the door and Mya nodded.

'We're going to take a risk and trust you with something. It may seem strange and hard for you to believe.'

Prynarra perched on her desk and folded her arms. 'Go on.'

'My sister, Jack's mother, was a spellward here for a while. Her name was Pria. Do you remember her?'

Prynarra studied her in return for a moment and replied slowly. 'Yes, I knew her. I taught her. She was a lively and clever woman who had an aptitude for healing. She gave too much to the Ward one night when she shouldn't have gone. She'd already done a double shift at the hospital.'

'You said she was clever; clever enough to know better than to feed that wraith of a spell when she had little to give?'

Prynarra shifted uncomfortably.

'The other day in the hospital, you almost let slip you're aware the Ward is killing people. It's been hushed up, but it is common gossip now all over the Valley, those with the Gift are being killed by the Ward. We've reason to believe those deaths are deliberate.'

Prynarra shot to her feet. 'Enough! I understand your grief but—'

'I can tell by the fear in your eyes you have your own suspicions.' Mya raised a hand and went on calmly. 'At this point in time, we just want to get to the truth. Why do you think this is being done?'

Prynarra looked from her to Jack like a trapped animal before sagging and letting out air loudly from her lungs. 'There are a few us who've had suspicions for a while that something bad is going on. We can explain a few accidents, but the rate at which we have lost spellwards? No, that is purposeful. We think… we think someone might be working with the Vallier to force people to give more power to the Ward as he is terrified of it failing.'

'But that makes no sense. What use is killing off spellwards and leaving us with no one to keep the Ward going?'

'Well… there is the forced recruitment—'

'And when they run out?'

Prynarra stared at her wide eyed.

Jack spoke up. 'When there is no one left with the Gift,

not only will the Ward fail, but there'll be no one left who can defend the Valley.'

'Why would the Lord Vallier want that?' Mya continued. 'I agree with you, he may have been involved in encouraging the feeding of the Gifted to the Ward out of fear, but I think he's realised his mistake and is terrified. We've important information that will change everything, but you must promise you'll keep it to yourself until we know who to trust. Can you do that?'

'Of course!'

Mya felt relief at how quickly and determinedly Prynarra answered. 'Someone has allowed a powerful fey into the Valley. They are working with allies amongst the spellwards to destroy the Ward and those who can defend the Valley. We know who it is but we need to convince you so you can persuade others of the truth, you'll not want to believe us.'

'Who is it?'

'What we'd like you to do is subtle, so you must watch everyone carefully. I warn you again, you won't like who it is, and won't want to believe it. Wear an item of clothing inside out and see as many people as possible tomorrow. Don't make it obvious, make it look like a mistake, and try to observe everyone before they see you so you can watch their instinctive and immediate reaction. Don't give yourself away by allowing yourself to be shocked by who it is. There's a chance you may not even get a reaction, and then we'll have to think of something else.'

'Couldn't you just tell me?'

'You'll need to see it for yourself.'

Prynarra frowned, and Mya let her think it through.

'Okay, I'll do it. But if by tomorrow evening I've had no reaction, you must tell me who you think it is, and allow me to bring a few of those I trust in on what you've said.'

'Agreed.' Mya nodded. 'We'd best go our separate ways. If anyone asks, I came to you this evening concerned my lesson hadn't gone well and I'm not good enough to be here.'

Prynarra took in a deep breath. 'What will you do when you've exposed the traitor?'

'Save the Valley,' Mya replied.

Chapter Twenty-One

Mya waited in her room for as long as her patience would allow whilst greyness seeped into the clouds on the horizon. She tried to read one of her books, but found she was going over the same paragraph without taking anything in. Finally, she gave up, and hurrying along the hall, she tapped on Jack's door. After a moment she heard the key turn and her nephew peered out at her bleary-eyed with his hair in disarray.

'Mya! What's wrong?'

'I haven't slept all night and couldn't stay in my room any longer. I'm going down to the dining room. Don't rush, just meet me there or in the library if I've gone.'

Lines creased Jack's forehead, but he nodded. 'I won't be too long.'

The stairway and downstairs hallway were deserted and Mya guessed most people made the most of their Seventh-day with a late night and a late morning. Breakfast hadn't yet been lain out, but she made herself some tea. When the first servant came in carrying a tray, she almost dropped it in shock when she realised Mya was there.

'Sorry.' Mya winced. 'Couldn't sleep, my first day exploring the city today.'

The young woman smiled and bobbed, but scuttled out as quickly as she could.

Jack came in, still looking tired, and almost pounced on the food as soon as they set it out.

'I'm sorry.' Mya told him. 'I should have let you sleep, I'm so anxious to get to the hospital and check on the others.'

'I didn't get off for ages,' he grumbled, falling on his food like a ravenous dog. 'Don't worry. Will we go to the stables first?'

'Yes, I think we should check with Feather in case anything has changed.'

They had to wait a while for Mrs Friend, but once she appeared and sat at her desk, she handed them their allowance with no delay. When they got to the stables, they found Reg cleaning out the stalls. Jack kept him talking whilst Mya wandered over to the pile of old harness and sacking.

'Feather, we're not alone but is everything okay?'

'Yes, my girl!' His voice was muffled. 'Get yourself on to the hospital.'

'Prynarra is following our plan. We'll be back later.'

She reluctantly walked away and re-joined Jack.

'Ready to go?'

'I am.'

They crossed through the gardens and the warden unlocked the gate to let them through. They headed straight to the hospital and found the small group of poor petitioners huddled in the street below the steps, some still slept. Mya's heart leapt when she heard a familiar cough and she had to stop herself from smiling.

'Your lungs don't sound good, old man,' she said.

'If y' can spare a few pence, kind lady, a nip o' whisky would do me the world of good!'

'I'll not waste a penny on drink for an old sot, but I'll ask what the healers can do.'

Immediately there was a clamour of voices as others pleaded for Mya to help them. Mya blushed as she pushed past to the doors, guilt gnawing at her that she was doing nothing for those who really needed it. She reminded herself that what she was here for would hopefully save all of them in the long run. She glanced back and caught Caelin's eyes, but immediately turned away to speak to the two guards.

'We're students from the Hall, here to help for the morning. We were here a couple of days ago, with Prynarra.'

'Aye, yeah, I remember you,' one of them said. 'Go on in.'

As soon as they were inside, they hurried straight up the stairs to the spellward's rest room. There was a woman there, drinking tea, and dressed in a nurse's apron.

'Excuse me, is Redda here today?' Jack asked.

'He's doing an urgent healing down in room two. Can I help you?'

'It's Redda we need, but we can wait.' Mya said. 'We'd like to pay for some of those people outside to receive treatment, though, if that's possible?'

'Really?' The woman put down her cup with a frown. 'We only have two spellwards here today, and they're exhausted. Me and nurse Westland could look them over and deal with anything minor. How much do you have?'

'Will you treat all of them for a Gold?'

'I'll see them all for that, but any medicines or supplies used will cost extra. We have to keep account–'

'Done,' Mya interrupted quickly. 'Can I let them in?'

'Well, I don't know, how many exactly are waiting? Maybe two at a time.' The nurse's eyebrows drew together across her nose.

'All right, let's get started.'

Without waiting for more permission, Mya strode to the door and threw it open.

'We're letting all of them in for treatment a few at a time,' Mya told the surprised guards.

Immediately there was a rush for the doors and Mya had to shout to make herself heard.

'You'll all be seen, but not if you push! Be patient a little longer. You, old man with the cough. The young lady there and the man with the scar.'

There were several angry protests from people that they'd been waiting longer, or they were more urgent, but Mya ignored them and the guards held them back. As soon as Ben, Caelin and Lissa were in Jack closed the heavy door leaving the guards to sort out the disorder.

'Mya!' Lissa pushed back her hood and threw herself at Mya, kissing both her and Jack on the cheek.

The nurse stood staring in shock.

'Old Flem!' Mya grinned at the old knight and hugged him fiercely. 'Caelin.'

He nodded at her in greeting, then surprised her by stepping forward and also kissing her cheek. 'Well done, Mya.'

'What's all the commotion?' Redda stepped out into the hall.

'Sir!' The nurse stepped in quickly to protest her own innocence. 'These two new students said they wanted to pay for the unfortunates outside to get some basic treatment. I don't know what's going on but–'

'Caelin!' Reda's eyes widened in recognition and immediately he called up power to form a shield.

'Easy, friend.' Caelin held up his hands. 'We're here for your help.'

'I don't help traitors.' Redda pulled the nurse behind him and backed up a step.

'That's the trouble.' Caelin lowered his hands. 'You *are* helping a traitor, without knowing it.'

Redda shook his head, but he halted in his retreat.

'It's true!' Mya said. 'Please, give us a moment to explain things. You're all in danger, we're just here to help!'

'We?'

'You obviously know Caelin and Ben Flame, myself and Jack are who we said we are, but we're not here as students but to save the Valley. This young woman here is called Lissa, she's daughter of the Druid of Ashgrove and the Dryad Queen of the Grove.'

Lissa stepped forward and held out her hand. The nurse clutched at Redda and continued to cringe away behind him. Redda looked the half-fey up and down, but didn't reach for her hand or drop his shield.

'Why would having a fey with you make me trust you more?' He asked.

'It wouldn't,' Caelin said. 'But Mya here thinks I can trust you with the truth. At the end of the day, what we needed was to get into the hospital to defend it from what's coming, and if need be, we can do that with you tied up out the way. We'd rather do it with your co-operation.'

'What is to come?' Redda shook off the clinging nurse.

'Revenants.' Mya stepped up beside Lissa. 'Now the spellwards are so reduced in number, our enemy plans to strike both here and at the Hall. The first step is to kill the strongest healers, here at the hospital. That means you. The second step is to feed the strongest of the students to the Ward. The Ward seal will be broken and an army of Dark Fey will enter the city with very little opposition and kill the human population; or take them captive for a lifetime of torment and servitude. You know things aren't right though you tried to stop Prynarra letting exactly how bad slip.'

'It doesn't pay to speak aloud of what we fear.' Redda stood up straighter and dropped his shield. 'People have a habit of disappearing. So, there have to be people on the inside to bring these fey in.'

'Redda.' Caelin stepped forward beside Lissa. 'When I attacked Kasira, it wasn't because I was jealous over her affair with the Lord Vallier, it was because I'd discovered the truth. *She* is the Dark Fey Queen for whom they created the Ward.'

Redda shook his head. 'No. No, she's a kind and gentle woman.'

'I don't think the Lord Vallier would agree, any more than Caelin,' Mya said. 'But if you want further proof, we've tasked Prynarra with discovering the traitor without telling her who it is. In the meantime, are you willing to let us stay in the hospital to defend against the revenant attack?'

'You've already made it clear you intend to stay here, with or without my help.' Redda sighed. 'If I'm to see the truth for myself, I'd best not be unconscious in a cellar. What's the plan?'

'We let those poor souls in to be healed and get them out the way as soon as possible,' Caelin said. 'Mya and Jack will help awhile, go shopping in the city as expected, then return to the Hall. There they'll decide they no longer need their horses and sell them to two men called Ash and Ferris who'll use them to run fast messages between here and the Hall as needed. You need to bring strong spellwards here discreetly to help us defeat the revenants. After, we'll head to the Hall to try to stop the Ward being destroyed. Jack and Myself will deal with Kasira.'

'I'm still not convinced it is Kasira,' Redda admitted. 'But I'll follow the plan as far as defending the hospital and the Ward.'

'Good enough' Caelin said. 'Can we trust this woman here to keep quiet?'

The nurse gave a squeal of alarm.

'She'll stay with me at all times,' Redda said. 'Shall we let our patients in?'

***

They spent the morning down in the cellar rooms doing their best to heal the poor. None of the magic users could resist using a little power although they were cautiously stingy. By the time Caelin insisted Mya and Jack leave to be about their normal activity, Mya found her respect for Redda and the other healers had grown. Redda himself was obviously still unsure of them, but she found she couldn't blame him.

'We'll probably not see you again before the attack,' Caelin said as they made their farewells. 'Have faith in yourselves and remember you're more than capable of doing this. The rest of us will join you as soon as we can after the revenant attack, myself and Lissa will use your horses to be all the faster. Good luck to you.'

'And to you,' Mya replied. She felt dazed as Ben and Lissa hugged her, but was determined to keep a smile on her face. She gave Redda a farewell wave, and he nodded in response. 'Ready?' she asked Jack.

'Let's do this.' He grasped the door handle and led them out into the street.

The steps outside the hospital were now empty, and the guards watched them with narrowed eyes as they made their way toward the city market. Mya wished they had better circumstances in which to explore the stalls and shops, but as distracted as she was by the thought of what was to come, they rushed through purchasing a couple of sets of luxury clothing each to keep up appearances. She insisted on buying a nice wine for Linda, and some sweets for Emon and Feather.

When they returned to Tower Hall, they found Ash and Ferris waiting for them at the boundary gate. Mya's heart gave a leap at the sight of the charcoal burner, but she scolded herself for being foolish, and composed herself to be completely formal.

'Good afternoon, I believe you're here to buy our horses?'

'We are indeed, Miss,' Ash replied with a small bow. 'This gentleman here told us you were still in the city and we were to wait outside the grounds.'

The gatekeeper took in a deep breath to puff himself up but Mya forestalled any bluster.

'Well done for taking such good care of our property and safety, but we're here now, so may we go in to fetch the horses?'

'Well, of course, Miss!' He opened the gate and stepped aside.

'How goes it at the hospital?' Ferris asked when they were out of hearing distance.

'Redda is dubious, but it's otherwise all set.' Jack told him. 'What will you two do?'

'Take the horses to the hospital and await the revenant attack.' Ferris shrugged.

'I'll come back here,' Ash said. 'I've no magic but I'm not going to leave you on your own when Kasira starts her attack.'

Jack bristled. 'We're perfectly capable of defending ourselves.'

Heat rose to Mya's face.

'I don't doubt it,' Ash replied calmly. 'However, I'm not someone who can stand by and not help.'

'Is that the Stable Master?' Ferris pointed.

'Yes, it is.' Mya waved at the man to let him know they wanted him. 'We've decided to sell our horses after all, as we intend to stay, and will have little time for them. We'll hand them over ourselves.'

'Would you like me to saddle them for you?'

'No, thank you, we'll do that, so we have a moment to say goodbye.'

The Stable Master touched his cap and continued about his business.

As soon as she was sure they were alone, Mya called for Feather. The discarded old tack moved, and the brownie wriggled his way out.

'Do things go well?'

'So far, so good,' Jack replied. 'What will you do, Feather?'

Feather rubbed his chin. 'I've been thinking, and whilst I'd like to stay with the two of you and help when Hassin makes his move, I don't think I'd be able to safely remain hidden with you and not give us away. I've decided to go to the hospital, with Ash and Ferris, and help out there as much as I can against the revenants. I'm sorry, Mya, Jack, my boy, but I think the revenants are a bigger threat than Hassin, it just makes sense for me to be at the hospital.'

Mya struggled to hide her disappointment. Feather might not be as powerful as her and Jack, but he had wisdom and experience that would have been reassuring. She knew they'd only be on their own for a short while, but she felt suddenly vulnerable. She caught Ash's eye, and although he said nothing, she could tell he was reminding her he'd be near.

'I understand,' Mya said. 'We can't risk the whole plan and the people at the hospital will need you against the revenants. There'll be two of us here against Hassin, we'll be fine.'

'And once Hassin shows his true nature, we'll have the whole school with us.' Jack added.

'We had best not loiter,' Ferris said.

Mya and Jack helped them saddle and harness the horses and Feather climbed into Ash's bag. The Stable Master came in to check on them, so their farewells were formal, and not what Mya would have wished. She watched them ride away and Jack nudged her.

'We best get back to the Hall. Are you changing into your new clothes?'

'Yes, we probably should,' Mya agreed. 'Early dinner?'

'You know me!' Jack grinned.

***

Whilst they were eating Prynarra appeared in the doorway; her face was flushed, but she was doing her best to appear calm. She forced a smile as she approached Jack and Mya.

'Did you have a nice day in the city?' She continued without waiting for a reply. 'I have those books you asked for, we can meet in my classroom to discuss them?'

'We'll be there as soon as we can,' Mya replied in concern. She noted the delicate lace shrug Prynarra wore was inside out, the seams barely noticeable.

'Super!' Prynarra's cheerfulness was too forced, but no one else in the dining hall appeared to be taking any notice.

Jack immediately wolfed his food, but Mya gestured for him to slow down. She'd lost her own appetite and had to force herself to chew and swallow each bite. As soon as Jack had finished, she pushed the remains of her dinner aside.

'Shall we see Prynarra about these books?'

They made their way to the classroom and Prynarra almost pounced on them as they entered, shutting the door quickly behind it and leaning against it as though she expected to stop someone else to burst in.

'Oh, my goodness!' She exclaimed breathlessly. 'It's true, isn't it? It's Kasira!'

'What happened?' Mya demanded. 'Did she notice you react?'

'No! No, I don't think so. I said "good morning" to her, she turned and flinched back as though I'd jabbed her with a pin! For a moment… for a brief moment I thought I saw very different eyes in her face. She backed away from me two steps, and I apologised for making her jump and rabbited on about my students. Oh, my goodness, she is really a fey? We're really going to be attacked?'

'Yes,' Mya said gently. 'As far as we know, it will be tomorrow. We've people in place at the hospital to protect it, and Redda is aware, although he doesn't quite trust us. There's a plan in place that… that someone here will take the strongest students up to the Ward and kill them by feeding it their power.'

'You know who, don't you?'

Mya glanced at Jack. 'We do. I think it will be safer for you, though, if you don't know who the traitor is and avoid Kasira. Keep an eye out tomorrow for any students being taken up to the tower, we should be among them–'

'It's Hassin!'

Mya hesitated. 'Prynarra, please don't take matters into your own hands. If we're found out too soon, Kasira could convince everyone we're traitors and dispose of us, as she tried to with Caelin. We need to allow others to learn the truth, but with us as in control as we can be, so no one gets hurt.'

'I understand.' Prynarra nodded. 'If I ran off to tell everyone, or attack Hassin now, I'd be locked up for being mad and likely found mysteriously dead in a matter of hours. So, when you go up to the tower, do you want me to follow?'

'We should be able to handle Hassin on our own.' Jack replied.

'I'm tempted to say bring your students up so we can work together, but you'd have to pass Kasira's rooms.' Mya thought it over. 'I got the impression she intended to be elsewhere to bring in her army of Fey, but I'm not certain.'

'I'll take my students to Kristin,' she said decisively. 'Tell him to keep them safe and come up to assist you. We should then get your students to testify to what they've seen to as many spellwards as possible.'

'Sounds good.' Jack nodded.

'Okay, well I guess we stay alert and try to act as normal as we can.' Mya took in a deep breath. 'We'll see you tomorrow. Good luck.'

***

Feather peered up at the healer whose eyes had grown huge.

'A brownie! But how can you be inside the Ward?'

'The same way Lissa can, fellow,' Feather replied. 'I was invited in.'

'A small flaw in the Ward that was kept quiet for obvious reasons.' Caelin leant against the wall in the cellar room with his arms folded. 'It's perfectly possible for a fey queen to be here and for her to call in revenants.'

'But Kasira!' One of the other healers who'd started her shift shook her head. 'I still find that hard to believe.'

'When you see through her glamour, you'll believe it, trust me.' Caelin stood up straight. 'Now, revenants. As you know they're powerful and there are limited ways to destroy one that take a lot of power. Can you all create a personal Ward?'

Redda and the other three healers nodded or said, 'Yes.'

'A good friend of mine accidently discovered a strong banishing spell we of less pure alignment can use. We're not sure exactly what happens to a subject; however, if you cast a Ward whilst touching a fey it seems to destroy it, or at least remove it, and it's less costly than a kill spell. It's advisable not to let a revenant within touching distance, of course, as it will try to drain your life away. So, my people will take turns keeping watch to allow you to go about your business. Try not to use too much power as you'll need it.' Caelin turned and strode away without another word, leaving Feather with the unsettled healers. He swallowed, looking around at the large and glowering strangers.

He cleared his throat. 'If you have any supplies, I could mix medicines for you?'

The healers looked at him with mixed expressions of shock and fear.

'Why would you want to help us?' Redda asked. 'After what we did to your kind?'

'Because I'm tied to a human who deserves my loyalty and help, as is the nature of us brownies. Also… as much as it breaks my heart to admit it, my old family didn't fight for me, Mya would have, Mya would never let me be cast out alone. I'd like to believe there are other humans like that, who are still within the bounds of the Ward.'

'Well,' Redda raised an eyebrow. 'Let me show you the mixing room.'

***

Lissa had taken the first watch and when she finished, she came down to join Feather. They worked together in companionable silence, crushing roots and distilling liquids, grating bark and infusing herbs. Occasionally a nurse would come in to collect something and disapprovingly look over their work. Somewhere outside a bell tolled eleven strikes.

'Is it that late already?' Lissa wiped her face with the back of her sleeve and stood up from bending over the workbench.

'Early for a brownie.' Feather smiled. 'It will be good to get back to a proper routine, it's been years since I had a settled home.'

'You couldn't find one in Ashgrove or any of the fey-allied towns outside the Ward?' Lissa regarded him with her green eyes.

'I was lost in the wilds; the Valley is a huge place for a tiny fey. I found some small villages, but the humans looked frightening and cruel to me.' Feather sighed. 'We brownies were made to live with humans, it makes me wonder, are we from this world or from the other?'

Both of them jumped as a shout came from somewhere above. Lissa ran for the door and opened it.

'What's going on?'

Ferris came running down the hall and grabbed her arm. 'Revenant attack! Get to our defensive position!'

'But it was meant to be tomorrow!' Feather froze.

Lissa turned and looked at him, her eyes huge. She picked him up, lifting him to her shoulder, and ran ahead of Ferris toward the stairs to the cellar.

'You should go down with the nurses and patients,' Lissa said to Feather as she knelt and held his hand to help him hop to the floor.

'No.' Feather shook his head stubbornly. 'I'll hold the back door with you.'

'Good luck.' Ferris took hold of the cellar door. Feather could tell by the set of the man's face he resented being sent to guard those with no magical Gift; however, this wasn't the time for pride, and killing revenants without magic was incredibly difficult.

Caelin and Redda had taken up a position near the front door at the other end of the hall, and Feather knew Ben was on the floor above to co-ordinate and back up the three healers there.

'Blessing spell?' Feather looked up at the half-fey.

'It's what I'm going to try first.' She nodded grimly.

Feather shivered, and he realised the temperature had fallen dramatically. The lamps on the walls dimmed and flickered, but struggled to stay alive. Their own shadows made a contorted dance against the flimsy door, and fingers of frost crept beneath it, snaking rapidly toward their feet.

Lissa hissed. 'We have visitors.'

Both of them called up their power and took a few steps back.

With a deafening crack the front door behind them burst into splinters. They spun around to see both Caelin and Redda ducking and wrapping their arms about their heads to protect themselves from the flying wood. The back door groaned, it was almost completely white with hoar, and bulging inward. Feather didn't wait, instead he called up fire, and putting as much strength as he could behind it, hurled it at the door. Instead of bursting inward the door was flung out in shards all aflame. Lissa released her blessing spell to repel the undead and croaking cries like those of ravens sounded in the darkness.

They had no time to pay attention to the sounds of battle coming from the floor above or the hall behind, the burning remnants of the door spluttered and died. Lissa called foxfire to compensate for their destroyed night vision, and at once movement caught their eyes. At first it seemed there was a deeper darkness in the night, but as they swayed closer on silent feet, Feather made out features. There were at least three creatures, possibly more behind where vision couldn't yet pierce. All three wore mouldering rags, the grave shifts worn by the buried poor. Grey flesh was eaten away to show the sharp white of bone and the yellow and black of teeth. A pale blue glow replaced eyes, and yet somehow still conveyed both suffering and rage, hands reaching forward for revenge and atonement. Lissa stood staring with both horror and pity on her young face.

Feather pulled elf-shot from his pouch and whizzing his sling above his head let fly. His shot 'thunked' against skull, the revenant's head jolted back, but it didn't stop. Lissa called ivy from the walls of the courtyard garden and compelled it to grow, wrapping around the legs of the revenants to hold them back.

'Do you not wish peace?' She cried out. 'What crime do you avenge?'

'I think I know,' Feather said with a shake of his head. 'You cannot reason with them, my girl.' He called up another fire spell and sent it at the nearest creature as it stepped across the threshold. The flames caught weakly in the damp cloth and decaying flesh until Lissa, with gritted teeth, added her own bright burst of fire.

'Take off the heads!' Caelin yelled from behind them. 'Ward doesn't work!'

Feather and Lissa glanced at each other, they had a tiny knife and a long dagger between them.

Feather swung another shot and this time the burning revenant fell back onto the one behind it. Lissa called up another banishing spell and Feather winced at how much of her power she put behind it. All the revenants still on their feet staggered back, one even turned and loped unevenly away. Lissa leapt over the burning revenant and, drawing her dagger, hacked at its neck. Feather threw two more shots as the other revenants started forward again. The fallen creature struggled to get up; ivy still grew slowly along its body and Feather fed it more power, directing it to fasten about the revenant's neck and squeeze at the same time as tangling its legs. Lissa leapt up as she finally cut through to the muddy flagstones, gore splattered her arm and her face was twisted with revulsion and sorrow. She sprang back as the second revenant caught fire, its scream was too human, and Feather let out his own cry of despair. They retreated quickly to the doorway, both of them out of breath and Lissa struggling to draw on more reserves of power.

There were three more out there, one still shuffling away after Lissa's strong banishing spell. The other two hesitated just beyond the heat of the burning flesh pyre, swaying like predators preparing to spring. Caelin leapt over Feather, power building as he drew heat to his sword, he swung before his feet touched the ground and he took the head off one revenant with a single strike. With surprising speed, the remaining revenant turned about and launched itself at the spellward. Lissa made a grab at its feet with some ivy, Feather called up all the power he had left and gambled it on a spell beyond the capability of most brownies. He reached up into the clouds and called down lightning. It struck the revenant, and it exploded outward, showering them all with bone and rotted flesh.

There was a moment of stillness. Feather's ears rang and his curly hair stood up on end. Caelin stirred, and running after the retreating revenant, cut off its head from behind. Lissa stood frozen, fingers and hands extended and shoulders hunched in repulsion.

'Ugh!' She exclaimed finally.

'Lightning, brownie?' Caelin stepped around the burning remains, wiping his sword with a rag.

Feather gave an embarrassed shrug.

'Dear God!' Redda exclaimed as he came up behind Lissa.

'Believe us yet?' Caelin asked, but without waiting for a reply, went bounding up the stairs to check on the others.

'I didn't think brownies were that powerful.' Redda turned to Feather.

'Those of us who didn't adapt outside the Ward, didn't survive,' he replied.

Caelin came back down the stairs followed by Ben and the three healers. One of the female healers had her arm cradled to her body from which blood dripped. Ben had a nasty-looking scratch across his face.

'Those wounds need purifying,' Lissa said. 'Give me a moment to clean this... this *stuff* off me and I'll sort it.'

'What now?' Redda looked around at them all.

'Find something to barricade those doors,' Caelin told him. 'When Kasira realises the attack has failed, she may send others. Get your door guards back up from the cellar and make sure they have sharp swords or axes. Myself and Ben will take the horses and make for Tower Hall.'

'As will I,' Feather said in a tone that would brook no argument.

Caelin looked down at him and nodded.

'And me!' Lissa protested.

Caelin sighed. 'Cleanse Ben's wound, then those of this spellward. Follow behind us with Ferris and Ash and take a moment to recharge a little power; you'll need it.'

***

Mya almost fell from her bed as she woke in shock to the pounding on her door. She grabbed a blanket to wrap about herself and hurried to open it a crack. Her heart stopped when she found Hassin standing there and her mouth turned completely dry.

'I'm sorry to wake you, we have an emergency! Fey are attacking the Ward and we are afraid it will fail. We need students to give it power.'

Mya realised her mouth was hanging open, and she closed it quickly. He was convincing; she had to give him that.

'Can I get dressed?' She asked.

'Quickly,' Hassin agreed. 'Meet us at the stairs to the upper floor.'

Mya's hand hovered over her new expensive clothes only momentarily, before she grabbed her sturdy walking boots and travelling clothes. She doubted Hassin would see any suspicion in that at this point in time. When she came out of her room, she found others gathered at the stairs, including Jack. Hassin was ushering another young man toward them.

'It was supposed to be tomorrow.' Jack bent to hiss into Mya's ear. 'Emon was in my room, I asked him to tell Prynarra when we're gone.'

'Right!' Hassin said in a loud whisper. 'We don't want to scare everyone so let's get up to the tower in a fast and orderly fashion. Follow me.'

Mya squeezed Jack's arm and then hurried forward so she was directly behind Hassin. They ascended the stairs to the plush hallway and Hassin unlocked the door to the tower. Some of the students had clearly not seen the pillar room before as Mya heard several indrawn breaths. As they passed Kasira's quarters, both Mya and Jack kept their eyes on the door, and Mya found her heart racing faster. The blood-tang of iron grew stronger as they ascended the last steep steps to the Ward room. Hassin disappeared into the pulsing red glow and, taking in a deep breath, Mya climbed up after him.

'Right,' Hassin's face was earnest, and had Mya not known his true cruel intent, she would have suspected nothing. 'What I want you all to do is call up your power. You'll feel a pull from the Ward, let it take a thread of your power and relax. I'll help you stop the flow before you lose too much. Go on.'

Mya and Jack looked at each other and both called up their power, instead of reaching for the Ward, however, both created a shield. At first Hassin didn't notice, but regarded the students with a pleased look on his face. When he realised what Mya and Jack were doing his posture stiffened.

'Come now, don't be afraid of the Ward, open your power!'

'Unfortunately, we know you've been killing spellwards by feeding them to the Ward,' Jack said.

Mya drew up more power, being sure to keep some back, even so Hassin's eyes widened in surprise and he immediately called up his own shield.

'Foolish rumours.' Hassin scoffed, although he took two steps back.

Most of the students were looking at them now, some decidedly nervous and others angry or confused.

'Mya!'

She glanced over her shoulder to see Linda was amongst the students.

'Mya I can't stop my power!'

That got everyone's attention and soon all the students were trying frantically to pull free from the Ward. One panicked and called up all of their power which the Ward greedily snatched. The young man gasped for breath and crumpled to the ground.

'Don't fight it!' Mya yelled. 'Just reduce the amount of power you're calling to as little as possible.'

At the same time Jack advanced on Hassin. 'Let them go and we might spare you, traitor!'

'I'm not the traitor, you are!' Hassin spat, calling up fire. 'Don't listen to them. You will all be fine.'

Mya felt anger and disgust at his nasty choice of spell. She and Jack had called up sparks of lightning that would stun rather than burn. There was no time to waste on more words, already other students were faltering. Jack blasted at Hassin's shield whilst Mya knocked aside the fireball, sending it spinning into the Ward where it dissipated. Behind her Linda broke away from the Ward and immediately set about helping the others free themselves.

Jack sent spark after spark toward Hassin, testing his shield and giving him little time to retaliate. Mya continued to block the spellward's attack, keeping anything from hitting Jack or the other students. Despite her efforts two fires had broken out in the Ward room and it was filling with smoke. Then Hassin grinned as he called up more reserves of power and sending a wall of pure force at Jack, he sent him stumbling backward, his shield buckling. Without hesitating, Mya stepped forward, and she ripped apart Hassin's shield, sending a wave of static into his body. He flew back and hit the wall, cracking his head on the stone. He didn't even have time to show any surprise.

Someone swore, and she turned to see Rutger, from her short-lived class, staring at her with his mouth open.

'Mya! What in Hell's name is going on?' Linda demanded.

'We are betrayed!' Jack answered for her. 'Kasira is the Dark Queen of the Fey and Hassin her minion. Help is on its way, but we must hold the Ward or all is lost!'

Chapter Twenty–Two

Mya checked Hassin's pulse. He lived, but blood still oozed beneath his hair.

'Where can we put him where he can't cause any trouble?' Mya wondered.

'Anywhere we put him he'd get out of using magic if he wakes.' Prynarra pushed through the students to join them. Emon held her hand but hid behind her. 'The best thing we can do is keep him where we can watch him.'

'Or kill him,' Jack said.

Both women turned to look at him and he shrugged.

'Do you know where Kasira is?' Mya asked Prynarra.

It was Emon who answered. 'She left when it got dark. I saw her from my window. She met a dark man in the garden and they went away.'

'Dark man?' Mya frowned

'He was made of shadows.' Emon gazed up at her wide eyed.

'I would imagine she's gone to meet her army.' Jack surveyed the room. 'She'll be expecting the Ward to fall.'

'She'll soon know something's gone wrong with her plan.' Mya sighed. 'I don't imagine we have long before she comes back here.'

There was a soft chuckle, and they turned to find Hassin watching them.

'Idiots,' he said. 'When the Ward doesn't fall, she won't come running back, she'll call the army through the Ward one at a time if need be!'

'It would take time, but it would work,' Mya confirmed.

'Where did she go?' Jack demanded.

Hassin smiled smugly up at them. 'She didn't tell me.'

'It's likely true.' Mya glared down at him. 'Why in the name of goodness are you helping her?'

'She's my Queen!'

'You can't reason with him,' Jack said. 'He's completely under her enchantment. We need to organise a defence of the Ward.'

'Students aren't enough.' Prynarra looked around. 'All of you, go downstairs and wake the spellwards, tell them what's happening and get them up here. Linda, you go get Mrs Friend and we'll get her to organise her household staff. I'll watch Hassin here.'

Mya had to smile at Prynarra's rapid, no nonsense approach. She doubted she'd be so calm and efficient in the teacher's position.

'You'll never stop her,' Hassin said. 'This Valley belongs to her.'

'It does to an extent,' Mya agreed. 'In actuality it's Nemeth's Valley.'

Hassin almost snarled, but caught himself, and forced a narrow-eyed smile. 'She never claimed it; her sister has a right to do so.'

'The Wild Fey rejected her.'

'Mya, leave it,' Jack said.

Reluctantly Mya nodded.

***

Feather clung to the horse's mane as Caelin blasted open the gate to Tower Hall with a force spell and urged the frightened animal through. The Hall itself stood ominously quiet, windows like woeful eyes, seeming empty. They halted and Caelin jumped down, picked up Feather and placed him on his shoulder. Ben, with Lissa seated behind him, joined them a moment later. Ben and Lissa regarded each other but no one spoke.

Caelin approached the front door cautiously and tried the large iron handle. When the door didn't budge, he called up power, but Lissa stopped him.

'Don't waste energy.' She warned. 'We'll try another way.'

Just as they stepped back, they heard the click and scrape of bolts and the door swung slowly inward to show the smallest of gaps through which a single frightened eye peeped. The door was pulled back dramatically.

'Sir Caelin!'

'Mrs Friend.' Caelin gave a small bow.

'They told me to look out for you. Oh, Sir! There's been such a commotion.'

'Out of the way, woman!' Ben grinned.

'Sir Ben!' Mrs Friend's hands turned to fists and rested on her hips. 'I didn't think you'd darken my doorway again, you old scallywag!'

Ben grabbed her about the waist and planted a kiss on her cheek whilst she flapped at him in feigned protest.

'Where's Mya?' Feather demanded.

'Well, I'll be!' Mrs Friend exclaimed. 'Is that really a brownie?'

'He is, and Lissa here is a dryad, both are here to help you. Now, as the brownie said, where's Mya?'

'Up in the tower room, this way, this way!' Mrs Friend lifted her skirt and ran for the stairs, she ascended them with surprising speed and was only a little out of breath as she hurried along the hallway to the door to the tower chambers. As they climbed the iron stairway, Lissa pulling her arms in tight to her side, they heard beyond the walls the sound of bells ringing.

'The alarm!' Ben glanced back over his shoulder at Caelin. 'The city is under attack!'

Caelin nodded and gestured for Ben to go on.

'The Ward is still up,' Feather said quietly from where he perched.

'She'd have to be near,' Caelin replied. 'For the attack to come so soon. She's obviously realised Hassin has failed.'

'Perhaps she always expected him to,' Feather mused.

The tower room was crowded when they entered and Caelin had to push through. Feather spotted Jack first; the 'boy' now reaching almost six feet in height was difficult to miss.

'You're here!' Mya called out, her relief evident. 'Hassin claims he doesn't know where Kasira's gone. Did you hear the bells?'

Caelin nodded. 'We have little time.'

'You!' Hassin tried to sit up and pressed himself against the wall.

Caelin dismissed him. 'Redda and the spellwards from the hospital are on their way with Ferris and Ash. I imagine the focus of Kasira's attack will be here and at the Vallier's castle; however, we cannot wait for her to bring all her army through. We'll leave the students here with a few strong spellwards but the majority of us must go after Kasira.'

'He won't tell us where she is,' Jack said through gritted teeth.

'She didn't tell me all her plan.' Hassin smirked.

'Unfortunately, he is telling the truth.' Feather sighed.

'Truth spell?' Ben asked.

Feather nodded.

'She isn't far.' Caelin looked over everyone gathered in the room to assess their strength as he spoke. 'Where is the Ward barrier closest to the city?'

'The sea,' Feather said.

'Of course. Everywhere else would be several days away. Prynarra, can you take charge here?'

The teacher's eyes widened, but she nodded.

'I'd get everyone to turn their clothes about and gather iron and salt,' Feather suggested. 'She will no doubt bring her most powerful allies through first, but don't underestimate the little fellows.'

'I'll get onto it right away.' Mrs Friend bobbed a curtsey.

'Prynarra, pick yourself half a dozen strong combat spellwards to stay with you and your students; the Ward must not fall. Redda and the other healers can stay with you when they get here. Everyone else, come with me at once.'

Feather managed a smile over his shoulder at Mya as Caelin headed for the stairs and ran down them. He had to clutch at the knight's collar to keep from falling.

Caelin hesitated as they reached the horses.

'Might be worth the gamble to gain time,' Feather said. 'But then we could lose in one go if you and Mya are overwhelmed.'

'She's probably called through a couple of hundred by now.' Caelin growled, clenching his jaw. 'We'll stick together.'

They hurried through the city, many people had come out into the streets, or watched from windows and doorways trying to find out why the bells were ringing.

'Get inside!' Ben shooed at them. 'Bar your windows and doors you idiots! Kasira is the Queen of the Dark Fey and we're under attack!'

There were incredulous protests, but just as many heeded the old warrior at once and ducked back inside their houses. Screams arose from the city ahead of them and the bells ceased.

''Ware!' One of the Spellwards who had come with them pointed up at the sky.

Feather squinted up into the darkness. With not even a moon for light, even with his good eyes, he could see nothing but a shadow moving across the stars. Lissa sent a flare upward even as Feather sent foxfire across the cobbles and up the walls of the houses.

In the blue-green glow, they caught the silhouette of a creature three times the size of a horse. It had an eagle-like head on an elongated neck, leathery wings, and a long serpent's tail. Furry legs were tucked beneath it with talons curled into fists.

'Cockatrice!' Lissa yelled. 'Its breath is poison!'

'Shield!' Caelin commanded.

All of them did so. Feather pulled out his sling and regarded it dubiously. 'We need Ferris and his bow.'

'A bow is not enough.' Caelin shook his head. 'They are creatures of magic and only magic can kill them. A kill spell or Mya's Touch-Ward might do it.'

'Aye, but good luck getting it down here to touch!' Feather replied.

The cockatrice passed over the street and Feather instinctively tightened his shield. Droplets of corrosive spittle spattered the ground about them and a fog of poisoned breath swirled about their shields. As soon as it drew level above them, Caelin called up a fireball and blasted it toward the beast. Its fur caught flame, and it was propelled upward with a furious roar. It came about, knocking tiles off the roof of a church tower as it sped back toward them.

'Can you protect me, brownie?' Caelin asked.

'I can.' Feather called up more power and expanded his shield.

Some of the other spellwards had summoned fire and Feather felt Caelin's jaw clench in either annoyance or concern. He sensed the shape of the spell Caelin was forming, but it was no ordinary spell. Mya was watching them, holding back and trusting Caelin to lead them in dealing with it. Jack, like some of the others, had drawn up an attack spell. It dove; breathing out its petrifying breath and turning to avoid several hastily flung fireballs. One spellward's shield faltered but Mya stepped up and rapidly expanded her own, even so acid droplets caught the man's arm and he screamed in pain.

Feather held steady as Caelin launched his spell. It looked to all appearances to be another fireball, but as the cockatrice flapped its wings to rise and avoid it, the fireball burst and lightning leapt from it in a bright net. Smoke rose from the serpent-bird and its wings collapsed.

'Move!' Caelin yelled.

They ran for the meagre shelter of the doorways as it fell to the cobbles. Feather grabbed at Caelin's collar and hair as the man drew his sword and leapt back to avoid the flailing wings. He darted back in, and sweeping his sword high, hacked down and severed the cockatrice's head from its neck.

'Genta is turning to stone!' One of the spellwards called out.

Lissa ran over and placing a hand on the stricken man quickly reversed the curse.

'Now listen up!' Caelin shouted angrily above the outbreak of chatter. 'We've much more to face before we even reach Kasira and we can't be wasting what energy we have! You and you.' He pointed. 'You are both to shield and protect Jack, he needs to conserve power more than any of us.' He placed his hand on Mya's shoulder, but didn't look at her, instead he caught Lissa's eyes and the half-fey nodded. It seemed Caelin wanted Mya's importance and strength hidden even from their allies. 'Feather, are you happy for us to work together?'

'I would be honoured,' he replied, and meant it

'Let's move,' Caelin said.

As they hurried onward, Feather noted Ben took up a position a step ahead of Mya, and Lissa to her left. Screams were coming from more parts of the city and Feather clenched his teeth. They had no choice but to ignore it and head for the source of the attack.

A scrabbling, skittering sound came from up ahead and from his vantage point on Caelin's shoulder Feather saw at once what it was.

'Powries!' He growled. 'They'll suffer iron, but a sword or a bolt will kill them well enough!'

The spellwards at the front of the group sent out a burst of flame whilst Ben hacked and stabbed at the fey dodging around him.

'Don't waste time!' Caelin urged. 'Nasty as they are, we'll have to leave them and press on!'

Even so Feather let fly a shot at two of them. Most of the Redcaps scattered across the city, looking for easier prey, but some stayed to harangue and torment them. Red eyes blinked from the gutters and tiny knife-sharp nails swiped at legs. Three of them launched themselves at once at one of the spellwards who cried out in alarm. They scrambled up her robe, but Jack caught one by its straggly grey hair and slit its throat. The spellward tore one loose herself and it bit her hand to the bone. The third had made it up to her shoulder and reached to slash her throat; Mya threw it back with a carefully aimed force spell. The spellward crouched and stamped on the one hanging from her hand by its fangs; once, twice, thrice. It released its grip and lay twitching.

'Get going!' Caelin commanded.

Tears were running down the spellward's cheeks, but she took Jack's hand to stand and stumbled after him.

'Nearly there!' Ben encouraged.

A man stepped out of the shadows and blocked their path.

All of them halted, except Caelin, who continued to walk forward until he was at the head of the group. Mya started to follow but Ben grabbed her arm to stop her.

Jack gasped. 'The shadow man.'

Lissa touched the ground and again foxfire spread across the cobbles although they stopped before the feet of the figure before them.

'We thought you might be about somewhere.' The voice sounded like stones grinding on a river bed. 'No one in this pitiable city has the ability to take down two succubae.' It stepped forward. The fey man was dressed in a ragged and mildewed suit and wore a wide-brimmed hat of straw. Its face was indeed made of shadows, or swirling smoke, in which yellow eyes gleamed.

'Out of the way, Bogle,' Caelin said. 'I am here on behalf of the Lady of Light and Life. this valley is Nemeth's and not *your* Queen's.'

'She gave up her claim.'

'Never her claim. She chose to leave the Valley to itself.'

'Nevertheless, she is not here and not my queen.' He gestured and two Black Dogs came slinking forward, ghostly muzzles drawn back to show phosphorescent fangs.

Feather swallowed and resisted the temptation to fumble for a bolt, he didn't dare distract Caelin or draw attention to himself. He sensed some spellwards draw up shields although they should have known better than to waste energy. There was more movement in the street ahead and a group of hobgoblins loped toward them.

Feather tried hard not to let his growing fear show. Caelin gave a sigh and a shake of his head.

'Don't waste my time, Bogle. You should know if I can beat two succubae, then you and this rabble won't be a problem.'

'Really.' The Bogle's yellow eyes darkened in amusement. He turned to his right and another figure, that had been leaning against the wall unnoticed, straightened up.

Mya recognised him at once and a blush rushed to her cheeks at the same time as she let out an angry cry.

Caelin let out a growl. 'You!'

'Me.' The man grinned and made a sweepingly low bow.

'Since when have you been subject to any queen?' Caelin demanded.

'Oh, I'm not.' The Ganconagh smiled ruefully. 'But Astol was so boring when you left and I thought it might be more interesting to observe what happen here.' He winked at Mya

Feather bristled and Caelin tensed. The Ganconagh was one of the most powerful fey there was, more than a match for most of them put together.

'What has Kasira promised you?' Caelin demanded defensively.

'Oh, only a chance at a little entertainment.'

Caelin stepped forward and grabbed for his sword but Feather pinched his ear hard. 'No, wait!' he whispered urgently.

The Ganconagh's eyes sparkled as his smile fell on Feather. He turned to Mya and gave another bow. 'My lady, you are wasted on these mere men, but I wish you luck in your endeavour.' With a laugh he turned and strode away.

For a moment the Bogle stared after him in stunned disbelief, then it spun about with its eyes burning.

Feather threw up his shield as the Bogle sent a blast of ice toward Caelin. Both dogs leapt forward, and the hobgoblins raised their bows. Contrary to Caelin's command, Lissa sent a strong blast of wind toward the goblins to throw off their arrows and Mya quickly shielded herself and the half-fey. From the corner of his eye, Feather saw both Ferris and Ash running up to join them. Jack attacked one of the Dogs and Feather saw Mya and Lissa went for the other. There was no time for concern that the strongest of them were being drawn into using up their power as the Bogle was focused entirely on Caelin. Feather concentrated hard on his shield as wind and hail battered it. Caelin was returning with fire, and Feather gritted his teeth at the weakness of the man's spell. He himself would have risked a powerful assault to get it over quickly.

Around them hobgoblins were falling to Ferris' arrows and Ash's well wielded stave. Ben had fallen in beside Jack, distracting the Black Dog with his ineffective sword.

'Feign your shield failing!' Caelin growled at Feather.

The brownie did so although fear stabbed at his heart. As he lowered his shield, Caelin staggered backward and raised a weak shield of his own. The Bogle laughed and strode forward, sending lightning flying out from both hands. Caelin sprang up and ran at the Bogle, Feather bringing his shield back up to full strength. Movement caught Feather's eye, Lissa was also running for the Dark Fey, he opened his mouth to shout a warning, but he was too late.

'Save your energy!' Lissa cried, and she hurled herself at the Bogle as she called up a kill spell.

Caelin faltered in shock.

Disbelief stabbed at Feather's heart and tears stung his eyes.

The last of the Bogle's power hammered at Feather's shield before it collapsed into a pile of steaming rags. Lissa crumpled to the road.

'Caelin!' Feather slapped the knight around the back of the head.

Caelin shook himself and took quick stock of their situation. Mya had banished her Black Dog, Jack and Ben had theirs pinned down. The slavering beast launched itself at Jack's throat, but before its jaws clamped shut, Jack reached inside its body and cast a Ward. Jack staggered back and Ben caught him. Hobgoblins still assailed them and Caelin drew his sword; Feather took his lead and pulled out his sling. Forgetting magic, they joined with Ben and Jack to form a defensive line of steel. Ash and Ferris joined them and the spellwards fell back behind them. Mya stood over Lissa with her fists clenched ready to call up power.

When the last Hobgoblin fell, Caelin turned at once and hurried back to where the half-fey lay.

'She lives,' Mya said, still breathless from the battle.

'A Dryad cannot use a kill spell!' His face was contorted in anguish.

'But she is half human,' Mya replied.

'After using that spell, they will never allow her back into the Grove.' Feather shook his head sadly. 'She has tainted her magical alignment. She has chosen her human side.'

Mya swallowed, her blue eyes fixed on his. She turned away, wiping quickly at her eyes and nose.

One spellward was staggering and covered in blood. Caelin looked about and beckoned Ferris over. 'Carry Lissa back to Tower Hall and keep her safe. Take that fellow with you, he can barely stand, never mind fight any more. You.' He pointed at another spellward, the one the redcaps had attacked. 'Go with them and help protect them. The rest of us… we go on to the harbour.' He picked up Feather and placed him on Mya's shoulder.

***

Mya felt Feather settle and his weight was comforting. He had one stubby arm around the back of her head to hold to her collar. They set off again, and she let herself fall back away from Caelin and Jack, to keep up her appearance of being insignificant. Ash dropped back behind her but said nothing. Her heart hurt at the thought of Lissa never being allowed to return to her home and her tree, but she couldn't allow herself to dwell on it. Ahead of them loomed the harbour gate and Caelin slowed down. The hairs on the back of Mya's neck prickled as she tried to look past those in front of her into the gloom below the iron portcullis. Nothing seemed to be moving, but she didn't believe it.

'I miss Lissa's foxfire already,' she whispered.

'I don't think anything is there,' Feather replied.

Without a word Caelin started forward again and passed cautiously through the gate.

'Ben, drop the portcullis,' Caelin instructed.

There were cries of protest from the spellwards when they realised they'd be trapped outside the city, but Caelin didn't heed them. As soon as they were all through Ben hacked through the ropes and quickly rolled away as the iron grid dropped.

The harbour was eerily quiet but for the shush of the waves and the occasional creak of settling wood. It didn't take them long before they came across the savaged bodies of sailors and four gate guards.

'Will she have taken a boat out do you think?' Mya heard Jack ask up ahead.

'She needn't go out to sea,' one of the spellwards replied. 'The Ward extends just as far as the lighthouse at the end of the rock-spit.'

'That's where we'll go,' Caelin agreed.

Feather shifted on her shoulder and she reached up to place her left hand over his tiny one. She could see the red glow of the lamp high in the lighthouse standing away from the rugged cliff to the left of the harbour. Between them and it stood a wide bridge, beneath which the river Ayre ran darkly. It was pitch black on the bridge and Caelin slowed almost to a stop.

'Give me light,' he ordered the spellward beside him.

The spellward sent two silvery orbs forward across the bridge and Mya heard several gasps. She pushed forward to find out what was happening and squeezed Feather's hand in fear when she saw the glistening shapes on the bridge. There were four of them, all as black as the river and dripping water. The kelpies were larger than any mortal horse Mya had ever seen, with overly long necks, red eyes and mouths full of sharp teeth.

'Myself, Jack and Mya need to get through to the lighthouse,' Caelin said. 'We'll fight our way through, but as soon as we can, we three will press on. Ben, you will lead the others. As soon as you can, come after us and give what help you can.'

'Sir.' Ben replied as he lifted his sword to a fighting stance.

'Come on, my girl.' Feather took in a deep breath. 'Let's cross this bridge.'

They crept forward, and the kelpies waited. One of the spellwards let nerves get the better of them and shot off a fireball. The kelpie screamed and reared, making an incredible leap away from the missile. All four of them seemed to grow impossibly larger as they charged the valley's defenders. Mya and Feather both instinctively shielded although the kelpies' attack was a purely physical one. She wished she'd learnt to use a sword as Jack had, as she ran and dodged. She knew she had to save her energy and get across at all costs, but she couldn't bring herself to just run and leave the others to face four kelpies.

Feather let fly a bolt from his sling as Mya ducked and twisted between two kelpies. She formed a ball of energy in both hands, one of fire and the other of ice, and set them to spin at a water-horse from two directions. Caelin sliced through one kelpie's leg as he charged across the bridge, and she couldn't help a twinge of sympathy. She threw a force spell at the stricken creature and knew as she did so, she would regret expending so much energy. It tumbled over the edge of the bridge and her heart lightened with the knowledge she had both committed an act of mercy and reduced the odds against her friends. She realised Ash was still right behind her and hesitated.

'Go on,' he said. 'I'll sort things here, but will be with you as soon as I can.'

She nodded and was surprised at the tightness in her throat and chest as she turned away and ran across the rest of the bridge.

Caelin was waiting and Jack came running up behind her with his sword dripping green blood. Caelin didn't wait, but immediately crept along the stone causeway toward the lighthouse. Mya spotted movement on the clifftop high above and gasped as she realised Kasira's massing army of Dark Fey waited there.

'Quite an incentive not to fail,' Feather said.

'Not that I needed more,' Mya replied. 'How are you doing?'

Feather laughed. 'I'm soooo way out of my depth I can't even feel scared anymore! I think I must be mad.'

'I know that feeling.' Mya smiled despite herself. She glanced across at Jack and there was nothing but determination on his face; pride lent her courage.

'Trouble,' Caelin warned them.

Mya peered ahead; small shapes scrambled across the rocks toward them.

'Gnomes!' Feather spat.

Caelin crouched and sent a sheet of flame broiling across the rocks. Mya stared open-mouthed at the careless use of power.

Feather tightened his grip on her collar. 'My Girl, don't be afraid but I think he is depending on you more than we realised. If I didn't know differently, I'd suspect he's intending to give everything he has to get you and Jack before Kasira; and Jack is just the decoy.'

Mya's mouth went dry. As much as she disliked Caelin for his bitterness, anger and seeming arrogance, she felt an unexpected, overwhelming love for him when she realised how much he was willing to give to save people who'd shunned him. She gritted her teeth and forced herself to stand up straighter as they scrambled over the uneven rocks toward the lighthouse.

As they drew closer, Caelin's pace slowed again, his shoulders were hunched as if to ward off a strong, cold wind. The door stood ajar and all of them looked around and up at the cliffs; some things, almost man-like, were hurrying down the steeply sloping hill.

Caelin turned and regarded Jack, Feather and then Mya. He said nothing but pushed open the lighthouse door and stepped in.

They found themselves in a storeroom in which a wooden spiral staircase started. They were not alone. An ephemeral figure floated above the stairway with elongated finger bones ending in claws, and silvery eyes like a melted moon.

Feather hissed. 'A Ghoul!'

Mya's heart sank; the person they needed most against such a creature had already sacrificed herself to take out the Bogle. Caelin glanced only briefly at Feather. Of all of them, the brownie was best qualified to banish such a creature; but to do so, to do so would take all he had, perhaps more, and leave him nothing with which to help against Kasira.

All of them shielded; the ghoul's smile widened to show blackened teeth. Despite knowing his own purity was questionable, Caelin chanted a blessing to banish the undead, and the ghoul rushed forward so swiftly it appeared to transport from one spot to another in an instant. Its long fingers wrapped around Caelin's throat and its mouth opened wide to suck in the man's soul. Jack slashed at it with his sword but the smith forged steel hit nothing. Mya circled, unsure what spell to choose but refused to panic. She sent a tentative force push and followed with a blast of lightning although she knew it might hurt Caelin. Jack looked at her helplessly and she could see in his eyes he was considering a kill spell.

'No!' she shouted even as she ran forward calling up a Ward.

Caelin tried his banishing, but it didn't succeed. His face had gone red and his eyes bulged from the strain of fighting the drain of his life force.

Feather let go of Mya's collar, and following in her imaginative bending of tradition, used all his concentration to force together a banishing and a blessing. As Mya reached out to cast her own spell Feather threw the last of his power at the ghoul, leaving only enough to remain conscious. With a wail the ghoul disintegrated and Caelin fell to the floor. Mya only just caught Feather as he, too, tumbled.

'Feather! Caelin?' Mya dropped to her knees and cradled the brownie.

'I'm all right,' Caelin rasped.

Feather nodded and then straightened himself up in Mya's arms. 'Still here,' he said. 'Though not much use to you now.'

Mya bent and kissed his head. 'You will always be of use, it's not your magic that matters to me.'

Jack helped Caelin up. The young man was deathly pale.

'On we go,' Caelin said, still barely able to breathe.

'Aunt Mya?'

'Go on,' she encouraged. 'Help Caelin take the lead.' She lifted Feather back to her shoulder and forced herself to stand. All of her instinct was screaming at her to get Jack away from here, to protect him as she'd always done; but there was more at stake than just her nephew, and she had to trust he was man enough now to decide his fate for himself.

There was just the barest flicker of light coming from above as they climbed the stairwell to the next level. The lighthouse keeper lay sprawled on the floor of his living quarters, still smoking from an excessively strong lightning spell. Caelin searched every shadow with his eyes before stepping forward into the room; it appeared to be clear.

'Pop me down,' Feather whispered. Mya did so.

Caelin crept to the foot of the last stairwell and peered up. Mya thought she could hear murmuring, but it might just have easily been the wind. Her heart was pounding and her blood rushed through her veins. She wiped her palms on her trousers and tried to steady her breathing. Caelin lifted his foot and placed it carefully on the first step, then began his ascent. Jack glanced at her and then followed the knight. Mya looked down at Feather and they nodded at each other. A cold breeze raised goose bumps on her skin and above them Caelin reached the top of the lighthouse tower. She sensed him raise his shield and instinctively did the same.

'So, you have finally stopped skulking with your tail between your legs and come back.'

She recognised the voice at once. Despite the words it was sweet-sounding and melodiously compelling. Mya gritted her teeth.

'And you have brought your little puppy with you; such a handsome, strong boy. I hope you haven't been telling him lies about me, my darling?'

Jack now stood at Caelin's shoulder and the two of them separated as though intending to capture a wary animal. Neither of them spoke and Mya heard frustration in Kasira's next words.

'Enough of this, you are wasting your time and putting off the inevitable. This valley belongs to the Fey.'

'It does,' Caelin agreed. Mya halted her creeping steps and held her breath. 'But every human here is descended from elves of the Dark Court, we are all Fey. You are not our rightful Queen.'

'Oh, pish! That boring little human's whore doesn't want this Valley!'

'She wants what's best for it,' Caelin replied evenly. 'And that's not you. As for name calling–'

'Oh, Cae! Not still jealous over my little indiscretion with the Lord Vallier? You know it's you I love.'

Caelin reached up to touch the scar on his face.

'I can fix that, you know.' Kasira's voice dripped honey. 'The Vallier is such a bore and a weakling. Come back to me, rule the Valley at my side as was always meant to be.'

Mya reached the top of the stairs but clung to the shadows. At the centre of the lighthouse tower the fire pit guttered and danced in the wind, the fuel running low. They were out in the open but for the pillars supporting the high, conical roof. Stars peered between the hurrying clouds and here and there the white peak of a wave shone far below. Jack was edging around to the right of the fire pit, and Caelin stood to its left. Kasira was almost hidden from view beyond the knight, but she wasn't alone. A barghest stood at her side, red eyes following Jack's movement. Mya bit hard on her lower lip.

'After all.' Kasira smiled at Caelin. 'We already have a son to rule after us.'

Mya gasped. All at once it hit her and she realised how foolish she'd been not to see it. The Vallier was dark, Kasira was dark; little Emon was as fair-haired and green eyed as his real father. She glanced down at Feather whose brown eyes caught the firelight as he gazed back up at her.

Caelin didn't move or speak, but Kasira took a seductive step forward.

Please, Caelin; please! Mya's nails dug into her palm she clenched her fists so tightly.

Caelin stiffened. 'You will never fool me again, Kasira!'

Jack called a spell so rapidly Mya barely had time to sense it. He sent both force and fire blasting toward the fire pit, sending ash, flame and magic hurtling toward the fey. Kasira ducked and shielded, the barghest was a little slower and was slammed backward into one of the pillars. Caelin and Kasira both hurled lightning at each other, holding nothing back. Jack sent a fireball at the barghest and Mya crouched quickly down behind the fire pit. Using all of her concentration she formed a fireball of her own out beyond the pillars and pulled it in toward Kasira. The fey queen's mouth opened in astonishment and she staggered forward, breaking off her attack to strengthen her shield. She looked around with a feral snarl before sending a blast of ice at both Caelin and Jack. Jack pushed forward against the assault, sending more fire at the barghest. Mya guessed he intended to try to get close enough to try the Ward banishing spell; it would leave him powerless but leave herself and Caelin to face Kasira.

Trusting her nephew, Mya turned her attention to the fey queen. She focused on the stone beneath Kasira's feet and summoned a force spell there. The stone cracked and shattered upward. Kasira fell back, but as she did so she sent out a force spell of her own, so strong the pillars and roof of the lighthouse exploded outward. Mya screamed as the fire pit tipped, but she rolled aside and gathered Feather up in her arms. As she lay stunned, she saw Jack, and the barghest had fetched up against the ruins of a pillar. Jack stared straight at her as he reached out his hand and threw all of his power into a banishing Ward. Emotion spilled out from Mya in hot tears even as she scrambled up and let go of Feather. Caelin had been thrown down the stairs, but was crawling up with his sword clasped in one hand.

'You.'

Mya turned to find the fey queen staring at her.

'You are nothing but a fleeting spring blossom.' Kasira smiled. 'A little frost will soon have you wilted!'

She sent ice shooting across the desolation of the tower. Feather ran for cover and Mya slammed up her shield, Kasira actually faltered and swayed backward, so shocked was she by the strength of Mya's block. Her smile turned into a mirthless grin as she increased the power behind her attack and added lightning to the ice storm.

Mya's chest hurt she was so afraid, but she set her shield firmly and when she was certain, she once again created fireballs behind Kasira and just beyond the tower.

Caelin pulled himself to his feet and threw a force spell at Kasira as Mya's fireballs battered her shield from behind. Feather hurled a shot from his sling but it was blown aside with no effort at all. Kasira dropped all glamour as she concentrated on the fight, her bones elongated and her eyes tilted upward, becoming hypnotically large. Caelin drew the last of his power and Kasira bent backward away from the onslaught of force and fire; but Kasira's shield didn't break. Mya tried to find a weak spot, sending ball after ball of fire from all directions but nothing seemed to phase the fey queen.

Caelin collapsed, barely able to pull together a shield. Kasira turned away from him and concentrated all of her power on Mya whilst still stalking toward the fallen knight. Mya sent her own attack of fire and force against the Queen but there was little strength behind it as she wracked her brain for something that might defeat her. There was nothing living she could manipulate through the shield as she had done with Nemeth; she could concentrate on her own shields and let Kasira waste her power, but she couldn't be sure she wouldn't be the one to drain all power first. Kasira was getting closer and closer to Caelin; the knight-spellward had his sword drawn, but a sudden blast of force from Kasira both broke his shield and sent the sword spinning from his hand. He stood as straight as he could in his battered armour and lifted his chin to bare his neck.

Scared to waste power, the lightning Mya sent toward Kasira was pitifully weak, and the queen laughed. She reached out toward Caelin and the iron of his breastplate melted away before her fingers. Caelin cried out as her nails pierced his skin and she grasped at his beating heart.

Mya found a roar exploding from her lungs as she charged at the fey queen, blasting her with lightning from her left hand even as she called up a kill spell deep within her chest. Kasira turned and strengthened her shield, refusing to lessen her grip on Caelin's heart. Mya's kill spell hit Kasira's shield so hard she felt as though she'd run into a mountain. Mya crumpled; all her power spent. Kasira's shield broke, but she stood there laughing, her hand squeezing tighter.

Then Mya stood and Kasira's mouth fell open and her eyes grew impossibly wider.

'No one! No human can stand after casting a kill Spell!'

Mya's ribs were splinters piercing her lungs, and her brain was being crushed by her skull. She pulled herself upright and the fingers of her right hand wriggled into her pocket and grasped the hilt of her small kitchen knife. Quick as thought, she struck, stabbing through Kasira's left breast into her heart. Kasira released Caelin and both of them fell back, dark blood trickled from the corner of Kasira's perfect lips and across her cream skin.

Mya collapsed to her knees.

Feather came running over, calling the tiniest trickle of power to his hands, tears blinding him as he reached for both Caelin and Mya.

'Heal! Heal!'

Mya fell forward and as sight faded, she saw Ash running up the stairs with his stave held across his body.

Too late, she though. *Too late*.

Chapter Twenty-Three

Feather woke to the worst headache he'd ever had in his life and almost wished he was dead. Almost. He blinked and squinted at the lamplight, and managed a tiny whimper to alert someone to the fact he was awake and needed assistance, thank you very much. The bed moved as someone sat beside him and a cool hand gently touched his forehead. He whimpered again and someone lifted his head from the pillow and a cup pressed to his lips. He drank as much as he could of the bitter brew before the nausea became too much.

'You should know better than to use up all your power, Sir Feather. I trusted you to be the sensible one.'

'Ash?' He struggled to open his eyes.

'Yes. Now you get some sleep.'

'But what about Mya and Jack? And Caelin an–'

'Mya and Jack are right here in the hospital with you; both of them sleeping off using all their power, like you. Caelin is weak but we think he will pull through. Lissa is recovering well but...'

'But?' Feather tried to sit up.

'Sir Ben is in quite a bad way. He defended the door to the lighthouse almost single-handedly from the fey climbing down the cliff.'

'*Almost* single-handedly?' Feather opened one eye to peer at the charcoal burner.

Ash stood up. 'Get some sleep, Sir Brownie. I'll come wake you if anything changes with the others.'

***

Mya paced up and down in her room. She'd been bullied into returning to Tower Hall to get her out of the way of the healers, despite her protests she could help. It had been three days since Kasira's defeat at the lighthouse, but many of the spellwards and people of the city were still in a bad way. Ben was still clinging on stubbornly, his wounds had been grave, but Redda had done much to repair the damage.

'You're making me dizzy!' Feather complained.

Mya smiled despite herself.

'Sorry, I hate not knowing what's going on.' She pulled a face. 'And I can't imagine it's pleasant for Caelin to be dealing with the Lord Vallier and his council.'

'Well, at least his council now includes Redda and Prynarra, rather than Kasira and Hassin!' Feather nibbled thoughtfully at a blueberry. 'Wish I was there though.'

'Ha!' Mya pointed at him triumphantly. 'See!'

Feather laughed. Then said soberly, 'It won't be easy, after this, going back to an ordinary life.'

Mya sat down on the bed. Going back to an ordinary life. But where *was* her life now?

They both jumped as someone knocked at the door. They didn't wait but opened it themselves.

'Mrs Friend! Whatever is it?'

'Oh, Mya! Good news. Sir Ben is awake.'

Mya jumped up and hugged the housekeeper.

'Oh, and you should know, Caelin and your Jack are back from the council—'

'Where?' Mya demanded, rushing out into the hall at once.

'They are heading for the library; the senior spellwards library!'

Mya barely waited for Feather, but knelt to help him up onto her shoulder before she bounded up the stairs. The solid, ornate tower door, wasn't locked and Mya made her way tentatively to the main library. She raised a hand to knock, but stopped herself, pushing the door open and stepping in. Amidst the shelves of books stood a beautiful dark-wood table set about with matching red-cushioned chairs. Caelin and Jack were already there, as were Ferris, and Lissa who jumped up to kiss Mya and Feather on the cheek.

'Well?' Mya demanded as she sat. Feather perched on the edge of the table at her elbow.

Lissa grinned, but Caelin held up a hand to stop her speaking.

'We have agreed the following terms,' Caelin began. 'The spellwards will return to being what they should have been, defenders of the Valley and healers for all. Redda's suggestion has been accepted, those who cannot pay may exchange goods or labour for healing, and I trust Redda not to exploit anyone. He will be made Head of Healers. I... I will run Tower Hall and oversee the training of new candidates and the defence of the Valley's people.'

'What of the Ward?' Mya asked.

'The Ward will be destroyed.'

'As it should be!' Lissa exclaimed.

But Mya and Feather looked at each other in concern.

'There'll be both Dark and Wild Fey who will exploit that and hurt people,' Feather warned.

'Indeed.' Caelin nodded. 'That's why removing the Ward will be a gradual thing and at first only certain fey will be invited through. Some fey will be selected to sit on the Valley's council, it's already been agreed Lissa will do so.'

The half-fey beamed at them all.

'And I–'

Caelin raised a hand to stop Jack's excited outburst. He looked at Mya with concern and her breathing slowed even as her heart sped up.

'I suggested the Order of Knights be restored,' Caelin said slowly. 'When Ben is well enough, I hope he'll be put in charge. Jack has a special assignment, he's to be both guardian and tutor to the heir of the Valley, Emon.'

'But...' Mya turned from Caelin to Feather and she saw Jack's face fall. Feather gave a discreet shake of his head.

'Emon is to be raised to be a Spellward and a Knight.' Caelin held her gaze. 'As a half-fey, he is the perfect heir to the Valley as it should be.'

'People will be told the truth about the history of the Valley,' Lissa added.

Mya glanced again at Feather and nodded. 'He will be the perfect heir,' Mya agreed.

Caelin sat back a little and experimented with a smile.

'Ask her!' Jack urged.

Caelin swallowed and glanced away. 'Mya, I... we would be honoured if you were to be a part of Emon's upbringing. You deserve a seat on the council at the very least, and I'd like you to be one of his tutors. Jack, Ferris and Feather have all been awarded the honorary title of Knight-defender; Ash declined any title. You'll of course be given the title of Lady–'

'No.' Mya stood up.

Jack stared at her open-mouthed. Caelin's breathing quickened, his skin flushing slightly beneath the stubble on his face. He looked down, raising a hand to rub his nose and hide his eyes.

'No. The city isn't for me. I want to go back to Briarton. I want to take my healing skills out to the edges of the Valley where they're needed. I want my quiet farm, with the mountains in the distance behind me, and my brownie to chat to in the evenings.' She smiled down at Feather.

'Your brownie would like that too, very much,' he replied quietly.

Both Jack and Lissa protested but Caelin held her gaze and nodded.

'I'm heading back to Ashgrove in a week,' Ferris said. 'I'd be honoured to escort you to Briarton.'

'Thank you,' Mya replied.

***

The days flew by with so much to do to repair the city of Ayresport. Mya spent as much time as she could with Jack and Lissa and tried not to be swayed by their hurt looks. There was no sign of Ash, and she felt both disappointed, and a little cross. She supposed she couldn't blame him; she hadn't exactly been friendly, but now she was ready to get to know him, he'd vanished. Caelin also seemed to avoid her, but that wasn't so unusual. She caught up with him in the stables where he went to escape from the demands of his new responsibilities.

'Good morning.' She leaned against the stall and watched him combing out Horse's tail.

He glanced up and almost managed a smile. 'Are you going down to the hospital again today?'

'I am.' After a moment she plucked up the courage to ask. 'Will you ever tell Emon the truth?'

'I will always tell the truth,' he replied evasively.

Mya laughed. 'You know what I mean.'

Caelin stopped combing and turned to give her his full attention. 'I don't know.' He sighed, his brows drawn down over his eyes. 'As yet I've not even said anything to the Vallier. Emon will be brought up to be the heir of the Valley, and I don't want to take that away from him. He has a chance to be raised with the influence of fey, the old codes of knighthood, and to be a spellward. I hope he'll be a good man. I hope he'll protect all the Valley and treat with the fey honourably. He doesn't need to know I'm his father.'

'I am not so sure,' Mya said. 'But Feather and I will say nothing of it to him. Do you think the Vallier guesses? When the two of you are together, it looks obvious.'

'I think he must.' Caelin leant back against the stall. 'He's been foolish, but is not a fool. He is young as I was once.'

Mya smiled, Caelin, and the Vallier weren't far off the same age. 'Well, whatever you decide, I'll honour.'

'Thank you. I wish you'd remain to help raise the boy, you did such a great job with Jack.'

Mya shook her head. 'Credit for Jack should go to Jack, and I have no wish to stay in the city. You'd be welcome to bring him to Briarton to visit though, and we could go on to Ashgrove. It's important he see how things are in the tree city.'

'I'm sure you'll be seeing us.' Caelin did smile then and for the first time Mya saw there wasn't the slightest trace of reservation. For a moment she glimpsed the man he'd been before he'd been wounded; that man didn't retreat.

Laughter intruded and Lissa and Jack followed it into the stables.

'Aunt Mya!' Jack halted, looking almost guilty.

'Are you heading down to the hospital too?' Lissa asked.

'I am.' She nodded.

'Emon has asked to come with us,' Jack said.

Mya refrained from looking around at Caelin for permission. 'Of course, he can. Are you riding down into the city?'

'It's such a fine morning I think we'll walk.' Lissa glanced at Jack. She slipped into Nemesis' stall and gave her horse a carrot, stroking its neck and nose.

'I'll see you later.' Mya smiled at Caelin and the spellward nodded.

Outside she found Emon waiting with Feather. The boy was chatting away to the brownie and barely acknowledged her. Lissa and Jack went on ahead leaving Mya to stroll behind the boy and the brownie. She realised Feather was telling Emon all about the history of the Valley, from the kidnap of the first humans and the settlement of the Valley, to the first attack of the Dark Fey and their queen and the invention of the Ward.

'So, Sir Ben was tricked into letting her in?' Emon asked wide eyed.

'He was.' Feather nodded. 'But Sir Caelin later saw through her enchantment and tried to warn everyone. She hurt him badly, and he had to go away to heal.'

'But he's better now.' Emon affirmed to himself. 'And he came back to save us.'

Feather glanced over his shoulder at Mya. 'Yes, my boy; he is much better now.'

***

When it came to time to leave for Briarton, Mya almost lost her resolve.

'Please stay.' Lissa pouted prettily. She had her arm through Jack's and Mya narrowed her eyes at the pair of them.

'You will come back soon, won't you, Aunt Mya?' Jack pleaded.

'Of course, I will,' she replied. 'And you will always be welcome to visit at Briarton.'

'Come here!' Ben picked her up in a bone-breaking hug, lifting her off her feet, his whiskers tickled her cheek. 'You look after yourself.'

'Take your own advice.' Mya grinned at him.

She hugged Jack and Lissa, whilst Ben said his farewells to Feather, and then stood before Caelin. She could see the muscles of his jaw clenching as though he were fighting back words. She stepped forward and resting her hand on his shoulder, placed a kiss on his scarred face. He put his arms about her and rested his cheek for a moment against her hair before letting her go.

'Thank you,' he murmured.

'Well, then.' Mya cleared her throat as Feather made his final farewells. 'I'll write when I can find a trader coming this way.'

She turned to hide her tears and stopped when she realised there were three horses waiting.

'I hope you don't mind, but Ash was going the same way,' Ferris said.

Mya looked at the charcoal burner and he gave a shrug. Her cheeks burned, and she tried to hide it by lifting Feather up onto Rusty's saddle and then swung up behind him.

Three times she turned to look back over her shoulder at her friends as they crossed the gardens, and three times she nearly turned back; but she didn't.

***

At first their journey was sombre and Mya's heart was heavy, but as they drew away from the city, back toward the forests and mountains of the northern valley, she felt a greater sense of peace and belonging. Ferris and Ash were capable companions, and as she lost her reservations, she found them to be enjoyable ones. Ferris had a surprisingly wicked sense of humour and he and Ash got on well. Mya found herself getting on well with Ash also, much as she tried to deny it.

When they came at last to her cottage, they found the garden overgrown and some storm damage both to the fence and the roof. Ferris and Ash insisted on staying a couple of days to repair the tiles and assist with any heavy work. When there was nothing left to do, and Ferris had to be on his way, Ash reluctantly announced he'd better see what state is own old home was in.

Mya gave Ferris a farewell hug without hesitation but felt decidedly more awkward saying goodbye to Ash. He touched her cheek and leaning forward gently kissed her lips in a way that made her whole body tingle.

'My Lady, may I have your permission to call on you?'

'Yes, I would like that,' Mya murmured. She growled at Feather and Ferris when she saw them both grinning at them.

Mya closed the door to her small cottage and added a log to the fire. She poured dandelion wine into an egg cup and some into her old battered tankard, then sat at the table beside Feather.

He lifted the egg cup. 'Here is to home, My Girl!'

'To home.' Mya smiled.

Firstly, a big thank you to you, the reader, for choosing this book and taking the time to read it. I hope you enjoyed it, if you did please leave me a review, reviews are incredibly important to us authors. I would love it if you said hello, come and find me in one of the places below:

Facebook https://www.facebook.com/TheWindsChildren

Twitter @EmmaMilesShadow

Instagram @emmamshadow

A big thank you to my friends and family for their continued support and to Rosie for her advice on editing.

Hall of Pillars was originally meant to be a standalone book, but I love the characters and the Valley so much (and have received so much nagging from my lovely readers) I have no choice but to write more. Mya and Feather's story will continue in 'Hall of Night' which I hope to have finished by the end of 2019. Please see my social media sites above for updates.

How much would you sacrifice to save your people? Your freedom, your home … power … love … your life?'

Four lands beneath the sky. A haven of peace, a kingdom of plenty, ravaged islands, and a nation of cruel, dark magic. One will try to devour them all.

Spring brings the ruthless Borrow raiders much earlier in the year, their attacks more ferocious, more desperate. When Kesta uses her magic to see in the flames who is really behind the raids the Independent islands of the Fulmers seem doomed to fall. Their only hope is to cross the sea to seek the help of the King of Elden and his dangerous sorcerer, the Dark Man; but what price will the king demand for his aid?

Wild Kesta has been raised to be a leader, trusted, loved, with the freedom of her cherished Islands. Can Kesta subdue her fiery nature and work with a man she hates, a man she fears, to stop the evil that will consume their lands and enslave them all?

Printed in Great Britain
by Amazon